Daughters of Babylon

Also by Elaine Stirling

Dead Edit Redo
The Mexican Saga
Percy and me 'neath the Yum Gum Tree

The Corporate Storyteller: *A Writing Manual & Style Guide for the Brave New Business Leader*

As Alain C. Dexter
Dead to Rights: A Circularity of Glosas

As Elaine K. Stirling
Unsuspected Conduct
Almost Heaven
Midnight Obsession
Foul Play
Chain Letter
This Time for Us
Sleepwalker
More Than a Feeling
Cross Tides
Different Worlds

Daughters of Babylon

Elaine Stirling

Daughters of Babylon

Greyhart Press

www.greyhartpress.com

BETA READER TEAM

The author and publisher wish to thank our beta reader team for their help with *Daughters of Babylon*.

Sarah Briggs
Kellie Fry
Misha Herwin
Jan Vincenc

For Abby, Nora, and Sam

If I could have a thousand years—just one little thousand years—more of life, I might, in that time, draw near enough to true Romance to touch the hem of her robe.
—O. Henry, "He Also Serves"

None of it is true. There are no people about whom you have been warned, and if there were, they would not be the Cairds. They have all died off and anyway they never existed. It is nothing but stories and stories are lies, as are songs and poems and promises of truth.
—Anne Cameron, Tales of the Cairds

We were always going to. We never did.
—Blythe Pendaris, annual address to TPA shareholders

BOOK ONE

The Queen of Heaven

The cook and I did meet 'neath the oleander tree
Till the cuckoo stole his eggs away to Galilee
Will the bread inside this oven ever rise?

—a Cossante, traditional fertility chant

CHAPTER ONE

A BARONIAL MANOR HOUSE
NEAR THE WELSH BORDER
HOLY WEEK, A.D. 1189

For as long as Eleanor could call up images of *Reine du Ciel*, she believed she could outrun despair. The priory at the far southern reaches of Aquitaine meant nothing to her husband and jailer, Henry, king of England, beyond the usual grain, gold, and *garçons de guerre*, of which her duchy had probably been stripped bare by now. The memory of Queen of Heaven had become her freedom on the head of a pin. Every day for fifteen years and eight months, Eleanor, in her mind, danced the farandole at harvest with the ruddy-cheeked and joyful. Every day, she recalled the names and faces of her court at Poitiers, her beloved court, and set to paper the quips and sweet flirtations in the tongues she'd heard them spoken, explaining to her sometimes nervous guards, "These are my Greek and Latin drills. Look." She would spread her arms. "No messenger birds, no agents lurking in the beeches to spirit my scribbles away." But Good Fridays were always difficult, and on this, the 52nd anniversary of her father's death, the scent of apricots in blossom eluded her. Imagination offered no mountains swept in mauve, no sheep or misty vineyards, only four people trudging.

She sat at her desk in the turret and closed her eyes.

They looked like pilgrims on an empty stretch of yellow road with low hills like flattened tin scrap to their left; the setting sun, a topaz nestled between slopes. If the sky were a woman's face, Venus would be a single hovering teardrop. There was a small, rhythmic clicking sound, connected somehow to the group of travelers, though she couldn't quite figure how. A cricket in the ditch along the roadside? Buttons or augury bones jangling in a pocket? No, the sound did not come from the unfolding tableau but from here in the turret.

Eleanor dropped the quill she'd been twiddling with and glanced beneath her writing desk. Nothing. She pressed the heels of her palms to its scarred oaken surface, rose and leaned forward to inspect the mortar that was chewed to lattice by worms and Heaven knows what manner of Mercian plaster louse. *Clickety-click-click*. No sign of crickets.

She glanced toward Leland, chief guard, who dozed at the top of the staircase in the center of the landing. His head had dropped forward, chin to collarbone, so that only his shoulders and bobbled knit hat were visible, and these rose and fell in consonance with his snoring, which was not in synchrony with…*clickety-clickety-CLICKCLICKCLICK*—

"*Maudit parbleu!*"

The elusive noise was coming now from deep inside her left ear. She shook her head and tipped it to one side and then the other, but as she strained and hopped about, the tintinnabulation swelled in volume and intensity, setting off reverberatory twitches in her right eye and at both corners of her mouth. The villagers of Cerabornes outside of *Reine du Ciel* used to dance and bang tin pots to ward off demons. Had some imp from Aquitaine smuggled its way in a sack of dried apricots?

I must tell Haldis, she thought, to cut back on the nutmeg.

Eleanor stepped away from the desk and pressed fingers to her cheeks. Her lips were twittering, pulling upward at the corners at a rate of seven, eight, nine involuntary grins per second. The ferocious winking of her eye called up the memory of a food taster from Limousin—Tibitard was his name, poor fellow. Over the years, he'd ingested so many toxins intended for his lordships that he became a jittering bundle of saliva-hurling palsies. He spent his final years suspended from a scaffold in a rye field to scare away the starlings.

She took small cautious steps around the landing with Leland's capped head like a mushroom at the center and considered the possibility of poison. Anything was possible, although she'd received no missives to suggest that her continued existence was irritating Henry more than usual. If anything, her staying alive served as a political pin cushion, a repository for barbs not currently required by an English king who preferred to live in Normandy. If he or their warring sons had outraged yet another vassal by pillaging crops

12

and castle, the murder of his estranged queen, about whom Henry was known to proclaim, apparently without irony, "She is everything to me," would snap tripwires from Hadrian's Wall to the Holy Land.

Eleanor came around again to the desk where her twitching gaze fell to the parchment, weighted by an ink pot and box of quills. The sheet had sat wordless for so long it had begun to curl in at the edges, as if reverting to the shape of the doe whose graceful curvatures it had once warmed. Only moments ago, before the twitches began, she'd written what she could remember of a *rubielo*:

To your pale cheeks, I shall restore
ere sunset over Christendom the bloom
of hearty pleasures and this long-stemméd love.

They'd put this one to music, although she couldn't be sure who'd composed the larkful iambs. Toward the end, there'd been so many cossantes, sestinas, and triolets flying about, it was hard to keep track... aah, yes, she remembered now. Wiley Forrest had made fun of "long-stemméd love", drawing out the phrase with bawdy dance steps that dissolved the court to mirthful weeping, but it was Arturo of Padrón who penned the piece and, pressing the jester to the wall, insisted that long stemméd love referred to "spiritual passion that extends across infinity, you buffoon!"

She'd prohibited dueling in the court with anything but words, but oh, how those verbal arrows sang! Eleanor smiled and pressed fingers to the page. Last she'd heard of her Irish jester, he was giving Sufis a run for their wit in Anatolia, but of the Galician, her knight, she knew nothing.

How much of Christendom Arturo was restoring to hearty pleasure, she would rather not know, but without him there'd have been no Court of Love, no heart of Aquitaine to match her mind. Long before the accolades and adoring ladies, he had stood apart, distinguishing himself. Had it not been for Arturo, Eleanor might have become an agreeable melancholic, like her mother: distant smile, vacant eyes, while bluebells drooped mid-summer at her passing, persuading bees to abandon joyful labours, spend their lives rheumatic and abed—

Clickety-click.

13

"Oh, no." Her left eye accelerated its frightful winking, like the thump of a hare's hind foot. She slapped a hand over it. The tips of a million icy needles pricked her chest and left arm, and drollness gave way to panic. Was this to be her dissolution then? Death by tic and sentimentality, the cables of her mind snapping like a bridge that's weathered too many crossings, too many spring melts. Eleanor gripped the edge of the desk and cried out, "Leland, *s'il vous plait, je crois que je vais avoir un coup de—non, non, non, pas français, englais!* Could you come quickly, please? I seem to be having *un p'ti dilemme.*"

Leland was Northumbrian, duty-bound and loyal to the marrow. He would halve his own gizzard without a second thought to prevent His Majesty's prisoner and sole charge from leaving the manor grounds or from conversing in private with anyone who wasn't a dead crushing bore. But he was also a good man. She did not doubt that, roused, Leland would pull helmet over cap and rush to protect her, dispatching orders to the knights and ladies arranged like flower pots down the cold, spiraling stairwell. Only he did not rouse. She called out again, but he carried on snoring, smacking lips, dreaming, perhaps, of Dorcas, his bride who, at this moment, would be elbow deep in sweet dough for the Easter feast.

Her entire body was clattering now. She entertained the possibility that her attendants had been drugged and were being carted away for the purpose of reaching her, unarmed and cornered. But whatever for? Or perhaps Leland and the others didn't hear her because she'd emitted no voice, only thinking that she spoke. Wasn't it Wiley who once jested, madness will ever outrun reflection? Reflection being a cold bed mate, keep running!

Running, alas, in a stone tower was not possible. The stairs were a horror and peppered with attendants, embroidering, or counting cracks in the mortar; and so she slid, juddering, onto the chair and gave her consent to the palsy, whatever it was, in hopes it would continue on its way when done with her.

After a few moments, the paroxysms began to lose steam. The maniacal grinning slowed enough that she could inhale fully between tics. She pulled herself to standing. Knees wobbled, heart raced, but bones and sinew held together. Perhaps a round or two of farandole would help: para-*pom*-pom, para-*pom*-pom…

The beat faded when her upraised arms started tingling. She dropped them and gazed through the high slitted window, the same window through which, as Henry's new bride, besotted and flush with pleasure, she'd thrown sprigs of lavender into the upheld arms of villagers. The Severn River, mindless as it ever was, meandered through pasture, beech and willow groves. Sheep grazed, cows dozed. If this were a plot against her, it bore an extraordinarily light touch. When was the last time Eleanor of Aquitaine flushed with pleasure? Or, more's the pity, laughed and amused another? Her *joie de vivre* extended no further these days than to the dutiful curtsy-bob of a maid servant laying logs or a dissolute baron trying to chuckle his way to a loan.

She tried her voice again. "Leland…my ladies, can any of you devoted stair-sitters hear me?"

The only reply was *clickety-clickety, clickety-clickety*, and it did not come from embroidery needles.

Tears splashed onto the parchment. Eleanor used the velvet hem of her sleeve to dab at her cheeks, to wipe away the drool. She rotated her neck from left to right, taking in the dimensions of the small, cramped landing. Apart from the chair and writing table, the room contained no other furnishings or comforts. Her only exercise, apart from a weekly ride of thirty minutes, would be the solemn descent from the turret across a small stretch of grass to the manor house for evening repast, devotionals, and bed. But why the sudden self-pity? Until this flibbertigibbet of nerves, she had been occupied with trying to call up the Pyrenees that cradle *Reine du Ciel*, but again, her mind's eye sketched four people on a road, in a vast stretch of land she'd never seen.

"Fine!" She settled on the chair. "If you are to be my new inner court, then let us begin acquaintance."

They walked three abreast and one behind, one man, three women. They were too sun-kissed to be English or Norman, though their features resembled neither the Turk nor Moorish races. The man was the front and central figure. He wore loose cotton breeches and a tunic, both white, and though his garb looked tattered from long wear and labour, his presence shone like a pearl midst the dark-jewel setting of shawls and skirts that surrounded him.

Variations in their height and levels of fatigue created an audible shuffle-swish as they walked, a point counter-point that called to mind the cossante when danced upon good hardwood floors. At the thought of Aquitaine, a small sound erupted at the back of her throat, like the single downbeat of a finch's wing. Her attention shifted to the woman who walked behind the other three. She couldn't tell if the woman's position was one of honour or subservience. The laryngeal croak came again, painfully this time.

Leland's bobbled cap jerked upward, offering a glimpse of the guard's slack-jawed face before returning with a snore and splutter to his chest. She touched the heavy linen at her throat.

"Have I become a habitation of pixies? Is it true what they say about the little people here?"

"I doubt that pixies would find you habitable at your age."

She glanced around. "I beg your pardon? Who said that?"

A figure had insinuated himself, without so much as a by-your-leave, between her and the stairwell of attendants. He wore full ecclesiastic robes and the expression of having eaten unripe persimmon.

"What in the name of St. Jacques are you doing here?" she asked. "This is England, not Purgatory."

Abbot Suger, chief cleric of St. Denis and counsellor to kings, snorted. In actuality, he had been mouldering in resins and fine herbs for decades, and thereby should have been incapable of snorting. But here he was, standing before her with as kempt a look of disapproval as she'd ever seen. "I wouldn't be too confident you're in England at the moment."

"In the absence of freedom and the collapse of one's senses, geography hardly matters. But if I've disturbed your eternal rest, Father, or the gleeful counting of your incorruptible treasures, please accept my apologies and be on your way."

"You really have forgotten, haven't you? All those opportunities for true understanding, spread before you like a Pentecostal feast, and you gobbled the sweet bits, tossed the rest behind like scraps of gristle." Abbot Suger flapped his upper arms and, to her astonishment, clucked. *Pwraawk, prawk, prawk!* Were those pin feathers peeking out from beneath his skull cap? "You're dimmer than *La Dangereuse*," he went on. "Now, there's one we'll not hear from again—another star that glimmered and winked out in your precious Queen of Heaven."

16

Eleanor's eyes flashed, and her spine straightened. "I will not tolerate the slander of my grandmother even from an apparition whose fowl nature I had, until this moment, only suspected."

"Scoff all you like. No one listens to your wordplays anymore, no one fawns or presses in for a glimpse of Her Benevolent Majesty. You lead your procession, day after day, from bed chamber to privy to this crumbling tower, a paragon of longsuffering, but your knights and ladies are scattered across Creation and your Court of Love is dead. Do you hear me? Dead, dead, dead! Those flapping tics and grins, they are your flaws of character assembling, your accursed selfishness that seeks to flee before you are called to Final Judgment."

The vile little man who, while he was alive, had never shown a mustard seed of original thought, twirled on gold-embroidered, silken slippers, his arms outstretched like the centerpiece of a *gateau d'amande* she'd once commissioned. The marzipan dancer had been Wiley's idea, the centerpiece attached to a dowel rotated by a page hidden under the table. The Sultan's envoy, who'd been cheated by wool merchants in Blois and Anjou and was on his way home to recommend war, signed a trade agreement for raw wool with the shepherds' guild of *Reine du Ciel* that night.

"And how do you waste your final days?" Suger clucked on. "You *imagine* movement of an *imagined* pregnant woman, knitting needles clacking as she walks behind an *imagined* threesome, and this is not what CHRIST our LORD would WANT to HEAR." What DAH-dah-DAH would DAH-dah-DAH. His phrasings had always called to mind the flap of an ill-fitting carriage door, but this was something different. The language of sound, the sound of language.

Eleanor sat back, flummoxed. This wasn't the dead abbot or even a ghost of the abbot showing her with three successive downstrokes of his knobby index finger: *Imagine. Imagined. Imagined.* Three decapitations, three clean severings of the heretic from the holy, the head of the serpent from the slithering spine. *The Power, the Glory, the Kingdom.*

A part of her shuddered. Another part, younger and far more disposing, yearned to throw her arms around his dimpled chicken neck and plant a kiss on his cheek. They had, after all, been friends once, long ago.

"How right you are, Father, how very right you are! I am, as you say, squanderous of opportunity. I can't thank you enough for reminding me."

And with that, he disappeared, whisked off-stage like a hose puppet, freeing her to peer anew at the tiny movement inside the woman who knitted, *clickety-click*, from a skein of turquoise blue wool while following her companions. Beneath those voluminous, striped skirts, she was pregnant! And within a heartbeat of that confirmation, there arose a corresponding flutter from her own lower belly. With a gasp, she placed a hand there.

The undulation was subtle but no less alive for that. Pleasurable feelings in her womb spread outward in concentric circles like a tide pool, filling the dimensions of the attic space. She, not quite in its center, could follow as it rose and circled elliptically. The orbiting spirals reached her heart, then branched off, unhurried, into chambers of inflow and outflow, halving again to quarters of pulse and resistance; and the quadrants pulled, drawing in, drawing in, as though calling others, more of itself, and strengthened by complicity of bone, muscle, tissue, continued upward to the inside of her crown where echoing refrains and towering exaltations called to mind angelic choirs singing *Alleluias*...and while this was going on, all she'd learned of pain, had accumulated and packed away; all the protestations she'd swallowed, for what else was there to do, time and again, but swallow; and the boredom she had railed so viciously and fruitlessly against—in their entirety, splintered. She watched them fall apart, crumble to powder like mouse-nibbled armour made of *papier mâché*, leaving in its place...

Leland shifted on the top step. She could hear her ladies-in-waiting conversing at the base of the stairs. Life was stirring around her again. Tiny drops of sweat beaded along the edges of her hairline, and she promised herself to ponder deeply, later, on how it all connected. For now, though, she needed to return to the foursome.

They were still plodding, stirring small clouds of yellow dust, yet something had brightened. They were still three in front, one behind, but she had undercalculated. How could she have forgotten movement, sound, the shape of things? Trembling, not with weakness now but with sweet, sharp desire, she dipped her quill into the inkpot and blew on the places where the tears had nearly dried. Bilqees, *femme de chambre*, dancer from the East, elegant and adored member of the court, had set Eleanor in front of a looking glass once and shown her, *de la manière la plus fantastique*.

Isolate the muscle, see the figures in your head. Because there are no starting points, you wait...you wait...you call the movement to you...while it comes, you take its measure...while it comes, you join its pleasure...when it comes—

And oh my, it had come! In a red-haired, lusty form from Normandy.

From the box of quills, Eleanor selected the taut, brown wing feather of a falcon. The linen of her headdress draped and folded so that light from the turret window suffused, pouring warmth into her aching knuckles, sanguinity to ink. To anyone observing—and they *were* observing—this was clearly a penitent in prayer and deep disconsolation.

Her script was swift, the ink flowed smooth, and the queen could scarcely keep from laughing!

LA HACIENDA DELGADO DE OBREGÓN
VERACRUZ, MEXICO; LATE SUMMER, 1972

The *Nagual* Lupo Sanchez worked, ate, drank, slept, dreamed, and made love with near equal fluency in Spanish, English, Nahuatl, Zapotec, Mixtec, and Chantal de Tabasco. He covered distances in rhythm.

> *Swatting at the midges*
> *that precede the woolly mammoth*
> *will not improve your chances*
> *when you finally meet the beast.*

Eight paces, that stanza had brought him. Eight paces closer to the hammock that awaited in his thatch-roofed adobe in Las Cuevas where he could rock away the ache of 18-hour days of swinging a machete, sweating, bending, swatting, squatting, stacking lengths of sugar cane, and coughing up dust while the soulless brute from Monterrey bellowed from the padded driver's seat of an air-conditioned Blazer through a rooftop bullhorn, "Speed it up, you lazy sons of—!"

Lippy dogs and trippy cats
and other cheap distractions…

Four steps further, Lupo crossed himself in deference to Euphenia, his dear mother, may she rest in peace, who'd never tolerated profanity from her only son, even when quoting miserable sons of bitches.

There were other verses to the nagual's narrative—

there's a clever little coconut
beyond the yellow door…

—470 to be precise, that he'd composed as part of his training with a *bruja*, witch, known throughout the Sierra Madres as La Pantera Negra, Black Panther. One might even argue that the rhyming ditties were his only training. Lupo wore through twelve pairs of *huarache* sandals to compose a rhythmic narrative that aligned precisely with a journey of 15.6 miles from the iron gates of the Obregón hacienda to the village well at the center of Las Cuevas, his birthplace. When he asked the witch, a brown-skinned dead ringer for Ava Gardner, why he wasn't learning curses and spell casting like a true sorcerer, she told him his joints were too gummed up with stupidity. He had to clear them first. Eleven pairs of *huaraches* fell apart before she explained with more detail the purpose of the nagual's narrative, and of course, by then, he'd figured it out for himself.

He met La Pantera thirty years ago, when he was eighteen. Mexico had entered the war against the Axis, and Lupo couldn't wait to enlist. He was going to drive Sherman tanks up and down the Rhineland, scything enemies the way gardeners of rich Americans rode motorized lawn mowers, sitting easy on the straight stretches, leaning deep into the steep bits. Unfortunately, a sexton with prophetic inclinations had warned his mother at Lupo's First Communion to keep her only son out of all military conflict; and so when he was six, she'd taken him, leaving behind four nearly grown daughters to live in New Jersey where, as an undocumented alien, he could be neither Mexican nor American. Since he'd come of age, she couldn't stop him, of course, from thumbing a ride to Mexico where he could do whatever he damn well pleased, but then there'd been that party in Ciudad Juarez, and tequila was new to him; and when he woke the next morning, he couldn't remember the poker game where, holding a full house of three kings and two aces, and nothing left to bet, he'd anted himself. The woman who'd been watching his idiocy from a corner of the bar knew the decks were marked but did nothing to stop it. La Pantera was twice Lupo's age and flirtatious, which led him to believe she must be Cuban because Mexican women never hung out in taverns unless they were whores. Turned out she was Zapotec and the proprietor of her own *cantina* deep in the western Sierra Madres. She'd come to the border town to pick up a 1940 Packard 120 and drive it back home. Wits anesthetized by the worst hangover of his life, Lupo agreed to accompany La Pantera Negra because she needed someone to share the driving—and because if he didn't, the *banditos* he'd lost to would have broken both his legs and sold him to a Colombian drug lord.

She told him on that heady road trip that he had the makings of a…something-or-other—like a shaman—he'd never heard the word before—and she was going to help him develop those skills. All he had to do in return was work off the gambling debt she'd covered on his behalf.

> *Pocket words and rock an ocean;*
> *tip the boat, you'll lose the motion…*

"How long is that going to take?" he asked La Pantera, somewhere on the highway between Parral and Durango.

"That depends," she said, freshening her ruby red lipstick in the rearview mirror. "You like the *peyote*, getting high, the *mescalito*?"

"Oh, yeah, man," he answered eagerly. Because Mamita would have skinned him alive, he'd never indulged in narcotics, but Longport, New Jersey, was a port town, and he knew of the Chinese opium dens, and the Moroccan hashish dealers with stilettos so sharp they could shave off an eyelash of resin, one inhale, and charge two bucks.

"Too bad," she said, "because you're never gonna touch it, long as you're with me."

That getting high would not be part of his training threw Lupo into a serious funk for months. Shamans and *curanderos*, after all, were notorious for partaking of the mescalito, of the peyote and toloache; for meeting and battling animal spirits—how hard could it be to convince anyone you'd fought Wild Boar and won? And there was that other thing Pantera talked about. Oh yeah, to break the boundaries of perception so that…well, so that one could say one had broken them, he supposed. But La Pantera Negra, whose cantina was named after her, showed no interest in his dog patch wisdom.

"First of all, you are not a shaman in training, you are *nagual*, which is something like the framework of the house where the shaman lives. It's hard to explain in words. Sending you to kingdoms of mind-bending plants would be useless, first of all, because you're too dumb to bring information back with you, and secondly, I need someone who can bring back far more than information. This world that's currently bombing itself to oblivion will reap the fruits of its action for the next hundred years, at least. You'd stand a better chance of survival if I smeared you with pig fat and fed you to coyotes."

"All right then," Lupo said, "how about vision questing? I could sleep in a cave and meet my totem."

"This is Mexico, not South Dakota. Trust me, you don't want to meet your totem in these deserts. Anyway, I have something much better in mind for you."

And that was how he learned to make tortillas—shameful, woman's work no self-respecting Mexican male would ever do—and to compose a narrative that, repeated a precise number of times, sang him from the gates of colonial oppression to the well spring that had washed his newborn body clean.

Years later, when he'd grown past the point of thinking with his dick, Lupo asked La Pantera why she'd plucked him from the path of violence and early death that awaited him.

"I could see you were a virgin," she said, "naïve as a duck egg, but your passages were clean." He laughed until he wept, then understood. There are many meanings to the word, passages.

Lupo nudged the tattered straw sombrero off his forehead so that the deep, curving brim rested along his shoulder blades and allowed the slight breeze of walking to dry the sweat off his brow.

The chatter will not leave you
  but the witches they will cleave
    and if you master the maneuvers
      there'll be fewer who can stream you...

He and his three companions were now 1.6 miles from the last paved intersection before Las Cuevas. Lupo stroked the length of his machete that was sheathed and holstered and riding his bony left hip. She'd performed like an angel for him these last six weeks with a whisper-sharp blade, never complaining, but he could feel her steel curves quietly contorting like a diver with the bends, like a Tarahumara who'd run a few too many marathons. She would need a good oiling before he settled for the night.

His stomach growled and his loins stirred, and he hoped that maybe after he'd tended to the cane knife and the hammock had rocked the heaviest of agonies from his joints, he might persuade one of the witches to deliver a massage with the new scented oil they were distilling. He wasn't fussy which one. Tita, Malvine, Deli, they all had masterful touches—masterful bites, too, when you crossed them—as complex and nuanced as the varieties of chili that go in to make a Veracruz *mole*.

The women walking with him were his counterparts. People in the region called them Lupo's witches, Lupo's wives, sometimes less complimentary things, but neither he nor any of the *brujas* bothered to set the record straight. They were the multi-celled vision of a single eye. Above all, the witches were loyal—not to him, so much, but to the construct of nagual that ran so deep and pure that it folded round the pulled pork of Lupo's exhaustion like a soft corn taco.

Never ask Napoleon
  to wash your brother's car;
    the bucket seats will throw him

23

They walked past a clump of cactus that always grew in the neighbourhood of the psilocybin mushroom. He felt the rhythm of Deli's knitting change behind him. She'd noticed the windfall too. "I'll come back for them later," she said, her needles clicking.

"Malvine can do it," he replied. "Is that all right with you, Malvine?"

"Happy to," said the woman on his right. "Dely needs to keep her feet up until the baby comes."

The warmth of the women's affection coaxed the tiny hairs at the back of Lupo's neck to rise. Mushrooms were but one small aspect of the joy in their lives. Employed in Meso-American medicinery since time immemorial, they brought his household steady cash from pharmaceutical companies and research universities across Europe and the United States. Rock stars and quacks too, unfortunately, were stampeding Mexico for the 'shroom, but La Pantera's insistence on keeping Lupo's passages clean had served him well. He knew which strands to pick up and which to leave alone.

"In the old days," La Pantera, who'd been gone now for many years, told him one evening, "mankind was of one tribe and one language. The world thrived. There were no limits to abundance, joy, creativity, prosperity. When the naguales, you could call them advisors or practitioners of the abstract, visited kingdoms of plant and animal, there was no fragmentation between there and here. They returned with blueprints for the pyramids of Teotihuacan; they brought guardian songs to the chacmools of Tula; they opened corridors to mastery for every branch of art, science, and commerce. That was many suns ago. Today, we are mongrels, declining and incomprehensible to one another. You, for example, you're half gringo and half mestizo, which makes you a cauldron of Oaxaca-Maya-Spanish...what did you say your father was?"

"Well, he never admitted to being my father," Lupo said. "I am told he was a petroleum engineer from Texas. I don't know where his ancestors came from."

"Scots-Irish, probably, which brings in the Vikings, Celts, all the way back to India and the Himalayas. You have no idea what floats inside the blood cells you inherit from your mother—it may be good, it may be terrible. But I know you have more important things to do with your life than to shake a rattle over rum-soaked alcoholics like a two-bit village *curandero*."

She had a way with praise, that one.

The first of Lupo's witches to hear the rumbling, not of his stomach but a four-cylinder German engine with dirty plugs, walked always to the left of the nagual. Tita had large, splay-toed feet that were impervious to footwear. Her slap-slap stride was the longest of them all, a disproportion she adjusted by slowing her walk and extending the swing of her arms. If Lupo carried the rhythm of nagual, she was its propulsion.

Tita was a Zapotec from Chiapas, daughter of a mechanic whose final exhalations, after a lifetime of knife fights and searing black moods, reeked of raw cane liquor and diesel. She was named Serafina at birth, and her mother died nine days later of breast fever, at which point Fulgencio Orozco, shattered with grief, took to calling his daughter Chiquitita, teeny little one, so the devil couldn't catch hold of her unshriven Christian name and steal her away to Hell. The devil did manage, however, to grab hold of Serafina's heel. How else to explain why "Tita" stretched and grew to the large-boned, freakish height of six feet in a village where the tallest men brushed five foot four, their dutiful women half a head shorter?

Despite her deformity, Fulgencio loved his only child. He taught her how to strain and purify motor oil and how to build carburetors from scratch. She learned to repel the evil eye—easy, you ignore it. She also learned with a mechanic's practicality when not to interfere with the order of things simply because she saw them coming.

A nimbus of stinking gray exhaust was approaching from the east on the only stretch of paved road outside the hacienda grounds. The vehicle would arrive at the T-intersection precisely at the moment when the Nagual Lupo Sanchez and her sisters got there (Tita had never been fond of the word "witches") and either turn left toward the hacienda—not likely, there were better access roads closer to the plantation—or right toward Las Cuevas. Unless, of course, the engine gave up its wretched, miserable existence first.

People and automobiles, Father had taught her, are essentially the same. Each is a system of component parts and functions: you have your strut suspension that distributes stresses and eases the ride through wishbone or compression links; you have heating and cooling systems that circulate and mirror each other and function, given the right lubrication, with minimal fuss. Every mechanical problem holds a solution until it doesn't, and then you find some way around or through it. Solutions within solutions, infinite retrieval, that was all one needed to trust and believe to be a good mechanic.

The 1968 Volkswagen camper van came into view. It was pumpkin-coloured with an off-white, pop-up roof. Only four years old, it should have been maneuvering the potholes with the easy indifference of a plow horse. Instead, it lurched and gasped like a fat *patrón* dancing cha-cha at his daughter's wedding. They were all aware of the intrusion now—Malvine, Delia, the *Nagual* Lupo Sanchez. They were all making miniscule adjustments, drawing conclusions, dropping them, formulating new ones in the continuous, moment by moment steering that is life.

Tita swung her arms and continued to walk. *Slap, slap, slap, slap...*

RUE DES MARTYRS DE LE SIÈGE
TOULOUSE, FRANCE
LATE SPRING, PRESENT DAY

Blinking neon tubes of blue and white and amber flashed through drizzle, every drop of rain reflecting headlights of a Friday night traffic crawl. Silvina Kestral stood at the window of her second-storey flat, filling in a spreadsheet on her BlackBerry.

Y172, Y266, B172, O172, O272, V172...
Yellow, Blue, Orange, Violet...

The final row of data read: *top tier, max teaching, 432 hours, new rate, fully booked,* ending with a sum in Canadian dollars in high six figures.

Silvie's thumb hovered over the currency icon, struggling over which would give the report its brightest sheen. She knew Blythe Pendaris was waiting. The CEO and founder of Tri-Partite Academy would be sitting at her 300-year-old mahogany roll-top desk, a gift from the king of Sweden, while Skyping with a shareholder. Or she might be crossing Bay Street, checking messages on her handheld, hoping for good news from Toulouse. It was only 5:00 p.m. in Toronto. Silvie's boss had hours of workday ahead of her.

Oh, what the heck—euros, dollars, they were still good numbers! Silvie selected Canadian dollars, hit save, send, looked up from her BlackBerry, and cried out, "Jesus!" She spun around and pressed herself against the wall.

Several feet away, Alphonse Térac continued to arrange documents in cascading rows on the coffee table. "Were you expecting Him?"

She slapped a hand across her forehead. "Sorry, I didn't mean to be profane."

Old-fashioned radiator coils gurgled and hissed to the left of her, while bass notes from a Georges Moustaki remix thumped through the soles of her four-inch Monolo Blahniks. Erotic whiffs of Gauloises made her wish she were still a smoker.

"Church and sex," Alphonse said, "eternal fallbacks for the disarticulated. Now, what genius said that?"

"You did." Silvie peered around the window frame. "It's been a long week. I'm not always disarticulated... I think you made up that word." The neon reflection was still there, still blinking—on, off, on, off—though what she'd seen emerging from the reflection was not. She glanced at the BlackBerry's idle screen. "I hope the report went through."

"Why shouldn't it?"

"I haven't heard from Blythe yet."

"It's only been ninety seconds."

"But Full Spectrum is her baby. First venture into Europe, it's a big deal."

Her assistant peered over half-spectacles. "FST is your program, Silvie, you developed it. Tri-Partite is merely your backer, and it's been global for years. Perhaps you are nervous about tomorrow, about *Reine du Ciel.*"

At sixty-four, Alphonse was old enough to be Silvie's father. The Franco-Algerian was a former bank president, retired advisor to the International Monetary Fund, and to the World Economic Forum. There were still moments when it astonished Silvie that he was now the Executive Coordinator of Full Spectrum Training—and a friend.

"Maybe I'm a little nervous—okay, a lot." She leaned over to coax off the heels she'd been wearing fourteen hours straight. Her arches buckled and spasmed. Silently, she mouthed, *Ow, ow, ow!* "I'd been looking forward to seeing Viv since the day I arrived. We were going to visit all the castles in Languedoc, do cycling tours and wine tastings… and now she's gone. I was eighty miles away and couldn't even go to the funeral." Alphonse's eyebrow rose, and she added quickly, "That's not what I mean, sorry. You told me to go—but I just couldn't."

"Have the police closed their files yet on the investigation?"

"They have. It's been ruled accidental. Blythe thinks it's bull. People don't fall down steps and accidentally die, she says, in the same way you don't walk into doors and get a black eye. I don't know what to think."

Alphonse brushed nonexistent crumbs off the documents, unscrewed a Cross black resin fountain pen, and gently set it down. "What do you know about her fiancé?"

"Dr. Shirazi? I've only spoken to him a few times, seems very nice. They'd known each other for years. He's the one who phoned me when they found her body."

"This Dr. Shirazi, will he be meeting your train in Foix?"

"No, he'll be at the house. There's a shuttle van from the winery that comes to the station. I'll be dropped off at Viv's door."

Alphonse placed both hands on his knees and rose with a popping sound from the stiffly upholstered faux velvet love seat. Silvie checked her BlackBerry again.

"Now, let us see what lurks in the shadows of Toulouse," he said, and crossed the room to the window.

"It's nothing."

"It's not nothing. Whatever you saw made you curse, spin up against the wall, and now you look as though you wish to dive into your smartphone. Technology will not save you, I can tell you that right now."

"Okay. I thought I saw a man bursting out of the bidet. He looked right up at me as if… I don't know, as if he'd found me."

"Bursting out of what?"

"Martini glass, is what I meant to say. Have you ever noticed," she said, massaging her numb toes, "how Elke Füme looks like she's sprawled in a… never mind." She laughed. "I've been in this country eight months. I ought to be accustomed to French plumbing by now."

Alphonse wiped a circle of condensation from the window with the elbow of his charcoal tweed jacket. "*Elle qui fume*, she who smokes. It is a clever wordplay, typical of the Languedoce. Myself, I prefer the Imuhagh humour of my homeland, it's less riddlesome, more…" He punched a fist twice into his open palm and said something that might have been Berber. "So this man, you say he found you. How intriguing."

"He probably looked up to see if it was still raining."

They looked out the window together. Elke Füme was the name of the pub downstairs where undergrad students from the University of Toulouse drank, debated politics, and flirted across rickety wooden tables, making her feel old at thirty-seven, when she popped in sometimes for late-night nachos. But it was Elke's strobing reflection in the print shop across the street that Silvina had grown accustomed to: a fantasy in neon, lolling naked in a martini glass, her shapely legs dangling, one arm thrust boldly upward. The cigarette holder she once brandished had broken off, giving the impression with what remained that Elke was giving the world the finger.

Beneath the halo of a streetlamp, a young couple were making out in a sinuous tangle of leather and black denim. Behind them, under the print shop awning, a man in a light-coloured fedora was scrolling his mobile with a large cardboard box propped on one leg, one glove pulled off. He put the phone to his ear, jammed the glove underneath the twine that held the parcel together, and tested its weight like a suitcase. He wore a dark jacket with the fur collar turned up and moved slowly along the sidewalk, looking around in the drizzle as if taking in every detail. He did not look up at the window above Elke Füme again.

"The guy who's walking away, that's him," Silvie said. "I've never noticed that Elke's reflection is centered on the print shop door. No one ever comes out after hours, so when he opened it…"

"His only exit was through her plumbing," Alphonse said in perfect deadpan.

"Exactly." She switched off her BlackBerry and headed toward the documents arranged on the coffee table. She sat in a faux velvet chair that let off a slightly higher popping sound than the matching loveseat. "Crikey, I will not miss this furniture. So what do we have here? Anything I should read on the train?"

"On the train, you should read nothing. You should eat beignets with fig jam and dream of unicorns." He pointed to the first stack. "These are contracts for next term, followed by testimonials—initials only on the latter, please. Here we have expressions of interest for FST from Stockholm, Berne, Cologne, and Salamanca. It is as I told you, Silvie. Full Spectrum is awakening EU's hopeful spirit."

"That is nice to hear."

"And lastly, the sublet papers in French legalese. I have reviewed them, they are in order. If you would be so kind as to sign at the Xs, *s'il vous plaît*."

While Silvina scanned and signed, Alphonse retreated to the kitchenette. She picked up an email from the expressions of interest pile.

Esteemed members of Tri-Partite Academy: Attention has come to me by way of the French ambassador of a program you have initiated with great success called Full Spectrum Training. I am the owner of a small clock manufacturing firm and survivor of a terrorist bombing...

The second letter came from an IT specialist in Spain who'd been downsized with a severance large enough to seed a new business. *I look at my young children and do not wish to leave them a world that shames me. Your organization suggests to me there are better ways of doing business...*

They'd been receiving messages like this for weeks. Silvie had even shared a few with Vivian, who'd been her first mentor. She was fighting the urge to check for new texts when Alphonse appeared with a tray bearing one snifter of cognac and a small unwrapped parcel.

"This should help you relax." He slid the documents aside and set the tray in their place.

"Thank you. Aren't you having any?"

"It's airplane Courvoisier, I only had the one bottle in my pocket." He handed her the parcel. "Claire-Elise insisted I should be present while you open this." The parcel was wrapped in white, crochet-trimmed cotton that had been gathered at the center, so that the needlework created a frothy, ivory-coloured posy. "She sews the fabric giftwrap herself."

"This is beautiful. I have clients in Toronto who would love this."

"My bride prefers to keep her talents quiet, but I shall tell her what you said."

Alphonse's voice swelled with emotion whenever he spoke of "his bride". He kept a photo on his desk of their wedding day some forty years ago and a collage on his wall of their travels; but there were no recent photos, for Claire-Elise suffered from acute agoraphobia and had not left her bedroom in the suburbs of Toulouse for over a decade. Alphonse, who'd survived two major heart attacks and a quadruple by-pass brought about by work stress, negotiated an early retirement package and sold their mansion in Switzerland weeks before the 2007 economic collapse. He was Silvina's first graduate in Full Spectrum Training, and her first hire.

Inside the box was a 5x7 photo in a plain wooden frame. Two rows of young people hammed for the camera on a sloped field with a backdrop of stone ruins and bushel baskets of fruit in front of them. Bell-bottom jeans, Indian cotton skirts, and long hair placed the shot at early to mid-seventies.

"Who are these people?" Silvina asked.

"Can you distinguish no familiar faces?"

There were three men, four women, and sitting in the front row, a boy about six or seven. A woman with a round face and beaming apple cheeks had her arm around the boy. "Is this Claire-Elise?"

"It is, indeed."

"She's gorgeous." Silvie peered more closely at the dark-haired child with hands folded in his lap. The Téracs, she knew, had four grown children. "One of your sons?"

"No, I did not know her then. She was scarcely twenty. He may have been one of the local boys, I did not think to inquire."

Silvie felt a tightening of her ribcage. "This is *Reine du Ciel*?"

Alphonse smiled. "Where you will be in twelve hours."

"Oh, my gosh."

She had been hearing about *Reine du Ciel* for years, long before imagining that she would one day see it for herself. The Queen of Heaven, a place where apricots grew in unimaginable abundance, where walnut trees dropped nutmeats the size of baseballs, and opium poppies—God's blood to the locals—erupted from the stony ground like divine, open wounds. According to the only two people she'd known who experienced *Reine du Ciel*, it was a place without boundaries, an amorphous patch of land steeped

31

in violence and strange passions. "Blythe and I called ourselves Daughters of Babylon," Viv said, "because of the abundance."

"What about the guys?" Silvina asked. "Were they the Sons?"

"No. The guys never bothered with a name, but we were thick, closer than family." She shook her head. "I've never known anything like it since."

Vivian Lansdowne left Canada before Silvina knew enough to ask, what did you mean by thick? What kind of strange passions? When she asked Blythe a couple years later to explain where Queen of Heaven was, she was told the far edges of Aquitaine but further south, before you reach Navarre—"Not there, a little further north," Blythe said, poring over an atlas. "…hmm, no, that doesn't look right either"—as if the locale were meta-geographic, some mythic core of sovereignty crumpled in the high valleys between France and Spain. Silvina asked how large was the priory, and Blythe said its lands stretched across the Pyrenees to the meanders of St. James, over tribunals, past witchhunts through dynasties of generations of crumbling Cerabornes. Whatever all of that meant. Trouble was, Blythe only waxed freely on the topic midway through a second—sometimes third—bottle of Château Latour, and if she made it to Spanish coffee, exaggeration would give way to twitches and small choking sounds as if a fishbone had lodged in her throat.

Sober, Blythe Pendaris, President and CEO of Tri-partite Academy, 128th of *Fortune 500*'s most influential women, hardly mentioned Queen of Heaven and only then as "Q of H"—or as Silvie heard it for the first few years, "Cue Vaitch". Unlike Viv, she never spoke of the Daughters at all.

Now that Silvie knew what she was seeing, both women became recognizable. Blythe sat beside the young boy with her legs outstretched and lips puckered, in a playful Betty Boop pose. Her orange cotton skirt was bunched at the knees to reveal long tanned calves. She was still a brunette then, with long wavy hair to her waist, and a low-cut peasant blouse that accentuated the majestic, braless globes of her breasts.

Vivian was freckled with a frothy ginger halo. She stood in the back row between two young men, holding a tambourine to her midriff and head thrown back, grinning at the young man to her left with such unabashed affection that it made Silvina's eyes sting. The focus of Viv's attention had one hand resting on the headstock of a guitar. With his other hand, he was making bunny ears behind her head. Silvie wondered if the guitarist had been her boyfriend. She wondered if he knew that Viv was dead.

"Are you all right, Silvie?"

She pressed knuckles to her lower eyelids. "Overtired, a little emotional, I'll be okay." She glanced at her watch. "Oh gosh, it's twenty past twelve, and I haven't finished packing."

"Then I shall take my leave now." He picked up a briefcase and stuffed the documents inside. "Are you sure you don't want a ride to the station in the morning? I'm coming into the city anyway."

"No, thank you. I've booked a cab, it's all arranged." Silvina pressed the photograph to her heart as she walked Alphonse to the door.

"I do not want you to worry about TPA, FST, VAT or any other acronyms, while you are away," he said. Her strain must have showed, for he added, "Give no more thought to Blythe. She will come around."

"I hope so. I thought she was upset because I'd be missing the strategy sessions. When we first landed the Toulouse contract, she said, 'This is fabulous, you'll be able to visit my old stomping grounds.' But since Viv died, she refuses to talk about the place, and she's not happy about me going there."

"She's right you should be careful, but you are a grown woman. The seventies were a strange decade, even in Algeria. It was the middle child between peace-and-love sixties and economic hostage-taking of the eighties. Perhaps she fears exposure of some muscular enjoyment from her past."

"I hope that's all it is." She lifted Alphonse's overcoat off a hanger and handed it to him. She looked at the photo again. "Please give Claire-Elise my deepest thanks. I feel like a part of me knows *Reine du Ciel* already."

"She will be happy to hear that."

"Was your wife one of the Daughters?"

He stopped buttoning his coat. "I don't know. She was a Cerabornes, of course."

"I don't know that word."

"Cerabornes is her family name and the name of the village nearest *Reine du Ciel*. Her parents owned the grocery store. They helped to sell and ship the produce that Claire-Elise and her friends grew. Their ancestors have lived in those mountains for at least a thousand years."

33

"I would love to know more. Do you think Claire-Elise might agree to meet me for an espresso one day?"

"If she did, it would be magnificent." He kissed Silvie on both cheeks, then rummaged through his pockets and pressed a tiny glass bottle into her hand. It was a second Courvoisier. "Save this for a night when the wind blows cold and *la maison de la montagne* feels ready to share her secrets. *Bonne chance*, my friend."

CHAPTER TWO

A small, stout fishing boat slipped through the pre-dawn waters of a quiet cove, sails down. The vessel was in need of paint, the man and boy on deck, in need of sleep. Their gazes swept the nearby shallows.

"When hunting the serpent," the man was saying, "first thing one must find is a good wreck. The more mangled, the better."

"How does one find such a wreck, *tío* Benicio?" The boy leaned against the boat's hull, chin resting on his forearms.

Silhouetted against a pinkening sky, his uncle kept one firm hand on the rudder and slowed *Nuestra Senhora de Graza Perpetua* to a crawl. With his other, he tapped an ear. "By using this, Arturo."

"But what does she sound like, the serpent? Does she hiss, make bubbles?"

"It is not the serpent we are listening for." He gestured toward the waters of the calm, dark bay. "Can you not hear them?"

Arturo stood on tiptoe and craned his skinny neck. He could hear the gentle slap of waves against the hull; he heard Father rummaging through tin cookware belowdecks; he heard nothing, however, to suggest a mangled wreck or the conger eels that inhabit them and fetch a fine price at market. "I think I will never make a good fishermen," he said. "I hear nothing."

Benicio placed a hand on the boy's shoulder and lowered his voice. "When I was your age, I felt the same way, but then my uncle shared a secret with me, one that is known to only a handful of the finest Galician fishermen."

"What is the secret, *tío*?"

His voice dropped to a whisper. "If I tell you, you must promise never to reveal it to another soul, except, perhaps, to a nephew, should you find yourself on foreign shores similar to this one."

Arturo crossed himself. "I swear upon the holy relics of Santiago."

"Very well, then, here is the secret: when brave men die, especially at sea, they leave a trace at the very spot that their ship goes down . . . and that trace can be picked up by anyone—throughout eternity— who knows how to listen."

The boy's nostrils quivered, while he allowed the splendour of what he had just been told to settle. "Why would brave men do that? Why leave a trace, where they could be hunted down?"

"Why, to help other seamen, of course."

Everyone in Padrón knew that Uncle Benicio wove outrageous tales, especially when he'd enjoyed a quaff or two, but a thrill coursed through Arturo nonetheless. He cast his gaze across the water again. A predawn mist was rising off the sea like wood smoke, hovering over whitecaps of fine spun sugar. Though he couldn't be sure, Arturo thought that maybe he detected some echo of a skirmish, some whirling desperation in the vicinity that his uncle had pointed out.

"Are you sure those men died bravely, *tío*? I think they were drunk and fighting with each other."

"If they were Galician, they were heroes, drunk or sober, but even a vessel of frog-sucking Franks will house decent eels. Serpents aren't fussy."

"What kind of swill are you feeding my son now?"

Plutarco de Vila de Padrón climbed out of the sleeping hold, scratching a knit cap pulled over salt-encrusted hair. Darker and more wiry than his younger brother, he smelled of sweat, cod and sour red wine.

"About time you joined the world, Tarco. I think we've found her."

The smaller man peered, bleary-eyed, across the bay, and Arturo knew that his father couldn't see the way Uncle Benicio saw. With a shrug of indifference, he shuffled toward a wooden barrel and lifted the lid.

"You haven't prepared the bait, Turo. What have you been doing? Wasting your time again, listening to your uncle's fish tales."

"You said we should wait until we've anchored, Papá. The serpent only eats—"

The backhand knocked him sideways like a charging bull. Arturo held his injured cheek and, staring at Father, drove the pain, as he always did, inward.

"I know what the serpent eats," Father said, "I don't need a child to tell me."

"Calm yourself, brother," Benicio said. "The boy needs daylight to slice fish. No more torches. We've used too much pitch as it is."

"I could slice bait with my eyes closed before the age of five and pull in nets with the best of them."

"Yes, yes, we've all heard your stories—so what? Aha, look, Arturo, sure enough, that log is a broken mast. See how she comes up at an angle?" He turned *Nuestra Senhora* so that her name would not be visible from the shore. "We'll drop anchor portside, right here. Help me lift it over."

Gratitude soothed the boy's aches. Everyone knew that Benicio was the strongest man in Padrón; on feast days, blessed by Santiago the Apostle, he could juggle anchors with a full wine bottle on his head and never spill a drop. Nonetheless, Arturo took hold of a tine of iron, weightless in his uncle's grip, and assisted with the motions of heaving it over. One second . . . two . . . he heard a soft thud.

Father grunted. "Any closer to shore, we'd have run aground. If the tide goes out—"

"The tide is coming in," Benicio said, "but this cove is deceptive, some say enchanted. The waters come in fast."

"What about them?" Father pointed upward toward the cliff along the shore. "Anyone can see us from there, and we are well within arrow range."

Arturo sucked in his breath. Talmont Castle was, indeed, becoming more ominous against the sunrise. A jagged edifice of towers and battlements, it thrust and sprawled across the horizon like advancing stone armies. The castle was home to generations of kings, princes and dukes of Aquitaine, and was his closest glimpse yet of foreign power.

"There may be an archer or two, but I see no colours displayed," Benicio said. "I don't think the family is there. It was the old *duque* who loved the place. No one else comes around, since he coughed up his last."

"It only takes one archer. And we are poaching."

"Plutarco, have you mislaid your balls again? We are humble fishermen, making an honest living. We can't tell one border from another, and I am sending our young innocent ashore to prove it."

"You're what?"

"Arturo," Benicio went on. "See those clefted rocks, the ones that now catch the light and shimmer, even before the sun hits them? You will find *bígaros* in the wedges that are so fat and succulent they would make the Virgin weep."

"I am going ashore?" Arturo clenched both fists to his sides, to keep himself from jumping up and down.

Father rose to full height. "You are not sending my son ashore. I forbid it."

Benicio stood half a head taller than his brother without trying. "Your son has been stuck on this shithole of a boat for three months without complaining—and must I remind you who is captain?"

Arturo felt a pang of empathy for his father. Sometimes *tío* Benicio was too hard on Papá whose loss of his own boat and those other debts were not his fault. Still, the prospect of stepping onto foreign, perhaps even hostile, shores set his heart thumping.

Father's eyes crept over him, scanning for signs of eagerness—or disloyalty, as he liked to call it. Arturo braced himself for a second blow, but none came. Instead, Father's shoulders sagged.

"You say the tide is coming in. How long can he stay ashore safely?"

"An hour or so. Arturo, listen to me. When the sun rests upon the donjon of that castle, the highest point, you must return to the boat, no dallying. Do you understand?"

"Yes, *tío*. When the sun rests on the highest point."

"Stay away from those grassy dunes and anything south of them. The marshes hide quicksand and riptides."

"But I'm a strong swimmer," Arturo said.

"Then the riptides will drown you even faster. Now jump from the stern here, no rowboat. Oars scare off the serpents." Benicio tossed him a gunny sack. "Fill this with *bígaros*, and tonight we shall feast with profit enough to sail home by torchlight."

Father knelt to double-knot the laces of Arturo's sandals. "Keep your shoes on, son. Those rocks will shred your feet—and not a word about this to your mother."

Arturo nodded, only half-listening, while he cinched the burlap around his waist. He climbed over the edge of the boat, let his feet dangle and took one final look across the watery expanse between himself and wedges full of *bígaros* that would make fat virgins weep. He pinched his nostrils shut and leaped; he paddled and waded to shore and saw within moments that *tío* Benicio was right. The *bígaros*, the periwinkles, were everywhere, heaped in clusters, and easy to pry off with a small stick.

Tide waters lapped the base of the clefted outcrop in small rhythmic swishes. Arturo's arms and legs tingled with salt spray, his nostrils with the scent of pine forest. Pools of effervescence bubbled at his feet. The first two or three periwinkles, he took time to admire. Grooved spiral bands lightened in colour as they swirled toward the tip; inside, the shells were pearlescent white, smooth as a lady's wrist. Longing that he couldn't quite name rose and fell—

—and a squeal pierced the air.

Arturo threw a hand to his ear and nearly flung the bag of winkles into the sea. What manner of Frankish demon could make such a noise? A second squeal was followed by chattering, and he realized with horror that this was no demon or rabid wild boar hurtling toward him—it was woman, and there was more than one of them!

Their conversation approached with intensifying waves from the hill behind the rock. Arturo quickly assessed his options. He could stay where he was and hope, by some miracle, not to be noticed, which, if they were coming to bathe in the cove, would be impossible. He could make a run for the water with only half a bag of *bígaros* and call it a day. If he made a dash for it, however, he'd call attention to himself and would be thrown into prison along with his father and uncle for poaching. Running was a coward's way out. If Uncle Benicio were in this predicament, he would relax, hold his ground, and charm the ladies. Arturo wished he'd paid more attention to how, precisely, that was done.

The chattering had ceased, and he wondered if they had seen him and were now planning to flush him out like a grouse—but no, Arturo had some rudimentary hunting skills, which included a prey's healthy sense of dread.

What he felt more than anything, so keenly that his teeth ached, was curiosity.

Securing the gunny sack at his waist, he crept along the base of the outcrop toward the hillside where the rock leveled off to a grassy slope ascending to the castle. He recalled Benicio's warning about the dunes; this appeared to be ordinary grass.

He peered around the corner of the monolith that lent him protection and gasped. Invisible from the bay was a copse of corkscrew willow that contained a small glade. Within the glade, tucked up against the granite wall was a hut built of rough stone slabs and a sod roof. The structure blended so cleverly against the striated outcrop that a person gazing down from the castle would see nothing but a quiet stand of trees.

The women had entered the hut. He knew this with bone-shuddering certainty when the small shuttered window burst open and a head popped through.

"Phew, this place reeks of dead fish!"

Arturo leaped back around the corner, not knowing whether he had been seen. He waited and listened through thundering heartbeats. Apparently, he hadn't been. Creeping around again, he heard no conversation. Either the women had stopped talking or the stone walls absorbed their sound. The complaint about the fishy smell had been uttered in Langue d'oc, the language of Aquitaine that Arturo knew from pilgrims who stopped in Padrón on their way to Santiago and from nerve-shattered veterans of the Crusade. Their tongue was less harsh than Frankish but no match for the beauty of Galician—then again, what was?

He heard a trill of laughter, lighter and clearer than the rest, and his mind was made up. This opportunity would never come again; he took a step forward. To spy on women, possibly nobles . . . he took a second step. Thinking of the stories he could bring home that would rival Benicio's, he crouched and scampered. If the stars were truly in his favour, it would be a bathing hut . . . he scuttled the remaining distance to the open window.

"This is where Grandfather and *La Dangereuse* used to meet. He had *chatilliontes* built specially for the two of them wherever they lived."

"Well, she wouldn't be impressed with the state of this one. We need to light a bonfire, burn all this rubbish. Look at the droppings!"

Arturo curled his fingers around the window ledge and slowly raised his head, high enough to observe two women criss-crossing his field of vision. They carted nets and baskets at arm's length and tossed them with noises of disgust through the open door that faced the castle. The shorter woman was plump with a sweaty pale face; a white linen touret covered her hair and forehead. The taller one, who'd remarked on the turds, wore a dark blue velvet gown and a circlet of pearls that held a sky blue veil. Ladies of the court, both of them—he was sure of it.

The first voice he'd heard spoke up again, but he heard no laughter in it now.

"It isn't just the state of things here, Jocelyne, it's everything. If *Grandpère* were alive, his rage alone would light bonfires. These lands are mine. They were willed to me by Father the day he died, en route to Compostelle. It was Good Friday, the day of Our Lord's death. I don't care if St. Peter himself comes down to argue canonical law with me. I know my heart's truth."

"Milady," said the woman in pearls. "It would be judicious, if I may say so, not to call down the wrath of Paradise at a time like this."

"Then tell me, on what occasion should we call down the wrath of Heaven, if not at times like these? The Holy Father has forbidden the people of Aquitaine from taking the sacraments, and now they fear for their souls and the souls of their families. Why? Because the Pope and my husband snort and paw the ground like bulls in rut and cannot be made to listen to reason."

"But they have divine authority, Madame," said the fat, sweaty woman who reminded Arturo of his maiden aunt Constanza.

"And what do I have, Marie-Thérèse? Is my authority not equally divine?"

And with those words, she came into view, centered in the window frame, profiled toward the sunrise; and the first thing Arturo saw—no, felt—was dazzlement. He had never seen hair that shimmered in currents of scarlet and gold, nor curls that tumbled luxuriant to the waist without a cord or ribbon to bind them. She was lithe and tall and proportioned in a way that men noticed—in a way, he suspected, that everyone noticed. Her wool gown of mulberry with tight sleeves and bodice was the least adorned of the three women, and yet he would have known—knew already—that he looked upon a queen.

THE INTERSECTION OF CAMINO DE OBREGÓN
AND CARRETERA 14A, VERACRUZ, MEXICO,
LATE SUMMER, 1972

The turn signals of the sputtering, pumpkin orange Volkswagen camper never did reveal whether the driver intended to turn south toward the Delgado de Obregón sugarcane plantation or north toward the village of Las Cuevas. Twelve yards from the T-crossing, the vehicle jerked hard and threw the front left wheel into a pothole obviously marked with a fresh palm frond. The sudden stop caused the van's suspension to judder, the front grille to hiss white steam. Plumes of black smoke coughed out of the exhaust, and as if the spectacle were not embarrassing enough, the cream-coloured roof extension popped up like a jack-in-the-box lid. The Nagual Lupo Sanchez half-expected a chuckle-headed clown to stick his woolly head through the canvas and shout, "Hello, boys and girls, welcome to wicky-wacky whozits!"

Lupo and the three *brujas* slowed their pace, stopped, and turned, as one, toward the wheezing van, maintaining the time-honoured Indian tradition of somber to the point of mournful non-expression. Delia gave off knitting the turquoise Phentex baby blanket and placed two hands on her bulging belly. Tita, who towered behind the others, had already worked out where and how she might obtain the best spare parts and what, given the US plates—Philadelphia, she was fairly sure—she might charge for labour.

The youngest and most petite witch stood in front of Lupo and muttered something under her breath.

42

"*Qué dices?*" he said, from behind her right shoulder.

Malvine LaVendrye jackknifed forward at the waist, removed a *huarache* sandal from her small high-arched foot, and shook out a nonexistent pebble. "I said," she said, pulling up a piece of horizon as she rose, "that Mictlantecuhtli and Cihuatl have arrived."

Lupo scratched the itch underneath his sombrero that always acted up when this particular *bruja* expressed herself. "There's a she in that thing?"

"Oh, yes."

Sure enough, although only a man had been visible through the windshield, both front doors opened, and from the passenger side stepped a leggy young blonde in khaki shorts and lavender top. She was wiping her mouth across the back of her forearm in a way that explained why a driver with perfect visibility would swerve into a pothole big as a rain barrel.

"Dely, Tita, stay here," Lupo said. "The baby does not need a close encounter with whatever these gringos are smoking, although personally, Malvine, I think that the god of death would carry less fat around the middle." He turned and patted Delia's tummy. "Rest, both of you, if you need to." He cupped a hand around Malvine's upper arm. "We'll approach as *indios bobos*. Are you willing to let me do the talking?"

The third witch did not reply. She had caved in her chest and curled her shoulders. She was chewing on a pinky cuticle with her hand twisted backward, her normally bright gaze dull as tin centavos. She had already switched.

The couple had taken note of their Indian audience, half of them barefoot, one hugely pregnant, but as they had no tow truck or other visible means of assistance—looked, in fact, as though they'd never seen a wheeled vehicle—the couple's interest was short-lived. The driver, sweat staining his U Penn T-shirt to riverine swathes of gray, cared more, at the moment, about damage to the wheel well. His passenger, holding waist-length hair the colour of corn silk off the back of her neck while fanning away flies, craved cherry cola. Neither noticed that two of the Mexicans were approaching.

Lupo figured the man to be in his mid-to-late forties, a few years younger than himself. Judging by his attire, a professor, tenured, probably on sabbatical; he had the melted candle shape of one who has forgotten what it's like to fear joblessness. The girl was the shy side of twenty, if that, and

43

from what he'd witnessed so far, Lupo guessed she was his—what did they call it?—research assistant. Yeah. Good name. Pairs like them were showing up all over rural Mexico these days.

There was no point in asking Malvine in her current state why she'd associated these two with the god and goddess of the Aztec underworld, nor in reminding her, jokingly, that she carried not a drop of Mixtec blood or religosity in her veins. What her twenty-two-year-old veins had known and survived was far more destructive.

The nagual had found Malvine three years ago, while on business in Mexico City. He'd been strolling through the Hotel Intercontinental, idly checking phone booths, as was his habit, for loose change and found her huddled on the floor inside a booth, trembling as if half frozen. She wore black leather hot pants and a studded denim jacket; she was hugging her matchstick legs and frothing at the mouth, her nostrils ringed with white powder like a pair of mini-*churros*. Lupo knelt to check her pulse and pull back her eyelids and knowing an overdose when he saw one, rose to call Security. But when he started to walk away, she grabbed his ankle, pulled herself closer, and clamped her teeth into his calf.

"*Chingada,* what the fuck?!"

He tried to shake her off, but she dug her teeth in and clung more tightly, arms wrapped around his shin as if he were the mast of a sinking ship. While he dragged his leg that was sure to draw blood once she broke through the fabric, she slid on red and yellow vinyl platform shoes in a squat that revealed far more inner curvature than strangers ought to see.

He glanced around the pillared lobby in search of help, but no one seemed to notice his predicament. Tourists draped in gold and jewels fussed with lap dogs wearing ribbons in their fur; businessmen with grim expressions and alligator briefcases criss-crossed the marble expanse as though Lupo and the spiky-haired rat hanging from his pantleg did not exist.

And so he yelled. It was a single word, nonsensical, and delivered with the full intentionality and momentum of a plank across the side of his captor's head. She immediately released her teeth from his calf, but then she howled. Hers too was a single sound, nonsensical. Unlike Lupo's, however, it went on and on, a screeching barbed wire tangle of noise that ripped the top layer of cells from his ear drums and swarmed his mind with images of

44

inbred mountain haunts where werewolves stalked and succubi slurped husbands' souls, and children died stillborn from hearing laments that they were not wanted; and with each escalating, crescendoed beat of her cry, another head in the lobby turned. By the time her lungs, which surely had the capacity and strength of a whale pod, emptied, every businessman, every hotel employee, every man, woman, and be-ribboned frou-frou dog was staring at them.

Her open palms dropped to the floor. She arched her back in a languid feline stretch, held the pose and then released it with a sudden exhalation. She looked up at him with huge black pupils ringed in crystal blue, moved her pouty bow lips in and out like a guppy. That she was engaging in well-practiced theatrics he had no doubt, but there was something in the girl's eyes, some optic trick of light that emanated like a spray of needles from an impenetrable center that was so precise, so infrangible he could have hung from a single beam and done chin-ups.

La Pantera Negra had told him such skills existed, but they were rare. She herself had never seen them, except in dreaming awake. Entire empires rose, thrived, and crumbled without a single sighting. These awarenesses, or assemblages of perception, crept along the surface of the earth unclaimed, like feral children, as castaways from prior suns, from lineages long ago self-destroyed.

Two security guards were swaggering toward them, one slapping a billy cub into his palm, the other resting his hand on an enormous holstered pistol. Lupo sized up the variables. The girl was young and pretty; she was unaccompanied and vulnerable. Addictions ruled her. To be stoned in public in Mexico City proved she was undisciplined, arrogant, maybe just stupid. The eagerness of the goons in cobalt blue to dispense their form of law enforcement showed itself in the shine of saliva on their lower lips.

Lupo could do the manly thing, if nothing else, and insist she had not troubled him. He'd startled her; she was clearly ill; her family must be worried to death. There was also the remote possibility—though it was infinitesimal—that this little *ratoncita* was the answer to a long-standing nagual conundrum. He had about 1.25 seconds to make up his mind. Luckily, he'd dressed that day in chinos, a respectable dark brown sports jacket, and white dress shirt.

With a nod to the guards, he squatted and picked up the scrawny, trembling woman by the shoulders and hoisted her to a standing wobble, murmuring stage whispers along the lines of, "My daughter, my poor sweet daughter, what have you done to yourself now?"

Surprise crossed her face, then suspicion. He wondered if this time she would chow down on his neck. But she did not bite again, and with a few well-placed words and gestures, techniques he'd learned from La Pantera Negra, he persuaded the security guards that he was the girl's long-suffering father from Guadalajara, widowed, doing his best as a modest importer/exporter. He even burst into tears of gratitude when the hotel concierge insisted on covering the cab fare as the distraught *papacito* had left his wallet at home. (That last bit was upstaging for his own amusement, but the Intercontinental was a huge chain. They could afford it.)

Malvine LaVendrye, though Mexican born, turned out to be descended from the French bluebloods who accompanied Emperor Maximilian and his mad wife Carlota to Mexico in the nineteenth century. Estranged from her son-worshipping family of lawyers, doctors and engineers, she returned with Lupo to Las Cuevas where she cleaned up her drug habit, absorbed the ways of nagual with a speed and efficiency that were probably aided by genetic quirks, and became his third witch.

Lupo placed a protective hand on the shoulder of his companion, who was clearly feeble-minded, and said in perfect English to the man and woman crouched at the Volkswagen camper's front wheel, "Could we be of assistance?"

Silvina Kestral looked up at the place she'd be calling home for the next few weeks or months—she didn't know how long—while Vivian Lansdowne's exuberant descriptions ran through her mind in a lusty Scottish brogue.

The house stands on a small rise, like the king of its own mountain, if you can picture a king of gray mottled stone with eyes of two front windows, tilting, strained and lazy from centuries of Pyrennean turmoil. He has a long narrow nose door painted dark teal—a colour that in the proper light, brightens to cyan, that shade we adore on a peacock's tail. He has a high, second story forehead attic with a porthole, where a monarch might be expected to cram the stores of his massive intellect, and from which, when the mood suits him, he might gaze out upon his vast holdings with a singular and divine third eye. Now my king also enjoys the common touch—he wears no crown, only the red-tiled hunting cap roof you see everywhere in Languedoc, set at a severe yet jaunty angle, adorned with a stove-pipe chimney that sends smoky plumage across the orchards toward St. Jacques de la Rivière. I cannot wait for you to see it!

What Viv had never intimated in their conversations was: *I cannot wait for you to see it after I am dead.*

Temperatures for the *Pyrénées Atlantiques* were being described as unseasonably low, but 42° Fahrenheit with a wind chill that made it feel like 38° was not why Silvina's teeth were chattering and her knees knocking like wooden spoons. It was because during the past hour, she'd fully expected to fly off this mortal coil herself half a dozen times.

The train ride from Toulouse had been lovely. She'd intended to get caught up on reading TPA reports but fell asleep with her laptop open and woke up in Foix with a dead battery and drool on the keyboard.

A smiling young man named Jean-Luc was waiting at the station to drive her to *Reine du Ciel*. Curly-haired, married, father of two young kids, he was the kind of chauffeur who loved to talk, and because she was his only passenger, he invited her to sit in the front of the Citröen mini-van.

Silvina had taken almost no days off since coming to Toulouse, but in her limited experience, she'd found the roads of southern France to be excellent. They'd clearly hit some kind of tax boundary: a few kilometers outside of Foix, they were deep into the mountains on single-lane sheep trails that were badly paved or rutted gravel, or greasy mud or fine gritty powder. Jean-Luc had one speed for all of them—maniacal—and while he careened along switchbacks and blind curves with one hand on the wheel, the other fiddling with temperature knobs—"Is that warm enough? Are you feeling a draft?"—he poured forth an endless stream of knowledge of the biscuit-coloured gorges and the rivers that ran through them, of the lupins that would burst into blossom any day now, the red-tailed fox and marmots, and the names of the hermits who lived in the caves from the time of the Crusades to the Second World War. "Not the same hermits, of course, haha! That would be absurd."

Jean-Luc braked for only one reason: sheep. Sheep appeared, it seemed, out of the gravel itself, carpeting the road in a vast, shaggy, slow-moving mass, on their way, apparently, to high sweet pastures that winter melt had in recent days made accessible. Silvina knew little about sheep, so until the creatures had proven they knew enough to part as well as bleat in response to oncoming crazy French drivers, she was certain they would be minced mutton.

She'd never seen so many varieties. There were black-faced sheep with prim little mouths; curly-haired sheep with bangs so long one wondered how they didn't just topple off precipices; there were prong-horned sheep and curly-horned sheep, red-haired, yellow-haired, and splotched black-and-white like Jersey cow sheep. Some of the world's rarest breeds were being introduced into this part of the world, Jean-Luc explained, and all were thriving.

Whether people too were thriving, Silvina couldn't be certain because she kept her eyes squeezed shut for much of the journey—toes curled and hands balled into fists too, for good measure. Of the eight people she did see, every one was a shepherd. Jean-Luc knew all the herders by name. The men who weren't gridlocked by their own sheep jams, he called over by gesticulating through the open window (the draft he never asked about) and pointing at Silvina with a great swing of the forearm as if to announce, "Found a live one, boys! She cooks, she cleans, doesn't talk your ear off!"

They were a handsome lot, all craggy and lean in their fleece vests and trousers tucked into high boots, but Silvina couldn't understand a word they shouted to Jean-Luc. Some were Basque, he explained; others still spoke old

48

dialects of Languedoc, the tongues of Aquitaine, with smatterings of Galician and Catalán thrown in.

"The culture of these peaks is unlike any other," he said, accelerating toward the edge of an escarpment. "They've been places of refuge for centuries, and nowhere will you find more honest men."

Silvie slapped a hand over her eyes one last time, certain she wouldn't survive long enough to confirm any of it.

At what point they entered the official boundaries of Queen of Heaven, she had no idea. The final few kilometers, past a thriving little community called St. Jacques de la Rivière, entailed a slow, steep ascent between walls of stacked limestone that pressed in on both sides. They came to a plateau that was high enough to make her ears pop, then drove through an evergreen forest so dense and pungent her nostrils stung. Finally, he stopped the car.

"*Voici le prieuré et la maison de ton amie.*" Here is the priory and the house of your friend.

Jean-Luc unloaded her suitcases and carried them to the front door, and then he received a call from his wife who wanted him to pick something up while in Foix, and he hadn't. Slapping his chest, waving a palm in self-defense, he thrust a business card at Silvie, then stomped to the van and, spitting gravel, drove off, leaving her alone at the edge of the woods in front of the house she'd waited too long to visit.

Silvina wiped the sweat from her hands. She lifted the dark brass ring in the center of the nose...of the king's...she lifted the ring in the center of the door, and knocked.

She waited and knocked again.

There were no parked vehicles around the house. The sprinkles of tiny pink blooms that spread across the scruffy lawn and ruts of driveway appeared uncrushed. She checked her watch. 12:52. Dr. Shirazi had been staying at Vivian's house since the accident; he'd been the one who arranged her transportation with Jean-Luc.

She rapped a third time, then stepped off the flagstones onto spongy ground to peer through a window. Pots and pans hung on a tongue and groove wall panel in a diagonal pattern, their copper bottoms gleaming. A basket covered in blue gingham sat on a marble top island. Bunches of dried herbs hung from the ceiling on swagging loops of brass chain. The kitchen, what Viv called a *foganha*, looked like a still life from a calendar that would

49

feature cassoulet recipes and tips for growing heritage tomatoes. She cupped her hands around her face and leaned into the glass.

"Hello!"

Waiting, hearing nothing, she picked her way through leaf debris to the side of the house. Tucked into the edge of the forest was a small stone outbuilding with a sagging roof that was too narrow to be a garage. Nearby, half buried in drifts of twig and dead needle sprays, was a hive-shaped bread oven. If it weren't for the thick black cable that extended from the second floor window to poles along the road, she could be standing in Languedoc of a thousand years ago.

She thought she heard a metallic click. Thank God! Silvina dashed around to the front of the house, tucking in long blonde tendrils that had worked loose from the knot at her nape. The door was still closed. Dust devils swirled like tiny galaxies at her feet, while a rash of anxiety prickled across her upper chest. Maybe the click she'd heard didn't come from a deadbolt but a safety catch from someone armed and intending to warn her off. She glanced across the road to a wall of limestone with stunted juniper and holly pushing through its veins. The property was surrounded on both sides by dense walls of cedar; she had no idea what or who lay further up the road. Perhaps that village Claire-Elise came from. What had Alphonse called it? Cerabornes.

Vivian Lansdowne had been no hermit; even from this secluded enclave, she'd maintained an active presence in British theatre and the film industry. But she did live by herself and had fallen to her death somewhere in these mountains, three days short of her 68th birthday. By the time they found her body—no, Silvina refused to go there. It takes only seventeen seconds to activate a chain of thoughts, and unless those links are going to pull you to something better...

She touched the door with her fingertips; this time, it swung inward a few inches.

"Hello, I hope I'm not too early. It's Silvina. We said one o'clock, right?"

Wind whistled like discordant pan pipes through the treetops; there were no other sounds. She pushed the door open and, glancing left and right, stepped inside. She kept the door ajar behind her, unable to shake the feeling that she was being watched. Whether she was safer inside or out was impossible to know, but it was a good stout wooden door with a modern deadbolt, a metal latch, and a sliding wooden plank as thick as her wrist.

The entryway was small and dark. Jackets of heavy tarp and wool piled atop each other hung from a row of wall hooks. Beneath them was a jumble of footwear: wellies and hiking boots, running shoes with thick cotton laces—sensible stuff for a country life. The house, according to Vivian, had been a toll collector's station in the 1700's, and centuries before that, the *ostal* of an influential family whose wealth would have been apparent to all by the luxury of a second floor, accessible by ladder.

The central stairwell, where the ladder might have been, was narrower than the corridor that led to it, reminding Silvina of something Viv had said in one of their phone conversations. "The stairs in this house are ladder rungs with backing nailed onto them. The first bed springs Tar and I tried to carry upstairs got jammed and had to be blowtorched to pieces."

On either side of the corridor were arched doorways with heavy ornate molding in dark wood. The house smelled of wood fires but held no warmth, of baked bread and sage that made her stomach growl, reminding her that she'd eaten nothing today but a small carton of fig vanilla yogurt.

The most startling feature was the colour of the walls. So this, she thought, looking around, is motion-sensitive blue. It was the same shade as the door, but the door was high gloss, while the matte teal on old plaster took on depth, almost an oscillating shimmer, with layers accrued in the way that eggs build colour when dipped into dye baths. The air itself seemed saturated with the hue, casting off glints like miniscule storyboards of graystone, deep forest moss and storming oceans.

Silvina shivered in the damp gloom. No lights were on in the entryway or stairs, and illumination from the front windows seemed to stop at the arches, creating an illusion from where she stood of dressing room mirrors, facing and reflecting each another. She pressed middle fingers into her temples with small circling motions.

"Is anyone here?" she called out again.

Obviously not. Well, too bad, she was, and there was no undoing it. She opened the door, pulled in her two suitcases and laptop shoulder bag, and slid them into the corridor. After checking that the door was firmly closed, she carried her luggage into the *foganha*, the kitchen, on her left.

51

She scanned the polished copper pots and one enamel dipper on the wall, the marble island with stools tucked beneath. The sink was of old porcelain, nicked and rusting with two long curving taps and a smaller dipper attached to a chain. There was a gas oven with two burners. Plank shelves on plain iron brackets held canned goods and spice jars, stoneware, mismatched tumblers and cocktail glasses. The wall plaster had crumbled away in places to reveal lath and bare stone, which may have been deliberate shabby chic on Vivian's part.

Across the corridor, through the matching archway, was the parlour, what Viv called, "our coziest, most delicious room." There was a deep stone fireplace on the side wall with a half circle hearth that arced into the room with quartz-studded flagstones in pink and dove gray. A large black cauldron hung inside the fireplace above a teepee of logs, and a set of iron pokers rested in a rack beside a basket of wood chip kindling.

There were bookshelves crammed with hardcover art books and figurines in clay and stone inside bell jars. There were pillars of hat boxes patterned in stripes, polkadots, and pastoral scenes. The coziest feature, which nearly compensated for the cold, came from a pair of oxblood leather wing chairs, angled and facing the fireplace. Beside one of the chairs was a cloth and wood rack that held balls of wool and knitting needles. On a side table, a crossword puzzle book lay open to a half-finished puzzle.

"Aah, there you are. How were the roads? Have they repaired the washout? I was afraid at St. Jacques they might stop you from..."

Silvina spun around, grabbing the back of one of the wing chairs to slow her momentum and to take in the stooped, slender man in the doorway.

"Dr. Shirazi? I'm so sorry, I tried knocking. The door was unlocked— well, it was open a bit, actually...I didn't hear you. I didn't hear anyone."

For a long, awkward moment, they assessed one another. He was staring through thick horn-rimmed glasses, not in shock or fear but confusion; and then he looked disappointed, as if he'd been awaiting someone who stepped out for a while, and she, most decidedly, was not that someone.

Silvina wondered briefly if Jean-Luc had dropped her off at the wrong house. What had he said at the end of the driveway? "Here is the house of your friend." But had she specifically told him in Foix who she was? Had he even asked?

If this frail, silver-haired man in Bermuda shorts and hand-knit knee socks was Dr. Tariq Shirazi, famed archeologist and scholar, he looked thirty years older than the photo Viv had sent of them, taken last summer on their holiday in Nice. Perhaps, she was seeing the effects of deep grief.

"I'm not sure about the wash-out," she said with a smile. "I'm afraid I had my eyes closed for most of the drive."

He gave her a wan smile, not much, but it was something.

The wop-wopping of Silvina's heart had slowed, and now she wondered how a man of such fragility could negotiate steep stairs, unnoticed, when she'd just passed the stairwell less than a minute ago. Maybe, convinced the house was empty, she'd had her own blinders on, while he, clouded by shock and careful of his footing, had not seen her either.

She crossed the room with her hand outstretched. "I'm Silvina. It's an honour to meet you, Doctor Shirazi." A few feet away from him, she stopped and dropped her arm.

When she was five or six, Silvie's grandmother bought her a ViewMaster at a yard sale. It was a hand-held plastic projector that one clicked to view colour images in 3-D. Her favourite slides had been the Seven Wonders of the World: click, the Pyramids; click, the Great Wall of China, click. What she was seeing now in dramatic succession might be called the Seven Desolations: loneliness, mistrust, sorrow, fear…

Dr. Shirazi did not want her to come closer. He had curled his upper body to one side, as if tracing an arc of protection with his shoulder. He had dropped his chin and was peering at her over his glasses, as if seeing her blurred made her less real.

"You have come to take her away."

"Oh, no, not at all, I'm not taking anyone or anything away." She paused to observe the effect of her words. "I'm only here to organize what Vivian has left for us. I'm here to make things easier for you and everyone she loved. Of course, if you'd rather I didn't, that's okay too." Blythe would probably like nothing better than to hear that Silvina had changed her mind and was returning to Toronto for the summer.

The angle of his shoulders shifted a few degrees toward normal.

"You're the girl she hired? The one who's good with patterns?"

Silvie felt a small, hard punch to the heart. Vivian hadn't mentioned anything about Dr. Shirazi suffering from dementia. She always spoke of him with the British endearment of "my", as in, "My Tar is at it again, we've enough caraway rye loaves to provision the French Foreign Legion."

"Yes, she did hire me once, a long time ago. I was only fifteen. I doubt that she saw much pattern potential in me."

"We were supposed to leave together. I have all the paperwork. I could show you."

"I'm sure everything is in order, Doctor. I'm also very certain that Viv would love some help in organizing those wonderful mementos you've gathered. They are going to bring you both much pleasure."

Pretending Viv was here and all was normal seemed to relax him. He released the awkward set of his shoulders, even straightened a little. "She insisted it be you."

"Pardon me?"

"There'll be people after I'm gone, she said, who will make claims and want to overturn things, but my Little Herring will know what to do. She'll slither right through them."

Silvina's vision went funny, as if she'd been driving and suddenly shifted her focus to the windshield instead of the road. "Viv said that?"

Dr. Shirazi nodded. "Her very words."

The spelling of Silvina's name on her birth certificate was Silviina, with two i's. There was probably no one alive anymore who knew that or cared. Only two people had ever called her *Pikku Silli*, a Finnish play on words that meant Little Herring. One of them was her grandmother, Helmi Kiviäinen, who died twenty-two years ago when Silvina was fifteen. The second was Vivian, who somehow extracted that detail from her in their first five minutes of conversation. Those two events occurred three hundred miles and several months apart, and though Silvie had not pulled them together in her mind for a very long time, she recalled her first impressions of Vivian now as if they'd taken place minutes ago. She'd had no inkling yet of the woman's identity—there'd been no introduction—but her bold square jaw, hazel eyes that pulled and plucked at you, the Scottish burr that sounded to Silvie like an army of Highlanders drumming through heather made her feel as though she'd landed not in the northern Ontario mining town of Sudbury but in some other century. She could feel the rolling Rs on the surface of her skin.

Your grrrrandmother did not give you a merrre nickname. She gave you a totem, you know, and a fine one. We have herrrrings in Scotland, call them kippers, when tinned. They're a skinny wee fish that can slither unnoticed thrrrough the tightest places. Would you say that describes you, then?

Silvina had no recollection of whether she said yes or no, only that she'd felt mortified and ill equipped. No one where she came from spoke with such intensity, with such fullness of being. She also felt excitement rapping—*IneedthisjobIneedthisjobIneedthisjob*—at her breast like a woodpecker. How she would love to say to Vivian now, "Yes, my grandmother named me well, though I'm still in the process of learning to slither."

Dr. Shirazi's gaunt face was taking on colour; his eyes were even twinkling a bit.

"I'm sorry I missed the funeral," Silvina said. "Was it well attended?"

"Standing room only and out into the parking lot. I know of at least three memorials in the planning stages, in London, Edinburgh, Broadway. What do they call them now—celebrations of life? Not everyone loved her, of course, but ..." He shrugged in the fatalistic manner of his Middle Eastern roots.

Viv had said once, "My Tar is Persian, you know. His family can trace their roots to Kayumars, first king at the dawn of Creation."

Given the man's frailty, Silvie decided not to probe the matter of people who did not love Vivian. "I know she was excited about returning to the dig with you."

"Oh, yes. Re-opening Tel-Hemat had been our fondest dream for years. We tried once before, I expect she told you. All the visas and permits were arranged, she had turned down I don't know many scripts, and then Saddam set fire to the oil wells of Kuwait." With his fingertips he tapped the part in his hair as if to be sure it was still ruler straight. "How kind the looters and tanks have been to the site of Old Bab-El remains to be seen— now, where are my manners? You have traveled all this way, Ms Kestral. You will take tea, a bit of refreshment before I show you the house?"

"Call me Silvie. I'd love some, thank you. Tea is what brought Viv and me together."

She accompanied him to the *foganha*, and because he insisted, please, to tell him everything she could remember of their meeting, Silvie recounted that the tea had been Twinings English Breakfast, and it came in little red envelopes that sat in a chipped sugar bowl that was sometimes used as a prop in the plays Vivian directed during her one and only season in Canada.

She was already famous in Britain for leading roles with Peter O'Toole and Alan Bates, and for her fiery affairs with politicians on both sides of the Atlantic—Dr. Shirazi, to Silvina's surprise, added that piece and seemed pleasantly amused rather than jealous. Silvie, however, had known nothing of Vivian Lansdowne's star quality the day she stepped off the Greyhound bus with a backpack and $7.42 in her pocket.

The local police in Silvie's home town of Thunder Bay had sent information across CPIC, the microfiche data system, to provincial and federal police forces: Missing, Caucasian female, age 15; height, 5'8"; weight, 110 pounds; blue eyes, dark blonde hair. But kids ran away all the time and when there was no evidence of foul play, no immediate family to keep the pressure on, cases like hers slipped quietly into filing cabinet drawers.

It was a shame, folks agreed in the Finnish-Canadian community on the north shore of Lake Superior, that something couldn't be done to prevent the bank foreclosing on Helmi Kiviäinen's boarding house; and if her son-in-law had kept a head on his shoulders and a certain something in his pants—after all, those rich American doctors and lawyers paid good money to fly in bush planes to Twice Past Sunset, his fishing camp—that poor child might have stood a chance. But people have to look after their own, and no, officer, I haven't seen the girl in this photo since her grandmother's funeral. St. Luke's Lutheran paid for the service, the meal, even a grave marker out of their compassionate fund, not that the family ever attended church. I don't know what direction she might have gone. Roger Kestral's fishing camp has been closed for years; I don't think the road's even open anymore. She's probably gone west, to Vancouver. That's where most teenagers end up these days, isn't it?

A few blocks from the bus station, Silvie noticed a sign in the door of the Sudbury Theatre Centre:

Box Office Manager Needed Immediately
Apply Within
"And so, within I went."

Dr. Shirazi set a small platter near the gift basket. "Would you do the honour? The pistachios and dried apricots from *La Sorcière de Miel* are wonderful."

While the archeologist prepared mint tea, Silvie arranged fruit and nuts on the dish and recalled her interview with the stage manager named Toby. "I'd never met a man with pink-tipped hair and black nail polish. And I thought he wasn't using his real voice.

"Within minutes, he had me near tears. No, I had no theatre experience, no, I had never worked in a box office—then why are you wasting my time, he wanted to know. I need someone to start in three hours."

Dr. Shirazi had a glorious laugh that rolled out of him in layers. Silvie was beginning to understand the attraction. They carried the tea things into the parlour and sat across from each other in the leather wing chairs, in front of the fireplace that, while still unlit, didn't seem so cold anymore. And she told him of the moment when an imperious figure in a full tartan cape swept past the open door of the office where Toby was chewing a cuticle and muttering of disastrous opening nights, and said in a voice that wasn't loud and yet rattled every corner of the room she wasn't in: "Is there no one in this shambles of a theatre who can make a decent cuppa?"

Silvina's insecurities blew apart in that instant, like a bird's nest struck by lightning. All that the stage manager had discouraged her from expressing, like the discipline it took to run a boarding house with her grandmother, cooking three meals a day, seven days a week for eight full-time boarders; and the joy she experienced rowing on the lake at Twice Past Sunset; and the fact that her grandmother used to act in amateur theatre when she was younger; and they loved to watch TVO's Saturday Night at the Movies together. And while most Finns drank coffee, those like her family who came from Karelia in the East, also enjoyed tea. And Silvie's favourite heirloom, that she'd been forced to leave behind when she ran away to avoid being taken by the Children's Aid and seeing the house she'd grown up in foreclose, had been the family's sterling silver samovar.

"I shot out of the chair, ran into the hall and called out to the retreating figure in plaid, 'I can make tea!'"

Dr. Shirazi threw his head back and laughed. "No wonder Vivian loved you on sight."

57

He poured them each a second cup, then pulled several large coffee table books from the shelves that contained tinted colour photographs of his palatial family home in Tehran and the various summer palaces where he'd grown up. Yes, it was true what Viv had told her, that his family could trace their lineage to the first Persians mentioned in the Shahnameh, Book of Kings, and they counted among their closest friends, Mohammad Rezā Shāh Pahlavī, the last Shah of Iran, and his wife, the Empress Farah.

And from there, he spun seamless tales of dervishes and djinns to the point that Silvie could no longer distinguish, and nor did she care, between metaphor and history, between stories of the Doctor growing up with a coterie of dressers and food tasters, and the summers he spent sifting through layers of Hittite civilization, until he fell in love with a young red-haired woman on the French Riviera, and though his parents were appalled at his dropping out of flight school and moving with a bunch of hippies to the south of France, because whatever Scottish Presbyterianism was, even if she was non-practicing, it certainly wasn't Islam…

Dr. Shirazi glanced at the mantel clock above the fireplace. "Aah, forgive me, I have allowed my love of reminiscence to overtake good sense. There is a ship waiting in the harbour of Montpelier. I sail with her at dawn. And of course, you must have questions about this task to which you have so kindly agreed."

She swallowed the last of her tea. "A few, yes."

"I have prepared contact lists, they are in the upstairs study. Keys to the house, the outbuildings, safety deposit, and so on are in the *foganha*, hanging near the phone…"

"Speaking of phones," Silvie said, gathering up the tea things, "do you have wi-fi here? I know there are places in southern France that are still dial-up."

"Wi-fi?"

"Wireless."

"Ah, yes, of course, in the bedroom. Reception isn't always the best, but on Friday evenings, Radio Free Europe comes in quite clearly."

Three short honks and two long ones came from a vehicle in the driveway.

"That would be Jean-Luc," the Doctor said. "He's taking me to the station. The house is yours until the first of September. I know you hope to be finished long before then. The furniture can stay, along with kitchen items. The new owners, I'm sure, would enjoy a turnkey operation."

Silvie was about to ask who the new owners were, when Jean-Luc honked again, more urgently. "He forgot to pick up some things in Foix," she said. "His wife was a bit upset."

"Oh, she's always upset with him. I'm going to tell him to turn the engine off while I give you a tour."

"But you have a train to catch, don't you?"

Dr. Shirazi bent over the plate of apricots and drew swirls in the air before selecting the plumpest. "Time waits for no man, except for the chauffeur of the Queen of Heaven. There's a trick with the attic pull I need to show you."

TALMONT CASTLE
THE DUCHY OF AQUITAINE
SUMMER, A.D. 1141

Arturo peered through the open window of the fishing hut. He could not tear his eyes off the woman in a mulberry gown, who paced across the small room, looking skyward with both hands covering her mouth.

"I did not mean to speak harshly, Marie-Thérèse," she said, "and nor do I wish to drag anyone to eternal damnation with me, if that is the price of speaking my mind. But . . ." Here, she paused to level her gaze. "I am once again being squeezed in the middle, and I find this situation intolerable. The Holy Father waggles his finger, ordering me to rein Louis in because he's still a boy, though he's eighteen and more than capable of manly things. And Louis, husband and God's chosen representative in affairs of state . . ."

The edge in her words while speaking of the king made Arturo's heart rattle like a cage with a moulting cockerel inside.

". . . throws his loyalty behind—not me, not his wife, but his dead father, Louis le Gros, and he was enormous, let me tell you. I have lost count of the times that Louis has sworn upon the head of St. James, while scourging himself through layers of brocade that he'd sooner burn in Hell than back down, then one snort from the Pope or the Count of Toulouse and he's simpering again. Even God with His infinite patience must recognize at some point, for it's certainly obvious to me, that not every royal head is equally appointed."

"Ooh, Madame, do calm yourself. Working up a froth will solve nothing." The Lady Jocelyne placed a fishing crate against the far wall and covered it with tarpaulin. "This is hardly a throne, but sit. You'll feel better."

"Thank you," the queen said, and continued her circuit from the doorway of the *chatillionte* to the back wall, knuckles pressed to her chin. Arturo did not understand the word *chatillionte*, but he had committed it, as he would every word of this conversation, to memory.

Arturo knew from his early years, having been scrubbed and tutored in a household of women, about the world's monarchs. Louis VII was king of the Franks and his queen was the illustrious Álienor or Eleanora, as they called her in Galicia. Their royal court lived most of the year at Poitiers in Bordeaux, many leagues north of here, but here she was, on her own land. He, Arturo de Padrón, was resting his eyes upon the Duchess of Aquitaine, in the very cove that his uncle had selected as the site for conger eels. And in that moment of illustrious pleasure, the queen swung round and saw him through the window. Her face froze, all colour drained, and she screamed.

Her royal shock ignited his. Arturo spun on his heels and tore from the hut across rocky ground toward the beach. Arms pumping, he leaped over boulders and plowed through sandy patches. *Tío* Benicio might call his decision to flee cowardice, but at the moment, he didn't give a fig's pip what his uncle thought. He skidded through puddles and surely would have outrun Queen Eleanora and her ladies in their ponderous gowns, had it not been for the grassy knoll he attempted to jump over.

He landed short, and the quicksand grabbed hold of him like a succubus, snaring first one ankle and then the other. The watery sludge squelched and pulled at him. Caught to the knees, his struggling accelerated the sinking, his legs splayed, mid-run, like a wishbone.

Arturo clawed at the air. He spat out every curse and prayer the fishermen and priests had taught him. Stretching his arms, he tried to wriggle toward a clump of bulrushes, and every effort threw him further out of reach.

The sucking accelerated, pulling him deeper the harder he fought. His shoulders slipped beneath the surface of the quicksand, then his neck, chin, mouth. Arturo's last breath was squeezed out of his lungs by the pressure of sand and sea. Salty ooze filled and burned his nostrils, the insides of his ears, even the shameful places where'd he soiled and peed himself in terror. His final thoughts rose and bubbled out: there would be no feast of big juicy *bígaros* to please *tío* Benicio and Plutarco de Padrón would return home with no son, with only the satisfaction of having been right about his progeny's ineptitude. With a final muddy pop, Arturo thought no more.

CHAPTER THREE

The colonists of Virginia in the 1600s, long before there was a United States of America with gringos hungry for oil and copper and sulphur and gold, long before teenage kids were smoking, snorting, dabbing tongues to dots on paper, anything to fly out of the emotional coffins that back-to-back world wars had nailed them into—those colonists called the vines that crept so pretty along split-rail fences, devil's weed. They also called it jimson, after Jamestown, where the first apothecaries, who couldn't yet communicate, if they'd even tried, with the Algonquian or Iroquois medicine men, were learning by trial and error how not to kill asthmatic, neuralgic, and hemorrhoidal patients with the seeds and leaves they called *Stranomium*. Thornapple, stinkweed, devil's trumpet, *manzana peruana*—there were more names for datura than Lupo Sanchez bothered to cram into his head; here, in Mexico, they called her *toloache*.

The *casita de toloache*, little house of datura, was the outermost dwelling at the far end of Las Cuevas, furthest from the sugarcane plantation, closest to the caves. Apart from the fact that the walls and roof were covered year-round by the flowering vine, the structure was no different than any other two-room adobe. The patch of land against an ancient stone terrace had been part of Lupo's mother's family since before the Conquest, with stewardship passing from mother to daughter and occasionally son, when sons-in-law, hepped up on the aggressive effects of datura, blew themselves up in revolutions, sometimes after committing bigamy with mules and launching assaults on armies of cacti. Lupo had owned the house since his mother died. None of his sisters, who were married and scattered across

Mexico, wanted anything to do with the place. Until a few weeks ago, he'd succeeded in keeping the *casita* empty and the toloache calm.

One day, having returned from a festival in Veracruz, Lupo decided to check in on his new tenants. It was a pretty little house, impossible to whitewash except for the front wall or to patch the adobe, except from the inside. The door and shuttered windows were painted aqua, a pastel shade of serenity and good fortune. The vines and branches of toloache encased the dwelling that stood against an ancient stone terrace with a tangle of spiky leaves and spectacular white trumpet blossoms.

Lupo was about to knock when he noticed two rubber balls beside the front door, lying half buried in straw and burro hair. One was blue with red and white bands around the center; the other, solid red. They looked as though they'd been lying there for years. Lupo picked the balls up and squeezed them. The rubber gave pleasantly in his hands; they hadn't been there long. He dropped the balls from shoulder height. The blue one hit a cobblestone, bounced straight up, and he caught it; the red one hit dirt and arced down the road, bouncing up a series of little dust storms before landing at the base of a prickly pear. He retrieved the red ball, blew the dirt off, and approached the house a second time.

The shutters on both windows were closed, so no one from the street could peer inside. Not that anyone would. Appearing to suppress curiosity was a high-ranking talent for the villagers of Las Cuevas, even though the professor and his "*señorita*", whom the more disparaging called "*la*", a female "the", were the spiciest topic of conversation since the Nagual Lupo Sanchez and his witches set up housekeeping. Karin Albrechtsson, eighteen and "white as a potato bug", came from a place called Sweden, which was near the North Pole. Bill "Call me Guillermo" Carver, at forty-four, was old enough to be a grandfather, but he too, scandalously, was unmarried. People knew from the sounds that leaked through the *casita* after dark—and sometimes in the afternoons—that he was no *maricón*, but given that someone paid him to follow honest working folk with a machine that steals voices, asking questions even priests had the decency not to ask, well, it made one glad for a half-acre of land and a good hoe.

Lupo stood at the door, juggling the balls. From inside the house, he could hear short aggressive clacks of typewriter keys, interspersed with silence. He had warned the professor before leaving with Dely and the baby

63

for Veracruz to get plenty of fresh air every day. "Yep, sure thing," Bill had promised. "We've just finished the first set of interviews. As soon as I've collated this data…"

Karin, thankfully, did not enjoy being glued to a desk chair. When she wasn't accompanying Bill on interviews or compiling field notes, she spent long hours with the witches. Dely noted she had a knack for herbs and beehives, and while Tita kept a wide berth from "*la vikinguita con ojos de iceberg*", the little Viking with iceberg eyes, Malvine didn't mind Karin tagging along to gather medicinals from the scrubland and caves.

"She's good company," Malvine said, one evening over supper. "I enjoy hearing her backpacking stories."

"But why has she come to Mexico?" Dely asked, spooning *lomito con mole verde* on her own plate after having served the others. "And to Las Cuevas? No one comes here, not even the bishop."

"Some musician in Stuttgart broke her heart." Malvine was cradling Dely and Lupo's newborn son Ívano, while scooping up sauce with a folded corn tortilla. "Karin has an aunt who works at U Penn. The professor's previous assistant backed out, and Karin wanted to get as far away from Europe as she could. Poor kid, she's just trying to figure things out."

"The same might be said for the professor." Lupo sprinkled dried habanera seeds on his *mole*, eyes tearing, both from the hot peppers and to see Malvine nestling her cheek against his son's downy black hair. "He makes a career out of lists, can you imagine? They even get published—of course, they're only read by other list makers."

"Don't complain," Dely said. "His money doesn't bite."

"Dely's right," said Tita, "and he's the worst haggler of any gringo I've met."

"I'm going to have to give him lessons," Lupo said. "Even Paquito, the shoeshine boy, is fleecing him."

The day Lupo agreed to rent the *casita* to Bill and Karin, the pair had been living in the VW camper, newly reconditioned by Tita, near the village well. Mid-afternoon temperatures were reaching their usual low hundreds with humidity when angry voices shook the air. Lupo was dozing on his front porch, enjoying Mariachi Vargas on the transistor radio with Ívano, five days old, sleeping in a bassinette beside him.

Karin's normal speaking voice was a lilting delight, but that afternoon her shrieks were those of a hydrophobic coyote. "If I have to spend one more minute in this fucking tin oven, I'm taking the next boat to Stockholm, and you can bet your fat ass I'll find my way to the Gulf!" The van door slid open, and backpack, shoes, and scanty bits of clothing flew into the town square, followed by Bill's plaintive, "Not the field notes, pleeeease!"

Karen stomped, beet-faced and sweating, to the nagual's porch followed by Bill who was a more purply shade under his Philadelphia Flyers baseball cap and gasping for breath. In a staccato duet of interruption and strained civilities, they begged him to lease that shady little—*pretty* little—vine-covered house standing empty at the edge of town—it's not quite at the edge—I've walked past, there's nothing beyond—before one of them ended up strangling the other. While Lupo listened, his head moving side to side while the pair lobbed their shots, he gestured to the street urchins who'd witnessed everything and slipped them a few pesos to retrieve Bill's field notes.

When the two had argued themselves out, Lupo invited them to sit on the two empty cane chairs. He turned off Mariachi Vargas.

"The house may look empty," Lupo said, "but it's not what it appears to be."

"What do you mean?" asked Bill, who'd taken the seat nearest the baby and was chucking Ívano under the chin.

"Well, for one thing, it belongs to Toloache. I would have to obtain her permission."

"Who? Everyone tells me it's your place, and who is this Tolo-whatever? Have I met her?"

"I don't know. She's never mentioned you."

Karin snorted and crossed one bare, creamy white leg over the other. "You're not talking about a person, are you?"

"Not exactly, no," Lupo said.

She turned to Bill and tipped her head in the manner of I-told-you-so's everywhere but in a pretty way. "If you insist on refusing to read Castaneda, you could at least brush up on Carl Linnaeus, Swedish botanist, 1707-1778. Toloache, indigenous term for angiosperm of the order *Solonales*, genus Datura. Am I right, Señor Sanchez?"

"I can't speak for the Latin, but yes, you have correctly identified the owner of the house."

Bill scratched underneath his ball cap. "But datura is a hallucinogen, and I thought you naguals weren't into that stuff." He'd Anglicized the Nahuala-Mixtec word, a practice strangely common to English-speaking academics, as *nag-walls*. Lupo was slowly learning not to wince.

"A few of us are not, but toloache is also a medicine, and we have *curanderas* in my household."

"Datura is part of my culture too," Karin said, "part of the Old Ways, that is."

"What old ways are those?" Lupo asked. He knew from the playful flick at his left earlobe that Toloache had already made her decision, but the couple didn't know that, and there was no hurry in telling them. Main thing was, they were both calming down.

"Herbals and magicks, communication with the awareness of all things. The Swedish government and church forbid such practices, but we all know they're real."

"So, are you saying this house is haunted by the plant?" Bill asked. Drops of sweat were plinking off the end of his nose like a rain gutter after a storm. There were no dry patches left on his khaki shirt and shorts.

"Plants do not haunt," Lupo said, "any more than emissions from a sulphur plant or a coal mine haunt. That doesn't mean you won't be affected by sleeping and living in its vicinity." But Karin, he could see, wanted to know more, so Lupo told them of the man who eloped with his mule and a few other stories, toned down to sound more believable until Ívano started to fuss. He lifted his son, swaddled in white cotton, out of the cradle. "*Oy, oy, mijito*, I shouldn't tell you these stories, should I?"

"I think they're great," Bill said. "Authentic folkways, credible eyewitnesses...we can sign a waiver, take full responsibility, if that's what you're worried about." Bill turned to Karin. "You okay with that?"

"As long as we're not in the camper, it's fine by me."

"Very well," said Lupo. "You can write up the waiver however you like. I will need three months' rent in advance." He named a figure about ten times the going rate for a two-room, cold water adobe, with the friendly expectation that haggling would follow. Neither of them blinked. Bill Carver pulled out his wallet and slapped cool crisp U.S. greenbacks on the table beside the radio. That was five weeks ago, and so far, to the best of his knowledge, no one had run off with a mule.

Lupo was all set to knock when a thick, foetid smell, a cross between rotten potatoes and orange blossom, thwapped him, full-frontal, as if the gnarly-trunked, flowering toloache that caged the house had sneezed. The propulsion pushed him back half a step and caused him briefly to see stars. He nudged his sombrero off his forehead and said to the plant, "That was rude. What's your problem?"

From inside the house came, *clackety-clack, clack-clack, clack, clackety clack-clack...*

"I see," he said, giving his moustache a vigorous rub. "So much for the waiver."

Until the thought, "I am not dead", wrapped around his wrists, Arturo may have been dead. He didn't know. Compressed and sinking in salt water sludge, the quicksand had forced his eyes and lungs shut, and yet a second thought affirmed the first, rippling like an air bubble from impenetrable darkness that two hands had reached him, slender, feminine hands, and he knew who she was and he fought to let her know: *I can feel you, I'm alive!*

Her voice descended through stuttering, disconnected sounds that traveled the length of his arms to his shoulders to meet up in the center of his chest where they solidified and formed into words. "You mu-must relax," Queen Eleanora was telling him. "Do not attempt-tempt-tempt to kick your way ou-ou-ou-out."

I'm relaxing, I'm relaxed! I can't breathe, hurry!

She tugged sharply as if he were a puppy on a rope, while the bubbly words echoed. "You're not listening. Let yourself loosen, or you will start to pull, pull, pull me in too . . . you'll drown all of us."

Arturo's lungs burned like a blacksmith's forge; salt water and sand scoured the lining of his mouth and throat and eyelids, as if trying to erase him out of existence. Everything in him yearned to struggle, but her voice held a sinewy strength that he trusted, so he pushed back his instincts, absorbing the sounds that translated as, "My ladies are here with me. We're going to ease you out slowly. Think of yourself as fine rope, silken ribbon, you bend and curve, nothing breaks you—that's it, rise, rise, nothing slows your flight. Breathe from the belly, the way you did before you were born, born, born…"

In the space between echoes, space grew…the more he allowed himself…he relaxed, he became…and relaxed, he became relaxation from inside the muscles, from inside his bones and the center of his chest, outward to belly and bowels, to thighs, calves, the tips of his toes; he imagined his arms linked with beauty, unbreakable cords, better yet, he and she, they were serpents, twins of the sea, conger eels, fluttering with ease through jags and hollows of an ancient wreck where the seamen stood guard. Meandering, he saw the mire as clear, turquoise ocean—imagined the two of them, weaving serene figure eights around the masts of broken ships whose seamen went down, sending messages through time. He felt his limbs flutter, torso, smooth as silk. He was rising, flowing toward her—

Splash!

—and his head broke through what felt like a tempest of broken glass and blood. With the first suck of air, his sand-filled lungs revolted. He shook his head, and the painful sting of salt in every mucus membrane nearly pushed him right out of his body; and perhaps he did leave, for the fight was gone, and she was laying him out, limp as wet laundry, saying, through tears, "Well done, my sweet one, well done."

Arturo could have hovered forever in that place, midway between sense and oblivion for the pleasure of riding the undulations of that voice. Were his eyes even open? He couldn't tell, but he could see her, bending over him, attendants on either side.

"You're safe now," she said. "I'm going to roll you to your side. You'll feel wretched, I'm afraid, but let the sick come out, let it all—"

His coughing and gagging drowned out her words. He expelled clots of mud and mucus that tasted like blood and rotting fish, but between all of that, there were parts of him breathing and alive. It was awful, but goddamn, he was alive!

And when the vomiting slowed and Arturo could draw a series of ragged half breaths, she pulled him onto her lap with the tenderest of movements and called him her brave young soldier.

His burning eyes still closed, he traveled in his mind the paradise of fine-spun wool being rubbed along his cheeks, his nose, eyes, ears, neck, arms, hair. When enough tears had flowed that he could risk a peek, the first colour he saw through sunshine was mulberry.

And then he met her eyes. They were sea green, flecked with amber, and she stared at him, gaze pressing like twin swords. "Who are you? You look so much like him. You scared us all half to death."

Arturo shook his head, not knowing how to answer. "*Eu non son ninguén,*" he said in Galician, with a scratchy voice that shamed him with its weakness. "I am nobody...your Ladyship, y-your Majesty."

She frowned, more in surprise than disapproval, and answered in the same tongue. "*Estou Eleanora.* I am Eleanor. The house on the hill is mine, I used to live here." She cupped his face in her muddy hands and drew him close to study him. God had poured the sea into her eyes. Curls of gold and copper framed a heart-shaped face and tumbled loose over her breasts and shoulders. She was muddy and pale with fright; he had never seen skin so flawless.

"Jocelyne, Marie-Thérèse," she said, setting Arturo to sit close beside her, "hasten to the castle. Fetch wine and food, some clean clothes." The ladies, their bejeweled gowns not nearly as shambled as their queen's, struggled to their feet. "Now tell me your name," she said to Arturo. "No one is a nobody."

"I am Arturo of Padrón, Madame."

She shook her head, as if something unwanted still rattled inside. If he knew what she'd rather hear, he'd have gladly said it.

"My brother was William...Guillermo. He was four when the quicksand took him, nearly on this very spot."

So that was it. She thought she'd seen a ghost through the *chatillionte* window.

"How old are you, Arturo?"

"Eleven, Madame, soon to be twelve." He braced himself, expecting her to say, as everyone did, that he was small for his age. But she didn't, and she stroked his sodden hair.

"If William were alive today, he would be fifteen. He was four years younger than I."

"I am sorry, Madame, that you lost your brother…and that I can't be him."

Eleanor looked at him, then laughed gently. He now had a collection of memories of the sound of a queen's laughter—and then he remembered. He looked up at the sun; it was fully visible above the castle. He looked toward the cove; the tide was coming in and bringing with it his father and uncle, poachers, in the rowboat. The queen saw them too.

"Madame, please, whatever you do, do not punish my father and *tío* Benicio. They are noble Galicians, fallen on hard times. We've been out to sea for months. They allowed me to come ashore for *bígaros*, and I—" He looked down at the soggy burlap mass still tied to his waist. "I have ruined them."

"Don't worry, there are plenty more of those to be found in this cove." Eleanor rose to her feet and held out her hand for him to do the same. "You are blessed to be Galician, Arturo of Padrón. If you were of these lands, your soul would now be dangling above the fires of Hell. Come, introduce me to your family, and we shall negotiate a price for whatever they have caught or intend to catch."

Benicio had climbed out of the boat first and was swaggering toward them. Father had removed his hat and was holding it to his midsection, walking with small uncertain steps. Arturo noticed that his uncle had combed his salt-encrusted hair and changed his shirt to one less stinking. Arturo adored *tío* Benicio and, until this moment, would have done anything for him. Now he felt the first angry stirrings of manhood.

Toloache, now that she'd snagged Lupo's attention, wasn't letting go. The nagual was aware of some kind of turbulence but had no images to go with it. He walked around to the side of the *casita* where the oldest trunks grew thick as a man's thigh. He lifted one of the white trumpet blooms with his index finger and lowered his face to it.

Datura shivered at his touch. She would not shiver for just any human, of course, but a plant knows when she is heard and seen. With multigenerational roots plunging deep to subterranean swamps and rivers, toloache, who owned this house, lived in a constant state of bloom, fruition, decay, and seed; her nations of dendrites, some no more than a molecule thick, extended to the tectonic plates of Mother Earth herself and kept up with events, could record and retrieve them as proficiently as an X-ray technician in a modern hospital. But there were so few to whom she could convey the depths of her affection. She was a lonely plant. Responding to Lupo's soft warm breath, to the perceptivity of his gaze, which, in itself, threw out tendrils, the six powdery tips of the filaments that grew from the bloom's ovary vibrated and blushed to a deeper shade of pink. Toloache loved her pleasures.

Lupo set down his satchel. "So how are our guests doing? Are you being gentle with them?"

He formed the questions and offered them; he did not speak aloud. A person walking by on the street would see an ordinary man admiring a flower. Recognizing Lupo, they might even exchange the flip-flop hand signal, universal symbol for *poquito loquito*, a little crazy, but only because real men do not smell flowers or change diapers—that such a man could find three women to live with him, it just wasn't fair.

Lupo had been deaf as a post when he began slapping tortillas and hating every minute. "How do you listen to something that has no mouth?" he griped once to La Pantera.

"A bow to violin has no mouth," she said. "Wind through trees has no mouth, but you can hear both. You have tiny hairs inside your ears as sensitive to vibration as the butterfly's antennas, long rivers of nerve behind your eyes that flow to brain and backbone and deliver the most succulent messages to your gut.

"Problem is, most people have sold their backbones, like burros for hire to bosses and wives and husbands, so their spine can't talk to their gut. They become like drunkards, kicked out of their own house. With no conversation between gut and backbone, we think we're abandoned… poor me, poor me. These tortillas are lumpy. My customers will shoot you. Roll out the dough and start again."

Lupo laughed at the memory, slapped a palm against his left ear, and said to Toloache, "Could you repeat that, please? I wasn't paying attention."

71

I said, they are not my guests, they're yours. I hardly notice them. She has potential—sometimes I think she even hears me, but him? I've seen more cojones on a wheelbarrow.

"Now, now, don't be that way. We've talked about this before. Life, for humans, is not all about sex."

We've talked about it, yes, but you will never be a great nagual until you learn better. In the old days, they knew it IS all about...

And with that, an electric thrill zapped Lupo's loins with such ferocity that he doubled over, hit his head on the wall, and grunted. "Ow, that was unkind!"

Apologies. I was merely attempting to hook you up.

"Hook me up?"

Close your eyes, I promise to be gentler.

Lupo, whose lungs were beginning to numb from breathing in the hallucinogenic pollen, turned his back to the street and with a flower resting in his palm like a miniature Victrola, he closed his eyes.

Simple geometry came to him first. Disassociated lines and curves in two dimensions. There were vertical planes, right angles, oblongs and trapezoids floating, suspended in a grayish void, hanging out, nothing much going on, like day labourers waiting near a truck stop to be hired. By holding and simultaneously unfurling his attention like a spider's anchor thread, his body-mind spun and laid out a grid with wide-open spaces that trapped the attention of the idling shapes. They drifted in closer and finding no resistance, fitted themselves into the grid like puzzle pieces. And the shapes absorbed depth, third dimension—*and the greatest of these is depth*—and grew solid, took on matter. The grids walled, and lightwaves undulated to produce an image that flowed along the rivers of Lupo's optic nerve of rolling countryside in ochers and a thousand shades of green. Finally, a manor house appeared with towers at both ends, sitting gray and remote— that is to say, it gave off remoteness with a feeble vibratory wash.

Toloache loosened her grip. *That's enough for now.*

"What do you mean? You haven't shown me anything. It's an oil painting above a rich gringo's sofa. So what?"

I gave you the whole kit and kaboodle when you knocked.

"But that will take me years to sort. I want to know more now."

Toloache sighed with a little plant crush. *Fine, but only for you.*

72

Within moments, a woman in green velvet appeared at the window in the tower of the lonely manor house as if she'd heard her name. He saw her from the distance of willows and beeches and heard their silent singing. The woman couldn't see him, of course, for no man was in her field of vision. He was only breezes and tricks of light—

Okay, you've seen her. That's enough.

Toloache brooked no argument this time. She blurred his vision, and the foetid-sweet smell that hit him like a powder puff moments ago was now a stench that rolled over him in waves and set off a sequence of bodily revulsions—gagging, contractions of the stomach, loosening bowels, and while Lupo had developed enough stamina over the years not to puke and soil himself, the blindness was beyond his control. Flashing lights attacked: infra-reds and harsh electric yellows, miasmic greens, dripping, garish purples. Lupo staggered to the limestone ridge at the base of the terrace behind the *casita* where he rested his head and forearm against the stone until the symptoms eased. Pushing himself from the wall, he wondered what all that was about.

"No, don't tell me. You're right. I couldn't have taken any more."

He returned to the front door.

Clackety-clack. Clackety, clack, clack, clack…

"Cmmm ihmmh!"

Lupo entered, relieved to find William G. Carver, Ph.D., upright and sitting at his desk with a pencil clenched between his teeth. Well, not upright exactly. With his back rounded, elbows out, shoulders hitched to his ears, he looked like a sea tortoise furiously trying to unwedge himself from the keyboard of a Smith Corona.

Bill paused to nod hello, then nodded with a couple side sweeps to indicate, *have a seat beside the desk here, you'll need to clear off the crap first, give me a minute.*

The main room looked much the way it had a few weeks ago when Bill and Karin invited Lupo and the witches for a homecoming thank you repast of Spaghetti-O's, Uncle Ben's Minute Rice stirred into ground beef with chili peppers, and tinned palm heart salad. "I would have made you smörgåsbord," Karin had apologized, "but Bill insists we use up these awful supplies first."

There were heaps of books, recording and photography equipment, folded beach umbrellas and camp stools—a little more of everything, maybe, but not enough to raise concern.

The simple dwelling with packed earth floors and no indoor plumbing had been upgraded in the 1920s to accommodate a team of petroleum prospectors from Texas, including one who took a shine to a widow with four daughters. The terracotta tile floors patterned in an ancient Olmec design to perpetuate good fortune had been laid by Lupo's grandfather, himself a *nagual*. The shutters on the side window were open to the toloache lattice, impossible to cut back, and Lupo guessed that the corresponding window in the bedroom was open too. He could feel, not a cross breeze—Las Cuevas had no breeze this time of day—but a slow, rhythmic contraction-expansion like the movement of a whale's lungs.

The room smelled of datura musk mixed with male sweat, mildew from old books, and the spritzy citrus of L'Air de Temps, Karin's favourite scent, according to Malvine. Five or six toloache flowers in various stages of bloom hung inside the house through the window. There was an electric hotplate in the corner with two lidded pots. He could detect no signs of cooking.

The professor removed the pencil from his mouth, drawing a long thread of saliva that rippled and bounced like translucent vermicelli. "Just give me a sec, nearly done here."

"No hurry." Lupo crossed an ankle over his knee and peered at the handwritten notes in a spiral notebook grown puffy from filled pages. Hand-drawn tables featured columns with titles like: Biol Fam with Rel, Biol Fam with Married Chil, Married Sibs with Fam, Unrelated Fams, Persons Living Alone, Misc. Comp.

Numbers had been entered in each of the lists. There was an overlay of sprinkles of pink eraser rubbings on the page, and tiny rubber mountain ranges were forming on the floor where Bill brushed them from the desk. But it wasn't the unkempt floor or barren kitchen that had Lupo wondering whether he ought to suggest that Dely come in a few times a week; it was the look of Bill Carver himself.

He'd lost none of the paunch that Lupo had associated with middle-aged American men since he was a wetback kid in Jersey. And his cheeks still held an endearing apple roundness, only now, fine blue lines had risen like a map of rivulets, like fissures on porcelain. The veins on his hands too

74

had become inky blue and prominent, as if too much was accumulating on the inside and straining to get out.

"There! Done!" Bill whacked at the carriage return, pulled out the page, and sat back, arms draped over the sides of his chair. "I think we could drill down further into Miscellaneous Composition, but for a first go-round, this isn't bad. Maybe I'll try talking to the priest again."

He turned to Lupo and grinned. "Sorry. I'm talking like you should be on my wave length. So how are you, buddy? How was Veracruz? How's the baby? What's his name again?"

"Ívano. He's good, loves his mama's milk. Dely sold all her *serapes* at the carnival."

"Hey, that's great." Bill stuck a pinky finger in his left ear and shook vigorously.

"So," Lupo said, "are you and Karin still okay with the house? Tita says you were having some problems with the generator."

"We were. The battery coils had been eaten by some kind of termite, but she replaced them, thank God. A cool house with lamps that work makes for a happy assistant. What time did she and Malvine leave for the caves this morning? Was it even daylight?"

"No, it was way before dawn. The caves they wanted to see, you can only enter when the dawn rays hit a certain series of stones."

"No shit! So those old beliefs, they're still being handed down."

"Well, you could call them beliefs. That's not what they are."

Bill raised a conciliatory hand. "Hey, Nag-wall, I may be an anthropologist, but I'm with you here. I've seen stuff with the Hopi and Navajo that would knock your socks off. What I mean is, and I'm glad to hear it, is that your people have retained modalities that predate the Conquest and influence of the Church." The capillaries on his face intensified while he spoke from a fountain pen aqua to luminescent cobalt blue. Excitement radiated from his pores like tiny electrical shorts. "Every new discovery, every hand reaching out from my border to yours, is a fork in the road to raise our awareness, know what I'm saying? I was trying to explain this to Karin the other day…"

Lupo stayed as neutral as he could. Agreeing with the professor in his current manic state, even a tiny nod, would only whip up a whole new line of chaos that the man would spin into questions to take out in the village

75

and irritate even more *rurales*, for the sake of his lists that no one gave two shits about. *Sorry, Mamita. I'll cross myself later.*

Thing is, Lupo liked the professor. He wouldn't hurt a flea, and his desire to know, to connect felt genuine. So he waited for Bill to talk himself out, and then said, "My people can't tell you anything about the sun's relation to the caves. They don't know about it."

"Really?" Bill was breathing like he'd run a marathon. "But they go to the caves all the time to gather guano."

"Sure, and they get bitten all the time by spiders and bats, and the bites get infected, and *indios* die. It doesn't matter whether they have access to the missionaries' medicine or the *curanderos'*. They die." Bill's respiration was slowing, the veins in his face fading, so Lupo continued. "When I was a kid, we lived in a town called Longport—all white, mostly upper class. My mother cleaned houses, and one of her employers had some kind of surgery. Mom wanted to bring her her mail, but the hospital had strict visiting hours. It didn't matter that the woman would have loved to open what were obviously get-well cards, or that my mother, who knew the room number, could have found the right corridor and delivered the mail, no harm done. She'd have been violating rules, and the hospital, in its way, would have bitten her. It's like that with the caves. They have visiting hours; they have boundaries. It's like that with anything, even people."

"Hold on, don't say another word." Bill leaned toward the far end of the desk and rummaged under textbooks and notebooks and pulled out a portable tape recorder. "Would you mind?"

"Would I mind what?"

"My getting this down on tape."

"But I've already said it."

"Are you kidding me? I want to know everything about caves and hospitals that bite, it's genius analogy. When Karin gets back, she'll transcribe our conversation into notes. They'll be verbatim. You can read them over for accuracy."

The toloache blossoms inside the window were shivering. Not that Lupo would have agreed to being taped, but they were letting him know, just in case. "I think it would be best if you let Karin tell you her experiences in the caves and whatever she's learned from Malvine. Some things are

76

clearer coming from women...speaking of witches." He held out the rubber balls. "Are these yours?"

Disappointment squashed Bill's features like a wedding cake left in the rain. "Where'd you find them?"

"Outside your door. They look like they'd been there a few days."

"Damn, that's the fifth time this week. I've tried ball point pens, compact mirrors—nice ones, too, pink with little rhinestones, Karin picked them out in Tucson. I know soccer balls go over well with the Huicholes, but you carry a couple of those under your arm, people can't keep their mind on the questions."

"What do you want me to do with them?"

"There's a box in the corner with all the—no, wait. Why don't you hang onto them? They're pretty good quality. You and your son could enjoy a few games of catch when he's a little older."

"You sure? Thanks." Lupo went to drop the balls into the satchel he always carried, but it wasn't there. He must have left it beside the house during the toloache episode.

Bill pushed a button on the recorder and the lid popped up. "While I have you here..."

He lifted out the reel and blew on it. He pulled out a foot or so of tape and held it to the light as if to inspect, or to make apparent that what he was about to ask would be, if Lupo insisted, off the record. "We were talking about the caves, it reminded me. In twenty-four years of research and field work, I've only come across this once or twice. *Curanderos* don't seem to know anything about it—well, they know the garden variety, obviously. Our doctors in the States do it all the time—take two of these, you'll feel better in the morning."

"What are you talking about, Bill?"

"I hope you won't think I'm out of line."

"Not at all, ask away."

Bill rubbed his nose with the back of his hand, which left a golden yellow smudge of what looked like pollen. He swiveled, leaned toward Lupo, planted elbows on his knees, and in a dramatic stage whisper said, "I want to know about the manny-opera."

"Excuse me?"

"The man-ny-ob-ra." It was a slight improvement.

77

Bill Carver's Spanglish was easy enough to sort; that wasn't why Lupo was stalling. "Are you saying *maniobra*?"

"Yeah, that's what I'm saying."

Now, *that*, he had not seen coming. Lupo flexed his fingers open and closed. "It means handiwork. *Mano*, hand, *obra*, work. Tapestry, pots, basket weaving…like what Dely sells on feast days. Unfortunately, in our subsistence economy, the quality of such work is declining. Even with tourism, it's not the—"

"I'm not talking about arts and crafts. I mean the real stuff, what you nag-walls do. The maneuver."

"Why would such a thing be of interest to you?"

"No reason, really. I mean, I have an academic interest, obviously."

That was the second time Bill Carver had used the word obviously. Lupo waited.

"Okay, I have a reason. There's this anthropologist turned bestselling author who's touring campuses these days, making a fortune talking about his experiences with a Mexican sorcerer. His sources are a little sketchy, if you ask me, but I've talked to friends who know friends of his, and they say, what he's doing, the whole thing, it's a maneuver, a calculated strategy that looks haphazard—"

At that moment, the door flew open, and Karin and Malvine burst into the room, chatting and laughing, carrying baskets with long-stemmed flowers and honeycomb peeking out from beneath squares of cotton.

"…and then he said, you should have told me what you wanted the first time."

With fresh shrieks of laughter, their heads came together, hands on each other's shoulders; they looked like a feminine *Arc de Triomphe*.

Lupo had never noticed the women side by side, away from the other witches. Both were petite and curvaceous, one raven-haired with multicoloured ribbons woven through her braids, the other platinum blonde in a touristy sombrero with red pompoms. In their matching playfulness, they reminded him of the West Highland White and Scottish terriers of the Black & White Scotch whisky ads.

On impulse, to counteract, perhaps, a sudden inappropriate craving, Lupo Sanchez lobbed both rubber balls toward the women. Without the slightest break in her engagement, Malvine extended an arm and the blue striped ball plopped neatly in her basket. Karin Albrechtsson didn't see the balls coming. The red one hit her on the right front pocket of her denim cut-offs and fell to the floor.

She caught it on the second bounce and pulled the ball up to her shoulder. Karin had stopped laughing. She looked toward the men, not knowing which of them had thrown it. She turned slightly at the waist and with a practiced overhand, threw the ball at Lupo. He caught it, and he caught the look in her eye.

The events that followed would be unobservable to anyone untrained in the ways of nagual. They might feel an awkward silence or the sensation of time slowing down. The technical term, translated from the ancient tongue, would go something like: *magnetic rock shatters, shower-song pours over parched land.*

Malvine LaVendrye, of course, observed it all, and her laughter too fell away. She glanced toward the window where the toloache blossoms bobbed jauntily in a nonexistent breeze, then to the nagual. She raised her eyebrows slightly: *Am I seeing what I think I see?*

Lupo Sanchez dropped his head. *I'm afraid so.*

PRIEURÉ DE REINE DU CIEL
PYRENEES, SOUTHERN FRANCE
PRESENT DAY

Wi-fi, wireless, it was an honest mistake, coming from a man who'd spent his life digging up 3000-year-old fertility goddesses with a toothbrush and sieve. The 1940s-era radio in Viv's bedroom crackled magnificently and must have been a comfort during the Cold War years. What disturbed

Silvina as much as the isolation was discovering that she had no numbers in her head, not even the main switchboard number for Tri-Partite Academy, her employer of twenty years. Speed dial and texting had wiped that part of her memory clean.

It took Silvie half an hour through long distance operators to obtain the TPA switchboard number. Blythe's home and mobile number were both unlisted. It was 8:30, Monday morning, Toronto time, so the chances were fairly good that Blythe would at least be in the building, if not at her desk. Silvie would find out as soon as she finished the slow, rotary dialing of twelve numbers.

Someone answered before the second ring. "Hello?"

"Oh, I'm sorry, I must have the wrong number."

"Silvina, is that you? Thank God!"

"Blythe? Is something wrong?"

Her employer never answered phones, even her cell, without identifying herself. And the hello had been incredulous, hesitant; it didn't sound like her at all.

"Wrong? No, nothing's wrong." Her laugh was a nervous hiccup. "It's just that when I saw the number on call display—there was no name, it just said 'out of country'—I had the awfulest feeling that it would be…well, of course, it couldn't be. Why are you calling on Vivian's phone?"

"You know this number by sight?"

"It was my number too for seven years."

True enough. Among Blythe's singular skills was a photographic, bordering on pathologic, memory for numbers. She'd admitted once that she trained herself not to look at licence plates while driving, or her head would be so cluttered she couldn't sleep or function in meetings. But still!

"I'm using Viv's phone because none of my technology works here. There's no dial-up, nothing. Even my adaptor plugs don't fit the wall sockets."

"Good grief, how are you going to function? Does Alphonse know?"

"Not yet. I'll call him later today. I don't know what I'm going to do. I suppose one advantage is that the publishers and agents and whoever else has been clamouring for access to Viv's life can't bother me."

"But you and Viv communicated by email."

"We did, and we talked on her mobile. She'd mention once in a while that she was in a coffee shop or a winery, but she never said it was by necessity."

"No, she wouldn't," Blythe said. "So, apart from archaic wiring, how is the house? At one time, there were eight of us living there, and we had no indoor plumbing. Can you imagine?"

"Sort of. It's a charming little place, middle of nowhere. She's put in some upgrades, and with the windows open, the most amazing smell of cedar and eucalyptus blows through. It's like living in a hope chest."

"Yes, I remember that smell and the physical ache of missing it for years afterwards. There is nothing like the air of the Pyrenees. I remember too when lupins appeared overnight like purple armies, poppies fluttering like sheets of red silk, the taste of apricots fresh from the tree…" There was warmth, this time, in her laughter. "Listen to me, going all nostalgic. Tell me, Silvie, what of your task? Any sense yet of how much of your summer this is going to consume?"

"Not really. The parlour has floor-to-ceiling bookshelves and pillars of hat boxes. If the boxes contain hats, clearing it won't take me long. There are armoires in the bedroom crammed with theatre scrapbooks and silk gloves and old handkerchiefs. I've only popped my head into the attic. It looks like a prop room with trunks, clothing racks and old lamps. Her study will be the biggest challenge. I don't think she ever threw away a receipt— or filed one."

"She always was a pack rat. Have you met any of the locals yet?"

"Apart from the chauffeur, no, though I am planning to visit Cerabornes within the next hour. Shops close at five, and the only food in the house is from a gift basket, most of which I've eaten."

"Really? Who's it from?"

"Some shop, I don't remember."

"Well, there used to be a couple in Cerabornes who owned a jewelry store. Their names were Louis-Bernard and Orsine. They were ancient then—or maybe they were only in their fifties and looked old to us. If they're still there, would you remember me to them? They used to call me *La Canadienne Solitaire*. They were the sweetest people."

"Of course, I'd be happy to."

"Hold on, I'm going to tell Liz I'm not taking calls." In less than a minute, she was back on the line. "So these publishers, what do you know about them?"

"I don't have the names in front of me, but they're major houses from both the UK and the States. They offered healthy advances, too. She turned them all down."

"Did she tell you why?"

"She said they were only looking for theatre rag—who slept with Burton, who partied with Princess Madge, that sort of thing."

"So you don't think they wanted to know about the Daughters."

The air thickened, and Silvie's lungs compressed as if she were breathing coal dust in a low-ceilinged room. It was no great haunting, just her normal bodily reaction to emotion. Known as synesthesia, some called the neurological cross-wiring of sensory perceptions a disorder. When her high school essays got flagged for including the smell of world events and the guidance counsellor had determined she wasn't a smart ass, he recommended meds or electro-shock. Her grandmother was incensed. "Nobody electrocutes my granddaughter! It's growing pains. She'll grow out of it." She didn't, but over the years, Silvina had learned to work with it.

Coal dust meant defensiveness. From Blythe's perspective, they were nearing dangerous emotional territory, and if Silvie answered too quickly, the conversation would fall apart. She waited until the air cleared before saying, "I can't imagine that anyone would care about a few young people who gardened organically forty years ago. Anyway, it's all on Google." That last bit wasn't quite true. Plenty was missing about those peculiar years at *Reine du Ciel*, but the statement was enough for Blythe to relax and change the subject.

"What about her legal and financial contacts? Have you been in touch with them? I know she had a theatre agent who was devoted to her."

"The agent died last year, and according to Dr. Shirazi, she fired her attorney and accountant about six months ago."

Timber wolf cornered, thunderbolts, translucent, frozen, held in check. Silvina needed to eat soon. Low blood sugar worsened the condition.

"According to whom?" Blythe said.

"Tariq Shirazi, her fiancé."

There was a sharp intake of breath, and she heard a word softly spoken. *Tar.*

"When were you speaking to him?"

"Yesterday. He let me into the house, gave me the tour."

"And where is…Dr. Shirazi now?"

"En route to Cairo, and from there to Iraq."

She heard a muffling, like a hand placed over the phone, and Blythe shouting, "Not now, Liz! Tell them I'll call back in five!" She came back on the line. "Sorry."

"No worries. I need to get going anyway."

"Silvie, wait. Listen to me. I know I've been a little bitchy since you agreed to being Vivianne's executrix, but I have my reasons. I wish I could go into them, but I can't. I honestly cannot."

Silvina curled loops of telephone cord around her finger. "I'm listening."

"Don't stay in that house. Rent a car, pack it with as much as it will hold, find a B & B somewhere. St. Jacques must have something by now. You can even expense a percentage. Just don't stay in that house."

Blythe's tendency to control was nothing new; Silvie felt more annoyed than worried and had no intention of mentioning the 30-year-old, one-speed bicycle with saddlebag baskets she'd found in the shed. "I appreciate your advice, but there's a perfectly good deadbolt, and a wooden plank that takes both hands and my full body weight to slide across the door."

"Shoot, it's Beijing, I can't miss this call. We'll talk later. Let me know when you've made arrangements."

Silvie had intended to ask Blythe for her unlisted cell and home numbers but didn't get a chance. She stood in the *foganha*, holding the receiver and heard a second click. Someone else had been on the line.

LAS CUEVAS
VERACRUZ, MEXICO
SUMMER, 1972

At the first rise of crescent moon, carrying only an empty gourd tied to a rope at his waist, the Nagual Lupo Sanchez visited the furthest series of caves for which the village was named. An hour's hike through maguey cactus, prickly pear and other barbed and thorny succulents, the caves he sought had never been dwelling places for humans, and the curanderos and naguales who'd frequented their chambers over millennia left no rock art or artifacts. The succession of domed rooms, though equal in grandeur to those of San Luis Potosí, had thus far escaped the attention of spelunkers and the Mexican Tourist Board. Snakes and rabid bats helped in that regard; so did the subtler biting things.

He slid on his belly through a horizontal crevasse in total darkness, feeling his way through air pockets, changes in surface texture, and gurgling patterns of water. Not that there was much chance of taking a wrong turn when, like the steps of cathedrals and places of pilgrimage, the crystal-studded basalt had worn to accommodate the human form. Lupo simply shimmy-crawled through the only narrowness that granted passage until his hands met air, and then he pulled himself forward, folding like a taco to release one leg at a time.

There was no natural light in the domed chamber known as *La Boca de Bruja*, Witch's Mouth, where stalactites thick as a man's thigh dripped from the ceiling to their stalagmite counterparts in a saline pool to create echoing, arrhythmic plings like a surrealist's bell choir. Lupo had brought flashlights and pitch torches in the past: he knew of the 1200-foot drop on the far side of the chamber, and the guano-slickened cat walk along the edges that could take a person into deeper auditoriums or allow them to peer into the bottomless and see all of one's conjurations about hell and damnation, but he hadn't come to explore his soul. And his was not the kind of vision that required light rays and retinas to meet. Lupo held out his gourd.

No insights came inside the cave. No rockets of inspiration fired while he walked home, soaking wet and shivering. Not until he was in his hammock beside Dely— *delicada y sabrosa, su amante preciosa*—who'd

84

received his gourd with the precious drops and hung it from a sacred place; who'd welcomed his sodden caresses in a tangle of cotton mesh and warm wool *serapes*, while their infant son Ívano slept in his own little hammock; not until he'd reached the blissful rocking state between wakefulness and sleep, did the toloache who'd sneezed her knowledge at him and cave waters...

> outside the circle of the ages
>> like cousins
>>> *ridicule awaits, rampages*
>>>> combine and offer up...

...cantilevered histories stretching and compressing, folding and unfolding through a single drop from aqueous, the multi-breast stalagtites, tetas, She-cave *is Shaddai to Hittites of Anatolia, precious Baal to the Phoenicians, seafarers of great Cana, Spider woman, she would be Chalchiuhtlicue to the Toltecs, consort of primordial nagual who dispenses Feathered Serpent knowing, crystalline the seeds among great rivers of the Maya and Mixtec, of Chimu and last Inca...single drop in the gourd of awareness enough for you to form a pearl, from thence to spread and travel sands of stone and time, to rise through edifices built by slaves, their muscled, sinewed muteness thrown to moats of snake-filled water, sad reward for toils done, the ramparts heaped with faggots for the burning and for archers, battlements, and architects of war they are—save one, save one—all gone...a Court of Love passed on, a single house, built not from cards yet joyfully a game from Gate of God, Bab-El, for none can be destroyed by utterance, a play of knave and queen and jester dealing freely, throw you One, I do, and W—no, double You! where Two and Three make Five, the women of the Sultan Eight—they eat divine of nectar and a bun, dance, yes, abundance, yes, I, la Cérida, grant you Thirteen spiral wishes—*

"Lupo, Lupo, wake up!"

"*La Cérida, axúdanos! Chingada*, what the fu—?" Even half asleep and disoriented, Lupo crossed himself and apologized to Mother.

"You're waking up the household, possibly the village."

He rolled onto his side and into the milk-sweet valley of Dely's breasts. "*Mmmffwwh*, what was I saying? Mmm, *delicada, deliciosa...*"

Lightly, Dely slapped his groping hand and giggled with the girlishness that grew him like a corn stalk every time. She slid her hand across his cheek, dipping her thumb into his mouth—"The milk is not for you," she chided, while taking hold of his manhood with her other hand. "You were hollering, crying out strange words…"

"Why would I holler? The dream was beautiful."

"It didn't sound like a happy dream."

"Tell me the words."

"I've never heard them, but they sounded like 'cel, *chuk*, cel, *chuk*!'"

Lupo rolled onto his back to enjoy the gentle manipulation. And even as desire filled him, tears poured in hot rivulets down his cheeks and into the whorls of his ears. "There was a boy, just a lad, he was running and running, so proud one moment, happy, and then—" His voice broke. "I cannot scrub the image…I do not want to see this."

"You shouldn't have gone to the cave. You know these things happen."

"This was different. The cave, the toloache, they sing of these lands, our lands, the tribulation and savagery of the soil beneath our own *huaraches*…but this was something else, Dely. An entire world cracked open and bleeding, every layer like the skins of a putrified onion. I don't know how to peel back this world, I don't know how to help."

"What makes you think you're supposed to?"

"I am nagual. For what other purpose am I here?"

Tiny squeaks and smackings of tongue and lip drifted from the hammock strung crosswise near their feet. Dely got out of bed and lifted the baby from his. Gently, she laid Ívano into his father's arms. "It is time for me to make tortillas. Rest with your son, Lupo. He will soothe your nightmares."

La Cérida, axúdanos! Lupo Sanchez was fluent in six languages. Of this one, he could catch the drift: "Someone, help us!" That was all he knew.

BOOK TWO

The Crusade

If you could hear
the stillness
of the footsteps of my lover
when she comes
to me at night,
you'd draw your sword,
you'd plunder
for a glimpse
or for an echo.

—*Arturo de Padrón of the Royal Order*

of the Knights of St. James,

Year of Our Lord, 1152

CHAPTER FOUR

Silvina leaned the single speed bike that she'd walked more than pedaled against a lamp post in front of a shop called LB & O. There were neon-coloured plastic lawn chairs stacked beside the door, and the sign on the window still read Louis-Bernard et Orsine in beautiful, flowing cursive, but *Bijouterie* on the stone façade had been painted over, replaced by *Quincaillerie*, hardware store, although the original letters still bled through.

Vivian, in her late sixties, had cycled to the village at least three times a week. Cerabornes was only a mile and a quarter from the house, not a steep ride but a continuous uphill at an already hefty elevation. Silvina held the lamp post and slowly raised one knee and then the other until her thigh muscles stopped seizing.

Small French cars were parked bumper to bumper on both sides of the narrow main street, but there were no more than a dozen people on the sidewalks. Most of the shops were three-storey stucco with graystone facades. A pair of oval-shaped older women in floral cotton dresses and handknit cardigans eyed Silvina keenly as they passed. One of them pulled her carrier bag closer, as if the foreigner might otherwise grab her carrots by their feathery green tops. A group of teenagers with multiple piercings and Koolaid-bright hair were gathered outside Chez Guillemette, *Salon de Beauté*, texting on handhelds. Silvie hadn't thought to bring her BlackBerry. She wondered if the teens had cornered Cerabornes's only hot spot.

A bell jingled above her head when she entered LB & O. A long, glass-fronted display counter ran along the left wall, and to her right, high rows of utilitarian metal shelves displayed nuts, bolts, washers, and nails. No one appeared in response to the bell. The plank floors worn to concave groaned beneath her feet. Inside the display case were thick leather gloves, hand-held tools that looked like portable vacuums, and shears with blades like butcher knives. There were posters with jaunty looking men in Australian drover hats that read, "*Ne vous fiez pas votre tonte des moutons à rien de moins que Whittier^MD.*" Don't trust your sheep shearing to anything less than Whittier.

A linen curtain in the back rippled, and a man stepped through. He regarded her a moment before greeting her in French, not Occitan, the dialect of the region. "*Bonjour, comment allez vous?*"

"*Bonjour, très bien, merci.*"

He went around to the back of the display case and, planting his hands wide apart in an inverted V on the counter, said, "How may I be of assistance?"

Back of the counter, retail etiquette from 1860, amazing! He looked to be about Silvie's age, mid-to-late thirties, but the plaid flannel shirt and suspenders added twenty years to his appearance. No part of his slender body smiled.

"I'm here from Canada," she continued in French, "and staying in the area awhile. I've been asked to pass along greetings from a friend to Louis-Bernard and his wife Orsine. Are they here, by any chance?"

"Louis-Bernard passed away over twenty years ago, and my grandmother, sadly, only last spring. I am their grandson, Olivier."

"I'm sorry to hear of your loss. Please accept my condolences."

"*Merci.*"

He picked up a rag and began to polish the glass top of the display case. Whether shy or rude, he did not seem inclined to chat, so she asked him when the jewelry store had converted to hardware.

"The early nineties. My parents ran the *bijouterie*. My family have been silversmiths and jewelers since the Second Crusade. I was learning the craft myself. But Cerabornes, we're less than four hundred souls now, and with St. Jacques taking what little business we have, not to mention *l'Internet…*" He shrugged in the Gallic way. *This is how it goes.*

"That must have been difficult. When my friend lived here, Cerabornes was enjoying something of a revival."

"Aah, *oui?* What years were those?"

"Mid-seventies."

His expression, though hardly chipper at the start, folded in on itself like a crumpled wrapper. He muttered something that seemed to go on and on.

"I'm sorry," Silvie said, "my Occitan is dreadful."

He rattled off a fusillade of idiomatic alternatives: *"Nid de la mare, le bunco, le flim-flam...*we have many names for *le cozenage* that destroyed the lives of many, including my grandparents."

If Sylvie had brought her handheld, she'd be jockeying the teens for their wifi spot to ask Blythe why she'd not mentioned that their years of growing giant zucchini were a sore spot with the locals. "I didn't know, I'm sorry." She looked around for a packet of seeds, something she could buy, but the counter top was bare, and she had no need for sheep shears.

"So why are you here?" Olivier asked.

"I'm a friend of Vivian Lansdowne who lived at *Reine du Ciel*. I'm staying at her house and organizing her effects."

At last, the fleeting passage of a smile. "Madame Lansdowne was *très gentile*. We talked often of ways to revive my family's craft. I was sad to hear what happened."

She waited for him to say more; he didn't.

"Do people talk about how she died?" Silvie asked.

"Of course, they talk. We are a small town. Are you here to ask questions? We have told everything to the police."

"I haven't come to ask questions, but I was a friend of Vivian's. I'm getting her house ready for new tenants. If there's anyone who might be willing to talk to me, I'd appreciate your spreading the word." She hadn't mentioned staying at the house, but Silvie was already wondering if she'd said too much.

Olivier tossed the cleaning rag from one hand to the other. "People do not like to talk about *Reine de Ciel*, even though she has many secrets that would bring in tourists of a certain kind...as it did once before."

"If tourists came again, would you want to resume silversmithing?"

"Very much." He dropped the rag and examined his palms. "Madame Lansdowne told me I have a gift, and I should not be selling shovels and plastic rakes."

"She told me the same thing once, long ago." Silvina reached into her purse and brought out a business card. "I offer a course in Toulouse for people who've been diverted from their passions. We're starting up again in the fall."

"Full Spectrum Training. I don't have money."

"We offer sliding rates and scholarships."

"*Merci*." He tucked the card into his shirt pocket. "And this friend who knew my grandparents, what is her name?"

Silvina decided to skirt the question. Blythe Pendaris was a billionaire—"Blythe Pendaris, Billionairess" as certain tabloids had been known to taunt. Extreme success, when accompanied by wealth, tended to trouble people, especially those who nursed disappointment like hot house orchids. It was one of the reasons downsized and scandalized CEOs and other executives felt comfortable in her FST sessions alongside musicians, artists, and entrepreneurs. They suffered and felt loss like everyone else, but no one was telling them, "You've got millions. Why aren't you on a beach somewhere?"

"She was someone who lived here when she was young, and who appreciated your grandparents' kindness. I'll pass her the sad news, and once again, my sympathies." She walked to the door, thought a moment, and turned. "Olivier, I know I've missed lunch and I'm too early for dinner, but are there any restaurants or cafés in Cerabornes that might be open?"

"On Mondays? The only place would be *La Sorcière du Miel*, two doors down. She may not offer table service at this hour, but she keeps sandwiches and pastries on hand. Everything is organic and quite delicious."

Silvina thanked him and walked to the store she'd passed when pedalling into the village. *La Sorcière du Miel*, that was the card in the gift basket, which, for all she knew, was left over from Viv's funeral. The restaurant had no graystone frontage but was all stucco, painted a pretty shade of apricot. There'd been a couple sitting at the table in the bay window. She remembered because they'd been framed by lace curtains, and the man wore black and she, a blonde, was in some frothy shade, and they looked, with their heads inclined toward each other, like a painting by Renoir. And Silvie had felt an ache when she saw them, the kind of ache that 16-hour work days generally kept at bay.

It was 3:40 p.m., and the sign in the window read, *Ouvert*, but the door was firmly locked. She sidled over to the bay window where the couple had been sitting. Tea accoutrements were still on the table, but the people were gone and there was no sign of activity in the café. A feeling of lassitude like thick jellied drippings poured over her. She shouldn't have waited this long to buy food. She walked Vivian's bicycle to the grocery store where Claire-Elise's parents, probably long gone too, had once helped a group of flower children sell the fruits of their labour. There seemed to be no point in asking the bored cashier or the lady with the worry lines who was slicing cheese, "Did you used to know...?" Silvie bought brie, eggs, butter, milk, fresh basil, mushrooms, and a baguette, and cycled home.

PHRYGIAN MOUNTAINS
ANATOLIA, ASIA MINOR
DECEMBER, A.D. 1147

On the morning of the slaughter, three days shy of his seventeenth birthday, Arturo de Padrón awoke before dawn. He lay huddled in wool and sacking on the frozen ground and gazed up at a clear, bright sky of constelled star ships, heroes and guardian beasts. The belt of Orion, great hunter, still prone these winter months, hid behind snow-capped peaks. He watched shooting stars arc across the heavens like flame-tipped arrows, like sweat from a steed shaking off a hard ride.

Surrounding him in the dark chill were five hundred sleeping pilgrims. Among them snored the lesser knights and squires, armed protectors interspersed among the weaponless. King Louis's tent rose high and proud in the center of the encampment, surrounded by the tents of his principal knights and entourage. At the corners of the camp and on the peaks of every tent flew the red and white banners of the Second Glorious Crusade, their mission to reclaim the holy cities for the One True Church. Queen Eleanor's sleeping quarters was not among them.

Arturo was neither knight nor courtier, and nor was he a pilgrim. He was the water boy, and more importantly, the tender of the queen's royal baggage and beasts of burden who hauled it. He listened to the coughs, the whistling snorts and bellows, and found that he could distinguish a few of them. Ezequiel, the old shoemaker, talked in his sleep, conducting dream business, perhaps, in the shop he'd left behind in Padrón. Isidore, a distant illegitimate cousin of the king, sounded like a jackal being flayed alive. Arturo listened for and was relieved not to hear the sobbing prayers of doña Maria del Carmen, mother of Lizibetta and her irritating younger sister, Catarina. Pilgrims who accompanied the Crusade en route to Jerusalem often prayed and grieved under cover of darkness, but they were not the mother of his new love, so they didn't pull him down into feelings of helplessness.

He reached inside a pillow of moss wrapped in canvas and felt around for two objects. The first was a dagger. An attendant of the royal baggage was permitted no unauthorized weaponry, although if it came to that, he would probably fight to the death to keep this one.

Arturo's mother had given him the sheathed knife on the eve of his departure from Galicia eight months ago. She had kept it sequestered behind the azulejo tiles in the kitchen for years, its existence known only to the women. He ran his fingers along the bumps and dips of the worn leather sheath. When they reached Mount Cadmos tonight, after all the watering and feeding and unloading was complete, he would find a quiet place in the woods and with a rag dipped in neatsfoot oil, restore suppleness to the leather.

The sheath, of course, had held less interest than its contents on the night that his mother placed it before him at the table near the fireplace.

"The time has come for you to have this, Arturo," she told him, unwrapping a long thin parcel of linen. "It belonged to your grandfather, for whom you were named, and now it belongs to you. It will keep you safe on your journeys."

Arturo stared at the beautiful object lying before him. Slowly, he wrapped his fingers around the polished bone handle and pulled out the dagger. It was Toledo steel, the world's finest, and hallmarked at the base. The blade was the length of a man's hand, curved and tapered to a point that drew blood instantly when Arturo touched it. The silver metal glinted in the firelight, showing off fine swirls from years of sharpening.

"I have never seen anything more beautiful in my life," he said, which lifted the weariness from his mother's face.

Father was dead three years now, having lost his fishing boat and eventually his life to poor business investments that Arturo was expected to pay off with years of indentured service. Uncle Benicio had managed with fists and other well-aimed negotiations to erase the debt and tried to persuade his nephew to carry on with the fishing trade, but Arturo couldn't do it. He didn't know why. The sea was not for him. Only Mother seemed to understand.

"Your grandfather was knighted during the First Crusade," she said, "although he began, as you will, with no rank."

"How did he become a knight?" Arturo asked.

She ran a hand up and down the sleeve of her perpetual mourning. "According to your Aunt Constanza, he crept into an encampment of infidels during the night and slit their throats while they slept."

Arturo drew in a sharp breath. "All of them?"

"All but the women and children." The sadness in her dark eyes, said to resemble his, deepened. "I want you to hear me now. There was never any proof that the people of that camp intended to attack the Crusaders. There were many travelers on the road in those days, driven from their homes by droughts, floods and pillaging knights. Your grandfather was haunted by his actions for the rest of his days. Do not let me hear that you have done the same."

Arturo held the dagger this way and that, taking in the heft and the balance. "Pillaging is for brigands, Mother. A true knight follows only the commands of God and king."

"So we are led to believe. I want you to look at the sheath." She waited until Arturo, reluctantly, set the knife down. "The finest craftsman in Compostela tanned and embossed this leather and when the task was complete, the Bishop himself blessed both dagger and sheath, imparting the humility of St. James to whoever used it."

Two strips of tan-coloured leather had been finely stitched with cord of a deeper hue to contain the curving shape of the knife. There wasn't a man in Galicia who wouldn't recognize the three scallop shells of Santiago, St.

James, patron of fishermen and the dispossessed, embossed on one side of the sheath. The symbols on the other side were less familiar to him.

Mother ran a finger, reddened from years of scaling and cleaning fish, along the image at the haft end. "This is the carpenter's square of St. Thomas, the apostle who doubted the resurrection of Our Lord until he touched the wounds." She traced the second image. "These are the crossed keys of the kingdoms of Heaven and Earth, entrusted to St. Peter even though he denied his Teacher three times. And this... this is the money pouch carried by Judas from whom the Apostles drew funds, as needed."

Arturo scowled. "But why would Grandfather include a symbol of Judas? He was the vilest sinner of them all."

"Yes, he was. Judas betrayed the Son of God, but in doing so, he set off a series of events that redeemed us all, one that we celebrate more than a thousand years later."

"I don't like hearing you talk that way, and I don't think our Bishop would approve of this money bag either."

She smiled. "Bishops, I assure you, have no quarrel with money bags. What matters, Turo, is that your grandfather selected these images after he left the Crusades, and he prayed for a son to whom he could impart their message."

"Father became his son when he married you."

"Yes, but they were very different men, your father and your grandfather. I wish you could have known both in better times."

Since joining up with the Second Crusade in Aragon in early summer, Arturo had used the dagger only for cutting and hunting, though in the face of arrogant squires and inebriated knights who could not keep their hands off female pilgrims, his fingers had often itched to draw blood. He slipped the weapon into his boot, as he did every morning.

The second object he removed from the pillow stirred a different set of emotions. The finger-length clay cylinder was a gift from Ezequiel and had once contained a mezuzah, a rolled parchment with the laws of God that every orthodox Jew kept upon his doorpost. Ezequiel claimed to be a *convertido*, no longer Jewish, although Arturo had seen him steal away on Fridays at sunset and suspected he had different reasons for traveling to Jerusalem. No matter. The cylinder made a perfect container for the poem he'd written and intended to give Lizibetta, as soon as he could work up the courage—perhaps today. He slipped the tube into a corded pouch he kept tied around his waist, threw back the covers and rose into the cold night air.

It took Arturo the better part of an hour to deliver buckets of icy river water to the pilgrims' encampment, and another to water and groom the horses in preparation for the loads they would soon be pulling through steep Phrygian passes to Mount Cadmos. There, they would reunite with the army vanguard, one hundred strong, led by Queen Eleanor and Geoffrey de Rancon, military commander of the Crusades. Fifty-four mares and geldings, perfectly matched in colour and temperament, pulled twenty-seven wheeled carts containing the personal wardrobes and possessions of the queen and her ladies-in-waiting.

Arturo checked all the bridles a second time. He could not understand why a king would send his queen, especially one as beautiful as Eleanor, ahead of him, deep into the land of infidels. Yes, he'd heard it was her idea, and tents, even those of royalty, were flimsy structures. It was no secret to anyone that Louis and Eleanor did not get along. Nonetheless, Arturo had perfected a routine of brushing, inspecting hooves and rewarding good behaviour with nosebags of oats so that when the time came for harnessing and setting out, the beasts, at least, would not delay the reunion of the monarchs.

Only one creature among the royal horses was spared the indignity of cartage, and Arturo always saved currying her for last. La Pistache, named for her love of the rich green nutmeat, was an Anadolu pony, bred of these mountains and the Arab lands to the south. She had been a gift to Queen Eleanor from the Byzantine Emperor in Constantinople.

Pistache stood just over 13 hands high and was a furry-coated sorrel with a long, cream-coloured mane that spilled over an enchanting pony face. Her breed was renowned throughout Anatolia for loyalty, endurance, and speed of the gods.

Arturo took a brush to the pony's coat and murmured endearments that cast Lizibetta's full lips and violet eyes temporarily out of mind. During their three weeks of rest and provisioning in Constantinople, he had been blessed to see Eleanor bring Pistache to a gallop at the Emperor's private track. They rode currents of pure joy, the queen's gold and copper locks streaming like a banner of flame, her pony more eager with every stride to please. She had even worn the divided silken trousers of the harem for riding. That had set the pilgrims' tongues flapping for days.

Eleanor had yet to recognize the eleven-year-old boy she'd pulled from quicksand at Talmont, and why should she? With six hundred Crusaders, attendants and pilgrims on the march, and Arturo forced, by virtue of his job, to bring up the rear, he had only been close enough to speak a few times, and of course, no commoner addressed a royal without being spoken to first. Although he was now Pistache's official groom and had delivered her, saddled and ready to ride many times, the queen had not yet addressed him with anything beyond the kind courtesies she offered to everyone.

Arturo wove his fingers through the pony's blonde mane and nuzzled her face. "Pistache, you are going to see your Beloved today. Do you know how much she misses you? I know because she whispers in my sleep how much she longs to ride you." The pony whickered and gave him a saucy peer from beneath long lashes.

A crunching sound on frozen grass came from behind them. Arturo grabbed hold of Pistache's bridle and swung around. Framed by long-needled mountain pines stood a silhouette of shawl and skirts, shivering a little. Arturo's emotions swung from fear to embarrassment to a heart that thumped happily.

"Lizibetta?"

The silhouette stepped forward. "Betta and I don't look at all alike. I don't see how you could confuse us."

"Cati . . ." Arturo sighed, hope plummeting. "You scared the horses, and you shouldn't sneak up on people. It's rude."

"I didn't scare anyone but you, and I think you're just worried that I might have overheard you."

"I don't care what you overheard! How long have you been spying?"

Catarina shrugged. "Not long. I was awake when you got up, but I know you don't like to be disturbed when grooming the horses, so I waited."

Cati was right. She didn't look like her sister. Lizibetta was tall and womanly with heavy-lidded eyes that gave her a look both sultry and intoxicating and far beyond her fifteen years. Catarina was smaller, built like a stick and younger than Betta by a year or two.

The two girls had accompanied their mother Maria del Carmen from Zaragoza where their father lay strapped to a bed, his mind vacant and his body withering from constant physical torments. The year before, the women had completed a pilgrimage to Compostela in search of a cure and received none; Maria del Carmen hoped for better results in Jerusalem.

"Why are you here, bothering me?" Arturo asked.

"We're breaking camp this morning, aren't we? I can help you harness the horses to the carts." Without being invited, she came over to Pistache and stroked her back. "You are such a pretty thing, look at you!"

Arturo refrained from slapping Cati's hand off Her Royal Highness's horse, only because Pistache seemed to approve. The pony turned her head and nibbled at Catarina's earlobe that held a small pearl stud.

"May I feed her?" Cati asked.

"How do you know she hasn't been fed?"

"Because you always groom the horses first, and her nosebag is over there." She pointed toward the pines where she'd been skulking.

"Very well," he said. "Make sure you use the special mix."

Catarina retrieved the bag that contained a costly blend of oats, ground sugar and pistachios and fed the pony from her open hand.

Watching her affectionate way with Pistache, Arturo had to admit that while it was fine to pride himself on all he could do single-handed, hitching the horses to the carts was tedious. The task was made lonelier by the pilgrims' aversion to the queen's royal baggage, which they viewed from their pinnacles of suffering as excessive. The knights and squires were no help either. In the absence of combat, they had far more time than Arturo, but they would never lower themselves to assist a waterboy.

"How does your mother feel about you sneaking around, unchaperoned?" he asked.

"She encourages anything that might get us to the Holy City sooner."

"Jerusalem could be months away. There's the weather to consider, and the Crusaders must first take Edessa, then Antioch . . ."

Cati rubbed the pony's nose while she looked at Arturo. "The queen's uncle is prince of Antioch. Why would we conquer a city that's already ours?"

"I meant Aleppo," he said, face burning.

She draped the nosebag around Pistache's neck and clapped her hands clean. "You like my sister, don't you?"

"Aah, erm . . ."

"No need to be embarrassed. She told me about the violets you picked for her, and I see you making cow eyes while we're on the road."

"Cow eyes!" The heat spread down his neck and across his collarbone. If Catarina was that observant, then she must also know that Lizibetta was not returning his long, adoring glances. He wasn't even sure she noticed them.

"She sent me here to offer my services as a go-between."

Arturo grabbed two grooming brushes and rubbed them together fiercely to dislodge the hair and to avoid looking at Cati. "Is that so?"

"Mother has marriage plans for Betta and does not want her reputation ruined. I happen to know the toad she's picked for her, and we both agree, my sister and I, that she ought to have a few moments of pleasure before she begins a life of kissing warts."

"You and Betta have actually spoken about this?"

"We have," she said, in her high-pitched, earnest voice. "It will work out very well. Mother doesn't care where I go or what happens to me. As a second daughter with no dowry, I'll end up in a convent sooner or later. Betta, though, has to wait on Mother hand and foot. It's hard for her to get away to . . . you know." She rubbed her nose with the back of her hand in a matter-of-fact way that suggested, yes, she had witnessed the trysts that went on outside the encampments of a Crusade after dark, and if he cared to challenge her knowledge, she was up for that, too.

"So what are you prepared to do as your sister's go-between?"

"I'll deliver messages from Betta to you and from you to Betta. I can make excuses when you need privacy." She rested a cheek on Pistache's shoulder and slowly stroked her back.

"In exchange for what?"

"No exchange. I love my sister."

There was something about Catarina that Arturo could not put his finger on. She was like a baby ferret, quick and unpredictable, who'd sooner nip than kiss you. Then again, there was a poem burning a hole near his trousers about the roses of Zaragoza whose perfume could never compare with the sweat of his Beloved, and they had camp to break with a long day's march ahead of them. He turned away so she couldn't watch and untied the pouch at his waist.

"You must promise on the blood of your ancestors never to read or tamper with anything I give you for Betta. My words are meant for her eyes only."

"I know that! What do you think I am—a child?"

Arturo held out the small clay cylinder. Cati looked surprised—he wasn't sure why—and opened her palm to accept it.

From a copse of pines, not twenty feet above them, a dozen pairs of eyes saw everything.

Silvina, standing at the teal blue door, jingled through her keys. She inserted the only modern brass key into the lock and turned the doorknob. The door wouldn't open. That was odd. She'd tested the door before leaving for Cerabornes; it had definitely been locked. She turned the key the other way, tried again, and the door opened. Maybe it had only been stuck, not locked. Old wood swells, and there'd been a lot of rain in Toulouse this spring. Maybe here, too.

She carried the groceries to the kitchen counter and turned the tap on, letting the rust clear out of the water while she unloaded the bags. She filled the blue and white speckled dipper and drank it half empty. The water tasted mountaintop cold and delicious.

The gift basket, mostly empty now, from *La Sorcière du Miel*, had included a bottle of Pinot Grigio that Silvina had placed in the refrigerator. She found a corkscrew in the utensil drawer, poured herself a glass, and prepared a plate of baguette and brie. The omelet could wait.

Silvie ate at the island facing the window that looked out at the escarpment across the road. The yellow-tan stone looked like stacks of giant pizza boxes. Juniper and holly and other tough little evergreens poked through the cracks, defying gravity and dearth of soil. In the twenty minutes she sat there, her brain orbiting from the recently completed FST sessions with the rave reviews to how out of shape she was—a mile and a quarter, for cripes' sake!—three cars went by, one of them Jean-Luc's shuttle van. She wondered how Viv did not go stark raving mad.

Silvina put her lunch dishes in the sink. Until the final year of her life, Viv only lived at Reine du Ciel six months out of twelve; the rest of the time, she spent on European theatre stages or American studio lots. If one viewed this place as a sanctuary for recharging and not 800 square feet of "Oh my God, where am I going to start?", it probably gave off a better vibe.

She was halfway up the stairs before she noticed. The sight of a second, perpendicular staircase blocking her way was so weird, she thought her senses were cross-wiring, playing musical chairs in a synesthesial episode brought on by electronics withdrawal. The stairs filled the second floor landing, crosscutting her access to the only bathroom in the house, which was where she'd been heading.

The attic stairs couldn't just fall. Dr. Shirazi had walked her through the mechanics and had insisted, after refastening the velvet pull to the bronze wall hook, that she try it herself while he watched. The purple velvet rope with gold tassel was wrapped three times around the hook and swagged over a second hook higher up the wall so it didn't hang loose in the corridor and strangle passersby. The far end was fastened to a ring on the trapdoor, held in place by a spring-loaded mechanism that required two to three good yanks before it released.

Faced with the certainty that she was not alone in the house, Silvie's head began to spin. She felt like the central pivot of an Escher drawing. Her need to pee intensified, along with an urge to flee, but where was she going to run, and to whom? Had there been a vehicle in the driveway when she returned from Cerabornes? No. At the end of her ride, she'd wheeled the bike back into the shed at the end of the driveway, and the little pink flowers were uncrushed. She had paused to admire them. Yes, the twelve-foot cedar walls on both sides of the house were thick enough to conceal an army, but she'd locked the door, hadn't she? Or thought she had.

Silvina girded her straining bladder, drew in a rattling breath, and called out, "Hello!"

Arturo thought up poems on the road to Mount Cadmos.

I listen to the sounds of melting, hope it is my—

No, that's not right.

I run to find you in the darkness, we are torn apart—melting heart, maybe is better.

Will she think it too common? She might.

I listen to the sounds of melting, hope it is my heart...

The rhythmic scrap of *cossante* he had been working on since their first rest stop chafed like the straps of old Ezequiel's satchel. He'd treated the satchel with neat's foot oil so it would be more comfortable for the shoemaker to carry. Repetitive movement like the rubbing of leather or the currying of horses usually inspired Arturo, but something was wrong. Holding the reins of the gentle bay mare that led the baggage train, he pushed at the inertia of the pilgrims ahead of him. Usually, by this time of the day, pecking orders and factions between family groups had worked themselves out, and they moved with, if not rigour, at least, steadiness. But today, the pilgrims were clustered into small tight groups and lagging, and the knights who would normally flank them for protection, or circle round and herd them like wayward sheep, were riding too far ahead.

We are torn apart, I listen—to the melting heart, I run to find you...

Part of the problem was this mountain pass. It was too narrow for five hundred people to travel with more than six or eight abreast. Sheer walls rose on one side with crumbling precipices to a thickly forested valley on the other. The trail was slick with ice and snow melt. People were twisting ankles on tree roots and stones; even a couple of the knight's horses had been hobbled, but King Louis was making no allowances for the difficult conditions. He hadn't even allowed fires to be lit and meals to be cooked during their midday stop.

And then there was the loneliness.

For the first hour of travel, Catarina had kept Arturo company, leading Pistache while they spoke, at Arturo's insistence, about her sister Lizibetta's likes and dislikes. Then, out of the blue, Cati informed him that her mother was not feeling well, which seemed suspect, given that an hour ago, the woman had been fine.

She tethered Pistache to the first baggage cart and sashayed off, and since then, Arturo only been able to catch glimpses of the three women. They walked arm-in-arm—Betta, his beloved, walked tall and stately on the left side of Maria del Carmen; Cati, twitchy as a flea-bit pup, on the other.

"We never should have come this way. There are easier routes." Ezequiel had broken from the ragged crowd to join Arturo, filling the gap that Catarina had left.

"I know," the boy said. "I nearly lost a cart and two horses a quarter mile back. This is his doing, you know."

"Whose?"

"His Royal Majesty's."

"Is it now?" The old man patted the lead mare's flank, his hand knobbly and red from a life of working leather. "What qualifies a waterboy to challenge a king's wisdom?"

They were walking far enough behind the others that no pilgrims or knights could overhear, but still Arturo lowered his voice. "It's something I learned from the fishermen's fleets, from my father and my uncle. The last boat to leave the harbour looks out for the other boats. Even when they're out to sea, the captain and crew of the last boat keep watch on the horizon for pirates and other threats, and if need be, they are ready to lead or change the fleet's direction at a moment's notice."

"So you think that Louis, king of the Franks, should be our last boat."

Arturo knew Ezequiel well enough to know he wasn't poking fun, but frustration still crackled in his belly like a blacksmith's fire. The procession *was* distorted and out of synchrony, like the phrases of the cossante that refused to come together. The girl for whom he pined had not glanced over her shoulder, not even once, and Catarina had, apparently, given her the poem hours ago. Perhaps it was the absence of Eleanor, queen of this Crusade, that dispirited the pilgrims and Arturo. For it was she, not Louis, who kept the disparate souls together with song and dance and merriment; who mitigated the dourness of clergy and the itching ambition of soldiers spoiling for combat. She should have been here with them, not a day's march ahead with the Crusade's dull knights and strategists.

"Why don't you let me lead the horses for awhile?" Ezequiel said. "My shoulder feels much better now that you've worked your magic on the leather. I've heard there are fine hunting trails for the next few leagues.

Perhaps while we inch and grumble our way forward, you could snare a few rabbits for the evening meal."

The thought of running, simply running, free of the horses, the carts and Betta's indifference, sent lightning bursts of joy through Arturo's limbs. They had come upon a straight stretch, with the trail even broadening a little. The sheer mountain wall sloped to a gladed, woodsy hillside with a brick-red carpet of needles, burnished to gold by the pale winter sun.

"Are you sure you can manage?" Arturo said. "The queen's pony can be headstrong. She'll work up the other horses if you let her."

"I'll summon your companion if I need help. What's her name again?"

"La Pistache."

"No, I mean your companion."

"My companion?" Was he speaking of Betta? Surely not. Companionship implied something steadier than an ache in the heart and a poem that would not come. He must mean Catarina. "Yes, Cati would know what to do. She has a way with horses."

"Then off with you, before the king and his men know you're gone."

The Crusade hadn't progressed a quarter league along the trail when Arturo, rope coiled at his shoulder, spotted a mountain hare nibbling at a patch of dried fern. He'd felt an edge of dread but shrugged it off; this was a grass eater, nothing to fear. He approached with soundless steps, careful to avoid the half-frozen rotted log that would have snapped—or maybe they weren't soundless. The hare's left ear twitched; her neck straightened, and with a flash of white tail, she leaped over the fern patch.

The chase was on.

Arturo ran with the vigour of youth, his strong legs pumping, spirit alight. Both he and the rabbit knew it was a game, for she would stop now and then, taunting her predator with a full-on look, letting him come sometimes within ten to twelve paces before setting off again in bold, graceful leaps. For a long, timeless stretch, he drank in lungfuls of crisp mountain air and exhaled plumes of soft white vapour. His thigh muscles ached and his mind sharpened with the effort of running on slopes that were treacherously icy in places and threaded with vines and old roots.

He ran and thought of Galicia where the fishing boats would be out in high seas. He thought of his mother, aunt, and sisters, pulling fresh loaves from communal ovens. He ran and thought of Lizibetta whose dark, disdainful eyes made him want her all the more. He leaped and cleared an outcrop of smoky graystone and thought of Eleanor, his queen, who would be watching and worrying from the encampment at Cadmos.

That he'd cleared the outcrop without a stumble, that he'd never once lost sight of his prey convinced Arturo that life held greater possibilities than a dead-slow march of a lackluster Crusade led by a king they hardly ever saw.

And then he saw the king.

Arturo skidded to a halt, the hare forgotten. He stood on high ground, looking down in astonishment upon Louis, king of the Franks. He sat astride a black stallion, surrounded by a phalanx of six knights with long swords and bows at their sides, silver-bright shields strapped to their horses. Their visors were up, and they were riding slow, some with heads nodding. Squires led the procession on foot; the tallest in the center carried the *oriflamme*, a fire red banner on a golden lance, announcing them, truncated from those ahead and behind, as the Second Crusade.

But what shocked Arturo more than this sadsack parade was the king himself. Dressed in the drab browns of a commoner, Louis wore no crown and no royal ermine graced the edges of his cape. He had greasy dark hair that curled at the shoulders, and he rode slump-shouldered, lazy. A wave of bile soured the back of Arturo's throat. This was their mighty sovereign?

Realizing that the slope above the road offered no concealment if the king or anyone else chanced to look up, he took several steps backward and crept toward the outcrop he had cleared moments ago. There he received his second shock.

The mountain hare who'd danced him a merry chase now swung in mid-air, head hanging. He'd not seen her doubling back, had, for the moment, forgotten all about her. She was still alive. The snare had caught her at the upper hind legs, and her long lean body twitched and bucked in the effort to free herself. At first, he imagined himself as liberator. He approached slowly, thinking it was only right to release the creature, in gratitude for the happiness she'd brought him. Then he saw that one hind leg was rigid, not engaged in the struggle; it was probably broken. She would be dinner to a wolf or fox before nightfall, and that he would not allow. He pulled his dagger from its sheath. The hare froze, as if aware of his intentions.

106

"I'm not going to let you suffer," Arturo said softly. "You are going to feed my friends tonight, and we will give proper thanks. I shall make a purse of your fur for Ca—for Betta, and if she'll listen, I will tell her the story of our merry chase." He moved in from behind and took hold of her neck. She was thin and bony beneath the gray fur, and with his other hand he drew the dagger swiftly across her throat. She gave one final spasm while her blood spurted and fell still.

A time would come when Arturo looked back on this day and know that the rabbit had saved his life. If she'd not been snared, if he'd chased her back toward the rotted log that was probably her home, he'd have run straight into the Seljuks who were creeping down the hillside toward the pilgrims.

The screaming began before Arturo understood what he was seeing. From behind, the warriors of Phrygia looked like women—it's what he thought they were! They wore no metal armour but long silky tunics of floral and quilted brocade. Their tightly wrapped turbans were scarlet and sapphire and emerald green; some wore braids that reached their waist.

What stopped Arturo cold, what nailed him to the ground with spikes of horror, was their silence. He *had* seen them—and not just now, while he approached, carrying a dead hare, but back then, when he felt a frisson of terror and shook it off. These infidels had been in the forest all along, hiding, watching and ignoring the silly boy with his coil of rope and grandfather's dagger. There were hundreds of them, flowing in a seamless shimmer like a quilt through the trees. This was no army or banner-toting regiment but a unit of indivisible, pure malice.

It was the scream of dying horses that finally jolted Arturo. He drew his dagger a second time and, throwing the hare aside, leaped from the same low cliff that his enemies were clearing, safe for the moment because all of their attention was focused ahead.

The ambush had been well planned. Seljuks landed upon the mounted knights first, slitting their throats with short curved swords and gutting the horses beneath them. Sprays of blood mingled with the chaos of pilgrims trying to escape, caught at the edge of the precipice.

Arturo's mind had slowed so that while he moved through the seething mass of men, women and children, he was able to ascertain that the invaders only numbered between thirty and forty. His thinking there'd been

107

hundreds was a mirage, a looping visual trick that was somehow part of their strategy. He looked around for Ezequiel and found the shoemaker holding a huge rock above his head while approaching an infidel, who at that moment was thrusting his blade into the belly of a pregnant woman.

The rock came down and the soldier staggered, but his crimson turban had cushioned the blow and he turned with a face diabolical in its serenity, and pulling the sword from the woman in a single unbroken arc, he sliced Ezequiel across the chest.

Arturo ran toward the murderer, dagger held high while a roar of pain and anger poured from his throat. In a moment of gloating satisfaction, the soldier had lost focus, and Arturo managed to slash his face from the left eye diagonally downward, puncturing his eyeball and severing his nose.

From that initial bloodlet, instinct took over, and Arturo moved between shouting instructions to the defenseless—"head for the baggage carts, hide behind them"—and driving his blade into the bare necks of warriors distracted by their own butchery.

He received slashes too, one across the arm, the face, and a long searing wound across his thigh, at the end of which he met the cold eyes of the Seljuk who did it. Once or twice, he was grabbed, but always managed to slip free, in every instance seeing a passage through the weaknesses of whoever held him.

What he could not stop and would never entirely stop hearing were the sounds of people and horses being driven off the cliff's edge, alive. They were high-pitched screaming choruses, ligatures of steel to the ear, keening endless with horror that somehow gathered momentum, pulling more of itself over the edge, as if the pilgrims were tied at the ankles in a single dying mass.

"Turo!"

He heard Cati's voice and swung around, his knife, hands and tunic drenched in blood. A Phrygian held her by the underarms while a second took hold of the collar of her gown and ripped downward. The flash of pale skin, of newly budding breasts, aroused more indignation in Arturo's heart than anything he'd seen yet. He grabbed the second soldier's braid close to the nape and with a ferocious yank pulled his head back, slicing his throat cleanly, as if he were a hare. The first soldier let go of Cati to attack Arturo, but Cati swung round and delivered a swift, hard knee to the groin. Arturo pulled her away and dragged her, both of them stumbling, to an overturned baggage cart where several bodies lay heaped over chests broken open and spilling with pearls.

"Where are your mother and sister?" he asked.

"I don't know!"

He peered around the cart and caught sight of Pistache, rearing and whinnying behind a heap of mangled carts. He took hold of Cati's shoulders.

"I need you to listen to me."

She nodded quickly, shivering beneath his grip.

He pulled his blood-encrusted tunic over his head.

"Can you ride bareback?"

"Yes."

Catarina struggled only briefly while Arturo pulled the tunic down over her half-naked breasts. With her long dark hair tucked in, she looked almost like a boy. Men dressed in skirts here; the chaos might be enough to save her.

Shock kept Cati silent, while Arturo spoke. "Pistache thinks she's pinned behind those carts, and she's terrified. If you can grab hold of her bridle, you'll free her easily enough. She knows you. I'm going to clear a path for you to reach her, and I want you to ride through the fighting—all of it. Ignore what you see. Ride until you find the king and his men. Tell them what's happening, but then keep riding until you reach the queen's encampment at Cadmos. It may be a half day's journey, I don't know. Pistache can do it."

Cati's mouth hung open. She was breathing hard, her gaze hooked on his, and then she rose, pushing down on Arturo's shoulders. "I can reach Pistache without your help. Find my mother and sister."

And just as surely as the hare had distracted and saved Arturo, something cleared a passage through twenty yards of butchery for Catarina to reach the queen's pony, to release and mount her, and to ride unharmed, eastward toward the king.

Arturo never found Maria del Carmen or his beloved. The Seljuks looted the royal baggage and slaughtered the knights and pilgrims who weren't young or handsome enough for the slave market. One of the old women who'd been left for dead told Arturo that Maria del Carmen had fought with teeth and nails to protect Lizibetta, and was among the first to be hurled off the cliff. Betta had been trampled by horses while trying to run. Mercifully, she had been dead or at least unconscious when she joined her mother in the river gorge below.

Of the five hundred travelers who'd made up the rear guard of the Second Crusade, sixty-eight survived. All but four of the horses assigned to the queen's baggage carts were dead. A makeshift hospital was set up near the outcrop that Arturo had cleared with a single happy bound less than twenty-four hours before.

Several days after the slaughter, King Louis, wearing a jewelled crown and ermine-trimmed cape, moved among the wounded, bestowing small crosses on bits of red cloth for the men and rosaries for the women. Arturo lay bandaged on a fleece pallet, aching and weak but alert enough to hear the kind of succour he dispensed. "Yes, dear sister, it is true what you've heard. Our Lord saw fit to save the Frankish throne by providing a tree for me to climb that would keep me safe until the infidels departed. We shall offer thanksgiving mass every morning from now to the end of our Crusade, so that we may continue to find favour."

Half dozing, Arturo was working and reworking how the Seljuks could have concealed themselves in an open forest of russets and brown while dressed like foot stools from a sultan's harem, when he felt a soft touch on his shoulder. He opened his eyes and saw the face he'd seen this close only once before, though he'd dreamed of that face many times.

"My queen," he whispered, through a throat bled raw from screaming.

She smiled and stroked his unbandaged cheek with the back of her hand. "My shining knight."

Tears filled Arturo's eyes, and he shook his head, hoping she would understand that he was no knight. He was a water boy and tender of—no, he was a failure. Most of the horses he'd been hired to tend were dead because he'd been too besotted and bored and selfish to stay at his post.

"Your friend Catarina reached me," Eleanor said, "and told me of your bravery. She and Pistache are both resting safely with the Emperor's knights."

Arturo opened his mouth to speak, but she stopped him with a finger to his lips.

"His Royal Majesty will be coming around soon to promote you to squire, first step to the knighthood I am certain awaits you. When we return, God willing, safely to Poitiers, I would like you and Catarina to join my Court." From the folds of her royal blue gown, she drew a small clay cylinder. "I'm not sure that my effluents are worthy of comparison to the roses of Zaragoza, but I do know we shall have need of beauty when these Crusades have run their course, and I sense that gift in you."

Arturo stared at the object in her hand. At first, he was confused, and then he was furious. Catarina had sworn an oath to pass messages to Lizibetta without intervention. She had assured him that her sister had indeed received the poem, adored it, and had slipped the clay cylinder between her breasts so that she might dream more sweetly.

Now Lizibetta and their mother lay dead in a heap of broken bones a thousand feet below them. She'd never seen the poem, and she'd never asked Catarina to act as go-between. There'd been no backward glances from the woman he loved because, to Betta, Arturo was nothing but a stupid water boy.

Queen Eleanor had been watching the turmoil of his thoughts; there was nothing he could do about that. And while he fully intended to wring the truth out of Catarina's scrawny neck, he could hardly tell his sovereign that the words of love she thought were written for her, weren't.

Then it turned out that Her Majesty's eyes were as readable as his. Arturo watched their tidal depths flow from tenderness to perplexity and finally, to surprise and pleasure. "I know you," the queen said. "We met once long ago, at the cove in Talmont."

Silvina heard the squeak of things that needed oiling. *"Allo, est quelqu'un là-haut?"* she asked again. "Is somebody up there?"

Wheels rolled along a bumpy surface, and footsteps grew louder, approaching the attic trapdoor. Standing midway up the stairs, she took hold of the railing with both hands, the way a non-swimmer grips the edges of a pool.

Black boots and black denim jeans, snug against a pair of long, lean legs descended the attic stairs—there were seven of them, stairs, not legs—she herself was on the eighth of seventeen—counting stairs, counting anything kept her senses orderly when they'd much rather fly off and switch places. He was coming down slowly, every ker-thump rattling the stairs and her nerves like the hunchbacks and phantoms in the black-and-white Lon Chaney films she used to watch with her grandmother. By the fourth step, there was no further doubt, anatomically, that the stranger in her attic was a man…in a dark leather bomber jacket with a fur collar. He was lean and tawny with an aquiline profile and raven black, shiny hair that he wore pulled back in a ponytail. Silvina stopped breathing and may have stopped counting. She descended backward a step or two, and the man disappeared.

It was a fluke of architecture. The attic trapdoor had been constructed at right angles to the central stairwell, which was only slightly wider than the ladder that had once connected the two floors. The bottom stairs of the attic lay beyond her sight line. If she'd been coming out of Viv's bedroom at that moment, he and she would be standing face to face and, in every sense of the word, trapped.

"If you think you're here to take something, we'll have to talk." Thinking of Vivian lent her courage. Thinking of how she died sapped it.

The man said nothing.

Silvina seized the opportunity during which an innocent, well-meaning intruder would explain himself to turn and hurry down the stairs, duck into the kitchen and rummage through the utensil drawer for something wood-handled and menacing. She returned, armed, to the base of the stairwell and watched the trapdoor judder. She heard a quiet expletive in a language that was neither English nor French. The loaded spring caught and with a *swoosh-fwump*, the stairs were swallowed like a tongue into the jaws of the attic. The change of air pressure caused Silvie's ear drums to pop and the house to give off what sounded like a moan.

The man held a stack of file folders in one arm and looked down at her. He stood framed against the bathroom door, sidelit by the windows in Viv's bedroom and the study at opposite ends of the corridor. Her synesthesia liquefied and poured him down the stairs, transforming him to a starry night, moonless and black and smelling of caramel. Sometimes, her disorder was utterly useless.

"Hello," he said, and came down the stairs.

Silvie was still holding her weapon of defense upright between her breasts when he reached the ground floor. He was smiling, and curiosity softened his angular face. He started to laugh. She looked down. What she'd grabbed from the utensil drawer thinking it was a murderous butcher knife was a wood-handled wire whisk.

She laughed too, then thrust the whisk into his arms and dashed upstairs. "Don't leave until we talk—sorry, I'll be right back."

When she returned, the whisk was on the counter in the *foganha*, and the man sat in the parlour on the chair that Dr. Shirazi had occupied two days before. He was riffling through papers in a brown accordion folder.

"Didn't you hear me calling?" she said.

"Cell phones don't work in this house."

"What? I don't mean on the phone. I was shouting hello, hello, and you didn't answer."

"Sorry, I thought you were getting poor reception on the landline. Why should I have thought you were talking to me?"

"Because you were in my attic?" she said, with an interrogative, adolescent flip at the end of each word. His chiseled Mediterranean features rearranged themselves, compelling her, awkwardly, to add, "I mean, Vivian's attic."

"Who are you?" he asked.

"Silvina Kestral. Who are you?"

"I am Gavriel Navarro." He rose and held out his hand.

Her palm met his, their fingers curled with just the right amount of pressure—or maybe a little too much. Her hand dropped, and she sank into the nearest wing chair. "I didn't notice a car in the driveway."

"I got a lift with Jean-Luc."

"That man takes everyone everywhere."

"Pardon me?"

"Nothing."

"I didn't hear you drive up either." Gavriel spoke flawless English with what Silvina guessed to be a Spanish accent.

"I don't have a car. Not here. I have one at home, in Canada."

"That's not safe. You should have a car. There are good rentals in St. Jacques."

"Why is it not safe? I used Vivian's bike today. It's old, but in pretty good condition."

Gavriel looked at her, appeared to think a moment, and shrugged. "Well, I'm done for now. I should let you go." He headed toward the door.

"Wait a minute." Silvie popped up from the chair. "You can't just walk out of here with those files. I don't know what they contain."

"They're just a few poems."

"Poems?"

"Yes, I'm translating them."

"Did you write them?"

"No."

"Then they don't belong to you."

Gavriel had thick, black eyebrows; the eyebrows came down. "How do poems belong to someone?"

"Copyright. I don't know. Look, I don't mean to be rude, but I'm Vivian's executrix. Nothing leaves this house until I've had a look at it."

"Sorry, I didn't realize that's who you were. You should have said."

"How did you get in anyway?"

Gavriel reached into his jacket pocket and pulled out a brass key on a white satin ribbon.

"You have a key to this house?"

"Yes, Vivian and I have been working together."

"On what?"

"A project."

"She never mentioned you."

"She never mentioned you either."

Silvina was having a hard time liking this man. She wondered how many other copies of the key to Viv's house were floating around the Pyrenees, or the world, for that matter, and she wondered if Olivier, grandson of Louis-Bernard and Orsine, knew of a good locksmith. Meanwhile, though, she had a more immediate situation.

"I'm sorry if I've come across like a banshee. I only arrived yesterday, I can't check my emails or send text messages, and I miss my friend." She smiled and gestured toward the wing chairs. "How about we have a glass of wine, some bread and cheese, and you can tell me about this project you and Viv were working on."

He looked down at the folder in his arms.

"Unless you're in a rush. Did I mention that no one in Cerabornes seems willing to talk to me?" She grinned, and finally, so did he.

"The wine sounds good, but I have a better idea," he said. "How about I take you first on a personal, guided tour of *a Raiña dos Ceos?* Have you seen it yet?"

"I don't know what that is."

"It's where you are, in Galician…the Queen of Heaven."

CHAPTER FIVE

THE POOLS OF ARTEMIS DAPHNAIA
PRINCIPALITY OF ANTIOCH, ASIA MINOR
MAY, A.D. 1148

In the droplets of cascading waters of the sacred springs of Daphne, two figures were reflected, walking arm in arm, Bowers of laurel arched overhead, protecting Eleanor and her uncle from the scorching sun like the interlaced fingers of a million Naiads, guardians of water and flow. There was a hush within the glade of moss and waterfalls, along the paths and foot bridges that kept the city out and felt to Eleanor like the stillpoint at the center of the grandeur of Creation.

People talked, of course. The pair had been coming to the pools of Artemis nearly every day for five months, as if their prince, Raymond of Poitiers, could afford time away from Council and the threat of infidels sacking Antioch, as they'd sacked Aleppo and Edessa, did not hang like the sword of Damocles over him. It was the kind of behaviour one would expect from the progeny of the old Duke. William IX of Aquitaine, troubadour and composer of shameless verse, and his married paramour, *La Dangereuse of Châtellerault,* lived under the delusion there was nothing more important than happiness, the pursuit of joy, unceasing appreciation of life, regardless of weather, tides and hellfire from pulpits. No wonder Louis, King of France, Eleanor's poor husband, lay prostrate every day before the altar of St. Anthony.

A pair of swans that Eleanor had named Leda and Narcissus glided to the edge of a pool. She scattered a handful of pine nuts along the bank, and the two birds waddled out of the water, claiming in humour what they lost in grace. Raymond let go of his niece's arm and sat upon a nearby bench, while she stooped to feed them from her hand.

"Why do you suppose, Uncle, that Daphne spurned the attentions of Apollo and begged to be transformed to laurel?"

"Now there's a question I haven't pondered in years. The common interpretation is that Daphne tired of the Sun God's endless desiring and saw no other means of escape."

"But why would one seek to escape desiring?"

Raymond laughed. "Answer that, and you shall win the boon of Artemis herself."

Eleanor glanced over her shoulder. "I am trying to answer it, and so far, you haven't."

Her uncle was a fine-looking man with chestnut hair and beard of a lighter shade, and kind gray eyes. Only six years older than herself, he was, at thirty-two, in constant agony from years of tournament and battle but never spoke of it. A decade ago, he'd been distrusted by the people of Antioch for what they called his loose Aquitainian ways. Now, they basked in the commerce he encouraged from the Second Crusade, and approved of his attentiveness to Constance, their princess, who had been a mere child when they wed. Such was the fall and rise of public opinion.

Eleanor had adored Raymond for as long as she could remember. Her father's only sibling, he included her in his play, while other boys thought the gangly Eleanor with her fondness for archery and falcons ought to stay inside and stitch with the women. He'd helped her with Greek and Latin, and composed stories of a Golden Age as if it were something neither from the past nor future but a state one attained from attention to the present.

She rose and joined him on the bench. "I'm waiting," she teased, slipping a hand around his biceps.

He covered her hand with his own. "Very well. So the question upon the table is desire. I believe it is in our nature, both man and woman, to desire and with each sweet taste of attainment to seek more, to climb, to aspire. Trouble arises, not in the action but the object and its unwillingness to participate. Every day, missives arrive of another stronghold fallen, homes and lives destroyed, booty in human flesh carted away, and I wonder if our fear of the Final Judgment is misplaced, that in our aggression to take, to claim, we create a world in which the greatest desire is to be left alone."

A dragonfly with wings of iridescent black lace hovered near them, hind end twitching. Eleanor held out her finger, and the insect landed. "Given

117

your interpretation," she said, "it would seem that my husband has achieved his ultimate desire. He can barely tolerate the sight of me."

"It devastates me to hear that. Louis shows spirit enough in Council, but not that of a husband…not even that of a king, truth be told."

"I can recall only two high points throughout our eleven years of marriage. There was the original confusing thrill, of course, to find ourselves wed and escorted to a chamber perfumed and strewn with rose petals. The second was at Vézelay, when Bernard of Clairvaux conferred the *oriflamme*, charging Louis and me with leading the Second Crusade. What a spell caster of words he was, that Bernard! I'm not sure that either Louis or I desired years of discomfort, danger, and travel, but we loved the sense of being desired by something holy."

"You know that Louis wants to carry on to Jerusalem."

"I do, and he still believes that he can persuade you to supply funds and men."

"It will not happen. I can't afford to divide our forces. Threats from Noor-ud-din grow stronger every day, and the Moorish occupation of Aleppo more brutal."

"I understand." She blew lightly on the dragonfly, and the creature tightened its grip. "I hope you know that Louis's support of your intention to invade Aleppo would not necessarily work in your favour. He has never recovered from events at Mount Cadmos, and the physicks sedate his nightmares with the juice of poppies. All this talk of penance, long hours spent in prayer and mortification, is not what it appears."

"Then what does he hope to achieve in Jerusalem? If anything, the unrest in that city is greater than all of Asia Minor."

"I have tried to tell him so, reminding him of his empty throne in France, but his cocoon thickens by the hour…and I no longer have the interest or strength to tear at it." The dragonfly shivered and lifted off. Eleanor watched her soar in great loops toward the waterfalls.

"I hope you know that you have sanctuary in Antioch for as long as you need it," Raymond said.

"I do, and thank you for it, but my presence as the estranged queen of a foreign land does not serve you either. I have been to see the Bishop and believe I've found a way to relieve all our tensions."

He looked at her with alarm. "Beware of extreme measures, *ma nièce.* Weak and thwarted men can be the most dangerous."

"What have I to fear? Death? When I am not in these glades, surrounded by Nature's perfection, I almost welcome it. Our daughter, Marie, lives in Paris and scarcely knows her parents. As queen, I have achieved nothing, and I come away from my rare occasions with Louis feeling even smaller. How much can a woman shrink, how little must she think of and for herself before her captor relents?"

Raymond wrapped an arm around her shoulder and drew her close. "My sweet Álienor, you are captive to no one, and what you describe is not the destiny that awaits. I remember you at four years old when Father and his beloved held court at Poitiers. The musicians were still warming up, and you were already on the dance floor. In the wee hours, when most of the palace slept from exhaustion, you would creep downstairs to catch the final, off-tune verses of the troubadours. Love rules your soul, my niece, not penitence."

Eleanor rested her head on his shoulder, imagining herself as the dragonfly at the moment of departing. "If that is so, then I should like to know what rules my heart, for the bars around it strain."

"We all feel that strain, but please, be careful in the matter of your husband."

"I will." She sat up and rotated her ankles while the lyrics of a farandole skipped through her memory. *I met a man who made me feel when I would rather think. He danced for me a pretty reel before I could scarce blink.* "What news have you of Grand-mère?"

"None, for some time. Receipts used to arrive with notes from the prioress, but with these latest hostilities, I suggested she refrain from sending anything that might be intercepted."

"The Queen of Heaven will look after her, and so will Grand-père."

"There are two ways to enter the Priory grounds," Gavriel Navarro said, as he and Silvina stood in the driveway. "We could take the road toward Cerabornes about half a kilometer. There's a parking lot and an old shepherd's trail. Or we could shortcut through the poplars, three minutes to the orchard." He gestured toward the back of the house.

"I'm all for shortcuts."

He pulled a digital camera from his jacket and tested a few settings. "Poplars it is, then."

They walked past the shed and outbuildings of stone and shingle that looked as though they might have housed chickens once. The coin-shaped leaves jingled like soft applause, like arboreal tambourines, and their smooth, gray trunks reminded Silvina of elephants. They had trees like these at Twice Past Sunset, her father's fishing lodge; she'd loved the sound and feel of them then, too.

"So you're a poet," she said, adjusting to Gavriel's long-legged stride.

"I am."

"Published?"

"Yes. Several books."

"That's amazing. I know nothing about poetry or poets. Do you write anything else?"

He paused and snapped five or six photos of a bright red cardinal that Silvina hadn't noticed. "Have you heard of *The Light Stalker's Handbook?*"

"Um, sorry, no."

"Well, that's my something else. Part autobiography, part inspiration. I wrote it to help fund a project, but so far it's proving to be a royal pain."

They came out of the grove into a shallow, bowl-like valley with scattered stone buildings in varying degrees of ruin. Most of the buildings were roofless, except for a few beams and crumbling red tiles. Small, gnarly trees were just beginning to leaf out, and the rocky soil and last year's grass created an aura of sepia.

"This is it?" Silvina asked.

"It's only the beginning. The priory grounds are laid out like beads on a string. This is the first bead. Excuse me, there's something I need to photograph." He wandered off about twenty feet, toward what looked like a stone fence. He got down on one knee, tilting the camera this way and that, moving in for close-ups.

Nothing prevented Silvina from wandering the grounds on her own; the land was open enough they could hardly lose each other. But the bead, as he called it, felt, not threatening, not unwelcoming, just…guarded, like the Ojibway lands in Canada where Dad used to buy tax-free smokes. She waited for the clicking of Gavriel's camera to slow before joining him.

"Do you know what all these buildings used to be?" she asked.

"Some, yes." He'd been photographing a patch of iridescent moss with tiny, star-shaped yellow flowers that draped over the graystone like velvet brocade. "This moss only blooms one day a year. I was afraid I'd missed it."

Silvina examined the ruins they grew on. The fence turned out to be walls of a circular structure about twelve feet across with enough broken graystone to suggest there may have been a second floor once. "So what was this?" she asked. "Some kind of silo?"

"It was a trysting place."

"Oh." She looked around. "Did you say trysting?"

"Mm-hm." He got up and brushed the dirt off his knees, then scrolled through the photos he'd just taken.

Gavriel's English was flawless, but she wondered whether he'd meant to say gristing… or int'resting. "This was a religious community, wasn't it?"

"I asked Viv the same question. She said it was a lay priory." The corner of his mouth twitched. Apparently, his comprehension of wordplay was flawless too.

"I see."

"Shall we continue?"

"Yes." They walked through clusters of small gnarly trees that seemed to have been planted in conjunction with the buildings as wind screens, shade, and, perhaps, beautiful views through windows. "Are these all fruit trees?"

"Fruit and nut. The priory was famous for apricots, walnuts, and pecans, with most of the root stock dating back to the time of Eleanor of Aquitaine, about eight hundred years ago."

"Cool. My employer used to live here, and she said the apricots in their peak years were larger than peaches, and always sweet, never woody."

"She was one of the Daughters?"

"Yes, her name is Blythe Pendaris. You may have read about her. Did Viv ever talk about those years, what it meant to be a Daughter of Babylon?"

"She talked about the friendships, the closeness, the creativity. There were guys too, you know. Everyone pitched in. That name the women took comes from old shepherd legends that say this land was first developed— no, that's a poor word—in Basque, they say *dinamizatzen*, made dynamic, energized, by refugees from Bab-El when the Tower fell and language splintered, and the group, they say, was led by daughters of the last high priest."

"You really know your languages."

"I wish I could speak them all." He laughed. "Frustration of a poet, I guess."

"Who is this poet you're translating?"

"The Galician? We don't know much about him. His name is Arturo. He may have been a knight, a squire, or just a regular plowman. Viv spent years gathering fragments of his poetry from villages in northern Spain, Aragón, all through the Pyrenees, and she always visited the shepherds. Even the young ones could quote Arturo's verses. She believed that shepherds may be our last living, oral archivists."

They walked through narrows, high elevation passes she presumed to be the string between beads, and they felt colder than the open grounds. There were swells of land that rose so gradually that Silvina wasn't aware until she felt exertion in her calves, and vast meadows that appeared to be empty until suddenly a new cluster of buildings would appear. Sometimes, she saw flocks of sheep in the distance that kept to the slopes and not the valley.

Walking over a small rise, Silvie snagged the toe of her purple Keds on a tree root, and if Gavriel hadn't been walking half a step ahead and gazing in her direction, he wouldn't have caught her like a toppled pine. She laughed and thanked him.

"*De nada*," he said. "Sometimes, we're walking on old aqueducts. The timelessness of this place is amazing."

"So you are Spanish," she said.

"I am from South America."

Gavriel had large, dark eyes framed by thick lashes that were somewhere between chocolate and forest green. His eyes reminded her of the north woods of Canada, layered, impenetrable, potentially dangerous.

Spider bites of fear moved up her spine, collecting in a knot at the back of her neck. Blythe had warned her less than three hours ago: *Get out of the house*. She'd come home to find a man *in* the house, and now she was out here in the middle of absolutely nowhere with him.

"We should be getting back," Silvina said. "It'll be dark soon."

"There's still hours of daylight, and you haven't seen anything yet."

"What more is there to see?"

"Did Vivian tell you about *La Tapiada*?"

"Not that I recall. What does that mean?"

"Come over here, I'll show you."

Silvina glanced back the way they'd come, wondering how long they'd been walking and how long she could outrun him, if it came to that.

If Gavriel was aware of her paranoia, he wasn't showing it. He trod on what appeared to be the same ordinary grass, only now he followed some kind of arc. "It's best if you walk where I walk," he said. "Until you know what to look for, the path is easy to miss."

"What path?"

He didn't answer. He did slow down occasionally to snap photos of small things close to the ground.

La Tapiada. Silvina rubbed the knot at the back of her neck and reviewed her internal Rosetta Stone for some clue as to its meaning. Tapioca was the best she could do, absurd enough to relieve her tension a little.

Sure enough, there was a path. A petal design of packed earth looped out and in, with contours of buildings that fit the flower shape. Once she saw that, Silvina noticed bits of cobblestone amidst the grass and gravel, some of it still tightly fitted, nearly pristine. Following Gavriel, she came toward what must have been the center of the flower, and she wondered with a jolt how she could not have seen it.

It was, by far, the largest and most intact of all the buildings. Hewn stones, three to four feet high, beveled on the edges, formed a long wall, and in the middle of the wall was an arched doorway.

"We're standing now at the heart of the priory," Gavriel said. "This building contained the refectory, the chapel, private apartments of the Mother Superior, and cells for the protected." He indicated a row of crumbling pillars that ran parallel to the wall. "This is the cloister gallery. It ran the entire length of this building as an enclosed courtyard, the kind you'd see in Moorish architecture, like the Alhambra."

Silvina wandered toward the pillars and stooped to inspect them. They looked Grecian in design with concave grooves like the Doric columns of the Parthenon. And beneath her feet were fragments of mosaic tile in geometric and floral motifs in deep and brilliant blue, like the *azulejo* tiles she'd ordered for her kitchen backsplash at home.

"I shouldn't be walking on these." She rose and lifted her feet, one after the other.

"It's all right. Frost and winter melt do far more damage, and villagers repair it with new tiles every spring. This would kill archeologists." He made a beckoning gesture. "Come and look from here."

She went to stand beside him at the priory entrance, and from that angle, even through the detritus of weeds, the pattern of the grounds revealed loops and whorls that wove through triangles and circles with an almost three-dimensional, star tetrahedral effect. The top of Silvie's head buzzed and tingled, as if someone were trying to fit a skull cap with hundreds of little suction cups. "Who designed this? I've never seen anything like it."

"This was all part of a Goddess culture, even the narrows, which weren't built for defense as you might think but as a means of directing energy or intent."

"What Goddess are we talking about?"

"Demeter, Ceres, Artemis, Inanna, even Mary, they're all aspects of the same Goddess. At the height of *Reine du Ciel*, they say, there was no competition, only abundance. You know how in the Old Testament, Jacob's sons would go to Egypt during seasons of drought, where there was always surplus? This was one of those places."

"And you hope it will be so again."

"I do, yes."

"I think Blythe must have hoped the same." Silvie placed a hand on a large beveled stone. "You said something about 'cells for the protected'. What did you mean?"

"Queen of Heaven was a sanctuary during the Crusades, the Inquisition, campaigns against the Cathars and other heretics. When certain skill sets needed to be protected, this is where they came."

"So this was a Templar priory."

"No. I thought so too, but Viv said the Templars and Cathars were, in their way, almost as rigid as the established Church. Residents of *Reine du Ciel* practiced something far older and, apparently, threatening to all of them." He looked up at the sky that was darkening with clouds. A chill wind had picked up. "A storm may be coming. Let's go see *La Tapiada*."

Silvie rubbed her hands to keep from shivering as they entered the ruins to a vast space that once must have been a magnificent hall. There were still remains of a fireplace and chimney.

"This was the refectory," Gavriel said. "There was an indoor kitchen on the other side. They say that she was walled here specifically so that any meals eaten or prepared in the vicinity would make a person sick from her eternal screaming. I didn't know that when Viv first brought me here, I just thought the smoked meat in my sandwich was a little off—"

"Whoa, wait a minute, did you say a woman was walled here?"

"Yes, that's what *La Tapiada* means, the walled woman. I thought you knew."

"I didn't. I should have asked."

"There's even a restaurant in St. Jacques called *La Tapieé*. Kind of tacky, if you ask me, but people do love the story."

"Who was she, and who did it?"

"She was the prioress, the Mother Superior. Local people walled her, maybe influenced by enemies, no one knows for sure."

Hot reddish tar pouring down from above her head, oozing like a fluid muzzle into her ears and nostrils, was how the synesthesia reconstructed the ruins. She felt revolted, outraged, helpless. "Can we go closer?"

"Sure."

The wall beside the fireplace was in the sturdiest condition of anything they'd seen, with a double thickness of mortared stone. But the masonry was cruder than the rest of the hall, suggesting something slapped together. "Is she still in there?"

"I expect so. There has been no excavation." Gavriel scrolled through photos he'd taken. "We've come nearly to the end of Queen of Heaven. There's one more place I'd like to show you."

Puffs of black cloud skiffed toward the snow-capped peaks in the distance.

"It won't take long," he said. "If we get caught in rain, I can get us to shelter in five minutes."

"All right," she said. Anything sounded better than standing here another minute.

There was one more complete orchard, the final bead, still within the bounds of Queen of Heaven. Here, the trees were most fully in leaf, and there were curly haired, ivory-coloured sheep grazing amidst the stately old trees. Gavriel led her with loping strides through a stand of evergreen and birch, and then the ground gave way abruptly to sky. For the first time since arriving, Silvina heard traffic. He walked to the edge, or not quite the edge.

Silvina remained where she stood, near a rusty old scaffold or derrick.

"You can't see it from there," he said.

"See what?"

Take what you need from the house and leave, Silvie. I can't stress this enough.

Blythe's warning repeated and rephrased itself, as the temperature dropped and trucks roared past, far, far below. If Silvie screamed, who would hear? Were the shepherds nearby? Would anyone bother to rescue her?

Gavriel's expression darkened. "You think I've brought you all this way to hurt you."

"The thought crossed my mind. It is crossing my mind. You can be offended if you want." She folded her arms, while her teeth chattered.

"I'm not offended. It shows you have instincts. I thought Viv had them too."

"What do you mean?"

He gestured toward the precipice. "This used to be a shortcut. Three hundred meters down is the village of St. Jacques de la Rivière. You'd have

126

driven through it with Jean-Luc. On the far side of the river is the winery, *Le Croix de Cinq Diamants,* with guest houses. I'm staying in one of them."

His description of the mundane helped. Silvina moved closer to the edge. First thing she saw in the tangled underbrush was a derelict cable car, nearly rusted through with the remains of a diamond logo on its side. St. Jacques looked like a toy village with tiny stucco buildings and red roofs, a blue silken river running through it. She dropped her gaze and saw, beside the cable car, carved directly into the rock, a set of stairs. They were impossibly steep and narrow, and would have been indistinguishable from the eroding mountain, except for the remains of a few iron stanchions and chain link railing.

"People used to climb these stairs?" Silvina said. "Were they crazy?"

"I don't know. Vivian's body was found at the bottom of these stairs by two young boys walking their dogs."

Her head began to spin, and she felt an almost magnetic pull to tip forward, follow where her friend had gone. She grabbed Gavriel's arm. "What was she doing all the way out here?"

He pulled her back a step. "I've been asking myself that same question for two weeks."

ROYAL PALACE
PRINCIPALITY OF ANTIOCH
MAY, A.D. 1148

Two small cedar chests sat on Eleanor's four-poster bed, side by side near the pillows, hinged lids lying open. Eleanor paused, glanced at the contents and walked on toward the hearth where a fire burned low, and Jocelyne, her *femme de chambre,* sat embroidering.

"You don't even want to look?" Jocelyne said.

The queen took the chair across from her. "I looked." The heavy canvas of the work in progress covered Jocelyne's lap and spilled onto cushions placed around her feet. She had two oil lamps for extra light, but even so, she squinted, shoulders curled in, back hunched. "Have you taken any breaks today, Jocie?"

"I don't recall, Milady. I'm quite sure I must have." She jabbed the needle from beneath the fabric with a small grunt. The tapestry that she had begun months ago was the scene of Prince Raymond welcoming Louis VII to Antioch. Working inward from the endless sand-coloured backdrop, she'd finally come to the principal characters. She pulled up lengths of thread with careful, tiny pinches.

Eleanor leaned closer. "Is that gold you're working with?"

"It is. Real gold thread from the Samarkand, and it's a torment. Whatever breaks must be gathered and remelted." She gestured toward a bowl of gilt flecks and scraps near the lamp. "His Majesty insists the *fleurs de lis* of his robe be authentic."

The Queen sighed. "I suppose the chests and this boon of exorbitant thread arrived simultaneously?"

Jocelyne looked up, and the sunken planes and shadows of her cheekbones removed any doubt of her exhaustion. "Your husband was most adamant that his gift be here when you returned from riding."

"With careful staging too, I see."

Her chamber maid looked as though she'd been jabbed.

"Aah, forgive me, I have caught you in our crossfire. You are doing a beautiful job."

"Thank you. How was your ride? Would you like some chilled wine? Marie Thèrese is reviewing preparations for dinner, but she should be back momentarily. Perhaps a nice foot bath..."

"I'm fine for the moment...truly."

Given that she'd spent the day riding through the hills outside Antioch with La Pistache, her sweet Anadolu sorrel, she ought to have felt tired but invigorated. The ride, however, had been a royal command by Louis to prevent her attendance on the final day of the Council sessions. Eleanor would have represented the nobles of Aquitaine, recommending that the Second Crusade be officially disbanded, the knights be sent home, stipends provided for any who wished to escort pilgrims still intent on reaching Jerusalem.

Louis, of course, knew what she intended to say, and because he'd lost nearly all capacity to look her in the eye, refused to join her for breakfast. A scroll tied in white satin ribbon came with a breakfast tray of fruit and warm, buttered lupin seed bread. The letter read:

> *My dearest wife,*
>
> *If it were within my power, I would build the walls of Antioch to Heaven to ensure no harm could come to your perfect being, no further sorrow to your eyes, nor distress to your loving heart. But since this cannot be, and I have witnessed with agony the toll these council sessions wreak upon your spirit, I have selected the finest of the Prince's Royal Guards with his full approbation, I might add, to accompany you for a day of riding and pleasant reprieve.*
>
> *I remain, forever, your devoted and beloved husband,*
> *L.*

La Pistache had been frisky and eager and would have given Eleanor a most pleasurable outing, but the knights—archers, fully armoured—none of whom she knew, refused to allow the pony to break into a gallop or Eleanor to lead—for reasons of threat to her royal person. They were hemmed in on all sides. Even at a canter, it felt like riding a hobby horse on a cart pulled by one-eyed oxen. The groom who received them at the stables, and who had none of Arturo de Padrón's finesse, bore the weight of Pistache's frustration with a kick to the forehead that knocked him cold. Eleanor stayed with the poor boy until he regained consciousness, but she'd not been able to shake the feeling that a single thread ran through this series of events—and that the thread was tightening.

"How did my husband seem to you, Jocelyne? Was he cheerful, morose?"

"Oh, most cheerful, Madame." She let the canvas fall to her lap. "He instructed that I make certain you know, the pearls come from the coffers of the Emperor, and that I arrange your hair for dinner this evening with the pearls of your choice."

"Really? This is the first I've seen of them."

Last October, in Constantinople, the Byzantine head of church and state Emperor Manuel Comnenos had hosted Eleanor and Louis for three weeks in the Great Palace overlooking the Bosporus. It was their first major rest stop of the Crusade, and while the first few days had been glorious, the excesses of stimulation wore on her more than travel. There'd been feasts of interminable courses, entertainments that made Eleanor's skin crawl of naked slaves, male, female, and eunuch cavorting with exotic beasts, while Orthodox monks chanted round the clock, doleful strains echoing. There'd been the endless signing of treaties with grandiose oratory, and at the end, a scolding in writing from Abbot Suger at the Cathedral of St. Denis to whom Louis had appealed for more funds. The slaughter at Cadmos occurred only a few weeks later, while Louis was still sulking.

"Let us have a look, then." Eleanor crossed the chambers to the bed where a chest of black pearls glistened beside a chest of white. She plunged a hand into the dark gems. They were not as perfectly formed as the white pearls, yet they held a lustre that came from deep within the stone. "You say my husband was cheerful. Was he also clear of eye?"

"Well, milady, a servant has not the liberty to gaze upon the face of a monarch, but I know your concern on the matter of the poppies, so I paid heed to his movements and to his breath, and he seemed to have some fresh resolve."

"Why do you suppose that is?"

"They are saying in the kitchens that Prince Raymond abandoned his quest today to liberate Aleppo."

"Abandoned? That does not sound like my uncle. Are you certain they didn't mean postponed until the weather is more favourable or the Seljuks are distracted by some holy day?"

"Marie Thérèse and I only heard the remark in passing, and we dared not seek more information, lest it should..."

"Lest it should what, Jocie?"

Feverish blooms rose to Jocelyne's cheeks. "Lest it should call more attention to your...feelings for the prince."

Eleanor dropped her face into her hands. "Where is the sin in adoring one's uncle?"

"They envy you, Madame. Not everyone knows such affection."

"Therefore, we must stomp it out in others? By now, I'm sure that everyone from the Holy Father to the beggars in Jerusalem know that Louis and his Queen Eleanor do not enjoy connubial relations. We have yet to produce a male heir, and heirs, as much as we might wish, are not windborne. But what does any of that have to do with today's Council? I saw the prince only yesterday, and he had no plans to back down…"

Thoughts began to take shape, and Jocelyne resumed stitching at twice the speed.

Eleanor moved the chests on the bed, so that she sat between two inestimable fortunes. "You mentioned that the king would like me to wear pearls in my hair tonight in a style of my choosing."

"That's right. He has arranged for a private dinner, the two of you, on the prince's rooftop terrace."

"Goodness, there is no end to the surprises. Have you any ideas for a coiffeur?"

"I've been mulling over a few. There were some splendid styles in the harem at Constantinople."

"Then first, we must draw a bath. I reek of Turkish pony. I also have a favour to ask."

"Of course."

"When dinner with my husband is firmly underway, I would like you and Marie Thérèse to deliver these chests to Prince Raymond with instructions that they be sent on the next ship to Talmont—tonight, if at all possible, and thence to *Reine du Ciel*. They should be well sealed and disguised as…I don't know, scrap armour or wholesale relics from lesser saints. He may take what's required from the pearls to cover expenses."

"Consider it done."

"Thank you." Eleanor unclasped the shoulder brooch of her riding mantle. "Now, I'm breathless to hear other details from Council that may have passed through the kitchens."

"It would be my pleasure, Madame."

"Are you Antoinelle Jenah?"

"Toinelle, yes. You must be Silvie. I'm delighted to meet you. Could you give me a moment, please? I have a client on the phone."

"Of course."

The woman with alluring eyes and a pink flower in her hair crossed the tasting lounge of *La Croix de Cinq Diamants* winery to one of a dozen high round tables scattered across the room. They were the kind of tables one saw in French cafés, made of distressed wood with a circular ledge to prop your feet. Toinelle's work station, as CEO and owner, was set apart from the other tables with a curving wrought iron half wall, filigreed with the vineyard's logo, a cross made of four diamonds, surrounding a diamond in the center, meeting at the points.

The room itself was underground, an extension of stone catacombs, brightened with track lights and skylights and niches with stained glass set high into the arched ceiling. There were no right angles and no straight walls. Signs above wooden doors informed in half a dozen languages: *Cellars this way. Steep stairs. Watch your head, please.*

"Thank you for waiting, Mrs. Robitaille." Toinelle typed swiftly while she spoke into a hands-free headset. "Yes, we can give you twelve cases of the Estate Corbières, it is the same red that you and your husband enjoyed most at last year's tasting ... 2008 ... *vraiment?* You must be so proud. Now, for your complimentary four, we have a blanquette, a light sparkling with a mint finish. Or you might enjoy our Minervois, a honey-tinted white...

The logo appeared everywhere on the vineyard premises, including the side of Jean-Luc's shuttle van. On the bottles, it was a work of art. On a label of pastel teal, the diamond shapes were etched in gold, and each of the sixteen points contained a pearl, all black except the four outermost that were a shimmering opalescent white.

Toinelle finished her call and rejoined Silvie. "Sorry to have kept you waiting. The order is going out to Quebec City. The Robitailles have been ordering our wine for forty years. You are from Canada, are you not?"

"Yes, from Ontario, the province next door."

"And fluent in French, *c'est magnifique*."

"As you are in English."

Toinelle gestured toward the bottle Silvina had been examining. "Would you like to taste the Gaillac? The grape variety is over a thousand years old."

"On another day, I'd love to. I'm meeting with a priest in Cerabornes in an hour. I have to say, though, I can't get enough of your winery's logo, especially the labels. Whoever designed it was genius."

"Thank you, we are quite proud of it. The cross of five diamonds is an ancient symbol that may even go back thousands of years."

"A symbol of what?"

"That depends on who you ask. The geometric shape, open red diamonds on a white field, was used on banners during the Crusades. That's what you'll see on our shuttle vans, packing boxes, and so on. But the pearls, now they are special. They honour the restoration of *Reine du Ciel* by our most beloved native daughter, Eleanor, Duchess of Aquitaine."

A breeze swept across Silvie's back, almost with a humming sound, like the air from a swarm of bees.

"Our vineyard," Toinelle continued, "is the oldest in Languedoc. It has been a known producer since the time of Christ. Our town is named for James the Apostle, who, according to Pyrenees lore, sat in Paradise beside Our Lord and mapped out portions of the Way to Compostela where the greatest likelihood of good fortune and miracles might occur. These catacombs were a favourite rest stop for pilgrims. You must visit our museum one day. There are wonderful displays of medieval daggers and items from the priory." Toinelle checked Call Display on her handheld. "Give me thirty seconds?"

"Of course," Silvina said. She thought about dropping in at the nearby Internet café and emailing Dr. Shirazi. He'd promised to be in touch once he made it safely to Tel-Hemat, but it had only been a week. He was

133

probably still settling in. If she didn't have easy access to satellite communication in the south of France, how much worse would it be in the Iraqi desert?

Toinelle turned off her phone and removed the earpiece. "So, would you like to see your rental car? We have it ready for you."

"I'd love to." She'd made the decision after several harrowing deliveries with Jean-Luc that her own set of wheels, four not two, would make life easier.

They climbed the stairs to a sunny garden that marked the main entrance of *La Croix de Cinq Diamants*. With St. Jacques at a lower elevation than Viv's house, the shrubs were in full flower. There were crocuses in lavender and deep purple and variegated tulips that looked hand-painted. They followed a path of crushed red tile to the parking area, where a flatbed push cart waited near Jean-Luc's van to unload twenty-seven hat boxes filled with props for the St. Jacques Amateur Theatre Company.

She had noticed the low-slung, burnished yellow sports car in the parking lot when she and Jean-Luc arrived—it was hard to miss—but did not understand why Toinelle had stopped beside it and was smiling at her.

"What do you think?" She jingled a set of keys. "I'm told she can reach 0-60 in under 3.7 seconds with a top speed of 202 mph. Not that you'd want to try it on these roads."

"Um…this is a Lexus, Toinelle."

"Yes, an LFA, crystal gold, specialized colour—lovely, isn't it?"

"But I ordered a four-door Renault Clio." She peered through the tinted passenger side window at the leather upholstery and dashboard that looked like something from a Marvel comic. "There's not much space for…well, anything."

"I know, and I do apologize. If trunk space is an issue, we'll replace it as soon as we can. But we had a lovely elderly couple in our guest house whose rental from Toulouse broke down, and they needed to drive to Andorra for their daughter's wedding. I gave them the Clio. This is all we have left. My brother Stephane bought this for his girlfriend in Dubai, and they've since broken up. He didn't think she deserved to keep it. Of course, I'm not charging you anything beyond our agreed rates."

"But this car is worth a fortune, the insurance alone…" Silvina earned a healthy salary at TPA, but all the cars she'd ever owned were mid-price and unsensational. "I've never driven anything so…low to the ground. My boss's Jaguar is a hearse compared to this."

"Your insurance is up-to-date, you gave us a credit card number, there's nothing to worry about. Like I said, there'll be no change to the rental rates."

"But, Toinelle, I don't understand why you would do something so exorbitant for a stranger."

"Stephane and I have our reasons."

"What?"

"We are both alumnae of Tri-Partite Academy. When you called the Business Centre and said you were a friend of Viv's, I Googled you—we are all spies to one another now, aren't we?—and saw that you work for TPA and that you've developed a new branch, all on your own. I'm hoping you'll tell me more about it one day."

"When did you attend Tri-Partite? We only entered France eight months ago."

"We were children, ten and eight. It was the very early years. These huge boxes would arrive from Canada filled with workbooks and markers and audiotapes. We couldn't wait for the next lessons, but we had to because Madame Pendaris was still developing them."

"Holy cow, you were in on the pilot. How did you learn about her?"

"She'd lived here at *Reine du Ciel*, of course. She was one of the Daughters. My father and she were, apparently, something of an item at one time. Then everything ended abruptly, and she returned to Canada, but they stayed in touch. Fact is, Silvie, our business would not be where it is today, I would not be the person I've become, were it not for the Academy."

"I don't know what to say. Blythe should be hearing this."

"You can tell her, of course. I've kept my maiden name, Jenah, brother is Stephane…and I'm hoping now you feel better about accepting this roadster until we can find you a Clio?"

"I, uh…yes, thank you."

Jean-Luc and Gavriel appeared just then from the area of the guest cabins, chatting like old friends. The curly-haired chauffeur grinned and patted the roof of the Lexus. "Lovely, *non*? She handles switchbacks like a dream."

"You knew about this?" Silvina said.

"I did, but Toinelle made me swear on the relics of St. James not to tell."

Gavriel Navarro was carrying a tripod and wearing cameras around his neck. He glanced from the Lexus to Silvina and gave a low whistle. "Nice choice. Will you give me a spin sometime?"

"Once I've gotten the hang of not driving into a tree, I'd love to."

"Off for the big shoot, are you?" Toinelle said.

"Not so big, a few photos." To Silvina, he said, "I'm going to *Reine du Ciel*. Perhaps, I could call on you later, take you up on that invitation of wine?"

Olivier, the hardware store owner from Cerabornes, had changed the door lock a few days ago, and Gavriel had turned over his keys. He'd shown her the poems he was translating from Galician; poems was all they were.

"I have a meeting in Cerabornes," she said, "but I'll be home this afternoon."

"Wine." Toinelle gasped with girlish delight. "Gavriel, you must pick up a bottle of our Estate Gaillac—better yet, a case." She slipped a hand under his arm and steered him toward the tasting centre. "You know, we offer a 15% discount for our cottage guests with delivery to your door." Jean-Luc and Silvie laughed as Gavriel was led away, powerless.

"She'll sell him three cases," Jean-Luc said. "And probably shares."

Silvina headed for the Business Centre to fill out the rental documents. Forty minutes later, she knew how it felt to sit behind an idling V10, 552 horsepower engine, staring eyeball to eyeball at a gridlock of sheep. Gold Lexus FLA roadster or not, she was going to be late for her date with the parish priest of Our Lady of Perpetual Succour.

"Ay, ay, ay, ay! Canta y no llores! porque cantando se alegran, cielito lindo, los corazones." The blended voices of Mariachi Vargas, Bill Carver, and Karin Albrechtsson filled the VW camper van with a sort of Old World-New World, NATO-positive free trade in the making, kitsch. The Nagual Lupo Sanchez hummed along, head bobbing and rocking in a serene figure eight, while Ívano, nestled in a reed bassinette on the floor, gnawed teething gums on a hunk of sugar cane.

The nagual, the witches, the professor, and his Swedish assistant were on their way home from the Guelaquetza festival in Oaxaca where Dely danced with a Zapotec troupe wearing a crown of pink and red carnations, and Tita haggled with lazy mechanics for spare auto parts, and Malvine sold honey and witch's brew to tourists, who were titillated at the idea of fruit juice steeped by a *bruja*. The carnation wreath sat on the little camper fridge beside Dely who sat across from Lupo in the "living room" behind the driver and passenger seats. She still wore her white embroidered blouse with puffed sleeves and petticoats of cotton beneath a skirt woven with deep reds, purples, green, and gold stripes. Malvine and Tita rode in the back of the van on the convertible bed seat, one watching scenery, the other half-dozing while listening for unwelcome pings in the engine. Karin was behind the wheel.

"Did you know," Bill said, when the song on the radio finished playing, "that 'Cielito Lindo' was inspired by the courage it took for people to travel through *bandito*-riddled territory in seventeenth-century Spain?"

"I thought it was a Mexican song," said Karin.

"It is. It was written in the 1800's. I'm just saying, the *ay, ay, ay* is not all sweetness and light."

Karin glanced at Lupo through the rearview mirror. "Are we driving through *bandito* territory now, nagual?" She asked this in a hopeful way.

"What would you do if we were?" Lupo was admiring Dely's evenly spaced brown toes.

"Watch."

Karin glanced into the driver's side mirror and tapped the brake at a tail-gating diesel truck carrying a load of live pigs. The truck driver responded with three angry hoots of his air horn. The eighteen-year-old Swede rolled down the window, thrust out her arm, and gave him a playful finger wave. Even with a tan from three months in Las Cuevas, she was twelve shades lighter than most anyone around her, and her nails were lacquered hot pink, and she wore beaded macramé bracelets on her slender wrist. The trucker slowed down and drove into the oncoming lane of the two-way highway. For a few minutes, pigs and truck rode alongside camper, while the two drivers engaged in hot and heavy Swedish-Latino flirting until a school bus heading toward Oaxaca forced the trucker to pass the van and drive off.

"*Eso,*" Karin said in her fast-improving Spanish. *I would do that.* She blew on her nails and buffed them on her skimpy tank top.

Dely smiled at Lupo and shook her head. *Youth!*

Malvine leaned forward in her seat. "We're coming up to the *finca de nopales.* Our guests might enjoy seeing it."

"That's a wonderful idea," Dely said. "We'll buy *agua fresca.* Ívano will love it."

The anthropology professor couldn't crane his neck all the way to the back row of passengers, so he asked Lupo, "What are *nopales*?"

"*Opuntia,* prickly pear."

Tita, who'd been snoozing, bolted upright and mumbled something in Zapotec. She glanced around and seemed surprised to find herself inside a camper van. "I thought I saw a mule. I must have been dreaming."

"Why does one farm cactus?" Karin asked. "They grow wild everywhere."

"It's not just the cactus," Lupo said, "it's the *cochinilla* insect that's used to make red dye. The nests are little woven baskets developed by the Zapotec ages ago, about the size of your finger. You hang them over the cactus, bugs lay their eggs inside."

"Oh, yeah, carmine red, the cochineal bug. I've heard of that," Bill said. "I'd like to see the place."

"We're nearly there. There'll be a gate house on the left."

The flat expanse of a prickly pear field, fenced with barbed wire, came into view. Standing in rows, the cacti resembled green, upright, ping pong paddles. The gatehouse was a white-washed, colonial style arch at the edge of the highway.

"Better slow down," Bill said. "Signal."

"I'm on it," Karin said.

There was a cluster of oncoming traffic less than a quarter mile away, with plenty of time for her to shift into second gear and turn left. She wasn't driving fast when the boy and his donkey, laden with baskets of cochineal pupae, stepped out from behind the gatehouse, but they were only four or five feet in front of the van. Karin slammed on the brakes and swerved hard to the right into a drainage ditch that caught the front wheel and catapulted the vehicle like a swimmer off a diving board. They rolled three times over rows of prickly pear with little reed nests, and the passengers flew around inside, and the terrified *burro* hee-hawed, and the boy ran toward the van yelling for help; and it may have been the mechanics that Serafina "Tita" learned from her father that saved the Volkswagen camper from blowing up like a fireball.

THE PRINCE'S PALACE
ANTIOCH, ASIA MINOR
MAY, A.D. 1148

Stone urns lined the edge of the rooftop terrace, spilling over with white, night-blooming jasmine and thrusting spikes of orange lily with deep brown leopard spots. The round marble table and two chairs had claw feet made of solid gold. Oil lamps and torches from the streets of Antioch lent a flickering shimmer to the night air, while the slash of Milky Way, an unblinking cat's eye, observed them all.

Eleanor sat at the table, spine erect, hands folded. In front of her was a bowl, still untouched, of iced cucumber soup garnished with sprigs of mint and lavender, and a platter of flatbread and olives. The plain linen headdress that she'd worn for the walk from her chamber to her uncle's private terrace lay folded on a bench. An enormous black eunuch, their server for the evening, stood in the shadow of the stairwell.

Louis paced an arc back and forth behind her, never quite entering Eleanor's field of vision. "Interesting elaboration of braids and coils," he said. "Not French, certainly. A touch of Arabesque, perhaps? I dare not presume you would deign to styles Byzantine."

"I confess to ignorance," Eleanor said, "of the coiffeur's origins and hope Your Majesty will forgive the inclusion of gold thread. They are only the broken pieces, and we kept count. I was most impressed with Jocelyne's skill at creating an illusion of wholeness."

"No need to address me, my sweet, even amidst this troubled patch, as anything but husband. On the matter of Jocelyne's talents, I agree. Her artful placement calls to mind the net of the fisherman, our first Holy Father, the Apostle Peter. On the other hand, I admit perplexity at your choosing a majority of dark pearls over light. Do they represent blots upon the soul? Hinting, perhaps, at a desperation to confess?"

"A smattering of pearls," she said, "could hardly represent the blots upon my soul, which I am sure outnumber the stars. Sit down, husband, and let us begin this meal. The broth looks refreshing, and I am famished from a day of—" *Riding dirge* is what she nearly said. On another night, she wouldn't have bothered to hold her tongue. "—riding."

Louis sat across from her. He'd clearly taken extra pains with his appearance, the first time in months, looking elegant in a doublet of cobalt blue, quilted with silver thread. His dark hair, freshly washed, curled behind his ears, and his beard was trimmed. He offered the plate of flatbreads and asked about the knights who'd accompanied Eleanor and her pony. They behaved as *chevaliers* of the highest degree, she assured him. Tearing the bread, she inquired, guileless, about the closing sessions of Council.

"On all major points," Louis said, "His Royal Highness has been persuaded to see reason."

Her husband's pupils shone black as olives, with only a thin blue rim of iris, but it was night. Her eyes probably looked the same. She sipped the aromatic broth, relieved to note that her hand holding the spoon was steady. "That is good to hear. On what major points, if I may ask?"

Louis dipped his bread into olive oil and talked while chewing. "Plans to invade Aleppo have been postponed, which will prevent much needless loss of life."

"That is hardly news. The invasion has been postponed almost weekly since our arrival."

"True, but now the prince's sights have turned to the greater prize of maintaining and defending the City of Our Lord. His Royal Highness has entrusted me to deliver relics of St. Jacques to King Baldwin himself and the Queen Mother when we arrive in Jerusalem." He rolled his tongue around the inside of his cheek, looking square at Eleanor before adding, "He has also made full confession."

He was waiting for her to flinch, but her uncle and the bishop were best friends. His Excellency was a native son of Aquitaine, loyal to the memory of the old Duke, her grandfather. If Raymond did agree to visit the bishop, they probably enjoyed a round of piquet with their feet up.

Poorly concealing his disappointment, Louis continued. "So, now for the best news. Our departure date for resumption of the Crusade is confirmed. You and I will be leading a modest contingent to the Holy City five days hence on the Feast of St. Matthias. A most auspicious day, we are assured by palace astrologers, to begin a pilgrimage."

Eleanor, once again, was obliged to rein in the sharp tongue she had, against her better nature, cultivated. Matthias was the Apostle who replaced Judas Iscariot who hanged himself after betraying Christ. As Abbot Suger liked to quip over jellied pork and beetroot every 14th of May, Our Lord Saviour may have died and gone to Heaven, but the Church still needs a treasurer. She took several quick swallows of claret to calm herself and keep listening.

"Raymond and I took pleasure in negotiating which knights would be best suited to safeguard our pilgrims, given that we have no plans for warfare on this leg of the Crusade. Your safety, of course, is also paramount, *ma femme*."

"You are too kind." Eleanor glanced toward the skyline of the terrace where the Milky Way seemed to be pouring white curds over Antioch. "I also have tidings to share."

"Oh, yes?" His eyelids were already drooping with disinterest.

She began with the usual sycophantic preludes, expected in the French court, of offering deep thanks to the King for his benevolence and generosity, and to God for the protection of their royal selves and their daughter, and to His Royal Highness, Raymond of Poitiers, for his hospitality, and finally she came to the crux. "I hope you will forgive my speaking plainly on two matters. I am not accompanying you to Jerusalem, and I have made petition for annulment of our marriage."

The spoon, halfway to Louis's mouth, froze. "Have you lost your wits?"

"My wits are not at issue. Appropriate authorities have confirmed that you and I, as fourth cousins, should not have wed, consanguination being prohibited by the Church. On the matter of Jerusalem, then, travel is impossible for we would be living in a state of greater sin, holding knowledge of these facts and disregarding them." She signaled to the eunuch in the shadows. "We are finished with this course, thank you."

The muscled Nubian disappeared behind a curtain, reappeared, and brought a tray to the table. In sleeveless gauze and crimson silk, he walked with a wide-straddled gait that would have been manly were it not for his hairless arms and tints of rouge.

Louis's jaw pulsed while they waited for the slave to remove the soup accoutrements and set down silver covered platters, which he presented with a flourish, of lamb, stewed figs, and rice. Salaaming, he backed away and returned to the place where he would pretend to hear nothing.

Seething, Louis leaned across the table. "He put you up to this, didn't he?"

"He?" Eleanor sprinkled salt across her meal. "Are you speaking of my uncle? If so, you are mistaken. Raymond is of the opinion that rumours of our indiscretion would best be laid to rest by my accompanying you to the Holy City. And while my intentions to dissolve this marriage distress him, he would prefer that I tend to the matter of annulment after we've returned to France. He does not like the idea of his niece being deprived of sovereign protection while in these troubled lands."

Louis fell silent for a long while. He stabbed morsels of lamb and lifted them to his face on knife tip, inspecting this way and that, but he did not eat. Finally, he spoke in flat, low tones. "You are my wife. You are queen of the Franks. Joined to me in holy wedlock, by the authority of the Holy Church of Rome, and the Church does not err. You will accompany me to Jerusalem because that is my desire and my command. We will not speak more about it."

And they didn't. Speak at all.

With each course that was whisked away and replaced by another, Louis complained to the slave. "The fish is underdone…goat too bony." But he did not address Eleanor again. When the eunuch brought sweet wine and honey pastries, Louis refused both and ordered him to bring a hookah and balls of gummed poppy. "Enough to fill this," he said, bringing his palms together and curling his fingers into a bowl shape.

The slave glanced at Eleanor who had determined to enjoy the meal and the night sky, regardless of the company. She shrugged: whatever the King desires. After he'd backed away with flourishes to carry out the order, Eleanor removed the napkin from her lap and laid it on the table. "Smoke yourself into a stupor, Louis. See where it takes you. Perhaps tomorrow, we can discuss our respective futures in an amicable manner."

She took up her headdress, threw it over her arm, and returned to her chambers, heavy of heart that there had been no glimmers of reconciliation, only glum retreat. Jocelyne and Marie-Thèrese did not have to ask while loosing the elaborate braids and removing layers of gown and underskirt how the evening had gone. Their queen did not protest a warm infusion of valerian to help her sleep, and once she'd nodded off, the ladies-in-waiting promised each other to watch over Eleanor through the night.

In the darkest hours, there came a quiet rap on the door. Marie Thèrese, who'd been dreaming of cassoulet with fat chunks of sausage, rose to answer. It was Sir Isidore, knight and distant cousin to the king. A dashing man, court-cultured, though not as tall as Louis, he held a tray with three goblets and a plate of pastries.

"Sir Isidore," said Marie-Thèrese, surprised.

"By order of His Majesty, I bring refreshment for the dedicated ladies."

She eyed the food and drink and her mouth watered. Jocelyne came up beside her, put a finger to her lips, and said, "Our Lady is sleeping."

"I promise not to make a sound," he mouthed, and with a movement of his shoulder and a smile that undid them both, he sidled into the room.

The ladies-in-waiting, whose instincts in their way were as formidable as his, formed a side-by-side barrier between Isidore and their charge. He caught a glimpse of the figure in the bed and bowed without spilling a drop. "How is Her Majesty? The king worries. She fell ill at dinner. He's not been able to sleep a wink."

"She tossed and turned for hours," Marie-Thèrese exaggerated.

Jocelyne relieved Sir Isidore of the tray and carried it to the table near the hearth. King Louis's robe of gold *fleurs de lis* in miniature was three-quarters complete, the scraps of gold thread she'd removed from Her Majesty's coiffeur returned to the dish, all accounted for.

Isidore refused an invitation to sit, insisting that the two women make themselves comfortable. "I can watch over Her Majesty from here," he said, his back to the fire. "The wine is lightly chilled. You will find it most invigorating."

"But you've brought three goblets," said Marie-Thèrese. "Surely you will join us in a toast to Her Majesty's health."

"Oh, I could not. The third goblet was intended for our Queen, should she be awake."

Jocelyne, who'd never really cared for Isidore, thought it possible that Louis might have felt remorse. She picked up the wine glass closest to her and held it out. "I agree with Marie. You must join us. Her Majesty would insist."

"Well, since you put it that way." The knight accepted the proffered drink, made a toast in Occitan that brought a tear to Marie-Thèrese's eye, and swallowed the contents of the sole, unpoisoned glass.

The tasteless, odorless poison, though not fatal, was fast-acting. Both women slumped into their chairs in under a minute, and they would remain unconscious for the duration of their cartage by enemies of Raymond to a pair of camel drivers outside the servants' entrance. They would be well on their way to the slave auctions of Constantinople before they woke, and rumour-mongers, generously compensated, would, by then, have spread the tale of their defection, so appalled were the ladies of Her Majesty's behaviour with her uncle, the Prince of Antioch.

The queen was a trickier business. Isidore couldn't be certain that the assistants he'd engaged were loyal to King Louis—or rather sufficiently disloyal to the queen. Eleanor was the kind of monarch people loved for no reason, and he'd had to descend quite far down the pecking order of *mécontents* to find someone willing to taint the oats of her Anadolu pony. "You may use her carcass to feed your family," he told the progeny of a German knight and murdered Seljuk concubine. "Her meat will be sweet. The poison has no effect on humans." Fussy eater that she was, La Pistache, whom the King decided was too swift and too loyal to accompany their caravan, had taken nearly eight minutes to die.

Isidore gagged and bound Eleanor and with the help of two aides, wrapped her in coarse linen, stained to resemble the suppurations and bleedings of a leper. They carried her through the same servants' entrance at the rear of the palace to a plain wheeled litter, harnessed to two horses.

The entourage that passed through the gates of Antioch an hour before dawn numbered less than twenty. Among them was a king disguised as a mendicant monk, a handful of his most loyal knights and their squires, and a few pilgrims who, for modest sums, were willing to insist, should anyone ask on their way to Jerusalem, that there wasn't a drop of royal blood among them.

BOOK THREE

The Court of Love

Little Fiendy Whozit has a weeny voice;
he rips away his little gifts and claims he had no choice.

Little Fiendy Whozit thinks he knows what's right from wrong,
and he likes to teach you lessons with a big bang-bong.

—Wiley Forrest, circa A.D. 1170,
translated from Middle English by Vivian Lansdowne

CHAPTER SIX

White, white, there was too much white! On the walls, on the ceiling, on the screen between Dely's bed and the patient on the other side with a stab wound through the liver. The floor was black and white linoleum squares, a checkerboard that made ugly farting sounds against the soles of Lupo's city shoes. This was Mexico! His Delia *sabrosa, mujer amorosa* was Mexican—where were the goddamn colours?

Best question you've asked all week.

Go away! Lupo's inside voice had been silent since the accident. Nights of prayer, days of sacred ceremony, flowers at their doorstep, gifts of food and rosaries, special masses at the church, visits from the priest, nine days of supplication and caring muted through a waterfall of tears that no one saw and that never stopped. The Nagual Lupo Sanchez had been bested by a burro, a stupid donkey ass too dumb to look both ways. And still his beautiful, black-eyed Dely lay here, strapped and tubed and wired to a machine that translated vital signs into blips and bleeps and wavy lines but as for leading her to her own vitality, was no smarter than the burro.

It could have been so much worse. Seven passengers, four of them with bruises and lacerations, some muscle pain and whiplash, and not a scratch on the baby who was found lying on the pop-up roof in a bed of carnations. It could have been so much worse.

Nine days he heard this from people in Las Cuevas and here in Oaxaca where he was staying at the YMCA and spending every waking hour at Dely's side in the Hospital San Matías. The doctors took her off life support

149

because they didn't know her the way Lupo knew her; they said she'd be gone within the hour. Too many internal injuries. That was three days ago, and although Bill Carver's insurance plan with UPenn was covering expenses—the trip to Oaxaca had been anthropological research—Lupo could feel the *vibraciones* snaking up and down the hall.

That Indian palurda *has no business taking up bed space that ought to go to Mexicans with good education and light skin. Why doesn't she die already? If that gringo professor down the hall with a fractured cranium and both legs in a cast weren't asking about her every day, making it plain that whatever happened in the hospital with regard to his friend's care would find its way into journals and lectures read and heard by professionals with greenback $$ bank accounts and even lighter skin, they'd have emptied the bed by now. It wasn't as though she'd have felt anything.*

Lupo slipped his hand under Dely's hand, careful not to disturb the IV needle. Lupo was nagual; he knew the pulses and the passageways, the vortices and planes of All That Is, but he did not know this. Dely's hand was neither hot nor cold. He could feel, like the nurses did, for a pulse at her wrist and find one, but she had no beat. He wiped his eyes and squeezed her fingers. The waterfall was threatening to flood again. No good.

"Dely, *mi amor*, it's me, Lupo, your peskiest, most persistent *novio* and nagual." He spoke softly in Mixtec and Spanish. "I know you can hear me—no, I don't know that, but I hope you can. I'm thinking I should tell you the news from Las Cuevas and down the hall. The professor sends his best. He's enjoying the morphine. So far, no infection where they put in the steel rods.

"I spoke to Malvine. Ívano is doing well. He misses you, but he's eating, and he's eating so you'll come back and tell him what a good boy he is for eating and sleeping through the night. Tita is nearly finished repairing the van. The headlights she bought during the fiesta fit perfectly. It may always pull to the left, but as she explained to the professor, vehicles too carry trauma. Talk to your van, she told Bill. Tell her the accident wasn't her fault."

Lupo thought he heard a snort of laughter, although nothing of the sort had registered in Dely's hand or on the machine of blips and bleeps.

"*La suequita*, Karin, tried sleeping alone in the *casita*, but she gave it up halfway through the third night. Too many nightmares, she said, of shipwrecks and confined spaces—but they aren't just nightmares, she told me, they're all-the-time-in-my-thought-mares. You know what that means! But our witches' party is complete, I don't know what to do. Anyway, the *casita* is empty, just the way toloache likes it, and Karin is staying with the *brujas*, and seems to be more successful than the professor who sends his love—oh, I told you that already, didn't I?—in asking *rurales* about their bathroom habits."

Ha ha ha! To be a cockroach on the wall for that!

"—the hell?" Lupo crossed himself. "Sorry, Mother." He looked around the room.

You don't recognize me, do you? It's the whiteness, all that antiseptic—hurts my eyes just thinking about it.

"Pantera? La Pantera Negra, is that you?"

She is not here. You should know better. You are nagual.

"Who is not here? Are you talking about Dely?" Lupo's eyes began to sting. The odours of floor wax, quinine, sawdust, blood, disinfectant, urine, stale tortillas, sweat, and the gel-capped contents of locked cabinets vomited their warring selves into his eardrums and travelled through inner tubes and cavities to exhale their stink through his nostrils. On his subsequent inhale, he nearly passed out. "*Puta madre chingada*, how does anyone breathe around here?"

He couldn't even cross himself; the swimmy motion of arm to forehead, left breast, right breast would have toppled him.

Your mother's here. Swear away, she says.

"Mamita is with you?"

From the other side of the white curtained divider: "Could you keep it quiet, Mister? My husband took a knife to the liver, and it was not a healthy liver to begin with. He needs his rest."

"Sorry." Lupo hadn't known there was anyone in the room besides Dely, the stab victim, and himself. He was losing his touch.

You're not losing your touch. We need to go somewhere we can talk.

La Pantera's voice boomed around him, amplified and coming out of everywhere like a small earthquake, like the bullhorned emanations of the foreman at Delgado-Obregón, minus the weeny dick arrogance. Lupo wondered how the entire ward didn't shake apart, but everything around him seemed oblivious, unchanged, including Dely.

I told you, she's not here. She's dining in the house of the Giver of Life. Quite enjoying the tamales.

And in that instant of mentioning the Divine Provider, Creator of Flower Song, Giver of Life, Holy Cleft and pre-division form of Feathered Serpent/Smoking Mirror, time tunneled, space stretched out in front of Lupo with himself in the middle, staring down a length of furrows like a pulsing infinite parade of bangle bracelets. Then, just as quickly, the tunnel collapsed to a single bangle, circus ring, and he landed in the middle of…

…no where

…on no thing

…on his butt. Ow!

A yellowish, desert-like terrain surrounded him, and there was La Pantera. Or rather, two blurry, bilateral versions of her. One was the sultry-eyed cantina owner whose perfect melon breasts beneath a white cotton huipil and hips like swaying palms kept male customers drinking and hoping, and the birth rate in the Sierra Madres Occidentales higher than anywhere in Mexico. The other was her essence self, Black Panther, golden-eyed and richly whiskered, sitting on his/her haunches in such a way that his *cojones*—call them spirit balls, if you like—were fully evident.

"You'll have to single-eye me," she said, "one or the other, else the multi-sensory feedback will make you crazy."

Lupo checked himself for arms, legs and torso; he appeared to have them all. He covered his right eye; she was cat. Left eye, Mexican Indian pin-up goddess. He stayed where he was.

"Right, then," she said, and they were in her cantina after-hours or pre-hours with a full, dimpled canteloupe moon shining through the window onto a table for two with a bowl of lime wedges, salt shaker, and a row of tequila shooters. She spared no detail, that Pantera.

"You want Dely back," she said.

"Of course, I do."

"What if she doesn't want to come back?"

"She has a baby who needs her. I need her." He could hear the warbling cant of his neediness. It sounded like rusty water draining through algae-clogged pipes. He didn't care.

Pantera licked the web of flesh between her right thumb and forefinger with a long, slow, languorous tongue. "You are aware of *Guelaquetza*?"

152

"The festival? Sure, we just came back from it—or we were, until…"

"Not the dancing, eating, pseudo-nostalgic version. I mean the original, the Word Itself."

Guelaquetza.

It was a Zapotec word—that is, the Zapotec nation had inherited the word from an older, much older, originating tongue. It meant:

…*offering, sacrifice, presence, receiving, wholeness, standing, cycle, depletion, offering, sacrifice, presence, receiving, wholeness…*

That was the trouble with original meanings. They were always loopy. Step onto the loop any one place, it was hard to get off.

"I am aware," he said, "of *Guelaquetza*."

The nagual woman sprinkled salt on her wet skin, licked it off, knocked back a shot of tequila, and sucked a lime wedge between her lips in a single, fluid, erotic motion. "We have need of your knowing and your action."

"*Una maniobra?*"

"A maneuver, yes."

The maneuver was the most powerful act a nagual could take on, and the most dangerous. It could never be self-initiated, only requested, and never forced. Because it was an act that, once initiated, changed everything, the *maniobra* was not to be entered into lightly—or heavily.

"Who is we?"

"Names don't matter, numbers don't count. The more successful your maneuver, the larger the participation. I'm banking on Infinite."

"If I agree to this," he said, "will Dely return to Ívano and me?"

"You know better than to ask. No *maniobra* steals choice from another. We can give you some suggestions. Get her out of the hospital. Talk to the *gringo*, use insurance loopholes to transport her to the *casita*. She must not spend another hour in that cesspool of hypocrisy."

The part of him that was man, lover, husband, friend latched onto the practical. "I can do those things."

"And the rest?"

The nagual gave his answer by licking the wedge of skin between his thumb and forefinger and sprinkling salt. He gave his answer by knocking back the shot of tequila and slamming the glass on the table. He gave his answer by sucking on the wedge of tart, fresh lime.

"Very well," she said.

153

La Pantera Negra leaned forward, heavy breasts resting on the table. Her instructions were a combination of eye contact, breath, scent, flavour, touch, and things for which there are no words. Lupo fell into the loop of his mentor's *guelaquetza* like chunks of mango in a blender turned on High.

REINE DU CIEL
FRENCH PYRENEES
PRESENT DAY

All night long, Silvina Kestral dreamed of making money. Not in the sense of earning an income or cranking out banknotes in a national mint but making it, manifesting, creating, pulling out of thin air. On every flat surface of the house, wherever she laid her hand, stacks of dollar bills and euros piled up—dollars (US) from the right hand, euros from the left. She'd been quite deliberate in paying attention to which hand "raised" which currency. On the vanity in Viv's bedroom, beside the Bakelite brush and mirror, a stack of dollars lifted her hand like a rising tide. In the bathroom, on the tank cover of the toilet, where magenta petals of an African violet had fallen, euros amassed.

She descended the stairs, resting her palms lightly along the walls and money rippled out, cascading, gently carpeting the stairs like rectangular confetti, euros and dollars left and right. And they didn't just flutter and land, they interwove, coming together like two halves of a card deck in the hands of a croupier, self-shuffling cash. By the time Silvie got the water boiling for French press coffee, she'd figured out that money appeared only when she lay her palms flat, allowing her, thereby, to engage in ordinary activities like slicing bread and opening a jar of honey. The surface didn't have to be large. Every one of the copper-bottomed pots hanging on the tongue and groove wall panel in the *foganha* produced cash; so did the side of the toaster. The small speckled dipper at the sink and its larger enamel counterpart on the wall did not.

Silvie noticed, too, the bills weren't crisp, fresh-off-the-press stacks one saw in briefcases in thriller films but ordinary, circulating, individually worn legal tender. And then the phone on the wall rang. She picked up the receiver. "Hello?"

The phone kept on ringing. And ringing.

"Hello? Hello?"

Ring *ri-i-i-i-ng!* Ring *ri-i-i-i-ng!*

Silvie rolled over in bed, pushed hair from her face, and stared at the Big Ben alarm clock on the bedside table.

Ring *ri-i-i-i-ng!* Ring *ri-i-i-i-ng!*

The clock read twelve minutes past seven, and the alarm hammer was not knocking itself out between the two gongs. The only phone in the house was in the *foganha*, and there was no voice mail, no automated pick-up, no answering service.

Ring *ri-i-i-i-ng!* Ring *ri-i-i-i-ng!*

"I'm coming, I'm coming, hold on, for cripes' sake." She climbed out of bed, wearing an oversized red Canadian beaver T-shirt, and stumbled downstairs. "Hello?"

"Sil? Did I wake you?"

"Blythe?"

"I woke you. I know it's only seven, but if you were in Toronto, you'd already be checking your messages—okay, that's a poor analogy, since it's midnight here, and we'd be in the same time zone. But if you were in Toulouse, it would be seven in the morning there too, and you'd be submitting reports in your usual...er, um...timely and effective manner."

Silvina had known her employer long enough to move past the urge to blurt, "Have you been drinking?" and say instead, "I'm awake."

"Good." Blythe sucked in a lungful of air that sounded like she was smoking, but it was just a symptom of her inebriated respiratory. "I've been thinking, and I don't want to keep thinking. I'd like to go to bed and sleep this day off."

"Why? What's happened?"

155

"Apart from a 37% drop in stock prices? No, that doesn't count, TSX had rallied by mid-afternoon. It's the floods in Alberta, pipeline damage—not that we have a school there. Maybe we should. I like Alberta—the Stampede, not so much."

"Blythe…" Silvina pulled a bar stool from the island and placed it so she could either see out the window or rest her forehead against the wall. "I'm here, how can I help?"

"Have you gone through everything yet?"

"In the house, you mean? Good Lord, no, though I did make a small dent yesterday. There's an amateur theatre group in St. Jacques that is taking all the prop material—they'd like posters too, but I think I can sell those. And I met with the parish priest in Cerabornes, nice man. He'll take clothes and household items for their jumble sales and missions in Africa."

"Father Aloe?"

"No, Father Rudy. Father Aloysius passed away a few years ago."

"Sorry to hear that. We didn't like the guy much. He didn't like us, all that pre-marital going on. We called him 'allo of Perp Succ, he was a jerk…but I am sorry to hear he's dead." There was a sound of liquid sloshing into glass. "So what about journals, photo albums, that kind of stuff? Are there many?"

"The house groans with them, especially the attic. But they're not in any kind of order. I opened a trunk yesterday, and there were notebooks wrapped in curtains and tucked inside tube socks. You know those sheer beige drapes you used to see in suburban bay windows all the time? Viv wrapped her theatre scrapbooks in those drapes."

"Whose were they?"

"I have no idea. I've already given them to the church. Was I supposed to save them?"

"You gave her scrapbooks to Perpetual Succour?"

"No, the curtains and tube socks. I'm still at the stage of trying to make space. Apart from the *foganha*, there is no space in this house. I feel like I have to walk sideways and hold in my stomach."

"I think I've told you, Viv's a pack rat, though I worried she might have turned a new leaf. I need you, Sil, to find a specific set of journals, and I'm using that term loose, loose, loose. They could be binders, spiral notebooks, those exercise pads kids use when they're learning to print. I hope mice haven't eaten them. Anything written by boh."

"Beau?"

"b-o-h, lower case, boh. That was me, Blythe o' the Haggerty."

Silvie laughed. "Blythe 'o the Haggerty? That sounds so Braveheart-ish."

"Oh, it was. We were deep into mythology. Celtic, Norse, Anatolian— sturdy goddess warrior types, none of that sairy gapphic apple grove…gairy, Sapphic…airy Sappho, apple grove stuff—shit!"

Spillage, Silvina guessed. What Blythe was going on about, she had no idea. She also needed to use the bathroom. "I'll look for the journals, no problem. What do you want me to do when I find them?"

"Call me. Doesn't matter what time of day. Leave a message on my cell."

"Okay, and then? Ship them?"

"No, no, no, don't do that! Hang on. Keep them somewhere."

"All right. Blythe, I need to go. Was there anything else? Any TPA updates?"

"What?"

"Tri-Partite, FST? Any good leads on the instructor screening?"

More liquid being poured. "They're useless, they're all useless…"

Silvie's head was beginning to ache. It wouldn't be long, she knew from experience, another drink or two, before Blythe turned weepy and references to a place that sounded like Cue Vaitch began surfacing. Only now Silvina was at Q of H, and while she could appreciate the nostalgia factor for a rich, lonely woman four years short of seventy, there wasn't much she could see here worth weeping about.

"I promise to call you as soon as I find anything." Silvie peered through the kitchen window to the junipers growing from the cracks in the escarpment across the road. Morning mist blended the edges of their blue-green boughs into the café au lait limestone, like an Impressionist water colour. The place was pretty, she had to grant it that.

She heard the sound of a motorcycle approaching from Cerabornes with a powerful engine, much louder than a moped. Within a few seconds, it came into view. The bike was a deep silver-plum shade, futuristic, and gorgeous; the rider wore jeans and black leather. He slowed the bike, turned into her driveway, and parked beside the Lexus. He turned off the engine, removed his helmet and came toward the door.

"…I've probably told you this a million times, how Viv and I—"

"Gotta go, Blythe, sorry!" Silvie hung up the phone and raced upstairs.

The knock on the door wasn't as annoying as the ringing phone, but it was persistent. After tending to necessities, she whipped off the beaver T-shirt and replaced it with a turquoise sundress with hardly any wrinkles, ran back downstairs, and flung open the door.

"Hi," said Gavriel Navarro. "Sorry I couldn't make it yesterday. Have you been running?"

A DAY'S SAIL WEST OF ACRE
THE MEDITERRANEAN SEA
MAY, 1149 A.D.

Seamen, whose memories outlast the clay and parchment of chroniclers, were calling it the wildest season on the Mediterranean since the collapse of Delphi in the year 363, when a handful of oracles to Apollo escaped on a leaky boat and should have drowned—*would* have drowned if only the magicians in service to the Byzantine emperor had sorted out their curses.

"One of them Pythians," Eleanor overheard a bo'sun say, "the captain tol' me, she caught a lightning bolt bare-handed—no, not even with her hands. Middle of a storm, she leaps right up outta that skiff and catches it between her teeth like a dancer to a long-stemmed rose. And then she takes it with both hands, snaps the lightning bolt in two, sends both halves, now spitting mad and twice as dangerous, back to the wizards what sent 'em."

These days, there were no Pythians, no oracles to the sun god and magicians in the Byzantine court were admitting to nothing, so people were blaming witches, *le streghe*, as the Sicilian crew on the three-masted *barca-*

longa called them. Moorish, heathen, Norman, *cristianos*, didn't matter—witches was witches. Haggish women, they were, who conjured hail and thunderstorms and freakish waves that rose out of nowhere, attacking ships like boots to an urchin's backside, and flinging them to splinters, drowning all good souls aboard.

Eleanor sat on the deck of the *Santa Clara* beneath a fleece blanket in a tense, leaden twilight, pondering these things. Arturo de Padrón sat beside her, writing. It was their first full day at sea since leaving Acre, Palestine with the sister ship, *La Purezza*. The reduced French entourage of less than forty souls could have fit on one *barca-longa*, but Louis had thought it prudent, given the rough waters, that the king and queen of France travel separately. Eleanor, in the privacy of her thoughts, applauded.

The last of the French nobles of the Second Crusade may have traveled home in shame and disappointment—*les ignobles sans queue*, no tail, like the king, the crueler punsters were saying—but Pope Blessed Eugene III remained as devoted as ever to routing the enemies of Christ. He was, after all, a friend to Abbot Suger, who, one year ago, congratulated Louis on the deft handling of a disobedient wife by spiriting Eleanor to Jerusalem and stifling all further efforts to annul the marriage.

She watched homing pigeons thrown from the deck of *La Purezza*, some hundred yards away, their wings flapping madly to catch the evening currents. They could be en route to Crete or Greece, any of a thousand northwesterly ports, but she perceived their instincts arrowing toward Tusculum, in the Alban hills outside Rome from which Pope Eugene sent missives with equal fervour across Christendom, inviting any and all evidence of black magic, white magic, and any other nefaria that reeked of Satan's handiwork. Three, four, five birds at a time, they were an aviary onslaught, a barrage of cylindrical messages of twenty words apiece. She imagined the papal scribes in Tusculum yawning as they pressed with flat iron yet another unprovable assertion of bony female figures seen traversing the full moon, gray tangled locks and withered teats aflapping. The captain of the *Santa Clara*, thankfully, was thriftier with his messenger birds.

"I wonder if our friend ever considers the possibility of the pigeons being intercepted," she said to Arturo, who sat with parchment on his propped knees, ink pot wedged between chair slats. Friend was their code word for Louis.

He wrote a few more lines before replying. "I'm sure he does, but the messages are cryptic and carry no royal seal. He could deny anything."

"God knows, he has mastered that skill."

Arturo was kind enough to ignore the remark.

It was hard to believe sometimes that the scrawny boy who'd once spied on her through the window of her grandfather's *chatillionte* was now her scribe and personal attendant. He was nineteen now, older than Louis when he took the throne. In a strange, seemingly endless, turn-around-and-come-again, it became Arturo's turn, after her abduction from Antioch, to restore life to Eleanor. He'd been squire to Sir Isidore since the massacre at Cadmos, though she'd not known Arturo was part of the entourage to Jerusalem until they'd been on the road for a week.

For days, she lay in shock and depression in a closed, wheeled litter. They traveled as commoners, displaying no banners or finery. Another forty or so followed a few days later on the Feast of St. Matthias, the official departure date, but they too kept themselves inobtrusive, a far, sad cry from the thousand who'd set out, *oriflamme* blazing, from Vézelay, three Easters ago.

Eleanor had no memory of traveling through northern Syria. She floated in and out of consciousness, hovering near death, and it was said that Louis genuinely feared losing her. By the third morning, he'd ordered the restraints on her ankles to be removed and insisted the curtains remain open during cooler hours of travel. At the borders of Lebanon, dysentery swept through their camp and swiftly claimed Isidore, her kidnapper, and two pilgrims, a newly married couple, sparking in Louis a fear of divine retribution that nearly overwhelmed him. He was unable to sleep at night until someone, not Arturo—"I made sure I was tending horses, otherwise I'd have thrashed him to death"—administered forty lashes; and he wore a hair shirt beneath his monk's robes that in the heat of the desert caused such irritation that he moaned to himself for hours, rocking back and forth on horseback. Pain had become the king's official mistress.

Arturo earned Louis's favour by becoming the first and only person who could bring colour to Eleanor's cheeks. He walked alongside her litter playing a lute he'd purchased in Antioch and reciting poems he'd learned in Court and in the marketplace and stables, or poems he'd written and set to music by campfire, or made up on the spot. When the bloody flux hit their camp and the king and his subjects lay retching in pools of their own vomit and excreta, only three people remained healthy enough to tend the rest: Eleanor, Arturo, and Catarina, the young Zaragozan who'd lost her mother and sister at Cadmos and who rode La Pistache bareback through the slaughter to deliver the news to the queen and her vanguard.

Now there was no Anadolu pony—the queen knew in her bones that La Pistache was gone, but worse, she had also lost her two best friends. Eleanor had known Jocelyne and Marie-Thèrese since her First Communion in Aquitaine; they'd been her *femmes de chambre* since the day of her coronation. Even with Sir Isidore dead and buried in a hasty roadside grave, no one, not even Louis dared speak openly of the women's fate. Only Arturo had the courage to pick up the gauntlet. With his budding minstrel talents, he composed a *partimen*, a poetic dialogue, between an asthmatic flesh merchant in Constantinople and two female attendants from the Temple of Venus. He read it to Eleanor in a grove of date palms at an oasis in north Palestine. Throughout the telling, she wept and might have fallen again into depression; but at the end of the tale, when the women are sold, Venus Herself descends to assure them that all separation is prelude to union, all suffering the promise of joy. The first thing she did after covering Arturo's face with wet, teary kisses was to seek out Louis, who was in his tent, studying maps. The accumulation of atrocities and build-up of guilt had come to weigh so heavily upon the king's shoulders that agreement to her demands fairly tumbled from his mouth. "Yes, wife, you may take the Galician boy as your scribe and that Spanish girl as your lady-in-waiting."

During their year in Jerusalem, Louis and Eleanor performed as king and queen. They entertained and were entertained; they toured the holy sites and dedicated new ones; they worshiped, made speeches, and contributed to pageantry. But from the day Eleanor heard the *partimen*, they never again held a conversation.

She watched Arturo from her deck chair and waited until he paused. "So what, may I ask, are you working on now with such ferocity?"

He rubbed his chin and set the quill on his lap. "A ghazal, but I fear it's hopeless. The rhyme scheme better suits the word roots of Arabic and Persian, and I've a tin ear in both."

"Not according to my sources. Rabbi ben Eliezer was most impressed with the letter you scripted on behalf of the Armenians. There was that one question of a puddle where you'd meant to say…what was it again?"

"Unguent. I'd been attempting to elucidate points of commonality between Kaddish and Christian last rites. I spoke of vials of holy puddles blessed by the bishop."

They looked at each other and laughed until puddles of tears threatened to ruin Arturo's ghazal.

"Here, use this to sop it up." Eleanor lifted the fleece off her lap. "What about that poem you were working on during Holy Week, while we were touring?"

Arturo grinned, and a tawny flush rose to his cheekbones. "A poem during Holy Week? That would be sacrilege, my Lady. I'm quite sure I was composing prayers."

"I'm quite sure you weren't. I noticed the look in your eyes whenever you gazed off." She tugged at a corner of the curling parchments. "Is it in here somewhere?"

"It is. Wait." Arturo riffled through the pages. "It's only in Galician, so far. I'd like to translate it into Occitan, maybe Catalán and Spanish, see how the nuance changes."

"Please, I would love to hear it."

He cleared his throat and ran a hand through the shock of black hair that fell across his forehead. "*Ata os pétalos de caída tristeza…*"

Until the petals of sorrow fall from your eyes
I shall not dream content beneath the almond tree.

Until Heaven gives back the happiness she stole
I shall not string my lute, unless it pleases you

And only then for you eternally I'd play
So swears this poet from Galicia.

He kept his gaze downcast, his body taut and alert, as if stanzas were still pouring in from somewhere, with these being, so far, the ones he had caught and sealed. Eleanor could find no words herself, so she slipped a hand into his, and the rocking of the ship became their consolation and the pull of the oarsmen belowdecks the momentum that neither could quite carry yet. She'd known for some time that Arturo lost his unrequited love on that terrible day near Cadmos, but she didn't know whether he still wrote for her—Lizibetta was her name, a beautiful girl, difficult mother—and it was not Eleanor's place to ask.

And from the stairs, amidships, in sublime poetic timing, two women appeared, one of whom always had eyes for the poet from Galicia.

Catarina curtsied, a small precise bob with skirt plucked between thumb and two fingers, and a tip of the head, oh-so-Spanish in its formality. "Ahem."

The second *femme de chambre*, taller, long-necked and sinuous, opened her hands at her sides and slowly dropped her head.

"Hello, ladies, I hope you've come to join us. Arturo and I are enjoying the fresh sea air in these last moments of daylight."

"Thank you, Madame," Catarina said, "you are most kind. However, the captain has requested we pass on his apologies. He will not be joining us for dinner. The cook has laid out a cold supper in the captain's cabin, and he suggests we dine as soon as we are able. There are choppy seas ahead."

"An early supper sounds perfect. We will share a table, the four of us. Is that all right with you, Arturo?"

He slipped the poem he'd been reading in amongst the parchments. "Of course."

"Bilqees, you will honour us with your company, as well?"

Her newest lady-in-waiting dipped slightly at the knees. "As you wish, Madame. I have laid out your new purple gown. The portholes have been shuttered in the cabin, and it's quite airless. The gown is Arabian silk and breathes most splendidly."

"Excellent choice." Eleanor rose, threw the fleece aside, and glanced toward *La Purezza*. The sister ship seemed to be moving away from them. "Arturo, we shall meet you in the mess in half an hour. I hope you will consider reading for us."

He looked at the two women near the stairs and gathered ink and papers, fumbling. "As Your Majesty desires."

"Running?" Silvina said to Gavriel Navarro, standing at the door. "No. I'm still adjusting to clean mountain air and not knowing what time it is." She tipped her head toward the driveway. "New bike? It's pretty hot."

"You like? It just came in from Japan. I've been waiting for this colour for a long, long time."

"So it's yours, not a Croix de Cinq Diamants trade-up from a moped?" She opened the door wider, stepped back to let him in, but he stayed where he was.

"Yes, it's mine. Actually, I was hoping you might want to take a ride to my place. I have some things I'd like you to look at."

"Some things."

He laughed. "Not like that. I've been Googling your Full Spectrum Training. You work with patterns."

"I do."

"You help people restructure thought."

"That's right."

"Then you'll enjoy what I'm going to show you. It's part of what Viv and I were working on."

"I thought you couldn't talk about that."

"I wasn't sure if I should."

"And now?" Silvina didn't enjoy conversations in open doorways. Where she came from, it let in bugs. She stepped outside and closed the door behind her. "I was expecting you to show up yesterday."

"Sorry. Something came up." Seeing her expression, he continued. "Some people are hosting an event this weekend at *Reine du Ciel*, and we ran into snags. I spent most of the day texting, on Skype, or on hold. I didn't get any photos taken either."

"What people?"

His shifted his weight from one leg to the other. "My translators and…um, my fan club."

"Whoa-ho, fan club! That's got to be fun."

"It's heavy duty, you have no idea."

164

"Okay, you're off the hook. But before I change into something more bike appropriate, I've been wanting to ask, do you have any idea where Viv kept her mobile devices—cellphone, laptop, tablet? I've looked everywhere, and the only technology I can find is an antiquated desktop in her study— pre-Internet, connected to nothing."

"She kept them in her bedroom. All the chargers were there, and she liked to work at the window seat. She even got reception once, for about three minutes."

"So you don't have them."

"No. Why would I?"

"Don't know, just asking." She glanced at the sleek new shiny bike, the colour of Damson plum: juicy, stain your lips and dribble down the front of you purple. "I guess I should go change."

"Why?"

"I'm in a dress."

"This is the south of France. I have a spare helmet."

If there was one thing Silvie loved more than patterns, it was non sequiturs. "Hang on, I'll just grab my purse."

In the captain's mess of the *Santa Clara*, Eleanor swigged from a bottle of burgundy so sour that tears welled up at the back of her eyes. "Ecstasy, my grandfather used to say, is the meaning of life." She wiped her mouth with the back of her hand and passed the clay bottle across the table to Bilqees.

"All else is waiting for the caravan," said the newest *femme de chambre*, who took a healthy swallow while the ship rocked and pitched, and slapped a palm on the table. The daughter of a Shirazi scholar and a dancer from Tikrit, the former slave tipped her head, listening or feeling for something, then, as the ship descended into the next trough, she returned the bottle to Eleanor in a graceful swoop that looked like flying.

"My grandmother told me before I left Poitiers for Paris where I would meet Louis that I had warring strands of bloodline. She fell in love with my grandfather when they were both married to others. Their affair angered so many in Aquitaine, nobles and Crusade widows, they called her *La Dangereuse*—to me, she was Mamie. I was only four when the Duke, my grandfather died, but I remember so vividly when they came to visit. My mother, Mamie's daughter, would go to bed early, complaining of a headache, and I would charm my father into letting me stay up to watch the troubadours and join in the farandoles and cossantes." She turned to Arturo at her right. "I've shared some of my grandfather's poems with you, have I not?"

"You have, Milady. He is my constant inspiration." The Galician sat across from Catarina, clutching his bottle of wine—goblets were out of the question in these swells—but had stopped quaffing some time ago. Catarina had turned the colour of green pea soup, while she clung, white-knuckled, to the arm rests of her chair.

"Cati," said Eleanor, "you're welcome to retire for the night. I'm sure the sight of food isn't helping. Arturo, perhaps you could escort her to the berths."

Catarina shook her head. "No, no, Madame, I prefer to stay here, thank you. At least, the chairs and tables are bolted down."

"Very well—oops, here we go again."

The *Santa Clara* had been sailing headlong into waves since they arrived in the captain's cabin. A trench ran down the center of the rectangular table with cheese, meat pies, bread, olive paste, dried fruit and nuts on platters that slid into grooves. The food stayed more or less stationary, but in one moment, Eleanor and Arturo were the highest people in the room, and in the next, Catarina and Bilqees towered over them. Eleanor couldn't remember when she'd enjoyed herself so thoroughly.

She took another long swallow and passed the bottle.

"Did you have injunctions against alcohol in your family?" she asked Bilqees, who followed the path of Islam.

"No. Ascetics were never part of our Court. My father refused even to engage them in debate. The devotee who denies pleasure denies Allah, he used to say, and there is no greater sacrilege."

Bilqees had been Eleanor's lady-in-waiting for only a month, replacing the nervous wife of a Limousin knight Louis appointed, whose tendency to drop trays of cosmetics turned out to be early symptoms of leprosy. The King had been so horrified by exposure to the dread disease he accused the woman of witchcraft and wanted to burn her. Eleanor, incensed, apprised him that leprosy had been creeping its way through the royal bloodlines of Jerusalem for years, which he would know if he weren't spending so much time face down on the cathedral floor, and where the flakes of their diseased skin were known to accumulate. Within the hour, Louis was boiling himself in caustic baths and barking orders to arrange sea passage home. Her husband thus occupied, Eleanor visited the ailing French woman, already abandoned by her husband and children, and gave her funds to travel to a colony in the Judean hills where treatments were said to be humane and the residents tolerant. Then she brought Catarina with her to the slave market run by Coptics, and it was Cati who first noticed the long-limbed woman in chains with skin like dark honey and burnt almond eyes with long black lashes. That her eyes reminded them both of a certain Anadolu never needed to be put into words.

Eleanor made inquiries and learned that the woman was thirty-eight years old, though she looked a decade younger. She spoke eight languages, was well-versed in mathematics and astronomy, and had been a slave since the age of twelve when her parents fell afoul of the sultan in Baghdad and were drowned in the Euphrates in weighted reed coffins. She haggled the merchants to half the asking price—"Her molars are missing, look at those flat feet. She can't have much life left in her"—and covered her nakedness with a plain linen robe when the chains were cut and the deal done. During their carriage ride home, she gave Bilqees her freedom, offered her the position of lady-in-waiting, which the woman accepted; and she saw Catarina smile, truly smile, for the first time in months.

The *Santa Clara* took another great heave, and a greasy meat pie slid off the platter in the direction of Cati, who slapped a hand to her mouth. Bilqees set the wine on the table and tipped her head. "Do you hear that, Milady?"

"Hear what?"

"The pace of drumming in the rowers' galley has changed."

Bilqees was right. The POOM-poom-poom, POOM-poom-poom that had filled the aural background of their dinner was now a single beat: POOM, POOM, POOM, POOM. Eleanor became aware of pressure in her ears. The *Santa Clara* began to pivot, and in the next instant, the starboard portholes burst their shutters, and sea water sluiced in. Cati leaped from her chair, screaming. Arturo took hold of Eleanor's arm, while Bilqees gathered Catarina into hers.

"To the door, hurry, hurry," the Persian woman said. "There'll be rowboats. We can't stay in here."

Raisins and almonds skittered, while the four of them zigzagged across the floor of the listing ship through water already to their knees. Bilqees managed to push Cati to within reach of the door when there came a loud cracking and the low-pitched groan of timbers, and the ship overturned, hurling them like kindling. The tar that sealed the portholes and planks snapped like hinges of clam shell, and the chamber filled with the cold briny waters of the Mediterranean, trapping its occupants inside.

CHAPTER SEVEN

Gavriel Navarro's stone cottage sat nestled in a bend of the river named for St. James the Apostle. "Make yourself at home," he said to Silvie. He placed a cloth carrier bag on the breakfast bar and from it pulled a pastry box tied with string. "These apricot beignets from *La Sorcière* are still warm. I'll make us a Spanish omelet later."

"Sounds fabulous, thanks." Silvie sipped her take-out coffee and looked around while Gavriel ducked, literally, through a door to the bedroom. He was over six feet; the door wasn't.

The place was like an upgraded seventeenth-century tradesman's cottage with open beams, plaster walls, and flat screen TV mounted above a flagstone hearth. Behind the wrought iron dinette set were an electronic keyboard and two guitars on stands, classical and electric. There was a stack of books on the floor and a box beside them, piled with cameras.

"Looks like you've settled in for awhile," she said, when he returned with a pile of folders.

"What do you mean?"

"The instruments. That's a lot to carry on holidays."

"I'm between homes at the moment." He gestured toward the living area with modular leather sofa units and a large, glass-topped coffee table mounted on granite. "We'll have more room to spread out over there."

A slender soft-cover book lay open, pages down, on the coffee table, *Dead to Rights: A Circularity of Glosas* by Alain C. Dexter. Silvina picked it up, kept her thumb in the page, and riffled through it. On the title page was an inscription:

> *To Gav,*
> *a bro in the struggle.*
> *Thx for everything!*
> *Alain*

"Wow," Silvie said, "you know Alain Dexter?"

"Yes, he's a friend—Canadian, like you." Gavriel was sorting through the folders he'd spread across the sofa. "Do you know him?"

"Not personally. I don't read poetry, but he is our Golden Boy." She set the book down to the page where he'd left it. "When my grandmother came to Canada from Finland, she cleaned house for the Brougham family who founded the college where he teaches. We may have attended a few of the same cocktail parties. That's my six degrees of separation story."

Gavriel looked up at her.

"What?" she said.

"Nothing." He set four stacks of unbound paper on the table, facing her direction. "I think this is more or less correct."

Silvie moved her coffee to the floor and leaned forward, scanning the typed pages. "What am I looking at?"

He tapped the first stack on her left. "These are the poems I translated from Arturo, the Galician." He tapped the second. "These are random quotes, like affirmations, and fragments of verse. We don't know who wrote them. They were in a variety of languages and old dialects. Viv spent years and a small fortune having them analyzed. Those coded letters in the margin represent the languages, and there's a legend on the last page."

She read the top lines aloud. "*Everything is a loop. We became for a while a single eye.* What are they talking about?"

"That's what I'm hoping you can figure out." He pointed to the third. "These are the poems I've written since Viv and I met—not all of them, of course. Just the relevant ones."

"How did you meet her?"

"Facebook."

Silvie snort-laughed. "Get out! Facebook? Did she Like your poetry page or something?"

"Yes. What's wrong with that? You should Like my page."

"And you should attend my Getting Real with Social Media sessions."

Gavriel gave her something like a glare. "Maybe I will."

"No offense meant, sorry. So, what's this fourth stack?"

"Satiric verse, my least favourite, written by someone named Wiley Forrest. They were composed in Middle English, you know, from Chaucer's era. Viv did the translating, she may have had help, I don't know."

Silvie let her gaze slide back and forth across the pages. "Are all of these three, the Galician, multi-language, and satire from the same time frame?"

"We believe so, yes."

"Why did you put your contemporary verse in the middle?"

"What do you mean?"

"I mean, you spent some time sorting, you laid them out carefully. I'm wondering if there is some order beyond chronology that I'm missing."

"I see." Gavriel reached for his coffee. "Viv noticed in my poetry, there are phrases that correspond to Wiley Forrest."

"The guy you don't like. By correspond, you mean you used the same phrases?"

"No, she believed there was something like dialogue going on. I don't see it myself, but she was pretty adamant, so maybe I placed them this way...in Viv's honour."

Silvina picked up the Wiley Forrest stack and riffled through the thirty or so pages. Some had short poems, only five or six lines; others were several pages long. She noticed words like Interlace, Septrois, and Rubielo, placed as subtitles beneath the poem title and fanned a few pages out to show Gavriel. "English, French, Spanish, I'm guessing. What do these terms mean?"

"They are poetry forms, like a sonnet—you know what a sonnet is."

"*How do I love thee? Let me count the ways.*" Silvie winced at her own LA-la-la LA-la sing-song. "Sorry, I had horrible English teachers. A poetry form has rules in meter and rhyme and whatever, right?"

"Right. Well, these forms, which you'll find in the Galician translations, and the satire, don't exist in modern times. It's not that they fell out of popularity like the glosa, which your Alain Dexter resurrected, by the way— they don't exist anywhere."

"Is that a big deal?"

"To poets, yes."

"Have you written these forms yourself?"

"A few, but I'm not a big fan of form poetry."

171

Silvina experienced an uncomfortable sucking sensation between her ears, the kind one feels when a door is closed in a pressurized cabin. She ran her hands along the edges of the paper. "Were these printed on tractor feed paper, that old tear-off stuff?"

"Yes. Viv only used her desktop for this work. Apart from Skype and general topic emails, we never shared anything online."

"Why? Is there some kind of Poetry Intelligence Agency, some Poem Land Security who might feel threatened by—" Suddenly, Silvina burst out laughing, and it wasn't just a passing giggle. Hilarity had erupted from nowhere and was ricocheting through her insides like pinballs. The more she tried to pull it in, the louder the wails and caterwauls and sputters of, "Oh my gosh, I'm sorry, I don't know why I'm laughing," followed by quavering in-breaths and brand new spurts of cackle-snort with teary eyes and runny nose.

Gavriel stared as if she were having some kind of seizure—or faking one. Eventually, he ducked into the bedroom and returned with a box of tissues. He yanked out a clump and handed them to her.

"Th-Thank you." She wiped her face, took a few breaths, and sipped coffee. The worst of the episode seemed to have passed. The swirling in her mid-section was still going on, but it felt more playful than absurd, pinballs turned to dolphins calmly circling. "I don't know what that was about. Please, don't take it personally. I'm sure this is all very…" She waved a hand but couldn't think of a word to describe any of it. "I think I'll have that apricot beignet now."

Sea water filled the captain's cabin in the overturned *Santa Clara*, trapping inside two ladies-in waiting, one poet, and the queen of France. Eleanor pushed through fluttering waves of purple silk, searching for somewhere to breathe. Pages of poetry that Arturo never had the chance to read drifted like belly-up skate fish, while the poet tore at a porthole too small to swim through. Bubbles rose from Catarina's nose and mouth as she flailed in terror across Eleanor's field of vision. Of the four, Bilqees seemed the most focused. She crept along the mess ceiling below them like a salamander, searching, prying, scrabbling at the cracks between timbers.

Whether time slowed or the mind broadened at the threshold of death, Eleanor couldn't tell. But in this state beyond panic that was not quite surrender, she saw that she'd been dying like this for years, a bug trapped and treading in resin slowly growing solid.

"*Mamie, Grand-mère,* help us!" she cried from her heart, "This is not how things should end. I've not yet tasted ecstasy. You and *Grand-père* savoured every day, and all I've known is anger and frustration. I am a daughter of Aquitaine, I carry your passion in my blood, and I've pledged to bring these friends home with me. If I must drown, save them, at least."

While Eleanor pushed aside floating clay bottles that once held wine, a woman swam toward her with silver hair rippling. She wore a mantle of gray held with a jeweled seahorse brooch, and her arms outstretched.

"*Mamie,* have I died?"

"You are not dead yet," said her grandmother, who swam with elegance, just outside her reach, like a mermaid. "I heard your call. *Álienor, ma petite fille,* enough of this drowning! *Soyez La Dangereuse.* Be the dangerous one. Ecstasy is pulled from blood and bone, it is your birthright and your hope." The woman's crystal blue eyes burned with white fire. She rippled past and slid a bony hand that felt like seaweed across Eleanor's cheek. "Your tears belong to the ocean now, leave them behind. You are Queen, remember…the Queen, you are…be dangerous, the Queen…it's all you need, remember…"

Eleanor turned at the waist and pushed through folds of useless silk, determined to follow the retreating apparition, but as she turned, the dimensions of the cabin revolved around her in clicks and creaks like the tumbler of a Kashmiri locking puzzle, and Bilqees, who'd been creeping across the ceiling cried aloud, "Aaaaiiii! The ship has turned herself. We are upright."

The Persian dancer filled her lungs from a pocket of air that hadn't been there a moment ago, then dove down for Catarina, now unconscious. Arturo pushed off from the porthole and caught Eleanor's hand. They linked fingers, eyes locking for a moment, and together they swam to the surface, to life.

The men who kicked the door in moments later and carried the four survivors to the deck, and thence to a rowboat and nearby ship, were not the crew of the *Santa Clara*. Most of them, including the Sicilian captain, had drowned. Their rescuers were pirates of Greek Byzantium who'd seen the ship hit broadside by a freak wave and capsize. Masters of tempest, they threw two anchors from their ship *Nausicaa* to catch a side of the hull in such a way that the momentum of waves and their maneuvering pulled the boat up again.

The Greeks claimed ship and contents for the Emperor, but when their captain recognized the fair-haired woman in purple as Eleanor, queen of the Franks and friend of Emperor Manuel I Komnenus, they knew the Fates had smiled. The captain assigned sailors round the clock to tend to the hostages, building them makeshift cabins on deck where the air was healthier, and feeding them broth of cod and dried berries, while the sea fell to doldrums, and hot sun baked the upper planks of the towed *Santa Clara* dry. Try as they might, the pirates could not catch currents to their home port near Hagios Theologos, and they floundered.

Eleanor, regaining strength, found herself once again sitting on the deck of a ship at twilight. She'd forgotten most of the ancient Greek she learned as a child, so she asked Bilqees to translate a conversation with the captain, a terse fellow with palsy that pulled up one side of his leathery face.

"Ask him, please, if he or members of his fleet also overtook a sister vessel called *La Purezza*."

Bilqees translated and conveyed the reply. "He says they have encountered no Sicilian ships or any other since the storm."

"Does he have word of any going down?"

"None, milady."

Scarcely had their conversation finished when a fleet of war ships deployed by King Roger of Sicily bore down on *Nausicaa* and the disabled *Santa Clara*. By nightfall, after a brief combat and surrender of the Byzantine captain at knife point, Eleanor and her entourage became guests, not hostages, on yet a third ship. And still another eight weeks would pass in that freakish season on the Mediterranean before she would hear a sailor cry out, *"Terra avanti!"*, and watch from steering quarters as they pulled into the teeming port of Palermo. In all that time, she received no news of Louis or of his ship *La Purezza*, and Eleanor thought, surely this ill-fated marriage is now behind me.

❦

The apricot beignet helped. It was probably a blood sugar thing.

Silvina returned to the stacks of poetry, the convulsive laughter behind her, while Gavriel went to the breakfast bar and laid out onions, garlic, tomato, and fresh herbs for the omelet. She lifted random sheets of paper. "So what am I looking for, exactly?"

"Patterns."

"Of what?"

"*I only need to think of you, a garden grows.*"

"Excuse me?"

Gavriel was examining the blade of a long, sleek cutting knife. "It's from one of Arturo's poems, first stack on your left."

She read the opening lines from the verse that happened to be on top.

If you could hear the stillness of the footsteps of my lover…

"Wow, romantic guy. So we have a knight, probably, who knew his way around the ladies…and we have a satirist, Wiley Forrest. Jester in those days. Offhand, I'd say we're looking at a court structure, medieval org chart. Toinelle mentioned that Eleanor of Aquitaine supported *Reine du Ciel* financially. Everything around here seems to hold traces of her. Are these people from her court?"

"Most likely, but we have no proof. Hold on." He set down the knife and went around the breakfast bar to the pile of books she'd noticed earlier. He carried them into the living room, the stack reached his chin, and he placed them on the floor beside Silvina. They were a mixture of fiction and nonfiction, hard and soft covers, library discards with missing dust jackets; many smelled of mildew. "I want to get them out of here, but it's good you see them first."

"Where are they from?"

"Viv's library. They're all books about Eleanor or from that era, and none of them mention *Reine du Ciel*, Arturo of Padrón, Wiley Forrest, or poetry. There's almost nothing about the Court of Love and when it is mentioned, it's dismissed as legend, an exaggeration. Some say it never existed."

"The Court of Love...is that, like, chivalry, manners, jousting for your lady love, that sort of thing?"

Gavriel returned to the kitchen and started chopping onions. "No. Manners and chivalry were already a part of court life in Spain, had been for centuries. That's not what they created."

"By they, you mean...?"

"Her inner circle. The people who surrounded Eleanor." Wafts of tear-inducing onion crossed the room. Gavriel wiped his eyes and smashed a garlic clove with his fist against the side of the knife blade.

Silvina looked through the pages again. "I don't get the sense of a king in any of these."

"I didn't either. But she was married to two of them—the king of France and the king of England. She had lots of kids, I don't know how many, with the king of England, Richard the Lionheart being one of them, but the Court of Love was something separate. It was hers."

"That can't have been easy to manage."

"What?"

"All of it." She watched him slide the onions and garlic into a pan. "So what's your interest in this? I mean, we have this huge body of work, it obviously came from somewhere, but if it proves something about Eleanor, so what? Toinelle might set up a nice exhibit in her museum, but it's not like thousands are going to break the door down to come see it."

He whipped the eggs with a wire whisk and poured them in a spiral toward the center of the pan. "Multiple streams of abundance," he said. "Appreciation as primary sense. The vibrational power of sound and colour to restructure thought."

"You're quoting phrases from the Full Spectrum website."

"Actually, I'm quoting from the pages in front of you."

"Where?" She lifted random sheets. "Where?"

"How should I know? I'm cooking."

Excitement bordering on panic was scrambling her brain. Nothing she looked at resembled what she did with corporate executives, a sign to stop looking. "Okay, let me pull at other threads. You've told me this land was settled thousands of years ago by refugees from the collapse of the Tower of Bab-El. Vivian and Blythe called themselves Daughters of Babylon. In the seven years they lived at *Reine du Ciel*, orchards and gardens produced mammoth crops with continuous harvests. Are you suggesting that all of this..." She swept her hand over the table. "...is somehow related to Full Spectrum Training?" Her heart continued to thump like a puppy dog's tail.

"Now you're getting it. Your work is an extension of Tri-Partite Academy, is it not, what your boss developed?"

"Yes."

"Have you never wondered where she found those radical ideas that made her so wealthy? Or, better question, how she found them?" He tipped and shook the pan, set it down, and lowered the flame.

"By following the model of the Court of Love?"

"Bingo! Breakfast is nearly ready. The bathroom is through that door if you need to freshen up."

"Thanks." Silvie crossed the room and wondered why, after all they'd talked about and given her current state of agitation, the only word that kept flashing at the back of her eyelids was bathroom.

After they'd finished eating at the dinette table, Silvina was tucking the documents into a backpack Gavriel loaned her when her gaze fell to the box in the corner. A little larger than a bread box, it sat on broken twine with a fedora on top. A sprawling naked lady, flashing neon lights...

"Were you, by any chance, in Toulouse at a print shop about ten days ago?"

"Yes. Why?"

"Across from a student pub, call the Elke Füme?"

"Maybe. I don't remember what was across the street."

"You came out of the store with this box. You were wearing the hat and gloves. It was raining, a cold night."

"Where were you?"

"Across the street, upstairs."

"But why do you remember?"

She shook her head. "It was a silly thing, to do with French plumbing. You looked up. You didn't see me, though, did you?"

177

"I don't think so. I might have looked up to see if it was still raining. I didn't want the books to get wet." He gave the box a kick. "I should have let them dissolve. Waste of gas, waste of time."

"Why?"

He folded back a flap, pulled out a softcover book, and handed it to her. "These were supposed to be gifts for the translators at the Navarrosa event this weekend. It's only a draft, but I thought they would enjoy a preview."

The Light Stalkers' Handbook: Reflections of an Amazonian River Guide by Gavriel Navarro.

"You were a river guide? On the Amazon?"

He laughed. "A long time ago, yes. I was very young."

The cover art featured the kind of pastel forest in which one might find a unicorn or mushroom-capped fairy. "Did you design the cover?" Silvie asked carefully.

"God, no, there are no colours like that in the rain forest. But that's not the worst of it. Go ahead, look through the book."

She tried to flip through the pages, but it was spined on both sides. "Oh, no. All of them?"

"All fifty copies. She offered to redo them, but now that I've seen the final product, I don't want her near my work again. I should have designed the cover myself, but I've been busy, and she claimed to have a Fine Arts degree from the Sorbonne."

Silvina squeezed the sides of the mutant book together and peered down into the pages. "This is prose? Nonfiction?"

"That's right."

"No poetry?"

"A few stanzas here and there, why?"

"Are you okay with me slicing the book open?"

"If you want, but—"

"And would you have a spare copy of your published poems, something I could take with me and annotate?"

"Sure, hold on." He went to the bedroom and returned a moment later with a slender volume in soft blues and grays.

She studied the front and back covers of *The Wind and the Sea: Poems and Reflections on a Voyage of No Return*. She flipped through the pages and read a few lines. "This is more like it."

"More like what? I don't understand your sudden interest in my poetry."

"But it's all connected, don't you see? My grandmother scrubbed bathrooms in the college where Canada's most famous poet teaches. You burst through a neon martini glass I mistook for a bidet, and blocked my way to the toilet my first day at Viv's house. This book you've worked so hard on turns out to be crap. You asked me to look for patterns. I'm seeing them."

Gavriel looked as though he'd stepped in something. "Patterns of what?"

"A suppressed thought system. Something that works—or worked— extremely well at one time and is now being pushed down." She dropped the two books into the backpack. "It's quite possible you have something here."

"You will be careful though, right?"

She slipped the backpack over her shoulders. "Gavriel, no offense...but these are a bunch of poems."

LE PRIEURÉ DE REINE DU CIEL
ATLANTIC PYRENEES
SUMMER, A.D. 1151

Three women and two children waited in the garden of the cloister gallery for the Prioress. They wore plain wool mantels and headdresses of coarse linen; no one had paid them the slightest heed when they stopped at the winery of St. Jacques de la Rivière on the final leg of their journey to purchase a bottle or two. The older child was a girl of five or six with red-gold hair that many called *oriflamme*; she chased a bright blue butterfly. The younger one, just over a year, slept in the arms of a wetnurse. Sister Benedicta came into the garden, and her face lit up.

"*Álie, ma petite*, is it really you?" She opened her arms to embrace Eleanor.

"*C'est moi, Tantie* Ben. A thousand years older, but still in one piece." They hugged long and kissed each other's faces, and it seemed that the ground trembled a little.

The Prioress stepped back and held her by the shoulders. "You look so much like your grandfather. You'll have his laugh lines one day, mark my words. How was the journey? I'd heard the road from Foix was washed out."

"It was, but shepherds came to our aid. They walked us and the horses along a trail above the road, dismantled the carriage, piece by piece, and reassembled it where the road was clear. By then, it was too late to reach St. Jacques, so we spent a wonderful night in a hut in the mountains in the company of Basques and Catalonians. Marie has not been able to stop talking about the lambs."

The little girl, Marie, crouched at the foxgloves where a fat bumblebee had wriggled into a bloom. "How beautiful she is. She'll be tall like you."

"I think so. She keeps the court ladies busy letting out hems. Speaking of ladies, I'd like you to meet my *femmes de chambre* and dearest friends, Catarina and Bilqees. This is Sister Benedicta whom I've known since the moment I was born. She was my midwife, and then my wetnurse."

The women exchanged greetings, while the infant suckled at Catarina's breast.

"And this," Eleanor said, touching the baby's head, "is Marie's sister, the Princess Alix."

The prioress glanced into the shadowed eyes of Catarina, wetnurse, and saw what she had suffered in her own fertile years. "Aah, such a blessing. The baby is feeding well?"

Catarina bobbed a curtsy. "Very well, Reverend Mother, thank you."

"Now then," she said, with a brisk clap, "let me take you to your suites, and you will see what the bounty of two chests of pearls has made possible for the Queen of Heaven." She led them through the cloister gallery with its stately Grecian pillars and latticed ceiling, festooned with clusters of ripening purple grapes.

"It's quite safe to run, Marie," the Prioress said, "if your attendants are amenable. It is gratifying to hear the slap of young feet on tiles. Your rooms are at the end of the gallery. Álienor and I will catch up."

"So how is *Mamie*?" Eleanor asked, when the others had gone off ahead.

"She has good days and bad. She's been watching the sky for weeks."

"Did she think we would fly in?"

Benedicta laughed. "No, but she remembers how you loved the hunt as a girl. Whenever she sees a falcon, she knows we've had word of you."

"I like that augury. I hope it continues to prove itself."

"There was one night, two summers ago, where she screamed and tore the tapestries from the wall and nearly set fire to her cottage. I made note of the date, August 14. I felt it might be significant."

"Were her cries intelligible?"

"Oh, yes. They were banishments in the Old Tongue, as I've not heard since I was a maiden."

The colour drained from Eleanor's face. She paused at a pillar, placed her fingers into the grooves, and looked up at the latticed ceiling, at the bounty of grapes made possible, perhaps, in some small way, by a bounty of pearls.

"The night you speak of, *Tantie*, Louis and I were guests of Pope Eugene at his villa in Tusculum. We had been separated for months by tempest and were on our way home. The Holy Father showered Louis with accolades for his selfless dedication to the Crusade, which of course thrilled my husband. The Pope was also anxious to repair the ruptures in our marriage, and so he prepared a special bed for us sprinkled with rose petals and holy water, and reminded Louis that his duties to the Crusade included a male heir. Nine months later…Alix."

"Would I be amiss to assume the bed of roses was not rapturous?"

"No, Reverend Mother, you would not be amiss."

Sister Benedicta gave a soft sigh. "It always grieves to hear of the Church's intrusion on such matters. On the other hand, your little Alix is beautiful…and I am reminded not to be so quick in future to dismiss your grandmother's episodes."

"Thank you. May I see her now?"

"Of course."

With the children and ladies settled in their rooms, Eleanor followed the looping pathways to a small cottage in a grove of pecan trees. Sister Benedicta suggested that she enter after knocking, which she did. "She will become aware of your presence when she's ready."

The woman they still gossiped about in the courts and villages of Aquitaine sat near a window with a crocheted blanket over her legs. Lustrous silver hair fell to her shoulders, and her fingers worked imaginary stitches, while she talked to a pitcher of red roses on the table.

"Make sure he builds you a *chatillionte*, and pay attention to his bones. Willingness always shows itself in a man's bones. *Pos vezem de novel florir / pratz, e vergiers reverdezir* …because we see again, the plains are in bloom, the meadows greening. He wrote that. Have you ever heard anything so exquisite?"

"*Mamie?*"

The old woman turned in Eleanor's direction and carried on talking. "People think Guillaume and I spend all our time banging the cymbals of Demeter, plucking the joy strings of Hermes. How feeble imagination has become. And how cowardly the euphemisms, even among country folk, don't you find?"

"I…hadn't given it much thought, to be honest."

"Come closer, *ma poussette*. I am not yet fully blind, and the light slants so beautifully here."

Ma poussette, my little sprout. Eleanor's heart thrilled—she *did* know!

Her grandmother pressed a fist to her heart. "You have his stride. I can hear him."

"Whose, *Mamie?* Whose stride do you hear?" There was a low, three-legged stool with scissors and bobbins of thread near the fireplace. Eleanor moved them to the table and brought the stool close to her grandmother.

"Raymond's, of course. He was your uncle twice."

Anguish caught at Eleanor's throat. She had not seen this topic coming.

The two of them clasped hands. Grandmother's skin was paper-thin and cool. There was strength yet in the fingers, and although cataracts dimmed her crystal blue eyes, the woman people called *La Dangereuse* was still handsome. Eleanor kissed her cheeks. "You look radiant as ever."

Her grandmother appeared not to have heard the compliment. "Did you see him? You saw Raymond? How did he look?"

"I saw him, yes. We spent many happy months together in Antioch. He looked fit and hale, every inch the prince."

Did *Mamie* know? Eleanor couldn't tell. She hadn't thought to ask *Tantie* Ben if the news had reached them.

For Eleanor's small court of knight and two ladies, Palermo, Sicily had provided a sort of giddiness. They were the stranded guests of King Roger who had been kind enough to house the French queen and her attendants in a private villa, billeting the other survivors of piracy and a capsized ship throughout the city. One morning, though, Eleanor woke from a troubled sleep where she'd dreamed of a battle in the flooded captain's cabin. All her joints ached from kicking and wielding swords and maces; the bedding lay everywhere. Bilqees had left her a breakfast tray with a note: *I thought it best to let you sleep, Madame.*

She was still feeling anxious when she stepped onto her balcony with a cup of mint tea and saw Arturo creeping down the vines outside Catarina's terrace, next door. At first, she'd felt an anger so intense she nearly threw the hot liquid at him. Then Arturo saw her, and he looked so embarrassed, her turmoil dissolved.

"I believe a wedding may be in order," she teased, at which point Arturo lost his footing and landed in a prickly bed of juniper.

Catarina, who saw and heard it all, whooped with laughter, and Eleanor joined in, night terrors forgotten. Her besotted *femme de chambre* refused to allow Arturo to launder the shirt that was spotted blue with squashed juniper berries. Arturo insisted, as the ever virtuous Galician, on requesting permission from Queen Eleanor to marry Catarina.

"You have my consent, of course, if it's what you both want, but there is no sin in pleasure, Arturo, and you are both very young."

Ten days later, Cati, a radiant bride, held up her husband's stained shirt at their wedding feast. "Lest it be thought that only women leave evidence."

Arturo had not laughed as heartily as the guests, Eleanor noted, but he was shy that way.

Toasts to the newlyweds were still being proffered when a page summoned Eleanor to Roger's private chambers. "Please sit down, my Lady," said the king. "I have bad tidings, I'm afraid." And he told her of the Byzantine forces that had attacked Antioch, led by Shirkuh, the new ruler of Aleppo. Prince Raymond of Poitiers was killed during battle, his head later severed by the gloating Shirkuh and shipped in a silver box to the caliph of Baghdad.

After the initial hot irons of grief seared through her, Eleanor asked, "When did this attack happen?"

"About ten days ago."

"But when? The exact date and time, if you please."

"I don't recall off-hand, but I have the missive here." He went to his desk and read the small curled message that had traveled by bird. "The 29th of June, in the pre-dawn hours."

She thought back and calculated: yes, it was the morning of her nightmares. It was not the flooded cabin of a *barca-longa* she'd been warring against, but her uncle's enemies.

Eleanor wondered again how much *Mamie* knew and recalled Grandmother's odd choice of words. "What do you mean, he was twice my uncle?"

"Your grandfather William and I were both married to unhappy people when we met, and we were parents. If he'd had a choice, William would have been a troubadour, living by his voice and wits, but he was our Duke, and the people of Aquitaine adored him. I became pregnant, and neither of our spouses, your other grandparents, would permit a divorce. William did not want our progeny raised by a man who might, in a fit of pique, disinherit the child for not being his. So Raymond, our son, was installed as your father's younger brother instead of your mother's half-brother. The Duchess Philippa had her faults, but I will always be grateful that she treated Raymond as her own." *Mamie*'s voice broke. "And now my beautiful son is dead."

She knew; she knew. They grieved together, and then Eleanor rose to hang a kettle over the fire. While she crumbled dried chicory and mint for tea, wondering whether Marie and Alix had woken yet from their naps, *Mamie* rocked back and forth, crooning Grandfather's poems.

"*Ben deu chascus lo joi jauzir / don es jauzens...D'amor non dei dire mas be. Quar no-n ai ni petit ni re?*" All should enjoy what makes him joyous. I can't speak of love, but why am I deprived?

By the time she carried the steaming cups of honey-sweetened tea to the table, *Grand-mère* was composed again.

"You haven't found him yet."

"Found who?" Eleanor said.

"The one who makes your soul sing."

She dropped her gaze. "No, I have not."

"You have called upon the right winds. It's only a matter now of keeping your heart untroubled."

"I don't know how to untrouble my heart, and even if I could, I'm married to the king of France."

Mamie held the cup to her nose and breathed in the vapours. "Do you think our pain goes unheard? What do you think becomes of our cries for happiness? Why do I sing my beloved's poetry all these years after he's gone?"

"Because it soothes you."

"Of course, it soothes me, but I do it because we are infinitely stringed and divinely tuned instruments of God. I told you when you crossed the room that you have your uncle's stride. You also carry your lover's touch and the laughter of your granddaughters, and the shine in your eyes comes from every soul who is blessed by your presence—and child, you have blessed many. This valley has been singing of your coming for weeks."

Hearing *Mamie*'s words was to be four years old again, allowed to stay up for the poetry and dancing. "You say I called upon the right winds. I don't know what that means."

"No, you wouldn't, not with that Blessed Eugene and his vultures breathing down the necks of good people. Have you ever heard a more self-obsessed moniker—*Blessed* Eugene?"

Eleanor sprayed her tea in laughter. "Well, he is the Holy Father."

"And I am *La Dangereuse*, what of it? But you ask about winds, and I tell you, they are language. Language is the inner wind that drives the power of *Reine du Ciel*. Long before usurpers of the Good Shepherd planted their plush bottoms on the Seat of Saint Peter, we knew peace. We knew prosperity. It was all we knew.

"On this land of Queen of Heaven, no one in need has been turned away in four thousand years. When St. Jacques drew his maps to Compostelle, the river, it is said, changed course to touch the hem of Her robe, so that the miracles of healing and abundance would never cease.

"I know the miracles have felt thin on the ground for you, child, but they are amassing—I can see them, heaped around your grandfather and

185

uncle now, I see them." The entire time she spoke, *Grand-mère* rocked back and forth from the waist, like the Jews when they prayed at the Temple wall in Jerusalem, and her eyes were crystal blue and shining even through the cataracts.

Eleanor felt like a fledgling bird, a falcon, tiny beak open to capture every morsel of her grandmother's words. But still, she felt compelled to say, "There was a ship, a *barca-longa* that capsized during a storm in the Mediterranean."

The woman went on rocking, staring off into the middle distance.

"I was dining with my *femmes de chambre* and my scribe—"

"Know the power in your womb. It is the holy serpent's eye that guided Eve and the first wife. All the kings and judges since the Tower fell seek the serpent's eye. When found, they try to kill it. Beware what you weave into words, for every thought is a string, and spoken, triples in strength. *The Power, the Glory, the Kingdom.*" *Mamie* pointed toward a high cabinet. "Feel around at the top, and bring me what you find."

Eleanor did as she was asked and returned with a small lacquered box.

"Open it, please."

Wrapped in fleece was a silver brooch, a seahorse inlaid with ruby, sapphire and diamond. It was the seahorse worn by the woman who came to Eleanor in the flooding ship.

"This was your grandfather's first gift to me. He said he dreamed of seahorses for weeks before we met. Now it is your time for dreaming."

Eleanor folded her fingers around the brooch and pressed it to her heart. "Thank you."

"There is one other thing before you bring me those beautiful great-granddaughters. My name."

"Your name? I have never known it."

"That is because the carrion pickers, the Blessed Eugene vultures who deplore the womb and joys of life, are already ensuring that the beloved of William, Guillaume IX of Aquitaine, is lost to history. Names have power, Álienor. Identities have power, and none more so than to those who own them fully. They will try to do the same to you. You must keep your name and identity strong. Be remembered, and keep this place, *Reine du Ciel*, safe in your heart for when the pyres across Europe start burning."

"I shall do everything in my power, *Mamie*."

"I know you will. And now, my name."

"Is it safe for you to utter?"

"Oh, yes. It is a simple name, one that would have caused far less trouble than the epithet they gave me. I am called Rivette, the little shore."

CHAPTER EIGHT

On the eastern shore of Isla Mujeres, off the coast of the Yucatán Peninsula, the Nagual Lupo Sanchez held up his infant son Ívano, both of them facing the ocean, and pronounced:

> *This is who you are!*
> You are the Dawn of Life
> who chased the Sun to where
> she hid in the Cave of Shadows
> afraid of her own heat
> with the message, *'Rise! Rise!'*

Ívano wriggled his naked bottom, arched his strong, brown back and sent a golden stream arcing high into the Atlantic. The shudder of pleasure when he was done reverberated through his father's arms, down his torso and legs to the heart of Mother Earth, who smiled.

"Well done, Papucho."

Lupo laid the boy, ten kilos now of sweet fat and dimples, onto a *rebozo* woven in deep rainbow stripes. He turned, squatted, and lifted him, sling-like, onto his back, then wrapped the long cloth around and up over his shoulders in the manner that travelers of the People of the Essence had been doing since they were first storied into Being. He walked to the café/general store, Manuelita's, that served as the local post office and asked the kind proprietress who gave them leftover *frijoles*, tortillas, and canned milk at the end of the day, "Anything?"

Manuelita pulled out a drawer from behind the counter and riffled through the same General Delivery envelopes that had been there yesterday. "I'm sorry, Lupo. *No hay nada.*"

From Isla Mujeres, they ferried to Cancún and from there, walked south through the province of Quintana Roo, hitching rides sometimes on flatbed

188

trucks carrying sugar cane or in station wagons driven by pale missionaries with blond, freckled children. On the day that the former appointments secretary to President Richard Nixon testified at the Watergate hearings, Lupo and Ívano arrived at Santa Rita Corozal in northern Belize. He carried Ívano up twenty-two stairs of a Mayan pyramid between stone effigies of helmeted beings with flat snouts and heavy-lidded eyes and said:

> *This is who you are!*
> You are *jabalí*, Wild Boar
> who parts the grasses that bow
> and flutter in subservience to Wind
> and knowing you are servant
> to none, cry out, "*See! See!*"

In Palenque, Lupo descended with Ívano twenty-five meters into the Temple of the Inscriptions to the tomb of the great poet-king Pakal, where nine dynastic guardians stood watch and spoke on behalf of the guardians:

> *This is who you are!*
> You are Jaguar of the silent
> paws and twitching whiskers who
> travels the corridors of Nagual to the
> hearts of the bewildered and
> counsels, '*Hear! Hear!*'

For over seven months, Lupo and his son had traveled with no possessions, not even his machete, a circuit of 2200 miles from La Venta, center of the Olmec heartland on the Gulf of Mexico, northeast to Isla Mujeres, sloping downward through ancient Mayan centers in a boomerang shape toward the Zapotec kingdoms, northwest through jungles held by land-reform rebels to the Toltec power sites of Teotihuacán and Tula. They were on their second lap; Lupo had worn through eleven pairs of huarache sandals. Ívano had sprouted eight teeth and outgrown three clothing sizes. Still, there was no news from home.

In Monte Albán, greatest of the Zapotec cities, high above the Oaxaca Valley, Lupo and Ívano circumnavigated the Great Plaza along an unmarked oval, and Lupo said:

This is who you are!
You are Black Road, rift
of the Milky Way, from
between your great Void the
game of Life spills out, and you
remind us, '*Laugh! Laugh!*'

At the volcano of Popocatepetl, after a two-month trudge through the jungles of Puebla where both father and son caught and walked off malaria, Lupo rocked his sleeping boy, looked up at the snow-capped peak, and said:

This is who you are!
You are Smoking Mountain
consort to Iztaccihuatl, defender
of peace, volcano of passion
who serenades his beloved
tenderly, '*Sing! Sing!*'

In the city of Puebla, a street vendor gave each of them a cup of iced *horchata*, a milky drink of ground melon seeds, because Ívano was such a delight to behold—"*Mexicano guapito, tú eres bonito!*"—the vendor was still singing his jingle as they walked away, slurping their drinks. In the central post office, Lupo set his barefoot son on the cool tiled floor, Ívano could stand now, and asked the clerk to check General Delivery for mail addressed to Lupo Sanchez. The young man retreated to a room behind the grille and emerged with a postcard of painted clay pots in the Veracruz market. It was written in English with a green ball-point pen and dated yesterday.

Dearest Nagual,

Dely has returned to us. She is sitting up and eating bean soup and wants to know when her two favourite "muchachos" are coming home. Everyone is well. Bill says hi!

Your friend, Karin Albrechtsson

Silvina learned that she was homeless at Moulin l'Internet, a cybercafé that used to be a flour mill in St. Jacques de la Rivière. The massive stone wheel that once ground wheat, oats, and barley into flour for pilgrims and residents of *Reine du Ciel* now lay flat in the center of the turret-shaped café, with computer carrels like slices of a bundt cake around its perimeter. A century-old gingko biloba tree grew from the hole in the middle of the wheel toward the high vaulted ceiling, spreading its branches amidst the filtered light of stained glass windows. The acoustics of the café, which might have been mellifluous with two violas and a cello, amplified and threw back Silvie's cell phone conversation with Midfield Property Management like an out-of-tune bell choir.

"I didn't fill out-*out-out* the form," Silvie and her echo were saying to Hello-my-name-is-Jessica in Toronto, who'd put her on hold five times and cut her off twice, "because I'm in the Pyrenees-*ees-ees* and I've been offline. I have not been ignoring your messages-*ges-ges*."

Three windows were open on her laptop screen. One was the yellow MPM Claims for Damages pdf; another was a slide show from the *Toronto Star*, dated three days ago, entitled, "100-year Storm Deluges Toronto". Two Australian backpackers halfway round the wheel were scrolling through the same slide show, thanks to Silvie having gasped, "What do you mean, flooded? I live on the twenty-seventh floor!" and were joking about the ambiguous headline—"A hundred years, that's a lotta rain, mate!"

Silvie had stopped the slide show at image 14 of 68. It was an aerial shot taken from a helicopter over Lake Ontario of a needle-shaped highrise during the worst of the storm's pummeling. The plate glass walls that reflected cerulean blue on clear days were gunmetal gray, except for one jagged, apartment-sized hole, black as a rotted tooth, halfway up the building into which the Great Lakes storm was pouring her meanest. The photographer would go on to win awards; he had even captured fork lightning as it pierced the building's basement like a javelin from Thor.

The third open window on Silvie's screen was an email from Jack, a personal claims lawyer she used to date, offering to represent her in the class action being filed against MPM, the builders, engineers, architects, and City Hall. The inundation of Silvie's condo had damaged thirty-two other suites and exposed structural flaws in the two-year-old highrise that promised to keep Jack and his peers luxuriating in billable hours for the next decade.

"Yes, of course, I will fill out the form now that I have it, but it's going to take me a few hours. I can't see what's been thrown into a Toronto Dumpster from here, can I?" Silvie hit the print button. "Yes, I understand the flooded storage unit is a separate claim." Four copies. A printer across the room hummed to life.

It didn't much matter that she'd woken up with a sinking feeling on an otherwise glorious day, or that her eyes were drawn obsessively to the eight stained glass windows that divided the café into quadrants and again, shooting ever-shifting beams of ruby, emerald, sapphire, and citrine into the room like a kaleidoscope. Round and round she swiveled, phone to ear, taking in the knights and ladies dancing, feasting, and making merry in sloped meadows ablaze with wild flowers. In every second window there was a queen, probably Eleanor of Aquitaine, a circlet of gold in her strawberry-flaxen waves, wearing simple gowns of lavender and pale rose. In the window closest to Silvina, the queen stood beside her throne, one hand resting on the back, the other pressed to her lower belly, head thrown back in an expression of rapture, unassailable joy.

The call to MPM finally ended, Silvie turned off the phone. She typed a quick reply to Jack. "Thank you for taking the lead on this. Do, please, set things into motion. I'll be checking messages at least twice a day." She saved the aerial image of the home she'd lived in for only fourteen months before the Toulouse gig came up and shut down the computer.

Silvie was coming around the mill wheel with the printed documents when the café door burst open and a woman came through. She wore parrot earrings and wooden bangles on thin, deeply tanned arms and a bright orange dress. She was carrying a clipboard.

"Are you Silvina Kestral?"

"I am."

"Thank God! Toinelle pointed out your car, said to look for a woman who looked like the queen. I thought she meant Elizabeth. What do I know? I'm from California!"

THE ROYAL PALACE
PARIS, FRANCE
AUGUST, 1151 A.D.

Eleanor stood naked before a full-length oval mirror, arms extended at shoulder height, hands and fingers draping loose. Bilqees stood behind her, bare midriffed, in a deep blue divided skirt of the *harram* and a bustier ornamented with small silver coins that jingled and lifted the pomegranate smoothness of her breasts. Her fingers rested lightly on the Queen's pelvic bones.

"We haven't even begun," Eleanor said, "and I already feel like we're sinning."

Bilqees slid her middle fingers inward along the smile of Eleanor's lower abdominal muscles, then back again to her hips, down a finger's length and along the tops of her thighs until they met at the springy-haired Y-juncture. Eleanor felt a tingle along the lines she had drawn like baby birds nipping.

"This is your sacred cradle," said Bilqees, "from which all movement, measurement, and thought begin. In my culture, we begin training these muscles from the age of three, adding archery, poetry and sciences as the muscles strengthen." She cupped her hands at Eleanor's hips. "Now, lift up from the waist, pulling in your breath. That's it, very good."

Feverish red splotches appeared on the Queen's neck and hot high colour to her cheeks, recalling her to episodes with Louis she would rather not remember.

"I am now going to guide the movement of your hips," Bilqees went on. "You may breathe freely, but keep your waist and awareness high. Imagine your shoulders as the top of a tree, with you observing all that goes on below." She pressed her thumbs into Eleanor's flesh, and tipped her pelvis forward. Then she applied equal pressure with her fingers and the cradle tipped back. "Good, good, keep breathing. This rocking, we call cradling, is the movement of pure thought. Feel your arms as branches, your fingers the leaves, extending toward light."

After a few minutes of cradling, the pockets of cruel heat dissipated, and Eleanor felt lighter, as if air were flowing through her bones, and to her mind came summer days in Aquitaine when they sent out the falcons, leather jesses fluttering; the lapping waves at Talmont where shoes were never worn; standing ankle deep in the foam, aching to design currents of water and sky with her own hands and heart.

"Remember who you are," *Grand-père* used to say, spinning her, straight out, round and round, while she shrieked with fear and pleasure.

"What shape are you drawing from your cradle, milady?" Bilqees asked.

The queen drew in a deep breath, eyes closed. "A circle, I am drawing a circle."

"And now?"

A long ripple of satisfaction blew from her lips. "A cockleshell, from the outside in…a spiral shape." She opened her eyes a crack and peered at her hardening nipples. "Oh, my!"

"Waist lifted, milady, stay high—and now, what formation?"

Eleanor gazed at the tall, slender reflection of herself. Her skin tone had deepened to an opalescent pink and her eyes held lustre, while hips undulated in slow, graceful movements. "Eight," she said. "I am drawing a prone figure eight."

"Yes. It is what the ancient Greeks called *apeiron*, Infinity. You are drawing the infinite, inviting the roots of Creation to plunge into your sacred cradle…it is you who sends creation, once invited, out again to the

194

furthest reaches, wrapping like vines and opening in trumpet blooms of white, deep purity—aroused, to receive again all that you desire, in abundance, all you can imagine, ever climbing—"

There was a rap on the door. Eleanor and Bilqees ignored it, but it came again.

Eleanor sighed and felt the bludgeoning weight of being queen again. Bilqees released her hold of Eleanor's hips and handed her a robe on the way to unlocking and opening the door. It was Catarina.

The eyes of the younger lady-in-waiting widened at the sight of her Queen standing at the mirror, whose form she'd bathed and dressed hundreds of times. The absence of raiment was nothing new, but something in her Lady had changed.

"Madame?" She curtsied. "Forgive the intrusion."

"Not at all, Cati, what is it?"

"We have received confirmation that His Highness the Duke of Normandy will be arriving within the hour. I have come to help you dress."

Petals burst open in the cradle of her thoughts like a morning glory to the sun. "At last, we meet Henry, of whom I have dreamed."

The brisk tanned woman from California shot out an arm. "I'm Glorianne Iverson, president of the Gavriel Navarro Worldwide Fan Club."

"How do you do?" Silvina said.

"I've come to give you this." She handed her a clear acrylic cube about four inches square with a dried, dark red rose inside. "It's a Navarrosa. We give these to all of Gav's translators, workshop presenters, and as awards to our poetry winners."

A rose corpse, was her first thought. Sleeping Beauty in fake glass. "Thanks," she said, "so, erm...how many translators does he have?"

Glorianne tapped her chin. "Let me think...last count, thirty-four—Icelandic, the latest." She glanced down at Silvina's zippered laptop case. "Have I disturbed your on-line time?"

"Nope, I'm finished." She slid the damage claim docs in with the computer.

"Oh, good. I only need two minutes of your time. There are lovely little café tables outside, remind me of San Diego. I'm a Sacramento gal myself. I understand you're from Canada?"

"Yes, Toronto." *But with no home.* Silvina followed Glorianne outside and sat with her beneath Moulin de l'Internet's dark green awning.

"I went to Toronto with my high school marching band in 1991. I was lead majorette. We stayed at the Royal York Hotel."

"That must have been fun."

"It was a blast." She paused. "Something strange has happened, and I need to ask you a favour."

"Go ahead."

"You know about the Navarrosa weekend coming up, day after tomorrow?"

"I do."

"And you know it's going to be down in the orchards at Queen of Heaven. Well, this morning, the caravans, tent and Porta-Potties were delivered. After they were set up, the guys tried to drive out and discovered the parking lot and most of the access road were gone."

"Gone?"

"Yes. Sunk, as in sinkhole, a crater the size of four swimming pools. Luckily, there was enough clearing in the woods for the drivers to get out, but there's no way we can expect 318 people from around the world to enter the site from there, let alone park their cars anywhere nearby. I've talked to the local police in the village up the hill—what's it called?"

"Cerabornes."

"Yeah, and they're okay with people parking along the road on the east side where your house is, but they'd like as many of the vehicles as possible to use your yard and driveway. We'd also need to use the path behind your house for coming and going, from Thursday to Sunday. They're all decent people, no doomsday hippie freaks or anything."

"Sure, that's fine. Why would the parking lot sink? There's been hardly any rain." *Not like the century storm in my city.*

"Collapsed ruins, apparently. This place is riddled with tunnels and catacombs and what-not. They say it happens a lot." Glorianne flipped

196

through pages on her clipboard. "Would you like me to draw up a waiver, in case someone trips on your property and threatens to sue?"

"It's not my property, there's no need." A tiny, diamond-shaped point of intensity was beginning to pulse in the middle of her forehead. Silvina rubbed it.

"Are you all right?" Glorianne asked. "You're looking peaked."

"I've had better days, it's just a headache."

"You need Gav's poetry. You've read his work, right?"

"Haven't dipped into it yet."

"You have to read him. He's better than porn, hotter than romance—do you know he trained as a shaman in the Amazon?"

"Really? A shaman?"

"Oh, yeah, he was only in his twenties, lived with some tribe that's practically extinct now. That was before the perfume, of course. All of his poems are coded, did you know that?"

"With what?"

Glorianne blinked.

Silvina replayed the sentence. "I'm sorry, I thought you said coated. So his poems have, what, secret meanings?"

"They do. They're all about universality and self-acceptance. You should drop in to the workshops. I'm sure Gav wouldn't mind, you letting us tramp through your woods, and all. Let me find you a schedule of events…" She pulled out a glossy brochure with the Navarrosa rose on the cover, which was prettier, freed of its polymer prison.

Silvie scanned the events that began with Welcoming Remarks by Gavriel Navarro, followed by revolving sessions of *Poetry for Beginners, Intermediate Poetry, Master Classes* beside names she did not know. These titles could use work, she thought.

"Are the facilitators paid?" she asked.

"Paid?" Glorianne's nose wrinkled. "They're published poets."

"Well, yes, I should hope so. What I mean is, people pay to come, but are the instructors paid?"

Not the kind of question, obviously, that a volunteer fan club president enjoyed considering. "The poets who come to Navarrosa events," she said, "sell their chapbooks on-site. The session fees pay admin costs. That's how it's done."

If she weren't feeling so sorry for herself, Silvie might have smiled. During Full Spectrum Training, at moments like these, she liked to quote Blythe:

"*That's how it's done. That's how it's done.* I pay myself a nickel every time I hear, think, or speak that phrase, and that accumulation of nickels flowed me my first million."

She tucked the brochure under the rose. "Thank you, Glorianne. I'll see how the weekend unfolds…you mentioned something about perfume."

"Yes, perfume is how Gav made his fortune so he's able to finance poetry. When he was in the Amazon, he developed a floral essence made from all natural ingredients and sold it to a Brazilian perfumery. He even modeled for them for awhile. You've heard of 'g', right?"

"Gee? Can't say I have. I stick to tried and true, scent-wise."

"Oh, you have got to smell it—to die for! Hold on." Glorianne slapped a hand on the table, set bangles a-jangling, and dashed off to a nearby Peugeot. She returned with a box of sample bottles nestled in black velvet. The label was a lower case cursive "g", stylized to resemble the @ symbol. "Here, take two. It's the least we can do for your kindness."

"Thanks," Silvie said, as mounting stress bloomed into, not a headache, but a full-scale synesthesial episode. Glorianne morphed into a carrot with dancing twin macaw guardians, each whispering deep shamanic secrets into her ears while she bounced off like a pogo stick, wiggling her fingers and crying, "Toodle-oo!"

Arturo de Padrón sat in the Great Hall amidst ale-swilling, wench-grabbing, onion-belching Norman boors, supposedly his peers, and wanted nothing more than to find some abandoned stable and curl up with inkpot, quill and parchment. It was a day that would go down in history, when peace was finally brokered between France and the duchy of Normandy, springboard to the British Isles. It was also the day he understood that the birth of a poet can mark the death of the man.

Had there been the slightest fissure, hairline crack; had there been a moment's pause between the final toll in the marriage of Eleanor and Louis, and the arrival of Henry, Duke of Normandy, with whom they'd been at war for two years, Arturo would have plunged his dagger to the hilt and broken the gap wide open. He would have pressed his palms above his head and dived into the swirling depths fearlessly for the chance to prove he could stand beside Eleanor, his queen, as equal. But there was no such fissure, and the final grains of matrimonial sand were still dribbling when the boulder smashed the hourglass—that is to say, the moment when Eleanor, thirty, and Henry, seventeen, first clamped eyes on one another.

Because Arturo was scribe to the woman and not her royal office, he took notes seven months later at the assembly of bishops, where they dissolved Eleanor's marriage to Louis on the very grounds the king had refused before abducting her to Jerusalem. Because Arturo was her personal attendant, he had no choice but to assist in the arrangement of romantic trysts in cottages and country inns for the lovestruck couple; and to abide her girlish gossip with Catarina and Bilqees of the stocky, blond, bearded Duke, who, admittedly, sat a horse better than most Franks.

Not until the return of Eleanor to Poitiers, her birthplace, did the Galician feel glimmers of a deeper possibility. Twice, on the barbarous roads from Paris, their coaches were seized by would-be suitors intent on forcing the now available Duchess into wedlock. Thibaud, Count of Blois, Arturo bested in a sword fight at the edge of a wood and managed even to extort a bag of gold for his trouble. But with the second brute, he miscalculated. Geoffrey of Anjou, the swaggering, younger brother of Henry, had the gall to force himself upon his future sister-in-law, as they disembarked at an inn for the night. Arturo pulled him off before he'd managed anything more than a fumbled grope, but once he had the Count on the ground, dagger pressed to his jugular, beading blood, Arturo's desire to wipe out the Norman royal bloodline one scrawny neck at a time nearly overcame him.

Eleanor had to pull him off. "Arturo, stop! He is fifteen, he is only a boy!"

Catarina twisted the knife away from Arturo, who fell back on his heels, staring at the sniveling youth, and saw himself as he must have appeared all those years ago in Talmont, muddied and overwhelmed, a sack of soggy *bígaros* tied to his waist. And he looked at Cati, sister of Lizibetta, who, because of a few nights of Sicilian passion, had become his wife; and he looked at Eleanor who would always be a queen to him, with whom he'd not yet tasted the pleasures he dreamed of. And he felt a great rending, as of parchment torn from the Book of Life and saw himself, Arturo de Padrón, son of a fisherman, disappearing, unwritten, forgotten, between its jagged edges.

They moved like an elongated loop of happiness all day Thursday and into the evening past Silvina's kitchen window, pouring expectation, exhilaration, and certainties of fun down the wooded slope into the apricot orchard. Poets and lovers of poetry carried backpacks and tents, folding chairs and firewood, and tramped back to help others. A dozen or so cars had parked in Silvie's—Viv's—driveway and lawn, but most of the Navarrosa guests arrived in Jean-Luc's minivan. Gavriel had parked his motorbike beside Silvina's Lexus and placed a yellow and black-striped sawhorse barrier behind them with No Parking signs in four languages.

Silvina stood in the kitchen at sunset on hold with her insurance company in Canada. There was no more activity from this window. They'd all be settled now in the shallow bowl of orchard with guitars, wine, and plates of food on their laps. The poet-founder himself had made more trips than anyone, hauling coolers of wine, beer, and soda, wearing the straw fedora he wore that night in Toulouse. Glorianne, the Gavriel Navarro fan club president, had made endless trips with her clipboard, wearing cork-soled espadrilles that sent her toppling and crying through the poplars, "I never bring the right shoes!"

Your call is important to us. Please hold, and the next available agent will be with you shortly.

Once the next agent became available, it took Silvina the length of a feature film plus credits to sort out her claim, listing contents, approximate value and purchase dates of original art, home theatre components, designer suits she'd worn once, designer bedding she slept in mostly alone. In texture if not content, it brought her back twenty-two years when a different set of circumstances took away her home, and she knew, sleeping under the stars that first scary night as a runaway, that she would never see her family's iron cookstove or the silver samovar again. Silvie had found temporary solace at Twice Past Sunset, the derelict fishing lodge and cabins in the deep north woods where she'd spent so many happy summers with Dad. But then the Pop-Tarts and dried noodles ran out, and cold, bug-free nights warned her she couldn't postpone whatever lay ahead much longer; so with a resilience she didn't know she owned, Silvie walked back out to the highway and stuck her thumb out, pointing east, toward the Sudbury Theatre Centre and a formidable woman in tartan named Vivian Lansdowne.

She was next on the phone with Blythe when her heart leaped at the sight of Gavriel walking past her window with flowers in his arm. She started to walk toward the door holding the receiver until the cord reached its limit at the arched entry of the *foganha*. She placed the phone face down on the island, and the curl in the cord yanked it back to slam against the wall and dangle.

"Oops!" She bent down toward the swinging apparatus. "Sorry, Blythe, someone's at the door. I'll be right back."

The flowers were wild and hand-picked—asters, Queen Anne's lace, and chicory. Gavriel held them out. "I tied them with the twine, from the box I picked up, on the night our eyes met." He spoke it with pauses and emphasis that caused the back of Silvie's knees to go weak.

"Thank you." She held the bouquet to her nose and breathed in the sweet caramel tang.

"I picked them myself," he added, and they both laughed.

"They're lovely."

He wasn't wearing the fedora, and his hair was pulled back in a ponytail, and she noticed, not for the first time, how his eyes were like the forest at Twice Past Sunset. The shimmering play of light across river stones, layer upon layer of colours: russet, charcoal, hunter green, and flint. It was no freaking wonder he had thirty-four translators.

"I know you're busy," he said, "but we're having a bonfire tonight, and I wanted to invite you."

Workaholic panic grabbed her. "I haven't started on those poems yet."

"That's okay, there's plenty of time."

"Well, all right then, thanks…I'll see you later."

She returned to the phone, dangling where she left it. "Sorry about that."

"You have an admirer," Blythe said.

"What? No, nothing like that. He's just a…he's a…well, he's a friend."

"And you're writing poems!"

"God, no! Poems? Me?" Silvina cursed Jurassic-era phones that had no Hold feature. The flush behind her ears was practically throbbing.

Blythe laughed. "Chill, my dear. We all need some fun in our lives. Speaking of which, we need to set up a conference call with Alphonse."

"Sure, but what's fun about that?"

"Alphonse is fun. So is making money. Those expressions of interest from Stockholm, Berne and Salamanca are firming up as we speak, and so far, we have only one FST instructor— that is you. How thin can you spread yourself?"

"Thinner than is good for me, but that is fine news."

Jean-Luc's van pulled up in the space behind Gavriel and Silvina's vehicles, and out poured five more guests with backpacks.

"What are your plans when you've finished with Viv's house?"

"I don't know. Until a few days ago, I thought I'd be enjoying buskers and shawarma at the Toronto Harbourfront. You want us to move the teacher training forward?"

"I think we should. How soon can we set up a call?"

Silvina's usual, *I'll get on it right away*, popped into her head, and then she saw the wildflowers lying on the island, long-stemmed and perky, their perfume riding crossbreeze between the open windows. "I'll speak to Alphonse on Monday. I'm in the middle of something here."

There were two long beats of not liking the answer.

"I was hoping tomorrow," Blythe said, "but if you're busy, you're busy."

Silvie touched the fringed, cornflower blue tip of a chicory petal.

"So," her employer continued, "have you managed to come across those journals of mine yet?" Her question was broken up by a triple beep, the sound of Call Waiting, a feature Silvina didn't know the phone had.

"Um...no, I have been keeping an eye out, but so far, all I've found are Viv's daybooks, and they're all from her theatre years."

"Okay. Well, then, I'd better let you go. I have a Board meeting that started eight minutes ago. Silvie..." *Beepbeepbeep.*

"Yes?"

"I am sorry about your condo. Please let me know if there's anything I can do."

"Thanks, I appreciate it." She hung up, and the phone rang. "Hello?"

"Silvina, Ms. Kestral, I am so glad to have caught you at home. I hope this is not an inconvenient time. It's Tariq, Dr. Shirazi—how are you?"

THE COURT AT POITIERS
DUCHY OF AQUITAINE
NOVEMBER, 1172 A.D.

"To create, Madame," said Wiley Forrest, "requires an altogether different pattern than to sustain."

Eleanor, queen of England now and wife of Henry II for twenty-one years, inspected the variety of quills Wiley had spread across the table with inkpots and parchment. The sharpened wing feathers appeared to be organized in order, not of size, but of the raptorial nature of their original owners. Peregrine, kestrel, eagle, owl, swan, goose, jackdaw.

"Give me an example," she said, picking up a kestrel feather.

"Certainly." He ran a hand through a thick brush of copper hair that rose back from his brow like a tufted hummock in perpetual breezes. "Shall we take a fictitious situation, or would you prefer something more rooted in reality?"

"Oh, fictitious, please! Life has far too much reality for my liking these days."

They were in her private offices, well past the dinner hour, the palace wing locked and guarded. Downstairs in the Great Hall, *cossantes* were still being danced and wine jugs poured with great liberality for the emissaries from Navarre and Aragon-Barcelona.

Wiley had yet to sit down at the large oval writing table with Eleanor, Arturo, and Bilqees. An Irish poet and satirist, he had trouble sitting still. He much preferred to perch or squat, pretend to lean, relax, and then to spring, and it was this agility of movement in the one-eyed exile that prompted Eleanor to employ him as official court jester, even before she'd read his outrageously funny verse.

A highly trained Celtic *file*, poet or "one who sees", Wiley had taken up the dangerous art of satire, a form of poetry outlawed in Ireland because of its ability, believed magical, to unseat and disempower. If he'd not been born to seventeen unbroken generations of *filid*, a status of poets nearly equal to kings, the twenty-year-old would have been put to death; instead, the offended monarch ordered his left eye gouged, his "sorcerer's eye", and the poet, still bleeding, to be banished on a rotted coracle into the Irish Sea. After many weeks, Wiley landed, *sans* vessel and mostly dead, onto a beach in Brittany where he was carried to the palace of the Breton lord who admired Eleanor for her policies in support of ducal autonomy. That was two years ago, the year coincidentally—or perhaps not—that Rosamund Clifford, a Welsh noblewoman, replaced Eleanor in her husband's affections. She and Henry, the parents of five sons and three daughters, now maintained separate courts, he in London, she in Poitiers, city of her birth.

Today, in honour of their diplomatic guests, Wiley wore the embroidered eye patch of a spider with a lion's head and legs in alternating stripes of red and yellow, a playful composite of the coats of arms of Aquitaine, Navarre, and the Catalonians. It was one of his milder folderols.

"Very well," Wiley said. "Two steps are needed before one picks up the quill or the needle, whatever your intended form." He glanced at Eleanor with his flashing green eye and at the black and white feather she was twiddling.

"*Hop-là*!" Oops! She chuckled and set the quill down.

"Let's take the issue, for example, of the usurpation of power. Imagine that your lands are threatened by aggressive forces from all sides."

Eleanor looked over at Arturo who, for eighteen years now, had been *Cabaleiro* Arturo, Sir Arthur, of the Royal Order of the Knights of St. James. One of Henry's first acts after their coronation at Westminster Abbey in 1154 was to appoint Arturo of Padrón as Knight Dedicate to Her Royal Majesty in reward for services rendered in protection of the Queen's person.

"What say you, Arturo? Is the lust for Aquitaine by kings and noblemen real or figment?"

"That would depend on who you ask," Arturo said, pointedly giving no attention to Wiley.

"I'm asking you. You were present at Limoges when my husband confirmed possession of Toulouse to that butcher of a cousin, Ramon. You were present at the pre-coronation of young Henri, our second-born, as future king of England, Normandy, and Anjou—and you served at Henri's nuptials to the daughter of Louis, King of France, whom we both know, perhaps better than anyone. All these calculations and maneuvers, do they benefit or threaten Aquitaine?"

"They could go either way. For now, we should be grateful that His Majesty has allocated Aquitaine to Richard, who shows signs of quite a different temperament than his brothers."

"True," she said. "Richard is only sixteen, yet our people adore him. They are calling him their Lion Heart. He was conceived in England, did you know that, Wiley? It was the night the King and I buried our sweet firstborn, William. He was only three, died of the ague brought on by that accursed damp chill. I love the English, but I still can't get their weather out of my bones." Though the fire burned a steady warmth, Eleanor rubbed her arms and shivered. "I had not known until that day that grief could be ferocious and stir one's passion, but I knew within moments of our lovemaking that a new son was on his way."

Arturo rose to poke the fire. Bilqees nodded with a slow smile. Wiley's single eye rolled over them all. "Methinks a less contentious topic might be in order," he said.

"Methinks the same." Eleanor laughed and sipped her claret, a clear red wine from La Croix du Cinq Diamants in St. Jacques de la Rivière. "Wiley, you play the fool well. You stir up the sloth of ambitious courtiers who dread your keen eye. All this business of courting my husband's dream of a sea-to-sea, Anglo-Norman empire while ensuring the autonomy of duchies exhausts me, as I'm sure Arturo and Bilqees will attest.

"Nonetheless, despite my warring sons, despite 'that Clifford woman' as my supporters call her who fills my husband's head with notions of conspiracy, despite the fact that too much of our revenue sails to England to finance English wars, we have revived, here in Aquitaine, the Court of Love that began with my grandfather.

"Our Christmas *fêtes* leave no belly unfed, the country songs and dances are revived across the land. We are blessed with resident poets and troubadours from across Europe, Persia, the Arab and Byzantine kingdoms. It is only in our realm, they say, that verse lives, that its pulse can be felt in the soles of the feet." She leaned toward Arturo who'd returned to his seat and touched his cheek with the back of her hand. "No small thanks to you, poet of my heart. I still have the first one, do you know that? The poem in the clay cylinder."

The pulsing in Arturo's jaw slowed. "You do me too much honour, Madame."

"Quite the contrary. Now, I do not fool myself that this grandest of duchies with our unsurpassable wealth in fruits and grain, forest, sea, and pasture can remain unscathed while forces of ambition, envy, paranoia, and greed swallow hearts around us. But I am willing—nay, committed to taking whatever action is necessary to preserve the seeds we've planted here, and to find some small corner of the world where they can rest undisturbed until time and space aright themselves."

Wiley spun the chair across from her backwards and straddled it. "You speak with alacrity and foresight, Milady. Our task, now, is to call down the powers, the second of two steps." He looked at Bilqees who, in her sixties, still turned the heads of everyone she passed. "I have seen you achieve this with your dance, transforming a room, erasing conflict. You say it is mathematical."

"It is," she replied. "My dancing, like your jest, sources from the realms that precede manifestation. We do not tamper with harvests already sown."

"Is there a name for these realms?" Eleanor asked.

"In Greek, it is *metanoia*, forethought or preconception," Bilqees said. "In Arabic, sacred geometry. In my tongue, it translates roughly as 'the goddess become'."

"Leaping ahead, coming back toward," said Wiley, nodding. "In Gaelic, we call it Summoning the Intelligences or the Elements—fairies and elves, to the humbler folk."

"These poetic forms you are about to teach us," the Queen said. "Are they dangerous?"

"They can fall flat, like a house of straw."

"If all is carried out to the best of one's abilities, is success assured?"

"Of assurances I cannot speak, but failure can be incrementally weakened until—" He closed a fist, opened it, palm up, and there sat a dragonfly, live and shimmering, with translucent emerald wings. "—it becomes your ally."

Arturo crossed himself and looked away. "With all due respect, Madame, I believe that whatever this satirist-conjurer has in mind is not a worthy pursuit for a Queen twice wed to thrones of enormous power, and one who has vassals by the thousands ready in an instant to lay down their lives."

Eleanor picked up the kestrel wing feather again and turned it over in her hands, feeling the precision of shaft and vane, the downy barbs that capture pockets of air to keep the bird in flight. "Arturo, my friend, I love you dearly, always will. In some other life, perhaps too many to count, I am certain we have shared extraordinary adventures. And God knows, as Aquitaine's principal composer of love poetry, you have singlehandedly fertilized more wombs, my own included, than three centuries of invading knights."

Wiley barked with laughter, and Arturo flushed a deep aubergine.

She pressed on. "But do not speak to me of power, for what you describe and have observed more closely than anyone alive is the power to lord *over*,

207

to humiliate, to hold down and silence like a sack of unwanted kittens in a river till they drown—and, yes, I have wed such ignominy twice—the second, for a time, in love. As for vassals, I have far more interest in subjects who are willing to thrive and grow the land and dandle healthy grandchildren on their knees. If such desire be conjuring, so be it." She took a sheet of parchment and placed it in front of her. "Wiley, please, teach me what you know."

Silvina gripped the phone with both hands. "I'm well, Dr. Shirazi, thank you, what a surprise! I've wanted to call or email you, but there have been a few turns of events."

"Nothing too serious, I hope."

"Taxing and a royal pain, but no loss of life or limb, thankfully. How are you? Where are you calling from?"

"From Tel-Hemat, I'm pleased to report, standing at the twin pillars, the very Gate of God herself. At this hour of the day, when shadows lengthen, one can imagine the exact proportions of the cataclysm that brought the Temple down."

"Excellent! And has excavation begun?"

"Not yet, but I have a full team of diggers, basket boys, and all the technical expertise I need to commence work in a day or two."

"That is good to hear."

"Now, I shan't keep you. My reason for calling is to ascertain if there's anything you need from me. Are the people of Cerabornes and St. Jacques cooperating? Are you making headway with all that Vivian and I have imposed upon you?"

Silvie filled him in on what she had donated to the church, village library, and the amateur theatre. "I haven't sorted through her personal memorabilia yet. If the major drama schools don't want them, I'm thinking eBay and donating the proceeds to charity. What were Viv's favourite non-profits? I don't believe we have a list."

"Well, she supported a group for disadvantaged youth in Glasgow and a meals for seniors program in Toulouse, I believe. Scroll through her contacts, I'm sure you'll find more."

"I'm glad you brought that up. Apart from a wheezing, offline desktop, I have nothing to scroll through. I've asked Blythe and Gavriel, and neither of them know what's become of her laptop or devices."

There was a heavy pause. "Who?"

"Blythe Pendaris…you knew her as Haggerty. Gavriel Navarro is the man Vivian was working with in the final weeks before she died. You must have met him. He was translating poetry for her."

"My dear Silvina, I thought we were clear on the issue of involving others."

The chill in his tone surprised her. "I'm not involving anyone new. Gav already had most of the documents in his possession, and I have them now. Blythe only wants what was hers to begin with, and I'm not going to begrudge her that."

The archeologist sighed. "I must say I'm disappointed. The importance of discretion simply cannot be overstated. The house you are staying in, free of charge, the legacy you are privileged to investigate, I promise, will bring you untold benefits. I thought you, of all people, would appreciate this."

"Why? Why me, of all people?"

"Because Viv trusted you profoundly, didn't she? Trusted you more than anyone she's ever spoken of. Recall, if you will, what I said the day we met. People will ask you for things, not only the contents of what Vivian and I spent years creating, but also your time and your intelligence. Do not fall into traps of flattery and charm, I beg you. When you fully understand what you are seeing, you will appreciate my caution."

Silvina doubted it. His scolding made her feel sick and stupid; the only thing she could appreciate was that she was neither. "I will be more careful," she said, "and now I have to go. Goodbye, Doctor." She hung up before synesthesia transformed him fully into gray-green sludge with spectacles.

The day seemed to have drawn a solid yellow highway line down the middle with directional posts: Happy People with a Life, that way; you, Silvina, homeless and artful at pissing off old men, this way.

In Viv's bedroom, she fiddled with the vintage radio until she found the only static-free station. It was playing mariachi music. While the doleful

Mexican brass and weeping vocals took the edge off her woes, she poured herself a tumbler of white wine in the *foganha*, dug Gavriel's book of poetry from the pile in the parlour she hadn't touched yet, and returned upstairs to the cushioned window seat.

Knees propped, bare toes resting on cool wood, she gazed out at the sun-dappled view through poplars to the orchard brightened by tents and caravans of the Navarrosa event. When she craned her neck over her right shoulder, she could almost distinguish the heap of stones that Gavriel told her was a *chatillionte*, a trysting place. Opening to the first pages of *The Wind and the Sea: Poems and Reflections on the Voyage of No Return*, she wondered how long it had been since those stones held a space for secrets to be whispered and lovers to tumble into each other's arms. And then she began to read.

Last night in the distance,
after feeling that I almost had you…

At first, she thought the ceiling above the window seat had leaked. The front of her blue cotton blouse was soaking wet, and the wet was cold. Sunlight still dappled through the poplars, and the Mexican with the fabulous wail in his voice was still singing "*y tú que nunca fuiste capaz de perdonar.*" How long was that song?

Silvie hadn't looked at the Big Ben bedside alarm clock before she started reading. It was now ten minutes past six in the evening. The only progression she could measure was that she had finished reading Gavriel's entire book of poetry in a single sitting. Shaman or no shaman, it was the most romantic, heart-wrenching, intoxicating, erotic, tender, soul-searing use of language she had ever floated through.

She glanced at the tumbler of wine on the floor beside the window seat—still full, with beads of condensation suspended on the glass. She touched her cheeks and neck. The wetness all across the front of her were tears.

She swung her legs off the window seat, palms pressed to temples, and weaved across the bedroom to the box of tissues on the mirrored dresser. She'd intended not to look—too late. Her reflection resembled something that had been left on the roadside, made of wax with all the gilt and surface bits dripping, falling off.

Yanking half a dozen tissues from the box, she noticed the framed photograph that Alphonse's wife, Claire-Elise, had given her the night before she left Toulouse. She wiped the dust off the glass.

They must have been happy times, those seventies. She pressed her finger to a tall, leggy Blythe; a freckled, broadly grinning, ginger-haired Vivian who was eyeing the guy with the guitar and stood slightly turned away from the young man with glasses on the other side. Was that Dr. Shirazi before he became an archeologist, whom Blythe, she was pretty sure, had called "Tar"? She wondered who the boy was, sitting cross-legged in the front row between Marie-Claire and Blythe. If he was seven or eight when the picture was taken, he'd be about Silvie's age, a little older. Perhaps he still lived in the area. She ought to take the photo to Cerabornes and ask around.

Equilibrium slightly restored, she turned toward the window where she'd left *The Wind and the Sea* face down on the cushion.

The cushion that sat on a wooden structure.

The structure that formed the window seat.

And was probably, because carpenters of old made good use of space, a storage compartment.

She threw the book and cushion onto the bed. Sure enough, there were hinges at the back and neatly carved finger grooves under the lip. Silvie lifted the lid that hardly creaked and smelled the pleasant vanilla aroma of old paper. Inside, filled to the brim were journals of leather and cloth and spiral notebooks and diaries, tied in bundles. Every bundle was dated and labeled with a scrap of butcher paper, "Inklings by boh", Blythe o' the Haggerty.

She untied the string from the top bundle and took out the first few notebooks, dated April-June, 1975. She sat crosslegged on the floor and leafed through them, recognizing a girlish version of Blythe's every-which-way handwriting.

She quickly took out another two or three bundles, and felt again that strange sense of a solid highway line, no passing, drawn through the middle of her. On this side, all the traffic of Silvina's ordinary—and come on, girl, give yourself some credit!—successful life motored on, including her

211

twenty-year association and friendship with a woman considered by *Fortune 500* to be the 128th most influential entrepreneur in the world.

In all those years, Silvina had never seen Blythe read anything that wasn't a financial report, newspaper, or business magazine. On the other side of the solid line, where Silvie couldn't go, was a woman forty years younger who tended apricot trees and hoed zucchini and called herself a Daughter of Babylon. And from the look of every notebook Silvina had skimmed, so far, the only thing "boh", Blythe o' the Haggerty, wrote was poetry.

Friday morning at sunrise, the Moulin d'Internet had no other customers but Silvie. She sat before her laptop on the mill wheel, beneath the gingko biloba with an extra-large coffee nearby. The divided highway sensation had not gone away. A part of her was certain she'd stayed awake all night reading Blythe's journals. She also had a memory of joining the Navarrosa poets at their bonfire around midnight, sitting beside Gavriel on a log, their thighs touching, aware of eyes like lightning bugs flitting in the darkness, fixed on both of them. But when she woke, spread-eagled, on the top of the covers, she was still in the tear-stained blouse and grubby shorts she wore for hauling and packing. It was the kind of dislocation she'd suffered often as a kid, when doctors wanted to medicate but her grandmother refused. "It's just growing pains. Let her be."

Typing emails, Silvina ached in every joint. To Blythe, she forced enthusiasm: *I found what you've been asking for. Many volumes, in good shape! Awaiting direction. Thanks, Sil*

To Dr. Shirazi: *I've finished crating the art and history books that belong to you. Total weight, more than eighty kilos. Please advise on where and how you'd like them shipped. All best, etc.*

The Delivery Failure message appeared within seconds. She checked the email address for Dr. Shirazi that had pulled up automatically against the one she kept in her BlackBerry. They were the same and appeared correct. She resent the message to an address attached to Tel-Hemat, his archeological dig in Iraq. Again: *This message cannot be delivered. Account unknown.*

Silvina's sandaled feet were freezing and her fingernails blue, although the cybercafé wasn't cold. She felt an overwhelming urge to shut down her computer and hit the road, testing the limits of her pretty yellow Lexus. She

Googled the Tel-Hemat website. The banner photo of terraced ruins in desert appeared within seconds. The headline on the cover page read: *Has the original Tower of Bab-El been found?* There was a sidebar photo of a much younger, smiling Dr. Shirazi holding up a clay goddess figurine with the caption, "5000-year-old Inanna oversees restoration of her Temple." Clicking through the pages, the latest updates Silvina could find, in the form of, *this comment has been deleted*—they'd all been deleted—had been posted three years ago.

Keep going. Keep going. Returning to the Google home page, she typed in the text box, Dr. Tariq Shirazi, and held her coffee mug with both hands. The name brought up more than half a million hits, but the first, from the archives of *The New York Times,* was enough to wield the blow that Silvina had felt coming in her bones:

Death of Esteemed Archeologist Confirmed…arrested by Saddam Hussein for espionage during the first Gulf War, convicted, imprisoned in Baghdad. Diplomatic efforts to secure his release unsuccessful. In 2006…transferred to an undisclosed location where he died from untreated wounds inflicted during torture…excavations at Tel-Hemat, Shirazi's lifelong passion, believed by many to be the site of the original Tower of Babel, have been bulldozed.

The obituary was six years old.

BOOK FOUR

Daughters of Babylon

I know a place
of resolution, of repose
whereupon a Queen
may lay her burdens
down and from their roots
observe a freshening
orchard, brooks of silver
trout and deer, fair leaping
where the man she lovéd
into being takes her hand
and walks in tranquil
dawn beside her.

— "Rubielo de la Cérida",
A rubā'ī of Ceres, authorship
uncertain, attributed to
E. of Aquitaine

CHAPTER NINE

TALMONT CASTLE
DUCHY OF AQUITAINE
MAY, A.D. 1173

The clouds were moving in like galleons under full sail from the west—tall-masted thunderheads, bruised purple and pewter-gray, thinly outlined in crimson. Eleanor stood at the cliff's edge, overlooking the cove. The tide was going out. The dense razor grass of the dunes, waterlogged an hour ago, was now wind-pressed toward the hillside, blades rippling like lute strings.

The queen paced back and forth along the shoulder-height wall of the castle's private courtyard, outside the battlements. The thin fabric of her headdress swirled and slapped, refusing to stay pinned. Holding the linen at her throat, she worked the strategies and counter-plans again and again through her mind until they blurred, until they liquefied, then fear rushed in and she could not remember them at all. At last, she heard the stout oak door open, and she swung around.

"Thank God!"

The knight with touches of gray in his dark hair bowed. "Milady."

Eleanor rushed into Arturo's arms, as if he were the embodiment of sea come to greet her. Solid and broad-shouldered, born to a fisherman, the son of Compostelle, he was a knight, after all, to St. James. "I thought you wouldn't come. I feared they'd set an ambush."

"Be calm," he said. "We routed a few, they were skirmishes of children, but I am here, and all is well." He ran his hands along her back, briskly at first to warm her, and then with slower strokes from shoulders to waist, to the dip of her lower back and rising.

They kissed each other's cheeks and mouth, a hungry fervent planting, never stopping long enough to test the heat or depth, knowing only both were there; and with that same synchrony, they let go at the same moment, hands sliding the length of each other's arms until only eyes and fingers clasped. A court dance, wordless.

"I feared the same for you," Arturo said. "The castle looked deserted when I rode up, no banners flying. When the servant let me in, I saw no fires had been lit. I began to think it was a trap, and they already had you."

"Come, let us talk where the wind will not blow our words to Montpellier." She led him to a stone bench built against the wall. They sat with hands in laps, knees pressed against each other's, shoulders folded in like a single heart. *We are a single heart*, Arturo had once written in a poem. "How was your journey to *Reine du Ciel*?" Eleanor asked. "Has Cati settled in?"

"The roads are in desperate need of repair. We had to abandon the carriages at Foix and travel the rest of the way by horseback. The lay sisters welcomed us; the priory is holding its own after a harsh winter. Catarina seemed lost at first—she has been your lady for so long—but after a day or two, she started catching on to the rituals and routines."

"Will there be horses for her to ride?"

"Oh, yes. They have stables, and miles and miles of pasture, as you know."

"Then our Catarina will make an excellent prioress. It relieves me to know at least one of us is beyond the reach of madness."

"I wouldn't underestimate the reach of anything," Arturo said. "I spent a few days in Cerabornes and then with the shepherds—the Basques have introduced a new breed to the valley, long-haired ivory fleece. You would love them. Talk is, certain families in the village are allying themselves with Count Ramón, persuaded by the proximity of Toulouse and his friendship with your husband that he will deliver them from crippling taxes and conscription."

"Deliver them? Do they not understand that the King of England views Aquitaine as the fattest of his sheep? Not for meat or wool, fairly bargained—that would be acceptable—but as veins to puncture and bleed, with Ramón his primary leech. And once the able-bodied men are bled away, Louis will march in with his French armies and grind what bones remain for mortar."

"Some of them do understand. There are still old soldiers who remember, and Cathars who swear, by their various strange means, that your son, Richard *du Coeur Léonine*, is Duke Guillaume himself, transmigrated."

"I like that idea. It sits well in my heart." Eleanor smiled, tucking her headdress into place. "Sometimes I dream that Richard was our son, yours and mine. He has your patience, your gifts of word and song. He can charm pearls out of raindrops. How can a boy be so unlike his brothers, especially that insufferable young Henri?"

"I have had the same dream, Milady."

She looked up at him. "Have you?"

He pressed her hand between both of his. "Many times."

As recently as five months ago, Eleanor might have stepped onto the intoxicating pathway Arturo had always held open with its harmonies and sweet musics. Yes, she was a queen and married woman, fifty years of age, and she'd known Arturo de Padrón since he was a boy—more than thirty years now. And she cared not a whit for what people might say: there were plenty enough, enemies of her second husband or her first, or this or that disgruntled noble's wife, who called her Mélusine, enchantress, demoness, and her progeny, the Devil's Brood. Even Abbot Suger, may he rest far from here, would have regarded her dalliance with a knight, also bound in wedlock, as unsurprising. "The carnal lusts of women," he loved preaching from the pulpit, "know no bounds."

But she had not selected Talmont, her family's summer home, to indulge in romantic fantasy. Rather, it was closest to the sea, if worse came to worst. It was a defunct court, remote, and of no interest to Henry, King of England, or Louis, King of France, who, incredibly, was now sheltering all four of Henry's sons from their father in his Paris court. Talmont also lay deepest in the heart of Aquitaine among people who loved Eleanor as their Duchess, daughter of their soil, and paid allegiance to no other.

The crisis of loyalties, the heaps upon heaps of double deals and treachery, had reached their breaking point three months ago at Henry and Eleanor's court in Limoges in eastern Aquitaine. The rare family gathering had begun with promise. Young Henri, 18-year-old future king of England and Normandy, had traveled from Anjou with his young wife, Margaret. Brothers Richard, 16, Geoffrey, 15, and John, 6, were present, and the long-anticipated occasion was a brokering of peace and betrothal for young John.

Eleanor and Henry presided over tournaments and banquets almost like the happily married couple they had once been. No mistresses had come along; no mention was made of them.

Peace included a laying down of arms in Maurienne, a duchy in the Savoyard Alps east of Provence. Count Humbert, the ruler of Maurienne, positively glowed at being the center of attention in an assembly that brought great southern rivals: the king of Navarre, the king of Aragon-Barcelona, and Count Ramón of Toulouse, Eleanor's cousin, a nobleman as ambitious as Humbert himself. The pièce de résistance was the proposal of marriage between Humbert's daughter and six-year-old Prince John, youngest son of the English king.

The expressions of concord and homage became ever more elaborate over dinner in the Grand Hall, and Eleanor noted, with a twinge of maternal anxiety, how much young Henri, already Duke of Wales, Normandy, and Anjou, enjoyed being treated as the future king of England. At his court in Rouen, he was known mostly for debauchery, for endless tournaments, gaming and feasts that strained the coffers of his nobles who already paid exorbitant tributes to the elder Henry across the Channel.

Then, in the kind of silence that falls upon a crowd but rarely and never without significance, Count Humbert asked King Henry what lands young John would bring to the marriage of his daughter, and Henry, flushed with wine and power, announced, to the full hearing of everyone: "My son shall add Chinon, Loudon, and Mirebeau to your illustrious holdings, dear Count."

There was a collective gasp, a sucking in of air that seemed to visibly reduce the flames in the fireplace and candles in the chandeliers. Chinon, Loudon, and Mirebeau were castles of great strategic importance, located in the duchy of Anjou, young Henri's land. And his father had just given them away.

Eleanor was seated near his younger brothers and too far away to respond physically. Not that she could have stopped Henri from sweeping food and dishes off the table, leaping to his feet, and demanding his father at swordpoint to retract his words. Young Henri's wife, Margaret, daughter of King Louis from his second marriage, had no success in preventing it. King Henry watched his son's reaction and laughed, as if humiliation were the evening's entertainment, and ordered the prince to sheath his weapon or leave the hall.

Which only fueled young Henri all the more. He overturned tables and grabbed at the collars of guests; he shouted to his brothers, even to newly affianced, six-year-old John, sitting on cushions so he could reach his soup, to stand with him against their father the King, purveyor of lies and treachery.

Eleanor acted on impulse. She strode through the mayhem to where John was seated near his future in-laws, lifted him off the chair, and held him, propped against her hip, while ordering Richard and Geoffrey to leave the Great Hall with her at once—for their safety, she believed, as swords were zinging from scabbards all over the room. The teenaged boys possessed land and titles and bore ornamental arms for the occasion, but they were still boys, and in their state of shock, they obeyed.

Looking back, Eleanor acknowledged it was entirely possible she'd decided in that moment to conspire against her husband, whose years of perfidy, of endless battle and the mustering of armies, of dangling power before his sons, then yanking it away for the pleasure of seeing their disappointment, showed no signs of abating. Unfortunately, it had not yet become a conscious decision, and two people to whom she would never have revealed such an intention were the first to see it in her eyes: Count Ramón of Toulouse and her husband, King Henry.

"The storm is moving in," Arturo said.

"I know," said Eleanor.

"No, I mean that." He pulled her to her feet and pointed at the blackening sky. Fat drops of rain were splatting on the packed earth of the courtyard. Still holding her hand, he led her toward a wrought iron gate at the end of the wall.

"We can't get into the castle this way," she said, turning toward the door behind them.

"We're not going to the castle."

"Where, then? We'll be drenched."

"We're going to the one place that your grandfather made sure would not be visible from the road, the battlements, or cove." Arturo opened the gate and stepped through it.

"The *chatillionte*? It'll be a sty. No one's been there for years." Despite her anxiety, she laughed. "No one's been there, probably, since you eavesdropped on Jocie, Marie-Thèrese, and me. How old were you then? Seven?"

"Eleven, going on twelve, and I must differ with you. The *chatillionte* has been well tended. A fire burns, dinner awaits, and there is a warm place," he said, turning to look at her, "to lay your head if Milady desires."

A rush of excitement filled her. "But when did you—"

"It's why I seemed a bit late. I'd sent word ahead, but I needed to check for myself that all was in order."

She passed through the gate and gazed at the path, grown in but still visible, that led to the trysting place. That her cheeks felt flushed and her breathing shallow astonished her. "I'm not the young woman I used to be."

"Nor I the young man, but I've learned a thing or two since then, and so have you. I've had the pleasure of watching yours happen."

Was this love, she asked herself, or the delusions of an exhausted woman? She didn't know. These past months of pretending to continue to be the loyal wife and consort of Henry, of arranging secret meetings with outraged counts and despairing commoners, of traveling from Poitou to Gascogny, the borders of Castile to Aragón, with itineraries layered in subterfuge, had sapped her.

In the morning, she and Arturo would be setting out for Paris, to the court of Louis, king of France, her former husband, now father-in-law to her oldest son and protector of all four boys against their power-bloated father. Oh, she entertained no illusions regarding Louis's motives. Now in his third marriage, he had finally attained the male heirs he craved, and to his credit, had seen their own two daughters, Marie and Alix, marry into titles, if not happiness. But as a monarch with eyes toward rule ever more absolute, he had no greater rival than Henry II of England. In times like these, the enemy of one's enemy was the only option.

Meanwhile, she and her dear Galician, loyal to the core, had three hundred miles to travel across battle-ravaged lands, studded with brigands and mercenaries operating in concert, watching for a renegade queen with a price on her head.

For now, they had tonight.

They had each other.

Silvina emerged from the poplar forest with Pyrenean deer flies like instruments of small torture buzzing around her head. She swatted at the air and followed the scent of frying bacon and French toast into the main tent.

Live in the Momentum! Welcome to the Navarrosa Weekend of Poetry! read the banners in elegant black script, strung above the long buffet table. The flies came in with her. Somewhere, she'd read that agitation attracts biting insects. That she wasn't completely swarmed in a cloud of insectoid menace, was a miracle. There were maybe fifty, sixty people queued up for breakfast or eating at round, linen-covered tables. She couldn't spot a tall, lean man with a dark ponytail among them. She approached a pleasant-looking woman in a "Poetry is for Airheads" T-shirt who was setting up a book-selling table.

"Excuse me, have you seen Gavriel?"

"You just missed him, dear. He's taken some people on a walking tour." The woman frowned. "Are you okay?"

"Yes, um…yes, I'm…thanks." She dashed out of the tent—

—and found him near the ruins of an old hive-shaped bread oven with a dozen men and women, mostly women, slightly bedazzled, with digital cameras and notebooks. Gavriel was hunkered beside a long, loaf-shaped rock that stood on a flat rock, balanced on a single point. "It is never the action, but the intent beneath the action," he was saying, "and with poetry, emotion and image must also balance…" He paused, seeing Silvie. "…one another. Excuse me a moment."

He rose and came toward her. "Has something happened? You look awful."

"I know. I also know you're busy, but would you have a few minutes…sometime, like now?"

He checked his watch. "Sure. Did you want to come to my caravan?" He gestured toward a cluster of wooden trailers with charming decks and awnings, painted multicolours of aqua, lime, and gardenia pink.

"No, thanks. Could we just walk?"

Gavriel nodded and turned toward the people at the bread oven. "I'll see you back at the tent at ten. Feel free to wander the grounds on your own. Notice everything." He took Silvina's elbow and steered her deeper into Queen of Heaven.

They followed the same route, more or less, as the day they'd met, across intricate looping pathways, past traces in stone of a once thriving priory. And as they walked, Silvie told him about Tariq Shirazi, the man who'd called and informed her of Vivian Lansdowne's death. She told Gavriel of how much Viv adored the archeologist, how they'd known each other since the Daughters of Babylon years, then met again late in life and fell in love. How they were planning to travel to Tel-Hemat together, spend their golden years digging for the legendary Tower of Babel. And finally, she spoke of what she'd learned that morning.

"He's been dead six years, was locked in an Iraqi prison for years before that. But I met him. He's the man who let me in to Viv's house, he showed me around, told me about his Persian lineage. We ate pistachios and drank mint tea." Silvina sank onto a large gray stone, as if something had kicked the back of her knees.

"This is a good place," he said.

There were other rocks suitable for sitting, but Gavriel sat on the ground, crosslegged, and, leaning forward, smoothed out the clover and short grasses in front of him as if he were unrolling a map. While he pondered whatever he was pondering, explanations marched in thundering goosestep through Silvie's head. *You are a goose! This Tariq Shirazi you met was obviously an imposter, con man, bunco, sharpie, after Viv's money—after your money! You should have gone to the cops. What's this, running to a poet? He gonna write you up a pretty little sonnet, hex the bad man away? You don't know Gavriel Navarro from Adam, and while he may be cute, he was rumbling around in your attic while you were out, without permission. Have you forgotten that? You got no sense of self-preservation, girl!*

Eventually, the barrage of ridicule passed. It had to. Silvie had no retorts, no protestations, no explanation for why she had driven at greater than optimal speeds in her yellow sports car on mountain switchbacks from St. Jacques to Viv's house through flocks of brown, black, and white sheep that mercifully parted, and run through woods in search of a man she knew even less than the apparently dead, but real to her, Dr. Shirazi. Except for one chance remark by Glorianne, president of Gavriel Navarro's Worldwide Fan Club.

"I have a question," he said, finally breaking his silence.

"Ask away."

"You said he let you into the house the first day you arrived."

"That's right."

"Did he actually let you in? By that I mean, did he open the door and say hello? Did he step out into the yard and help you with your bags?"

Silvina thought back to the day, only a few weeks ago, when Jean-Luc left her by the door, while arguing with his wife on a cell phone—how did he have reception?—and she knocked and waited. She went around the house, thought she heard a click, went back and tried the door. It was unlocked.

"He did none of those things," she said. "The house felt empty when I entered."

"And did he hand you the keys? Like this." Gavriel extended his arm toward her, as if holding something.

"No. He told me where they were." She waited while he stared at the ground some more. "Have you come across this kind of thing…in South America?"

"Similar, not quite like yours. But the head shaman of the Coblán, the Indians I lived with, used to talk about such things. They were apparently quite common long ago when boundaries were thinner."

"What boundaries, what things?" Silvie felt icy cold. She also felt enormously, overwhelmingly tired.

"Inorganic beings, allies, elementals, djinns…the boundaries of time-space. There are many words to describe the beings; every culture has its stories, like Aladdin's cave in *One Thousand and One Nights*. Not everyone believes in djinns, of course."

"I don't believe in them, but that didn't prevent whatever this was from happening. So what is the relevance of keys and doors?"

"If he's a djinn or something like it, then he can't pass through thresholds such as doors or cave entrances. He can lure you in, or keep you out. But these energy forms cannot follow you across boundaries. It's Law."

Silvie feared she was going to be sick. She hadn't eaten anything and had only drunk coffee at Moulin l'Internet.

225

"Put your head between your knees," Gavriel said. "You'll feel better."

She did as he suggested; it helped a little. "What if a person is already inside? I mean, you talk about boundaries, and Dr. Shir—"

"Don't mention his name."

"Okay. So, this guy…thing, he can obviously move around inside Viv's house. He showed me all the rooms, except for the attic. I can't very well live up there."

"Now I understand why Viv never mentioned him," Gavriel said.

"Why?"

"Because names carry vibration, and vibration is power. The work we were doing, she didn't want him knowing…it explains the old desktop and why she printed off the poems for me to take away." Gavriel's expression shifted like clouds moving fast over the sun, like a deck of cards being riffled. And then he looked at her, dead somber. "You shouldn't stay in that house. I'm going to phone Toinelle, see if she has—"

"NO!"

He jumped at both her volume and vehemence. Silvina had scared herself a little too. But the shout from her gut had cleared the nausea and the fatigue and the icy chill.

"I'm not going to leave the house. Blythe told me the same thing. At the first mention of…him, come to think of it. I've since been flooded out of a 27th floor apartment by a freak storm, and now, with your warning, that makes three. But I can't keep running, I can't keep allowing people to push me out. I'm not fifteen anymore. I'm not afraid of foreclosure."

"Foreclosure? Silvina, we are not talking about a mortgage. This is a sorcerer's maneuver. Witchcraft. You have no idea what you're dealing with."

"You're right, I don't. But I know what to do, when I don't know what to do." She slid off the rock, tipped onto her knees and planted a kiss on Gavriel's cheek, feeling only the slightest tug to linger, to slide her kiss a little to the left—*yes, that way, sweetie! He's willing enough; he wouldn't disappoint you.*

"Where are you going?" asked the poet, while she brushed off her knees and stood.

"Home. And thank you, Gavriel! I owe you big-time."

226

Silvina turned and ran across the looping pathways, through and around the community of pup tents and caravans and into the poplar woods. Inside the house, she packed all the notebooks and journals labeled "Inklings by boh" into two cardboard liquor boxes and drove, encountering nothing four-legged and fleecy on the way, to La Croix du Cinq Diamants winery that had a business centre with photocopiers. And through all that, not a single deer fly buzzed.

Back at the house, armed with coloured pencils, paper, highlighters, sticky notes, and rolls of masking tape, she set to work. On the center island in the *foganha*, she laid out the four stacks of documents Gavriel had given her: the poems he'd translated from Galician; pages of random phrases in assorted languages; Gav's newest work, written since meeting Vivian; and the poems written by someone he disliked whose name was Wiley Forrest. There were also two more stacks: the photocopied pages of "Inklings" by a much younger Blythe Pendaris, nee. Haggerty and pages from *The Light Stalker's Handbook*, sliced from their double spine. She colour-coded each pile with a small mark in the corner.

If she were in Toulouse or Toronto, or pretty much anywhere but here, she'd be using a spreadsheet program developed by Tri-partite and wouldn't require vast expanses of horizontal space. Viv's house was half emptied, but expansive it was not. By eight in the evening, pathways of paper were snaking around the parlour chairs and up the stairs, along the corridor to Viv's study where books on the craft of poetry and a volume by Alain C. Dexter, fellow Canadian, joined the queue, relevant pages sticky-noted; then back into the hall to the bedroom where the final sheet reached the claw feet of the mirrored dresser, weighted with the small framed photo of Daughters of Babylon and company.

That was the first step.

Silvina went downstairs and boiled a pot of noodles in the blue speckled saucepan that matched the smaller dipper at the sink. She poured the drained noodles into a bowl, stirred in butter and asiago cheese, then washed the pot and returned it to its peg on the wall, amongst the copper-bottomed pots.

She ate while she walked the path of pages, pausing now and then to highlight with the neon markers she carried in a shopping bag over her arm. Sometimes, she'd rest on her heels and read more deeply and attach a sticky note with comments before moving on. She traveled the full circuit fourteen times, and with each lap she rearranged pages, sometimes, but not often, clear across the house. By 2 a.m., she felt satisfied with the sinuous order and sequence. In Tri-partite lingo, she had isolated head, thorax and abdomen of a single body of thought with clear divisions between them.

That was the second step.

Silvie brewed a pot of French roast and came across the mini-bottle of Courvoisier Alphonse had given her for a night when the house felt ready to share her secrets. She poured the cognac into the coffee and went upstairs to the window seat and wrote single-word headings on sheets of coloured paper. There were no campfires and no lights burning in the orchard; the poets were asleep. She wondered if Gavriel dreamed his poems, the way she had dreamed her FST procedures in spectral bits and pieces over the years.

Having climbed the stairs in Vivian's house often enough with packing boxes, garbage bags, and recycling bins, she knew how to divide the stairwell space evenly into seven. At each interval, on both sides of the stairs, she taped the fourteen headings, seven going up, seven going down. Then she sat at the top step, with all the lights on, and enjoyed her spiked java.

"*Ce soir, ma maison.* Your secrets, please." She entered the bedroom and sat crosslegged at the poem nearest the goalpost, the photo of seven adults and one boy in a happier time. She picked up the page. It was one of boh's short pieces from an early volume, called "The Decision".

Silvie read the poem and she read it again. Her mouth fell open, and her thoughts turned toward the kitchen, the *foganha*, directly below the bedroom. Layers of her mind folded back, one after another, like the petal folds of a woman in her most secret places, and with each progression, each new reveal, her mind grew more still, and then she switched into some kind of overdrive, where furrows rushed past at dizzying speed, and if she didn't keep her eyes fixed straight ahead, the collision, the obliteration would be more than her central nervous system could withstand. And when she reached what appeared to be a destination and slowed, bobbing like a cork on a wine dark sea, she murmured, "Sweet mothering Jesus..."

THE COUNTY OF BLOIS, FIVE DAYS'
JOURNEY SOUTHWEST OF PARIS
JULY, 1173 A.D.

Sherurd and Pascal called themselves soldiers of fortune, though they'd known little of soldiery in recent years and even less of fortune. Sherurd was a German veteran of the Second Crusade, who'd singlehandedly dispatched eighty-seven Saracens until a surprise attack by Turks nearly wiped his king and countrymen off the map. Pascal, a Breton, had enjoyed a cushy post as palace guard in Antioch until that city too met its foul end. The two men met in a veterans' hospital and enjoyed each other's humour. Once their wounds were healed, they set out to follow tournament routes across France and Germany, taking sword work wherever they could find it. For the past few years, Count Theobald of Blois had been paying them two pounds of dried lentils and a slab of pork belly per month as reserve guards and extensions of the royal ear, but lately the bellies were growing lean and the pounds lighter than they used to be. Then, at the festival of St. Barnabas last month, Sherurd was told by a sibyl that he would become a man of means on the day he let his soup grow cold. He'd been eating lentils cold ever since, which meant that he and Pascal didn't sup together anymore. It also meant that Sherurd, whittling at the roadside, waiting for his pease porridge to congeal, was at the perfect spot when a disabled wagon clackered into view.

Two men in coarse garb stepped down from the boxy, four-wheeled cart, pulled by a pair of swayback grays. Sherurd set down the half-finished whistle, tucked the knife at his waist, and ambled toward them.

"That's a lot of cartage for a pair of nags," he remarked.

"They're sturdy enough," said the driver, who stooped to examine the front axle and wheel.

"Retired war horses?"

"So I'm told. They've taken us twice as far as the last pair."

The second man, wearing a cowl so Sherurd couldn't size him up, had crossed the road and was pulling up handfuls of timothy grass. "So what's the problem?"

"The bearing is cracked. We're in need of a blacksmith, but we've passed no villages in two days—none, that is, with people in them."

Sherurd felt the tips of his ears twitch. "Yes, well, there's been some trouble last couple years. It's like that everywhere these days, inn' it?"

The man looked up briefly. "Yes, I suppose it is."

Darkish, swarthy—maybe Jewish, maybe not.

"I don't recognize your accent," said Sherurd. "Where did you say you're from?"

"We're Basques from Navarre en route to the Basilica of St. Denis."

"So you're Christians then."

The man pulled a rag and small jar of neat's foot oil from his tunic and rubbed the rag in the emollient with small circles. "We are. And you?"

Arrogant son of a bitch. "Everyone hereabouts is Christian. The father of our Count, may he rest in peace, was a personal friend of Abbot Suger— may he, too, rest in peace."

Sherurd saw no need to point out that the dearth of villagers and unanimity of faith had a common source in the blood libel of 1171, wherein Count Theobald oversaw the burning at the stake of thirty-one Jews. No one likes to hear about the blood of Christian babies baked into matzoh.

The driver finished greasing the axle and stood up, wiping his hands. "So how far is it to the nearest smithy?" His companion, by this time, was feeding the sweet grass to the horses, but Sherurd still couldn't catch more than the tip of his nose and his height and his slow way of moving.

"Given the state of your wagon," he replied, "about three hours too far. You won't make it before nightfall, which is when they close the city gates. But my friend and I have a small forge. We may be able to rig something up, and we've a barn if you're content with straw bedding."

The driver looked toward his companion, who nodded and said in a most unexpected voice, "We are fortunate to have come upon a Good Samaritan, and we shall accept your hospitality."

The old knight, if he'd been a rook, would have fell right off his perch. "You're a *maudit* woman! In a man's hose!"

230

"Mind your language," growled the driver, reaching for the very place at his waist that Sherurd kept his own knife.

"No harm done." She drew back her cowl enough for him to see the straight nose and strong jaw of an older but still handsome woman. "I am the widow of a shepherd. What you see is my working garb. The man you've been speaking to is my brother-in-law, Atze. We travel in this fashion because two men are safer than a couple, with fewer questions asked."

"I see." The questions he'd intended to fire withered at the back of his throat. Still, Count Theobald, if he were here, would be having none of this cross-dressing—not in his county, and a full report would earn them, at the very least, a fatter slab of belly. "Well then," he said, "our home is up the hill here. If you're willing to unhitch the horses, Ma'am, you can walk them along the path just past that stand of oaks. Your brother-in-law and I will deal with the cart."

"Thank you." She unbuckled the harnesses and, gathering the reins, moved the horses away from the wagon shafts. "We haven't much in the way of funds, but such as we have, we'll pay."

The sybil's prophecy flew into his head. *You'll become a man of means when...*

Apart from refinement in their speech, the couple displayed no outward signs of wealth, but no one in their right mind would travel these days with gold jingling in their pouches. And he knew for certain that his soup, by now, was cold. "It's the first cluster of buildings you'll come to," he said, with a tickle in his belly the size of a fist. "My friend's name is Pascal. Tell him that Sherurd of Saxony invited you."

As hosts of potential windfalls go, one would be hard-pressed to imagine a more butter-fingered, tongue-tied oaf than Pascal, the Breton. "I know that woman," he hissed to Sherurd, while the pair from Navarre refreshed themselves at the water trough outside the barn. "As soon as I saw her walking those horses, as soon as our eyes met, I said to myself, I know that woman."

"From where? From where do you know her?"

He scratched the ring of gray curls around his bald pate, setting off a halo of displaced fleas. "I wish I knew. I also wish we had more to feed them than beans and pork fat. Do we still have that cabbage?"

"I don't think so."

"Parsnips?"

"I don't keep track of the larder. That's your job. I'm going to fire up the forge."

"Duck eggs. I buried a dozen last month, and there's a hardy patch of chives…"

While the two knights ironed out domestic details, another couple were settling in at the castle they'd not seen for months. Count Theobald V of Blois and his wife, the Countess Alix, had returned from Chartres out of season to attend the nuptials of an old friend. Alix had been feeling poorly with nightmares and rashes and outbreaks of sweat, which the physicks had dismissed as nervous instabilities, not untypical for a woman her age. Treatments of fortified wine and bleeding were recommended, as well as taking care not to overtax her mind with unpleasantries.

"I'm going to get some air," she told her husband in the dining hall. Not that he noticed, absorbed as he was poring over ledgers, lamenting the money that had flowed out of Blois in his absence.

She walked the stone path along the dove and pigeon cotes, soothed by the cooing of brood hens. "What I would give for your peace, mother birds."

Her own mother, Eleanor, duchess of Aquitaine, queen of England, wife of Henry, was nowhere to be found. She had gone missing, and the Courts from Rouen to Toulouse were in high gossip. "They say she's fled to Greece…I hear the King of Aragón has granted her sanctuary…I have it on good authority she's drowned herself, despondent with the shame she has brought on womankind."

Meanwhile, Alix's four half-brothers, whom she scarcely knew, were guests, uneasily so, of her own father, King Louis, the poor boys never knowing from day to day whether they would see their dear *Maman* again. And the homilies from pulpits, inspired by that noxious Latin scholar, Peter of Blois, were united in their condemnation of women who revolt against their menfolk, "violating the condition of nature, the mandate of the Apostle and the law of Scripture…being the cause of widespread disaster…resulting in ruin…the head of the woman is the man [Ephesians 5]…for every kingdom divided against itself will be destroyed [Luke 11]."

The one reprieve to which Alix clung was that her husband, Count Theobald, was among the allies Louis was gathering to take up arms against the King of England, to secure the lands for her half-brothers that their

232

father kept selling out from under them. If her mother could only stay safe a little longer—God willing, in Aquitaine, where people knew and loved her as the granddaughter of Duke Guillaume, troubadour and poet. She wrapped her arms around herself. *Be in Aquitaine, Mother, where husbands do not round up innocent men, women, and children for the way they love their God, and tie them to stakes and burn them, as my husband did.* A wind was picking up; she walked faster along the path that circled round the mill pond and back to the castle. *Be in Aquitaine, where the Courts of Love, I am told with salacious detail, of chivalry and romance, of poetry and sweet musics, refresh hearts and minds and recall the Goddess pleasures of the hanging gardens of Babylon.*

"I never knew you like I needed to." She turned and, walking into the wind, spoke aloud. "My sister Marie, countess of Champagne, consorts with the Albigensian heretics, the Cathars, and Theobald forbids me from seeing her. Sometimes I have hated you for leaving my father, for leaving us, but I have also buried three infant sons and know what the coldness of a husband does to a woman's soul." Gates were slapping, shutters banging at the castle windows. A lone pigeon flew low over Alix's head toward the cotes, startling her. It was one of the homing birds. "Now, two fearsome kings are staring each other down, and your ten children moan in their sleep, 'Where are you, *Maman,* where are you?'"

The first bird had carried an advisory message, nothing more, to the chamberlain who looked after the Castle of Blois in the Count's absence. *Guests of unusual rank, possibly spies. Will update.* Sherurd had sent it, on the pretext of fetching more wine, while Pascal entertained their guests with tales of the joust.

"I still can't place her," Pascal whispered to Sherurd in passing, "but he is no shepherd, I can promise you that."

The revelation came to the old knight when he dropped the entire pot of parsnips au gratin in the kitchen behind the house. Sherurd knew this because Pascal, instead of cursing, cried, *"Je l'ai!"* I have it! And the guests who insisted they'd eaten quite enough after the duck omelet—"The meal was lovely, thank you," said the woman who called herself Garaine—were looking more discomfited with each passing moment.

Pascal came in with a square of linen and a bottle of cognac, the bottle they'd been saving for a momentous occasion. He placed it with an indelicate thump in the center of the table. "If you will forgive my rudeness, I couldn't help noticing, Madame, your deftness with horses."

The woman maintained a half-smiling expression. "I have grown up riding. I adore horses and falcons and trout, all living things."

Pascal lifted each of the wine goblets, checked them for contents, and threw the dregs into the fire, raising a hiss. And then he methodically wiped each one. "Quite," he said. "I too enjoy riding. When I was young, I worked in an eastern city in the employ of a Christian prince."

"Is that so?" said the woman. "Which city?"

"Antioch."

Oh, how the man who wasn't a shepherd bristled! Sherurd considered moving the cognac while the bottle was still in one piece.

"And the prince?" she said lightly.

"Raymond. Prince Raymond. But what I especially remember, Madame, was an Anadolu pony about thirteen hands high, and the young woman who rode her with such elegance."

"Except for one day," she said, "when a coterie of knights was—"

"Milady," said her companion. "You don't need to do this."

She placed a hand on his arm, which seemed to drain the tension from his body. "My dear heart, it's over. Two angry kingdoms, a dozen duchies and counties slavering for whatever scraps might be thrown at them in the wars that are certain to ensue, regardless of my action or inaction. I am tired. I need for this to be finished."

The man sat back and stared at the table, then thumped his empty goblet near Sherurd. "If you'd be so kind."

Sherurd sat dumbstruck. This was the queen? Queen *Eleanor*, the renegade, the revolting, disobedient, carnal-loving, sure-to-be-damned-for-eternity wife of the English king? Both he and Louis had posted rewards! One was accusing her of high treason, the other praising her as a stalwart daughter of France. He wondered if both kings would pay out.

All right, so this was a momentous occasion.

He poured the fiery amber liquor into all of their glasses except Her Majesty's. Her Majesty's! She'd placed her hand atop and shook her head.

"As I was saying," she said to Pascal, "my husband assigned a coterie of knights to keep the pony and me in check that day, and you were among them. What flank did you take?"

234

"Right flank, Milady."

"The side of the precipice, as I recall, most susceptible to covert marksmen. I appreciate your valour."

"Milady." Pascal blushed the colour of beetroot, then slid off his chair and with a few creaks and groans dropped to one knee. "To be in your presence again is an honour. The reputation of your fine Court at Poitiers precedes you."

"For now, I suppose it does, but reputations have a way of distorting and disappearing, faster than we know. Please, do get up. We're none of us as young as we used to be."

Pascal pressed his lips to her hand, then used her hand to leverage himself back onto the seat. "Erm, thank you, Milady."

"The pony's name was La Pistache," she went on, "and she was beautiful. My dear friend here, who will introduce himself if he chooses, once risked his life to save that horse. I am honoured to sit amongst great bravery tonight."

Sherurd choked on his drink, Pascal blushed again, and the wagon driver shrugged and raised his glass. "Greetings, *chevaliers*. I am Arturo of Padrón, Galician and Knight Dedicate to Her Royal Majesty...and may I say, this job is never dull."

All of them laughed, so much so that the Queen changed her mind and accepted a splash of cognac. They toasted to peace and equality and a good harvest.

"And a good chase," Eleanor said, setting down her cup. "Now I am ready for a night's sleep. Sherurd, if I may be so bold?"

"I am at your service, Milady."

"Homing pigeons don't like to fly in the dark, but I'd be most grateful if you'd send a second message to the Castle of Blois in the morning. There's a small possibility that my daughter, the Countess Alix, might be there. We haven't seen each other in quite some time. It will be good to catch up."

Chapter Ten

"Silvie, Silvina, wake up! Come back to us, please!"

Whoever invented this mattress needed to be taken to the deep woods and introduced to moss. It was like sleeping on alligator teeth. And why was Gavriel Navarro—it was him, wasn't it?—slapping her? She lifted an arm to fend off the poet.

"Geez, would you stop it already? I'm awake!" Silvie cracked an eye open, tried to rise from her face down sprawl, and howled.

"Careful!" He slid an arm across her solar plexus. "I thought you were dead. Shit!" He slid his other arm across the front of her thighs and lifted her about a quarter inch.

"Ow, ow, ow!"

"Sorry. I don't know how you could sleep like that. On the stairs. I'm going to roll you over slowly, get you into a sitting position. Just relax."

"I can't."

"You can."

"I can't." She could feel Gavriel wedged in beside her on the narrow stairs. She could almost hear his calculations as he looked for ways to relieve her zigzagged body. So acute was her sensitivity to movement, she could feel her veins unkinking and blood surging like rivers through a burst dam.

"What happened to you last night? Did you get drunk?"

"On one mini-bottle? Hardly." Her eyes were still closed. "I was finding patterns. Did I give you a key?"

"No." His breath was becoming audible under the strain, she supposed, of dead weight.

She lifted her arms above her head and stretched—ow! "So how'd you get in?"

"The door was unlocked. I knocked for five minutes."

She was now lying on her back with Gavriel holding her in the hammock of his arms. She wriggled her backside and found a step, so she was sitting, spine arched, almost back to normal. Silvie ventured opening an eye again, but the inside of her eyelids felt like sandpaper. "Is it morning yet?"

"It's nearly noon. I came to invite you for lunch and to sit in on my poetry session. Why is it all we ever do is exchange invitations?"

"Because life," she proclaimed with a flourish of her arm, "is continuous invitation, a flow of, would you like? would you like? 'Why, yes!' is all we have to say, and 'thank you, thank you very much.'"

"What are you talking about?"

"Wiley Forrest, jester to the Queen."

"Ugh, I still don't like him." He placed one arm across her lap, the other across her middle back, and folded her like an airplane seat to an upright position. "How does that feel?"

"Whoa! Like free fall."

"Rub your eyes gently. They're probably dry. Then open them, and tell me what you see."

She rubbed with the balls of her hands until her eyes felt lubricated, but the light, when she opened them, nearly made her scream. Rays streaming through the kitchen and parlour windows to the base of the stairs felt like solar flares. A few more minutes, her clothes would catch fire.

"What do you see?" he said again.

Gavriel's face was inches away, mostly in teal shadow. "Um, I see caring, worry…maybe too much of the latter, lots of travel."

"Silvie, you're making me crazy here."

"You asked me what I see."

He waved his hand in front of her. "I'm holding up fingers for you to count."

"Well, you should have said! Four." And then, in her peripheral vision, she saw the walls of the stairwell on either side. "Oh my God, I thought I dreamed this. I feel like I'm still dreaming."

"You are. You're awake and dreaming. Most people need drugs to do what you're doing."

Silvie craned her head in both directions to look all the way up and down the stairs. Every inch of wall space to her full extended height was covered with cascading pages of poetry, prose, and fragments of thought, arranged in columns. Seven headings were printed on coloured paper, ascending from red to violet on the left wall; seven again, descending from red to violet on the right. "I must have used a lot of tape."

"I think you've had a head injury."

"No, no, no, I know what I'm looking at. This is what I do—it's just usually in soft copy." She looked down at her bare feet; her toes were the colour of the walls under the poetry. She rotated her ankles until some pinkness returned. "Could you help me down the stairs, please? I'm kind of tingling."

"Sure." Gavriel lifted her arm over his shoulder and slowly raised her to a standing position. She felt as if she were made of petroleum jelly. Pins and needles shot through her legs every time she placed a foot down, and the feeling of being split between here and some other here complicated the task. But Gavriel kept a firm grip, and they made it to safety. "Hold on," he said, leaning her against the arched doorway of the *foganha*. "I'm going to get you some water. You shouldn't eat for a little while."

"Use the dipper." *Fewer dishes. Builds immunity.*

"Excuse me?"

"Never mind. A glass is fine." That remark about the dipper had sounded like Vivian, as if some invisible thread of camaraderie had slipped a bobbin from the seventies. Silvina had even rolled the r, Scots-like: *dipperrrr*. She felt like she could pull the thread too, tug at entire conversations that never left the house.

Gavriel pulled two bar stools out from under the island and brought them to the hallway at the base of the stairs, and made a second trip with two glasses of water. "Front row seats," he said. "How about you walk me through these patterns? If we wait until you're feeling normal, reason will kick in. You've worked too hard to let that happen."

Condensation covered the small arched window like a net embedded with tiny perfect pearls. Through distorting waves of glass, a 12-point buck wanted to be seen. He stood in quarter profile amongst the shadowed beech and oak, every muscle, every hair of his rich amber pelt alert.

Eleanor stood at the window and wondered if the magnificent creature, who'd been lingering near the lodge for days, knew when the king's horses and men, bows strung and quivers full, were arriving. She wondered if he felt their intent to kill through the clattering hooves and elevated pulses, and if he did, was his stepping forth an act of agreement?

She pressed the fingertips of both hands to the glass and felt cool miniscule rivulets flowing through the whorls. The shape her fingers left behind resembled the twin arcs of the top of a heart. Not a broken heart nor incomplete, but half above the surface, and perforated. All one had to do was draw a line continuous from dot to dot, and the heart would become clear.

"*Mon Dieu, Álie.*" She turned away from the window. The dream was dead. She might as well be. A captured queen, a traitor, enemy of King Henry of England, she had not been escorted here to the middle of a Shropshire wood as guest but prisoner. In less complicated times, she might have been burnt at the stake or pulled apart by horses, saving the Crown a fortune in upkeep. But Henry, despite his flaws and passion for the hunt, the latter of which was sometimes endearing, had never enjoyed butchery as spectacle. And they had, long ago, loved each other.

When she was brought, manacled and bruised from careless handling to his throne at Rouen, Henry ordered the fetters removed, and he did not insist on more of her obeisance than a bowed head.

"So we have come to this," he said, in doleful, almost gentle tones.

There was no trial and no argument. She had, indeed, attempted to unite her sons, if not unseat their father, and she'd failed. The consequences of her failure were only beginning to ripple out, and unlike the circles from a stone tossed into water, they would grow in strength, accelerate. The monks from Haughmond Abbey who brought her meals and, given their vows of silence, should not have been heeding worldly events and speaking of them, heard that Richard, to assuage his father, was now sacking the castles of the Aquitainian lords who'd supported the rebellion. Making foes of those who'd loved him, foolish boy.

"But I cannot think of these things now," she said aloud to the one-room lodge. "I have come too far and seen too much of goodness. I have found amidst the turbulence, pockets of such tenderness that I wonder how the heart doesn't fly apart." She walked toward the glow of warmth in the crackling log fire. "And I have known love."

On the morning that the soldiers set out from the Castle of Blois to arrest her, she'd issued her final, incontrovertible order to Arturo. That he leave her, that he make haste southwest to the court of Poitiers, to Aquitaine, and gather all written evidence of what they had created—every sestina, septime, octavo, rubielo—especially the rubielos. Bilqees and Wiley would assist him in the task, and the collection was to be taken by him and no other to Catarina at *Reine du Ciel*. Should events at Queen of Heaven darken, there were sister priories dotted across the mountainscapes of Aragón, Castile, and Navarre that would hold their proof. And she instructed that all of them: Arturo, her knight; Bilqees, her *femme de chambre*; and Wiley, court jester, were to take such remuneration as required from her private coffers to effect their freedom. The Court of Love was...

The Court of Love...

She could not even think the rest of the sentence.

The fire seemed to be growing hotter, though she'd added no new logs. Her face felt like it was burning, and the layers of skirt suffocating. Eleanor backed away from the hearth, one step, then another, and from the soles of her feet, she felt a kind of upward thundering, as of hooves gaining speed on a straight, solitary road.

She looked down at her slippered feet peeking out from beneath the black gown and envisioned them as the cloven feet of a satyr or fawn. She imagined them as delicate and tendriled like the dryads of the sweet pea and the English hedgerow. She walked around the room, weaving through heavy furnishings on the broad plank floor made of oak from this very forest and thought she caught a rhythm, the heartbeat of a people and language not her own, though one she'd come to love; and in that flow she saw, like jewels scattered cross a river bed, words. English words. *Palavres anglais*, as they would say in the old dialect. And though she had no writing implements—these would come, they would surely come—she spoke the words to air, into particles of space:

> *A version of myself beyond I draw*
> *in soft iambs, I am a Queen divine*
> *and erring, both...*

And the twelve-point buck came to the window, and between the dots of her fingertips, he pressed his moist nose to listen.

"It's a narrative and reverse narrative," Silvina said, sitting on a bar stool at the base of the stairs.

"What is?" Gavriel asked, seated beside her.

"All of this." She swept her arm in a large, counter-clockwise circle that took in the hundreds of cascading pages taped to the walls of the central stairwell. "Everything that I gathered here is not only patterned, it's part of a cohesive whole, even though about 40% of the poems were written centuries ago—I'm guessing, at the time of Eleanor."

"Are you sure? According to Viv, everything was written in the seventies by the people who lived in this house. Apart from my poems and translations, of course."

"But what about Arturo? Did he live in this house or at *Reine du Ciel*?"

"I don't know. There's nothing about him anywhere. I asked Viv where she found his work. She laughed and said, thin air."

"I don't think she was joking. How does it feel to translate him?"

"I can only do a few at a time. There's an intensity about his work that feels like, I don't know...pushing uphill into a headwind. Poets have to feel comfortable with emotion, but this guy...ooph." Gavriel shook his head

"I felt it too. It was beyond grief or personal heartbreak, it was like he was mourning an aeon. But your work interlocks with his, I can show you. Where he expresses despair, you create with hope. Where he's groping, you find toeholds. What was that term you used once—corresponds? It's that, like a partimen dialogue poem."

"Wow, you are a quick study." His expression turned thoughtful, almost sad. "Shall we go on with the tour?"

"Yes." She got off the stool, and the water in the tumbler she held started to swirl.

"Careful." Gavriel grabbed her arm. "You're not as recovered as you think."

"I can see that. It feels like the whole house is rocking." Silvina took hold of the bannister and focused on the water until it stilled. "I should be okay now. I promise not to let go of the railing." She led him halfway up the stairs. "And if I topple, it'll be straight into you."

He returned her grin. "Deal."

"So, here's the short lesson. Full Spectrum is an oscillation at a very high frequency. You can apply it to any thought stream, any situation, whether it's family life, an economic system, conflict, romance. The base assumption is continuous, infinite uplift, sourced from positive—that is, forward moving—emotion." She swept an arm along the seven column headings at the top in sequential light spectrum colours and turned to continue the sweep on the opposite wall. "Appreciation, Curiosity, Audacity…"

Appreciation	Curiosity	Audacity	Inclusiveness	Humour U	Humour P	Enjoyment
Enjoyment	Humour P	Humour U	Inclusiveness	Audacity	Curiosity	Appreciation

"Humour twice?"

"Yes. Five-two ratio, always. Now because seven frequencies are set up as mirror images, once you've inputted the data, you can spot weak areas right away. Then, with minor adjustments, you can start up, repair, or strengthen the flow."

Gavriel pointed at two oval sheets of paper, facing each other at the top of the stairs. "What do these mean, Crest and Trough?"

"They are a way to define pairings. For example, boh, who is Blythe, and a guy named Wiley Forrest both wrote a lot of satiric poetry. Wiley, who feels like someone from way back, has a stronger grip on Humour, both Universal and Personal, so I've placed his work on the Trough wall, at the base of oscillation where momentum builds. Blythe's sits at the Crest across from him because she says the last funny thing that can be said on a topic before it collapses to redundancy or sarcasm."

"Can the pairs switch places?"

"Oh, yes. Every pairing is an oscillation within the greater wave, and there's no leader/follower, it's just movement. That's what I meant when I linked you with Arturo. If he were still around, you could choose to dip into the dark stuff, and his work would lighten. There's no right or wrong, no better, worse—and most importantly, no competition. That's what we accentuate at Tri-Partite and my division, FST. The concept does not exist at these frequencies."

"What's the worst that can happen?"

"Good question! You see how there's a gap at both ends of the stairwell. If the momentum of full spectrum isn't maintained, someone can fall off the cliff, metaphorically. Taking you and Arturo as an example, something he did or failed to do in Trough position might have caused that printing screw-up with your *Light Stalker* book. But as a result, you could strike up a great working relationship with the printer who repairs the damage, and boom, the momentum is going again, and you're now Trough while Arturo Crests."

Gavriel lifted random pages from various rows. "This is cool. No one's work seems to be exclusively in any one column."

"That's right. It's an amazingly even spread of participants, which tells me this was…or is a deeply strategized, abundance-based system. And it seems to source from form poetry, that strict stuff where you count all the syllables and rhymes, whatever. The variety of forms is kind of boggling, even for me." She tapped on the central column. "Here, you'll find the most concentrated pairing, Inclusiveness with Inclusiveness. In FST, we call it the All in All, the most powerful part of the wave where acceleration and lift kick-up."

"Upward spiraling," he said, scanning the poems and fragments. "Sestina, septimes, octavos, septrois…a few of these are new to me, too. What's this—*rubielo de la Cérida*?"

"Oh, gosh, this had me stumped, but I had to crack it because, look, the greatest concentration of rubielos is here at the center, Heart, green light of the spectrum. I eventually landed with the translation, *rubā'ī of Ceres*. Goddess poetry, *Femme de la femme*. Demeter, Inanna, Ishtar, Ceres, they were all aspects of the Goddess of grain and abundance. La Cérida may have been an old dialect name for her." Silvina grinned. "Ceres would be the Chick, capital C, that stimulates eternal lift, if you get my drift."

"I get it." He laughed a little, not as much as she would have liked at her spontaneous rhyme.

"Rubais, I mean, rubaiyat, as I'm sure you know, are ancient poetic forms from Persia, Turkey, the Arab countries. But here's the funny thing." She leaned a forearm against the wall and riffled through them. "The poems labeled as rubielos are free verse, almost conversational, but they're all inter-connected. Each one seems to pull from the center of a predecessor in theme, which grows the next rubielo and the next, until, taken together, you have something like the scales of a snake or a dragon, overlapping, elongat-ing, eternally oscillating. Whoever wrote these rubielos, Gavriel, they are vibrant. There were times I thought I could see the words dancing. That probably sounds crazy."

"Not at all. That's what the best poetry does," Gavriel said. "Then all of these other forms spin off the rubielo serpent like stars from the center of a galaxy or water from a whirling fountain."

"Exactly. And what's also hot is that the forms build on numerical strength as well as that Fibonacci shape you're describing. Sestinas are based on the number six, septimes on seven, octavos on eight and so on. There's even a glosa by Alain C. Dexter that reads as if Eleanor wrote it. Makes me think he might be a closet shaman, too."

Gavriel looked at her. "Now I understand why you passed out." He descended the stairs, holding the railing. "I need to think for a few minutes." He sat on a stool and guzzled water until the glass was empty.

"Careful, you could get cramps." She laughed. "But seriously, I feel more energized than ever, as if I could fly off a mountain or lift an ocean liner with one hand."

"Tripping a little, are we?" He set the glass on the floor and eyed her askance. "You feel like Superwoman."

"I do, and why shouldn't I? What we have here, Gav, is a genius system, a poetically-based creation of superior human beings, the core of a society where everyone is included, everyone enjoys life at optimal capacities that just keep getting better." She slapped the wall a bit harder than she intended. "*This* is the Tower of Bab-El. It's the reason Blythe, Viv, and whoever else, gave themselves the title Daughters of Babylon. It also explains why, when the poetry died and the friendships fell apart, Viv had her heart set on traveling to Tel-Hemat with Dr. Shira—"

"*Nooooooo, Silviiiiinaaa!*" Gavriel leaped off the stool, arms outstretched, his face contorting like a diver with the bends.

"—zi."

"You called?"

The air had turned oily. Silvina could feel it, slimy and oozing, on the surface of her skin. There was a faint briny smell like seaweed, like an ocean beach at low tide. But otherwise, the presence of Dr. Tariq Shirazi was as real and indisputable as Gavriel's had been an instant before—except the walls of the stairwell were now bare, and there were no barstools at the bottom, and Gavriel, poet-shaman, was moving around the ground floor, arms and legs slowly flailing as if he were tangled in an underwater marsh.

"What have you done to him?" Silvina tried to push past the archeologist who was wearing the same tacky Bermuda shorts and hand-knit knee socks as the day they met. But the man she'd believed to be a spry senior citizen stood in the middle of the step, rooted as an oak. "He's drowning, dammit—get out of my way!" She punched him in the chest; it was exactly like punching said tree.

"He's not drowning." The man-creature, whatever he was, examined his fingernails. "You're sharing a memory."

"Of what?"

"Oh, puh-lease, after the night you just spent, don't dumb yourself down. You'll get spit out like sour milk, and we don't have time."

It was quicksand, I thought you were the ghost of my dead brother…

Oh. That memory.

"What are you, anyway?" Silvina asked, feeling again the splitting off she'd experienced while reading and sorting poems. "Some kind of resident monster?"

"Actually, your buddy from the Amazon explained me rather well. We live in the boundaries, the land of djinn, beings who can go either way— deeper into spirit, shallower into flesh. Free will, everywhere you look. Short answer? I am the ally of Vivian Lansdowne. We made our acquaintance in your terms in 1974, the year that the Daughters—what is the phrase you people like to use?—got their shit together."

245

The djinn version of Dr. Shirazi had the grace of a Persian scholar, mellifluous voice, dignified cadence, but his choice of words seemed to emanate from some smarmy sarcastic place, where words and rancid fish oil meet.

He turned his back on Silvina and started walking down the stairs.

"Where are you going?" she called out.

"I already told you. We don't have time."

He descended slowly, holding the railing, his steps cautious as one might expect from a man near seventy, but he wasn't making progress. He just kept on descending the same seven stairs, as if they'd become an escalator going the opposite way.

Silvina looked behind, and there was no upstairs, no five more steps to the second floor corridor with the attic trapdoor, two rooms and a bath. It was just a miasmic grayish-teal, colour before it decides to be colour. She had no choice but to follow him.

And sure enough, when Silvie took a step down, the Doctor moved ahead one step. Six, five, four, three…they both stood at the bottom in the central corridor between the parlour and the *foganha*. "Why don't we have time?" she asked. "What's the hurry?"

He extended his arm with a grandiose gesture toward the kitchen. "Take a look. See for yourself."

She turned and heard a great cracking like an earthquake, and her grand levees of reason, walls of rationality that had served Silvina, assured and promised her, things like this cannot happen burst their seams, and a deluge of oceanic, chaotic, unformed-but-forming, kinesthetic thought blasted through her muscles, through her bloodstream, through her sinews, bones, and organs, thoughts, beliefs and fears. Smithereens came to mind. Whatever smithereens were, she ought to be them by now, little human bits and pieces scattered everywhere, only she'd spent the night sorting rubielos from sestinas, septrois from octavos, which may have been the reason she was not washed away. It felt only slightly worse than standing in a fast-moving weather front. Rain falls, wind blows. Done.

Except for the gaping hole.

Silvina walked into the kitchen. The wall that held the copper pots with polished bottoms was gone. Everything else looked tidy and untouched, but the tongue and groove panel had been replaced with an entrance to a dark, dripping tunnel of stairs, giving off a blast of cold that was numbing Silvie's nose and fingertips. And though she knew Dr. Shirazi was standing beside her, expecting her to exclaim something along the lines of, *oh my God, what is this*, she had no intention of fulfilling his expectation. Because she'd already seen it, read it over and over in a rubielo until she knew it to be more than a pretty collection of words, and she'd taped it to the stairwell in a state beyond awe. What she'd not anticipated was standing before the facts of the poem, or of being reminded of its title, "The Decision".

There is a corridor
behind the Big Dipper
you can travel unseen.
I've left a lantern at the portal
to light your way, the width
of the passage is made
for one, admits no
shadows. Are you
brave enough—I think
you are—to meet who's
waited all this time
to love you?

The transcriber of the poem had made only one small error. Or maybe two. She couldn't see a lantern. The darkness beyond the natural light of the *foganha* looked absolute.

She turned to the djinn-ally-being who stood beside her, looking smug. "You think I'm going down there, forget it. This is not some stupid Gothic novel, and I'm less blonde than I look."

"What were you planning to do instead?" said the Doctor. "Bake a cake?"

"Maybe." He had a knack, she noticed, for eye holds. Once you looked at him, it was hard to look away. And as eye contacts go, it was not pleasant. Silvie could feel the lines of fear and doubt marching in like army ants, traveling, she supposed, the optic nerve, which led to the brain and spinal column. They weren't her fears and doubts—or maybe they were. Maybe they were Viv's or the grand accumulation of every person in a million years unfortunate enough to have summoned a being from the boundaries.

Peripherally, the kitchen was intact. Reaching out, she could feel the center island. The masking tape was there, the scissors and the coloured markers where she'd left them. So although she couldn't see him, it was also possible that Gavriel was around.

"Really," said Dr. Shirazi. "Once again, you disappoint. Do you honestly believe your poet friend is lurking around in some shamanic non-space, looking for ways to rescue you? What makes you think he didn't cause this in the first place? What do you really know about the man, apart from a book of poems and what a California nut-case in parrot earrings told you?"

She'd been thinking too loudly. She tried not to think, which sounded like, *dontthinkdontthinkdontthinkdontthink*, the kind of rhythmic, slapping screen door sensation that either signaled or brought on full-fledged synesthesia...and maybe this was a massive episode of cross-sensory malfunction, but holding the idea of a medical opinion didn't solve a hoot in hell.

"Please come in," said a voice from inside the tunnel. "There's no one else who can help me. You're my last hope."

She saw the lantern first, a ball of light inside glass, swaying from a metal wire handle. Then the arm holding up the lantern came into view, a blue and yellow striped T-shirt, scuffed-up jeans, and high-top sneakers with red laces on a boy about seven or eight. He stood inside the corridor, looking at Silvina.

"Oh my God." She dropped to a squat, which placed her a few inches shorter than eye to eye, because if she hadn't, she might have passed out again the way she had on the stairs, and if there was one thing she needed to remember in this god-awful mess, it was to stay conscious. "I saw you last night when I read the rubielo."

"I know. You swore pretty bad. Mom would never have let me say sweet mothering Jesus."

"No need for you to say it either. I don't usually swear, but I was shocked. Can you tell me your name?"

The boy looked past her, presumably at Dr. Shirazi whom she could feel behind her left shoulder like a slow-breathing, raspy stick insect.

"If you can't tell me, it's okay. I don't need to know. I'm Silvie."

"Isn't it fascinating?" Dr. Shirazi said. "Allies and djinns, we come in all shapes."

"I'm not a djinn," the boy said. "My name is Thomas Haggerty."

If there'd been a floor—there was, of course, or maybe not—Silvie would have fallen through it. Whatever lay beneath her and nothing, held. "Haggerty. Are you…?"

He nodded. "My Mom's name is Blythe. I'm all she has, and I'm the reason she—"

Silvie reached across the threshold and pressed a finger to his warm, utterly genuine, boy lips. "No, that's not true. You're the reason she loves you." He'd been about to say, *I'm the reason she drinks,* and from a Jungian point of view, he was probably right. In twenty years, Blythe Pendaris had never mentioned being a single parent with a son. She only obsessed, when three sheets to the wind, about a place called Queen of Heaven, Cue Vaitch—miraculous, but with no joy.

"Why are you in that dark place, Thomas? What happened?"

"You have to come in," he said. "There's no time."

There's no time. Why did people keep saying that? She looked over her shoulder at the archeologist or rather, his impersonator. He wasn't really Viv's boyfriend or Dr. Shirazi. She turned to gauge Thomas's expression. Rising to her feet, she decided. But before Silvina stepped across the space between the *foganha* and the corridor, she yelled something at the top of her lungs. Dr. Shirazi yowled like a wounded bobcat and shoved her, and the stone stairs he pushed her down were cold and slippery and the bruising agony went on and on. At last, she landed—*hard*—and picking herself up, felt consoled by the knowledge that, if nothing else, she'd chosen her last five words, in a space with no time, carefully.

The corridors of sound to word, of rhythmic clicks—*the prioress walks soundlessly along the open corridor of the cloister gallery*—were not devoid of light but more like infra-red, the colour of a photographer's darkroom. What had become of Thomas and the djinn, she didn't know—*holding a*

ring of iron keys close to her heart. That she was being watched, she knew, but why? There's nothing here of me to see. All my life I've done my job, I've done it well. What more is there to do do do do do do do do…?

The night is cold but windless, and the coarseness of her wool habit reassures like an old friend. The plainsong of the women, their cantus firmus *sharp and clear as crystal, settles across the pine and oak forests of Reine du Ciel, rippling with the river whose current, swift with winter melt, crashes and foams to the orchards below.*

The she that was beyond Silvie paused to absorb what she was receiving in word, thought, and image, but she didn't understand, so she continued to walk through looping, coiling, tube-like halls, like boilerworks, with furrows made from bands of light. She ran her hands along the bands; they rippled, sending up small electrical charges that flared into honeycomb shapes in her brain.

A long row of flickering candle sconces light the northeast wing that does not smell of boiled turnip, caustic lyes but deeper musk of battles, outside world, man. The prioress stops outside a door, raises her hand to knock.

"It's open," he says.

Dr. Shirazi appeared at her left. "It's good to walk through the valley of the shadow of death and fear no evil, is it not, especially if it means we can know what happened to our dearest friends?"

"Why am I here? Where is—" She stopped herself in time, this time. No mention of the boy. "—the door to get out?"

"Oh, we'll reach the exit soon enough. These corridors may seem endless, but so does a long dull afternoon at the office."

The low-burning fire in the guest cell gives off the sweet essence of cherrywood. The man sitting at the edge of the bed looks up briefly, then returns his attention to the leather boot he is buffing with a scrap of chamois.

Silvina stopped, while the corridor kept bouncing softly like a spring. "Arturo? Is that you?" A few of the honeycomb cells ignited. She wanted to look deeper, beyond the need to understand why she knew the knight's name. She knew the knight's name because she knew the knight.

His silver hair is brushed and pulled back with cord, the chain mail that still fits him well glows with a soft filigree. The prioress drags her gaze from the weathered hollows of his face while taking in the smell of mutton grease and other unguents needful to an old soldier.

250

"Be careful," she heard Thomas say. "Auntie Viv thought it was okay that Uncle Tar used poppies to remember. He boiled the flowers and smoked the tar. That's why we called him Tar, it wasn't just his name. He thought it was a game to think he'd been a king named Louis with a queen…"

Through lingering scents of mutton grease, Silvina caught glimpses of Thomas peering through the circular bands of light, the places in between the furrows where Arturo and the prioress conversed. "How did you end up here?" she asked the boy.

"Mom wrote poems for us every day. She'd rock and rock, and the vegetables grew, and the apricots and pecans were making us rich. Some of the villagers didn't like our remembering. The priest said we were evil, but Mom and the other Daughters didn't care."

"I've been dreaming," says the prioress, "of lands on fire, humans tied to stakes, the stench of burning flesh. I came to warn you, but perhaps you have no need of dreams from me."

"To the contrary, Reverend Mother, you have always kept my spirit on course, and your dreams speak truly. Villagers from Cerabornes beat two shepherds to death last night, accusing them of heresy, theft, stealing wives and babies. We have a saying in Galician…"

Silvina felt a shudder of nausea that turned to confusion and then excitement as she mouthed the words along with the knight she recognized from somewhere. *"Cando os pastores están en perigo, a morte de Deus non pode estar moi lonxe."* When shepherds live in peril, the death of God cannot be far behind.

"Well done." Dr. Shirazi patted her left shoulder. "Rewarding, isn't it, to recover one's proficiencies. You were lucky to have a grandmother who kept you safe from doctors."

The djinn's commentary made it hard for Silvina to keep track. Thomas resided in the light bands, the medieval events took place in the dark; only the djinn seemed capable of traveling the corridor with her.

The knight pulls on his boots, stamps his feet a few times, and rises. Thrown over a chair is a long woollen cloak. He lifts the cloak and beneath it is a bulging leather satchel.

"Do you see it?" whispered Thomas excitedly.

"See what?" Silvina felt a pull of urgency but didn't know where it was coming from, and Thomas didn't answer.

"*To leave now would be folly,*" the prioress says. "*The moon is not half full, the stairs slick with ice.*"

"*The orchard path is clear, and I know it well enough. God willing, I should be well past St. Jacques by daylight.*"

"*Well, at least, let me gather provisions for your journey. Two to three days' worth will keep you off the main roads until you cross the border.*"

"*There is no time for that.*"

"*But I have not heard from the Reverend Mother Eusebia for months. For all we know, our sister priory in Aragón may already be ashes...*"

A crackling, rhythmic stomping sound outside the cloister distracted Silvina. Not quite unified, except in the colour and shape of their intent, their minds were pushing in, squeezing the dimensions of old *Reine du Ciel* from all sides, like a fist around fruit. She could see them. They were the men of Cerabornes, the ones who'd beat the shepherds to death, only now they were greater in number, carrying clubs and sacks of stone and mortar, crosses round their necks, blessed by the priest, they trudged up the hillside.

The leather satchel is heavier than it looks. Arturo grunts as he lifts the strap over his head.

"*Do you have them all?*"

"*I took whatever was in the vault.*"

"Now do you see it?" A series of furrows lit up, turning the corridor from gloomy infra-red to a miasmic yellow. She suspected it was Thomas who made that happen, running off ahead, the way happy kids do when they're excited.

"Do I see what?" she said. "The leather bag?"

Arturo throws the cloak over his shoulders and pins it shut, concealing the satchel. "*Your loyalty will be well rewarded, Reverend Mother.*"

"*For the love of saints!*" *Tears spill down the old woman's cheeks, and she claws at the starched tight fabric at her neck.* "*Would it be so great a sin in these remaining moments for you to call me Catarina—or is your heart is still tied to her?*"

His face crinkles into a sad, beautiful smile. "*No, dear wife, it would not be so great a sin.*"

And it suddenly dawned on Silvina what the men of Cerabornes were doing, hiding in the bushes with cudgels, stones, and mortar until Arturo departed, not giving a rip about the old knight. Gavriel showed her that first day the ruins of stone in the refectory that stood thicker than the rest. *La Tapiada*, he'd called her. The walled woman.

Eleanor had never known what became of Catarina. How could she, sequestered and mouldering for eight years at that point, and still Henry's prisoner in England? Silvina leaped with the combined strength of who she'd been and who she was—not so terrible a thing, knowing—toward the dark bands to warn her former lady-in-waiting, but as soon as her feet left the floor of the corridor, her being, her entire physicality fell apart. She pixillated into hexagons of light, confetti, bits of tiny coloured memory, and all that remained were random, floating senses.

"I told you to be careful!" Thomas cried out, his voice wracked with distress. "I thought you'd be smarter than Aunt Viv and my Mom and the rest, but you're not!"

And all around her was a click-click-clicking, the sound of a triumphant djinn laughing.

CHAPTER ELEVEN

The boy and the shaman-poet in his light body crept along a band of spectral frequencies, one behind the other, that arced over the hut of the dying *bruja*. In realms of time, the scene they observed, unnoticed, as if from ceiling rafters, was taking place in the year 1182 A.D., the season, winter; location, the mountains of Gudal in Teruel, Aragón. And vastly, across space, upon the throne of Aragón-Barcelona sat Alfonso II, friend of Richard the Lionheart and composer of verse, a troubadour in his own right.

A storm had moved in from the southeast, bringing pellets of icy rain that pushed through the crumbling mortar of the *caseta*, whistling gusts of cold air through the chimney. A cauldron of white bean soup bubbled softly from an iron hook over the fire. The woman sat on a three-legged stool and threw in her last handfuls of kindling. She poked at the logs shooting sparks and flakes of ash into the air. When the fire went out, she would lie down, cover herself in fleece and let the cabin grow cold. If she felt so inclined, she might savour bean soup one last time.

While into the court of Alfonso, her king in Barcelona, *rubielos de la Cérida* were slowly making their way—small, dangerous poems, rousing and intentional, said to draw from the power of pre-Christian pockets of terrain still ruled by *La Diosa*, the Goddess Ceres. Troubadours spoke of one knight in particular, former Dedicate to the imprisoned Queen of England, whose skill at *rubielos* was so pronounced, so immediate and all-encompassing in its effect that Creation itself could be renewed. And if the king's sources were correct, he was somewhere at this very moment in the kingdom.

"Hmph, how about that?" Gavriel said, from his spectral vantage.

"Shh," said the boy. "The lady's a witch."

The wafting aromas of garlic and onion caused the old woman's belly to rumble, while the storm drove a solitary traveller to the only hut with smoke wisping from the chimney. People used to journey often to the house of the *bruja*, high on the mountain pass, and she herself had traveled every year to the painted caves where carnivals were held, and she would set bones, cure fevers, and cast stones of fate. But those days were gone. The Cistercian order was spreading its dark, humourless wing across these mountains, and soon, the secret places of *La Diosa* would be discovered and destroyed, and women with her skills and inclination would become kindling.

"Do you have a line yet?" the boy asked the shaman, whose ear for Catalán and Iberian rhythms, in general, brightened their location to a hopeful green.

"A scattering of words, no lines. There's so much coming in, I don't know where to look."

"Yeah, it takes some getting used to," said the boy whose name was Thomas. "I've been at this awhile. Stay close behind me, and don't focus on any one thing for too long."

"I don't understand why you've brought us here," said Gavriel, who'd watched his friend Silvina vanish before his eyes, fully flesh and vibrant one moment, a vacuous shimmer like a heat mirage the next.

He'd understood it was her naming the djinn that caused the rift, suspected too that she had created an unintentional corridor of power through her intricate assembling of poetry, a vortex of energy he'd not anticipated. And he also felt responsible.

Then he heard her shout from the *foganha*: "Look behind the Big Dipper!" He thought she'd meant the constellation, some kind of metaphor. But it was midday, no stars to be seen, and she'd mentioned a dipper moments earlier, a small one at the sink, partner to its larger counterpart hanging on the wall panel.

A crowbar from Jean-Luc's toolbox in the van exposed ancient stairs and a tunnel in short order, but Silvie was not there—the wall clearly hadn't been opened in years—and 340 people in caravans and tents were expecting his return. Gavriel decided in a shaman's maneuver to split himself, appearing to function normally at the Navarrosa event while searching energetic pathways for his friend. No sooner had he made that decision than Thomas showed up in his mind's eye. "I can help you. I've seen her." He also knew about the djinn who'd attached himself to Vivian and was now accompanying Silvina. After fourteen hours of real time, Gavriel had yet to catch a glimpse of inorganic being or woman, and he was having trouble believing he would find Silvie in 12th century Aragón.

"Just keep watching," Thomas said.

The old woman carried the stool to the small table at the center of the room. From a shelf beside the hearth she took down a bowl and ladle. She was lifting the first spoonful of soup to her mouth when there came a pounding at the door. She was so startled she forgot to blow and burnt her mouth. The pounding came again.

Who, at this hour, would disturb an old woman? Some brigand, a king's guard, his wages guzzled, intent on pillaging her meager possessions. If she did not answer the door, he or they would break it down.

She picked up the iron poker and crossed the room. At the door, she spoke in her clearest *bruja* voice. "Who knocks? Declare yourself."

"I am a traveller, man of words, who…his way."

The wind had made off with part of what he said, but she caught enough to sense his turmoil. "I have no horses and no money."

"A few moments of warmth is all I ask…some directions, if you would be so kind."

Perhaps this was a test, a final rigour to determine the levels of Paradise to which she'd be entitled. She slid the bolt across the door and opened it.

The broad-shouldered man in a long woollen cloak towered over her even with his head bowed. The hood of his garment was pulled close against the wind, and in his right hand, he gripped a walking staff. Without looking up, he stepped across the threshold, nodding his thanks, then faltered.

She reached out to steady him, and a heavy leather satchel swung out from inside the cloak, walloping her across the shoulder and breast, nearly knocking her over.

"Forgive me," he said, pulling the bag into the folds of his cloak and wincing as he caught her, mid-fall. His breath was raspy, and she saw with a healer's eye that every move and word cost him dear. He dragged himself another step or two, enough for her to close the door and to understand the cause of his suffering. From the middle of his back, there protruded the long quivering shaft of an arrow—

"That's it!" said the boy, who dove across the arcs of light as if they were cascading waterfalls, and he, a lithe young salmon.

For Gavriel to follow into realms of such high frequency, even with his training, was impossible. The boy was gone. But he could see the final moments of the man he'd once been, and his heart wrenched at all that

Arturo de Padrón had achieved and failed to do. He poured strength and gratitude to the old woman who'd wanted nothing more that night than to fall asleep and not waken. He watched her remove the arrow—shot by whom, he didn't know and didn't care. Tears fell onto the empty page of his notebook where he'd written three lines of a rubielo since the boy asked.

I find you scattered cross
the river bed, translucent
stones of pink and violet

The notebook sat on Gavriel's lap in his bed at St. Jacques de la Rivière, the Navarossa weekend with its workshops and gala award dinner over, his mind and body exhausted. He never should have asked Silvina to pick up where he and Viv left off. If he'd known there was sorcery involved, if he'd known she would take his request so damned seriously—but he hadn't.

Gavriel watched the frail, kind, determined woman lay Arturo's scarred and battered body across the floor where she washed him gently with warm water. She placed copper coins, her last, upon his eyes, wrapped gauze around his head and chin, and spoke the prayers to La Cérida she'd known since childhood. When there was nothing more that could be done, she climbed into bed, pulled the covers over her face, and closed her eyes. If the *bruja* noticed during her labours that the satchel on the table shimmered, oscillated, and disappeared, she gave no sign. All things, Gavriel thought, find their way home.

and bitter green, a gown
once radiant, a smile worth
the crossing of a kingdom
swordless, while my paying
guests the ones I guide
they want to know the value.
Are they gems? I tell them
no, the only lie that lies
between us now.

The cross between a giant upright earwig and segmented humanoid didn't bother to impersonate Dr. Shirazi anymore. It bobbed and clicked along the furrows of its primordial kingdom carefree, relaxed, boasting of the millions upon millions over millennia who'd sought the powers of abundant Creation, summoned a djinn, and messed up. They always messed up, and for the same tired reasons—greed, fear, shame, and self-doubt.

"Shame is the worst." *Click, click.* "Shame, blame, guilt, fear…shameblameguiltfear. That's what brought the Temple down. Not arrogance, not thumbing their noses at God, but shame, feeling bad for feeling good, afraid of the heights of limitless abundance, screwing up their minds and thinking that joy is a silent thief that takes from others, leaving them with less." *Click, click, click.* "It's how they lost the boy, those women and their friends. The Daughters of Babylon, they'd been doing so well. Not since the Courts of Love at the time of the Good Queen had *Reine du Ciel* so thrived. We allies were flocking to the boundaries like bees to pollen. "Let us help, let us help!" We reached across, joined with their success, and grew it; we brought them secrets direct from Ceres and Bab-El, the Gate of God, through poetry, through balance and wisdom of soil, fruit, and nutmeats.

"Young Thomas was the brightest, always curious, always happy, everything about Queen of Heaven, he appreciated. The village was coming to life again, the vineyards were more prosperous than ever—and then one day, someone said, wouldn't it be nice if people saw us as something more than hippies, and we could persuade governments, historians, and scientists that we're on to something. And Tariq started harvesting the opium poppy…"

Silvina tuned him out. The ability to turn her senses off or on was all she had since she'd made the error of attempting to prevent a historical event—and not even quite historic, the walling of Catarina. No one remembered her name. How long ago Silvie's faux pas occurred, she didn't know, but ever since, she'd been holding in her mind the full spectrum of Enjoyment, Humour Personal, Humour Universal, Inclusiveness, Audacity, Curiosity, Appreciation, and its mirror image—holding, holding—letting the djinn talk, for he loved to talk, and whatever one loves is the place to begin. The more she focused on the spectrum of abundance, the further along the light prism they traveled. The corridor that had begun as infra-red and dungeon-like had passed through orange, yellow, green, and when the vibrations reached the All in All Inclusiveness of Green, Silvina began to feel physicality return, her self cohering with the cellular recomposition of blood and bone and pulse and flow. The creature kept on talking, and she followed. Thinking bold and funny thoughts, appreciating, brought them to deep violet and deeper still, till suddenly—

The djinn stopped. "What's this?"

"The end."

He turned and saw Silvina fully formed. He shrieked and leaped on hairy, insectoid feet as if the ground had turned to fire, but ultra-violet is cool. And so were her thoughts. Silvie had walked away all fear; the cause that brought the Tower down, she had no more.

"Vivian walked this far with you too, didn't she?" Silvina said. "All those years alone in that house, researching, trying to retrace their steps, reclaim what they'd lost—and for awhile, you were helpful."

"That's not always how we are seen."

"We humans don't see each other that way either, but it's true. Djinns, allies, inorganic beings, all of us have an equal right to be."

While they stood regarding one another, the djinn had begun to reassemble the appearance of Dr. Shirazi, possibly because the look had pleased Vivian who'd genuinely loved the archeologist. And possibly because he knew that earwigs were not considered dapper by humanity. So his smile was pleasant, his expression convincingly sincere.

"You are correct, Miss Silvina." It was the first time in these realms that he'd used her name. "The great actress, Miss Lansdowne and I also reached the end. I told you it was coming, didn't I? A djinn can do many things, but unlike you, we cannot lie."

Silvie peered over his shoulder. "Behind you are the steps carved into the mountain that lead from *Reine du Ciel* to St. Jacques. They're the steps where Viv fell and broke her neck."

"I pushed her."

"I know. And you did so as a favour. She knew she'd reached the end but thought she had achieved nothing. It's like you said. Shame crept in, convincing her that she and the other Daughters had done wrong, fallen short, then *blameguiltfear* pushed up from behind, and you're an ally, obliged to help. You can only reinforce a pre-existing thought flow."

"She'd have been stuck here forever," he said, "like the boy, but worse. She begged me to push her. I told her it would be dangerous. She said it didn't matter. She'd made arrangements with a poet from South America and a businesswoman from Canada who'd once been a teenaged runaway. I agreed to stand in as her old boyfriend, whom she kept alive in her heart, I'll have you know, until her dying breath."

"So was it fear that caused her to lose her footing?"

"Yes. There was a chance until the final moment in her leap from No Time to Time that she could have recollected herself. Even during the tumble, hundreds of feet down, she could have…" The djinn gave a crickety sort of shrug.

"She could have appreciated and enjoyed." Silvina smiled. "I think I'd have had trouble with that contrast too."

"Nonetheless, it was possible."

"Thank you. You've been very helpful. And now it's my turn."

"Do you know what to do?"

"I believe I can do whatever I like, so if you wouldn't mind stepping aside…"

The djinn did as he was asked, and the shimmering violet haze, roughly circular but moving like an oil stain on water, became fully visible.

"My grandmother used to call me Pikku Silli, Little Herring. It's one of the first things Viv and I talked about when she took a chance on me, twenty-two years ago."

"Are you well-versed in the behaviour of little herrings?"

"Oh, yes."

He gave her a gracious Dr. Shirazi smile. "Then you'll be fine."

Silvina had decided during her sojourns through Humour that a crazy running leap would work best. And so she backed up about a dozen steps and started to sprint, picked up speed, and by the time she reached the boundary of No Time, hair rippling, lungs strong and clear, she ran with full oscillation and the joyful cry of Little Herring, "Sliiiitheeeerrrrr!" resounded across the peaks of Queen of Heaven, and she landed, not at the base of 800-year-old steps but somewhere green, peaceful, and quite horizontal. As she lay face down, exhilarated, breathing in the fresh, dewy scent of grass and purple clover, something cold and wet with long corkscrew curls nuzzled her cheek and said, "Ba-a-a-a-h."

∽

The Land Rover with Silvina and three Basque shepherds pulled into the driveway behind her yellow Lexus on a Wednesday, four days after she'd vanished from the hallway into No Time. All the Navarrosa vehicles were long gone, although there was a dark blue Clio parked beside Gavriel's motorbike.

"You're sure Monsieur Navarro will not mind signing all these?" said Eneko, who sat in the back with a pile of books between him and his cousin Dunixi. He'd brought not only his own copies of Gav's poetry books but his Mom's, aunts', and sisters'.

"I can't imagine why he'd mind," Silvina said, while Josepe turned off the engine, looking as though he intended to stay in the vehicle. "Please, all of you come inside, meet the other essential party of the rescue team." On a phone conversation, Gavriel had read her the rubielo he wrote of finding a woman scattered into jewel-like colours across a river bed. "That's it," he said, after she'd described her experience. "My revised edition of *The Light Stalker's Handbook* is going to be all rubielos, once I've figured out what they are."

Silvina led Dunixi, Eneko, and Josepe into the *foganha* and found Gavriel sitting at the island with his laptop, a garage door sized hole in the wall behind him where the pots used to hang. He'd forewarned her—"there's been some renovation"—but it was still a shock to see the physical facsimile of something that occurred far beyond the physical. In her sojourn with the djinn, she'd forgotten to worry whether Gav heard or understood to look behind the big dipper, lower case, not the Big Dipper in the sky.

"Silvina!" Gav's face lit up, and he came around the counter.

"Ah, the tunnels!" exclaimed Dunixi. "I used to lose my dogs in there all the time. Once, we lost fifteen head of sheep, never saw them again." His cousin poked him in the ribs and said something in Basque, probably, "Shut up!"

The hug between Silvina and Gavriel went on and on, plunging roots and sending out great branches; they both cried a little and leaves unfolded, buds swelled and burst to flower.

"How could I have forgotten?" Gavriel said, holding her face, taking in every detail, as if they hadn't laid eyes on one other in centuries.

"You never forgot. Have you read your own poetry?" And flowers turned to fruit, green and tart but certain, as all things do, to ripen. They finally let go of each other, and Silvina wiped her eyes. "Phew! I should disappear more often."

"Please don't," said Gav, laughing.

She introduced him to Dunixi, Eneko, and Josepe. "These guys are your biggest fans. I think they were more excited at the prospect of meeting you than finding a teleported woman in the middle of their Basco-Béarnaises." That was the name of their breed of long-horned, curly-haired sheep, whom she intended to visit with treats as often as possible.

"Teleporting is not that unusual in these mountains," said Josepe. "It happened to my uncle, though no one believed him when he landed in the bed of his best friend's wife."

The men groaned and laughed and punched one another, and Dunixi told Gavriel how his poetry had brought him, a shy shepherd, a beautiful wife. And Eneko insisted that the fertility issues he'd been having with his spouse Anika were cured by reading *The Wind and the Sea* aloud to one another.

"Our twins are now three-and-one-half. Would you like to see pictures?" He whipped out his cell phone.

"Sure!" said Gavriel. "I'd love to."

Silvina, who'd seen the photos and heard stories from the shepherds that were centuries old and seldom shared for fear of being thought strange, including tales of djinns and a temple far to the south that fell, wandered into the parlour. A woman in a red silk skirt was sitting in the high-back wing chair, facing the fireplace. She had a laptop open with a full screen video playing.

"When did we get Internet connection in this house?" she said to no one in particular.

"Sometimes it's best not to look into things too deeply." The woman peeked her head around the chair. "Hello, Silvina."

The room spun a little. "Blythe!"

The president/founder of Tri-Partite Academy set the computer aside and rose. Tall, elegant, silver hair pulled back in an S-shaped swirl, Blythe Pendaris walked toward her, arms outstretched. "You scared the bloody, freaking crap out of all of us."

"I know."

They hugged and cried, and the tree that Silvina and Gavriel grew in their moment of reconciliation and remembering dropped its fruit and orchards spread in pure, unrestricted abundance. *I could get used to this*, she thought, and sank into the other wing chair.

"So why are you here?" she asked Blythe. "You must have a million things on your plate at home."

"Gav called me as soon as you disappeared. I took the next flight to Paris."

"You've been here since…?" She gestured vaguely. Time still felt flimsy, like a cardboard sign stapled to a stick that people agreed to carry around. Her day and night reclimatizing in a shepherd's hut at 2600 meters felt like a month at the Riviera, and the time before that? No such thing, though memories, thank God, of all she'd seen there and here seemed intact.

"Since Sunday. I'm staying at the winery B&B. It's gorgeous! We talked about that way back when La Croix du Cinq was almost unknown." She laughed. "Toinelle and her brother were still in diapers then."

Her friend's lightness of spirit was wonderful to see, but Silvina knew she hadn't come all this way to await the return of a missing employee. "Blythe, while I was gone, I encountered someone." She waited for the pain she'd witnessed so often to rise. Instead, Blythe's expression grew even more vibrant.

"Did you see Viv?"

"No, I saw Thomas."

Hands flew to her mouth. "You saw Thomas! I wondered if that might happen. How old was he? What was he wearing?"

"Erm…about seven. Striped T-shirt, high-tops."

"Blue and yellow, red laces, exactly what he wore the day he went missing." The light in her eyes faded some, and she looked away. "We could

263

be so thoughtless, at times. None of us realized how literally kids take things. I'd been scribbling poems for months, long complex things that seemed to lay out a new economy or an old one, we didn't know which. Viv and Tar, they were the researchers, the mad and fearless scouts. They wanted to find evidence of the people we were dreaming about, a Galician knight, an Irish jester—Wiley was my favourite. I felt sometimes like he and I shared the same backbone, pumped from the same heart. You know, of course, that Eleanor of Aquitaine is beloved like no one in these parts, and locals believe that *Reine du Ciel* was part of the network of her famous Court of Love. But historians claim there's no evidence, it's just a legend." Blythe looked down at her hands folded in her lap. "And one night, when I thought Thomas was asleep, I said to Viv and the others, wouldn't it be nice if we could find one piece of incontrovertible evidence that the Court of Love was real? I went to check on him later, and…" She shook her head. "Beauty and joy died for me that night, Sil. I never wrote another poem, never read one…left everything I'd created here."

And then she told Silvina of her drive to create a multi-million dollar business, a unique creative school based on recent developments in brain theory, so that she could post a standing million dollar reward for information that led to her missing son. Thomas Haggerty's picture had been on milk cartons in North America for years; on Interpol files; she hired teams of private detectives who brought her hundreds of false leads.

"Then, two nights ago, walking along the river at St. Jacques, I get a phone call from Sydney," Blythe said. "The man asked if I was Blythe Haggerty. I said yes. Were you once a Daughter of Babylon? In forty years, no one has ever asked me that question. That's when I knew." She turned the laptop around on the small table so they could both see the screen with a stopped video of a handsome bearded man on a tall-masted sailing ship with two smiling children.

"Oh my gosh, what a gorgeous family!" Silvie said.

"Thank you. Thomas grew up in Australia with foster parents. He had a different name and no memory of anything that happened before the age of seven. Then, when he turned twenty-one, he changed his name legally to Thomas Haggerty, not really knowing why. He's a software developer, has his own company, divorced, two children. This video was shot yesterday, two days after Thomas picked up *Fortune* magazine in the tall ship lounge and read about Tri-Partite Academy." She clicked on the Play button, handed Silvie a box of tissues, and the YouTube came to life.

"Hi, Grandma, we're having a great time," said the boy, who looked about nine. "Dad wants to catch a marlin, but if he does, Rayna wants him to let it go." A girl, maybe two years younger, mugged for the camera with thumbs in her ears, fingers wiggling. "We can't wait to meet you, Grams. Love you!" Then Thomas, fully grown, came on screen and said a few words, an arm hooked playfully around each of his children. Silvina couldn't take her eyes off the man he had become. His eyes were blue-gray, he had a wicked sense of humour—things a camera can't always pick up, but a heart with open memory knows.

"Their names are James and Rayna," Blythe said, when the video ended. "Can you believe it? I'm a Grandma."

And before Silvina could gather the sodden tissues from her lap or think of anything to say beyond, "Congratulations!", Blythe's phone rang.

She checked the caller ID. "Oops, gotta take this."

Gavriel strolled into the parlour, the shepherds having gone their way, and sat at the flagstone hearth, elbows on knees, looking every bit the relaxed conspirator.

"Yes, she's here—looking great…well, maybe, a little stunned. I wouldn't ask her what day it is." She placed a hand over the phone. "Silvie, I'm sure you'd like to shower and nap, but the third Daughter of Babylon would really like to meet you, and she has a great dinner planned for this evening."

"There were three Daughters?"

"Yep. Viv, me and Karin Albrechtsson—redhead, brunette, and blonde. Scots, Canadian, Swedish."

"Um…holy cow." *Enjoyment, appreciation, enjoyment, appreciation.* The spectral loop had kept Silvie conscious, sane and grounded for immeasurable stretches of No Time; they could do the same for her now on a random, inconceivable Wednesday.

A few hours later, Silvie was filling the small dipper at the sink when Gavriel came into the *foganha* carrying a bulging leather satchel. "Sorry, I'm a little late with this." He thumped it down onto the counter. "I got waylaid in Aragón. Go ahead," he said. "Open it."

265

Blythe came up behind him and watched Silvina open the flap and, scarcely breathing, slide out sheets of parchment, centuries old, of poetry written in contemporary dialects of Aquitainian, French, English, and Galician. The documents from Eleanor's Court of Love felt soft and pliable. She could almost smell the ink. She could, most definitely, hear the joy, especially from the page that read, in a smattering of tongues that Silvina, for the moment, could read with no effort: *Abbot Suger came to visit me in the turret today. Of course, he is not really AS who has been dead for years, and anyone who reads this will be certain I am mad.*

"Where did you find these?"

Gavriel pointed to the hole in the wall. "Wrapped in oiled cloth and tucked in a niche…behind the bigger dipper."

Blythe grinned. "It seems you have inherited an ally."

Karin Albrechtsson, the proprietor of La Sorcière de Miel, had closed the restaurant for the party of four that included herself. Students from Lycée Professionel de Cerabornes dressed in formal catering attire served crudités and fresh bread sticks while Gavriel and Blythe studied the menu and Karin studied Silvina. Not in a disconcerting, judgmental manner, but in the way that one might observe a guest who'd just returned from six months orbiting the Moon.

The fine-boned, pretty blonde known for serving the best food in Cerabornes didn't look anywhere near mid-sixties, which was about the youngest she could have been as Blythe and Viv's peer. She sat across from Silvie with Gavriel and Blythe on either side. The scrutiny felt odd, too, because Silvie had grown accustomed to being vaguely snubbed running errands in the village, a hold-over, she assumed, from angry investors who'd built a cable car and silk-screened *Reine du Ciel* tea towels for a boom that went bust. Karin wore a smile that appeared to be an effort to hold in.

"Viv and I had always intended to sort the poems," she said, dipping a celery spear into garlic dip. "We got as far as wrapping them with elastics.

Blythe, of course, leaped straight into financial wizardry and hasn't had time to pull the trail up behind her, as the nagual used to say."

"Aah, the nagual," Blythe said. "I haven't heard you mention him in decades. What was his name—Cuco?"

"Lupo. The Nagual Lupo Sanchez."

"Is he still alive, have you kept in touch?"

"Oh, yes. His son Ívano is the new nagual, but Lupo, nearly ninety, is spry as ever—they all are...and since we're on the topic, I have a confession."

Gavriel looked up from his menu.

"While I'm proud and grateful to be a Daughter of Babylon and a prime shareholder in TPA, I am not actually Karin Albrechtsson. My name is Malvine Lavendrye. I am Mexican of French descent and a member of the party of *brujas* of Lupo Sanchez." Her grin broadened. "I'm also not a natural blonde."

"What?" Blythe set down her breadstick. Gavriel's eyebrows rose. Silvina felt as though someone had plugged her feet into electrical sockets.

"Karin and I exchanged identities in 1972. She came to Mexico with a professor on sabbatical and after a rough start, showed a flair for *brujería*, and I'd always wanted to see Europe. The nagual, meanwhile, had been asked by his mentor, La Pantera Negra—" She paused and turned to Gavriel. "I believe she visits your dreaming, now and then."

"She does." He smiled ruefully. "She is relentless."

Malvine returned his smile. "The nagual was asked to launch a *maniobra*, a sorcerer's maneuver of extraordinary complexity—I'm quite sure nothing like this has been attempted in thousands of years—in response to a queen imprisoned by her husband in the 12th century."

"This was Eleanor's doing?" Blythe asked.

"It was all of us. You can pick up the thread anywhere, including the chance meeting of flower children in the seventies and a nagual in Mexico who nearly lost the love of his life in collision with a donkey."

While her guests enjoyed quail bisque, Malvine explained how the intention of a *maniobra* by an impeccable nagual produces results across time and space that can, in effect, link Creation to Infinity with entirely new configurations.

"So that's why we had three harvests every year and Europe's biggest zuccinis?" Blythe said.

"And why poetry flowed from you like a volcano, yes."

"Then why did we fail?"

"We didn't. Viv enjoyed a stellar career on film and stage, Tar found his beloved Bab-El, and look at you, happy Mom, who is now a Grandma."

"A *maniobra* continues," Gavriel said, tearing a cheese brioche in two. "Once launched, the unfolding maneuver becomes as permanent as a galaxy and like the Universe, continuously expands."

"Well said," said Malvine. "And if you haven't already guessed, you and Silvina are the next generation of an ongoing strategy of pure intent. Which brings me to the next topic." She signaled to one of the wait staff who delivered a zippered leather briefcase.

"Oh my God, not another satchel," Blythe joked. "Please, don't tell me you're selling your shares."

"Never. TPA is the best investment I've ever made." Malvine took out a laptop, a computer tablet and cell phone. "I know you've been looking for these, Silvina. They belonged to Viv. As soon as I learned of her death and how it happened, I removed them from the house to reduce the chances of it being overwhelmed by inorganic beings. I know it sounds like *bruja* crazy talk, but djinns can manipulate technology like you wouldn't believe."

"I have no problem with *bruja* crazy talk," Silvie said.

"You're welcome to take them if you believe your ally is truly on your side."

"We'll see over time, I suppose, but I don't need to poke through any more of Vivian's life. I'm nearly done with what I came to do."

"In one sense, yes, but now we come to the most important piece." Malvine pulled out a large, thick manila envelope. "You've been readying the house, as you know, for new owners who were scheduled to take possession in the fall. You have far exceeded expectations on that score." She turned to Gavriel. "Acceptance of your offer to buy the house has been conditional on your ability to build a bridge."

He nodded. "That is correct."

"A bridge?" Blythe said. "Where?"

Silvina's eardrums began to pound.

"Between the work of the Daughters of Babylon and the future," said Gavriel. "Is that how the agreement was worded?"

"Precisely," said Malvine. "I think we can agree, given the splendid unfolding of recent events that the bridge is built and looking sturdy. Gav, you will also recall that co-ownership was part of the deal."

"As long as I agreed to the co-owner, yes."

"She is, at the moment, sitting to your right. Silvie, in thanks for what you've achieved, the house is yours in perpetuity with Gavriel, if you're interested."

Silvina and Gavriel stared at one another. "Her?" he said, at the same time that she said, "Him?"

Blythe burst out laughing. "That is one hell of a negotiation, Karin, or whatever you said your name was."

"You can both take time to think about it, of course."

"I have no objections," Gavriel said.

Silvina recalled the day she met the poet, when the attic stairs were down, blocking the bathroom. No, it was her last night in Toulouse when he stood in the rain—no, no, no! It was way, way before that. "Me neither," she said. "As long as we fix those attic stairs."

EPILOGUE

THREE YEARS LATER

The private jet, a refurbished DC-3, took off from the airport in Montego Bay and smoothly headed west toward Mexico. Sometimes, the plane was full of squealing happy children; it seated twenty-four plus crew comfortably. At the moment, there were only two passengers: Silvina and Gavriel, on their way to visit Las Cuevas, Veracruz. Gavriel was working on a poem.

"So how are the honeymooners?" he asked, without looking up from his laptop.

"Doing great, thanks. How's the poetry?"

"Mmph?" He'd stuck a pen between his teeth and was looking something up in an enormous poetry reference book beside him.

"That good, huh?" She undid her seatbelt and reached under the seat for her carry-on.

"I'm working on a new form. The kids are gonna love it."

She was certain they would. Gavriel Navarro had an enthusiasm for teaching poetry to children that had transformed him. His change in direction had been as dramatic as hers when she met Thomas Haggerty, fell crazily in love, and married him. Their two-week vacation in Jamaica with her beautiful stepkids, James and Rayna, had been a first anniversary gift from Grandma Blythe. From there, Tom and the kids would fly to Toronto, while she and Gavriel visited the first Mexican Navarrosa Centre for Poetry and the Arts in Business. The original school, now in its second semester, was a beautiful complex at Queen of Heaven built between the ruins with a cable car to Cerabornes and bike trails through sheep country to St. Jacques.

Gavriel had a special fondness for the Mexican school, built on the land that had once been the Delgado-Obregón sugarcane plantation. With the old colonial family bankrupted by falling sugar prices, their land destroyed by narco wars in the nineties, *El Centro Navarrosa*, a working plantation and school, was on its way to becoming the Latin American model for education and enterprise. All corporate clients who wished to attend the program, affiliated with Tri-Partite Academy and Full Spectrum Training, had to support a street kids program and a youth employment initiative, both for ten years. Queen of Heaven already had a three-year waiting list.

Silvina opened her tablet and scrolled through emails. "I have two pieces of happy news. Do you want to hear them now or later?"

"Now, of course."

"Thanks to the influence of our Canadian poet friend, Alain C. Dexter, we're going to have a Navarrosa Centre in northern Ontario, probably by next year."

"Get out! Where, exactly?"

"My Dad's old fishing lodge, Twice Past Sunset, is Crown land and available for leasing. It's only a few hours from Brougham College where Alain teaches. He's agreed to be a guest instructor. He even wrote a septrois to celebrate the venture."

"Could I see?"

She handed him the tablet, knowing what would come next.

Gavriel pored over Alain's message that was two-thirds business, one-third poem. "This is amazing. Septrois is one of the hardest poetic forms. If you don't find the right seven-line host, it just sounds stupid."

She laughed. "You poets, you're all madmen."

Next, from her carry-on, she brought out a flat rectangular box that held three smaller boxes nested in velvet. "These are from Olivier, the jeweler-hardware store owner in Cerabornes. They are only samples, but I think he's done a great job, and they're much more representative of the Navarrosa spirit than dead roses in plastic. Mine fell to powder, by the way."

Now she had his attention. The silver lockets, heart-shaped, oval, and cartouche, rested on *rubielos de la Cérida*, written by Arturo de Padrón eight centuries ago.

"I asked Olivier to select his three favourite rubielos. I'd have probably chosen the same myself."

Gavriel looked up, and his eyes shone with that deep woods intensity that always made her swoon a little. "I never imagined that Arturo's words would be read again."

"Read and loved, never to be forgotten." She took back the tablet.

While she was in Jamaica, Silvina had downloaded a new app called "On This Day in History". As the jet descended toward Veracruz, the latest post appeared in her Inbox:

On this day in 1189 CE, King Richard I of England, also known as Lionheart, released his mother, Eleanor of Aquitaine, after sixteen years imprisonment by her husband, Richard's father, Henry II. Eleanor was sixty-seven and would live another fifteen years, working tirelessly for a better, kinder world.

"Thank you," Silvie whispered, looking out across the turquoise Gulf of Mexico. "Thank you."

ACKNOWLEDGMENTS

Creating the meta-world of *Daughters of Babylon* has been a twenty-year adventure that began with sitting on a kitchen floor far from home and wailing, "I can't do this anymore!" to a sunny August Saturday when the book, astonishingly, was finished. I would like to thank every person, place, and circumstance that brought me to this Saturday, and single out a few, in particular.

Many books have been written about Eleanor of Aquitaine, and a surprising number of letters to the queen of France, and later England, survive 800 years after writing, most of them chastisements at her behaviour by humourless clerics and scholars. To our great fortune, however, a new book has been written that shines a kinder, more intelligent light on an incredible woman. Thank you, Helen Castor, for writing *She-Wolves, The Women Who Ruled England before Elizabeth.* I am forever grateful for the depth of your research, unstinting attention to detail, and your willingness to challenge attitudes that should have been mothballed centuries ago. The events I portray from Eleanor's life, while based on fact, are fictional and/or conjectural, though in many cases, this required toning things down for believability. Such a life that woman lived! Any factual errors, of course, are completely mine.

One of the principal characters in *Daughters of Babylon*, Gavriel Navarro, is a poet and friend in real life, who not only encouraged me to finish the book but dared me to, in writing, in two of his published volumes of poetry. In depicting Gavriel, as with Eleanor, I fictionalized an extraordinary person whose real-life adventures and depth of spirit, one could never seriously hope to plumb or capture. To reread *The Wind and the Sea: Poems and Reflections on the Voyage of No Return* was pure joy, and I thank Gavriel for excerpting *Daughters of Babylon* in his second book, *Fire and Earth: Poems and Reflections on the Nature of Desire.* For those of you with an interest in the esoteric and indigenous, I highly recommend Gavriel's most recent book, cowritten with Norman W. Wilson PhD, called *A Shaman's Journey, Revealed Through Poetry.*

Among the serendipitous joys of this journey, has been meeting Lauren Bradford, artist, jeweler, life enthusiast, and founder of Heartsmith, a company devoted to creating high quality lockets. Lauren has been a champion of this book since she first heard the title, and like me, she believes that the marriage of lockets to poetry is a most natural pairing. Heartsmith's "Live in the Momentum: The Navarrosa Collection", based on *Daughters of Babylon*, now offers rubielos (medieval form poems with connections to the Goddess) written by the medieval knight you met in this book, Arturo de Padrón. You can find these works of art at www.heartsmith.com.

Finally, I wish to thank Tim C. Taylor for being the kind of publisher and editor that every writer dreams of, and seldom finds. I truly did not know the meaning of the word "anachronism" until he'd pointed out, with great kindness, how adept I am at writing them. Tim is a staunch supporter of the idea of restoring poetry to the modern mind; he is a fan of Eleanor; he's never anything less than cheerful and helpful—and very often, funny. To feel so championed in the final laps of a writing project is, like I said, the stuff of dreams.

And now, a word about the poetry. It is my fondest hope that if you weren't already a lover of verse, that *Daughters of Babylon* may have sparked an interest. I've introduced a number of medieval forms because they are amazing, and invented a few, for the fun of it. In the following pages, you will find, for your reading pleasure, original sestinas, septimes, septrois, octavos, glosas, satiric rhyming couplets, mitotes, and sonnets, all of which contributed in ways large and small to the energy of this novel and its grateful author.

ROOT PROCESSES OF
THE TRI-PARTITE ACADEMY
AND FULL SPECTRUM TRAINING

**Written by boh,
resurrected by S.K.**

Refunding Fire I: A Sestina

"For we are not pans and barrows, nor even porters of the fire and torch-bearers, but children of the fire, made of it, and only the same divinity transmuted and at two or three removes, when we know least about it."

Ralph Waldo Emerson, from his essay, "The Poet"

Volte-face: This being a labyrinthine fragment of a convoluted map, while true to form, lies, by necessity, three removes from the title's premise and cannot, therefore, guarantee reprieve or escape from situations that exist or may have existed prior to the reader approaching this work. Re-reading may or may not be of further assistance.

My task began, as many do, with meaning well;
some learn by sight, others by repetition of sound,
I, of latter bent, having been for so long blanketed
had not heard the Titan who stole fire has a twin,
dull-witted thunk, Epimetheus, who goes about
unsetting fires, never quite managing but bad enough

that a magus named Pythagoras saw fit enough
to ask for volunteers none too bright who might, well,
consent to go to hell, and since I'd had about
enough of people's whines & mockery, the sound
of someplace deeper held appeal. Have you a twin?
Pyth asked, before I signed. Nope, just me! Blanketed

thus with solitude and ignorance of how wet-blanketed
our species had agreed to be, I brought enough
of twinéd rope and kit to wend my way along twin
spirals that descend to nether studios so well
entrained in resonance—this is hell?—that no sound
can be heard and no thing can be talked about.

You'd think in such a place—Xibalba, Hades—about
which we are warned from infancy, still blanketed,
there'd be no sights, no complementary sound
apart from souls on fire, crying out, "Enough!"
This home to deviants where not quite perfect d…well
were monochord in their deploring of the hindsight twin,

brother of Prometheus. What comes before twin
thinking, Foresight, matters most, yet you fuss about
the done and did, as if the world had darned well
better know how miffed you are! Now you're blanketed
in afterthought, fires erupting everywhere, enough
to make you think there is, or that you're in, hell! Sound

familiar? They were looking straight at me, their sound
of perfect fifth, just major third, while a trepidatious twin
inside my head was twanging. I do not know enough
of theory musical, although I paused when talk about
harmonic ratios to Mayan myth conjoined. Fire blanketed
creates the Smoking Mirror, Pythagoras knows this well.

Their harmonies were sounding off, as if cacophony that lay about
Prometheus's twin multi-hatched with them. Already over-blanketed
with enough—no, too much data, I could not see things faring well.

Refunding Fire II: A Septime

"For the Universe has three children, born at one time, which reappear under different names in every system of thought, whether they be called cause, operation, and effect; or, more poetically, Jove, Pluto, Neptune; or, theologically, the Father, the Spirit, and the Son; but which we will call here the Knower, the Doer, and the Sayer."

Ralph Waldo Emerson, "The Poet"

The tone read, you have reached the end
of conversation. Greater Diesis now says
you may proceed. With what, wha, wh…? Even
echo was giving up in my spiraling effort
to return fire to the Customer Service
nether gods with no hind end in sight
to guide me, I could only grope and hope.

Welcome to twenty-three degrees. We hope
you have enjoyed the fright. The effort
to speak without speech, to view sans sight,
I don't care what anybody says—
the jar of fire surged—here resides the end
of lies! Don't try that again, mortal. Disservice
the gods, what, you think you can get even?

The place was neither hot nor cold. Effort
to think sucked away out the bitter/sweet end
of where I used to have fingers and toes. Hope,
Pandora, last thing in the box, in dreary service
to hubby, Epimethius, fun-killer, myth says,
but do we listen? If none of us can even
fathom truth, what's the diff, hind or foresight?

Sightless, imagination had come to my service.
Three surrounded me, only numbers uneven
seemed to rule in these chambers. No effort
conjured a macaw with man's face; the sight
of Diotima, Socrates's teacher, gave me hope;
the third, unsmiling old man, set of keys, says,
Call me Rock. How's it feel to reach the end?

Pyth had warned me of the trap. Whoever says
the stupid earthly things, keep in your sight.
I nudged the urn forward. We've come to the end
of uses for this fire. We cook with microwave, hope
that eating raw will slow down time, even
though we must know better. Can you service

my request? Three pinwheels spun, a sight
that made my ears pop. Too few carry hope
for mankind; this once mighty fire can't service
like it used to. Fire power, huh! You can't even
imagine—I shut my no-mouth in an effort
to remember, this is a place of forgetting, End
of all ends, who cares what a paltry human says?

The guy named Rock jangles his keys. Even
Macaw Man rattles at that noise. Service,
by custom, requires exchange, calmly says
the priestess Diotima. To meet your end
you must give up the means. This no-sight
of humans creates and sustains no hope,
though to your credit, you are surrendering effort.

To hope or pray I can convey the sight
of fire's service vanishing is beyond my effort
though goddess says, firmly, there is no end.

Refunding Fire III: Four Octaves

"It is a secret which every intellectual man quickly learns, that beyond the energy of his possessed and conscious intellect he is capable of a new energy (as of an intellect doubled on itself), by abandonment to the nature of things...If in any manner we can stimulate this instinct, new passages are opened for us into nature; the mind flows into and through things hardest and highest, and the metamorphosis is possible."

Ralph Waldo Emerson, "The Poet"

So you think you know the secrets of desire,
mastered all the words & moves designed to capture;
or perhaps you've given up, made way for rapture
of a lesser kind: I'll eat and buy, no new fire
awaits, so what's the point? From passion I retire,
yet even so you check the horoscopes, in case
the Universe has spared a crumb or two, inquire
through proper channels, might you find for me a place?

Expand your range! Each day, toss out the rhyme schemes of
yesterday, and spring anew. The funds to fire all
you dream and hope, they come by seeing first. Recall
what's yours, not others'. Be the object of great love
by sweet Creation. Disregard below. Above
is where the fun of life begins, begins again.
Three things I've learned: that push does not rely on shove;
there's no such thing as wrong & goodness never ends.

Renewing fire from the fund that never dries
like drug-free magic carpet rides will help you soar,
will guide you through Prometheus's door.
From both ends of the telescope you may apprise
by feeling thoughts of joy, you'll entertain surprise.
But surely none of this excessive pep is new!

You brought it with you on the day you came, bright eyes,
and through these octaves, you'll remember what to do.

Begin by disaccommodating thoughts of lack,
replace them in this moment with the possible—
a teeny crack, to gods is fully plausible.
Tend every tiny evidence that you're on track
as if the Universe now had (it does!) your back.
A forethought of the good is mightier than gold;
give favour to abundancy and watch it stack.
You ARE the star, the greatest story ever told!

The Seven Sisters Mercantilia

Firstborn: the Merchant of Images

The Merchant of Images plies her wares
transacting 'neath canopies of dragon
fly wings with coinage of silver too quick
for you to count the change; she'll bide your stares
in exchange for a taste from your flagon,
but don't be deceived: affection's a trick
of the eye from a deck she's stacked with all
that you've pilloried, all that you've loved; she's
tested your market, she knows what you'll buy.
You may try to outfit her like a doll
or outwit and unseat her—she will freeze
until you leave or learn to humbly supply
what she needs. Neither choice will disorder
the firstborn of this familial quarter.

Second-born Twins of the Sisters Mercantilia

The Guardian of Supply

The Guardian of Supply is plain of face.
You'll pass her in a crowd and not look twice;
on this she does rely, while all the while
she notes your attitude and keeps apace
providing more and more of avarice
toward joy or grief, she cares not which. Your style,
like the buttons on your coat she'll push or
fashion new ones when from happiness you
burst—the choice is yours, and no one else is
gathering to limit or suppress your
bountiful experience of life. Do
not be taken in by feudal classes'
antidote. The merchant guilds of fraud die
neglected by sweet sister of supply.

Dominatrix of Demand

Oh, how her sibling does enjoy the trend
of those who think they hold an upper hand
by means of pain. The Dominatrix true
rejects the trivial, does not pretend
she cannot hear you when you ask. Demand
is our twin sister's mastery, her view
of vortex unimpeded, she is brash,
intolerant of lack, loves imagery
of best and most and happiest; she breaks
the weakness of timidity, she'll smash
the indecisive, throw monotony
like tepid water out the window. Fakes
she can't abide, there is no concept in
our family of flaw, regret or sin.

The Executrix of Pause

Demand is high, supply unsure, three kin
of Mercantilia stimulating pulse
and drive, you feel alive, a need to buy
or interject, you've wrecked before, again,
so what? The knee jerk of a mad impulse
restores the balance to—but wait! Just try
this once not acting or to think in haste
and watch who comes, who's curious at what
you've done. The fulcrum, fourth of seven, seeks
to leverage thought to higher ground, not waste
through argument what's done before—no but,
just more and both. Reduce from years to weeks
the evidence of commerce practiced clean
by living the abundant Golden Mean.

Sister Five, Sequencia

Sister Five, Sequencia, says nothing
of the world as it is; to some she's mute
observing from nucleic center all
that spins, she's singular, unwed, she sings
to her equivalent, no less. Refute
her calls to trade and be assured of fall,
for data she engages includes all whose
limbic centers, 3-legged stools, are wobble-
free. Monopoly cannot be ruled save
in a fishy bowl, guaranteed to lose.
Continuous alarm, selling trouble
is a karma-based economy, grave-
headed. Only "con sequencia", by
sequence deep-observed can plenitude fly.

The Sister of No Permission

Sister Six you'll seldom see amidst her
sibling company, she has small use for
gatherings, she is the scout, the comet
head who flies, advancing with no other
aim in mind but joy, momentum-sped. Your
slow considerations will never get
between her and her light, your sordid talk
of shadow is the back end of the cave.
Good luck with that! If anti-trust makes cents
to you, invest—if not, fire up, unblock
those wings suspended for too long. Behave
as though permission were a sin. No fence
to climb or break, begin! The sisters six
plus one have heard your ascent to magicks.

Salt of the Earth

I am the seventh sister of the clan,
Cantilia is my name. I flow within
the bloodstreams of the race you call mankind.
You are my sea, la mer, the reach you plan
as if you weren't already here, undimmed,
full content closer than a thought. You'll find
the sisterhood has unspelled words like heal
and seek. You are not ill, you're lacking naught!
Supply, demand and imagery who live
the other side of pause know how you feel—
do you, or are you pillared salt? They've got
you covered. Let go my hand now, and give
your heart to pure abundancy. You're free
to recreate Bab-El's society.

Little Fiendy Whozit

by Wiley Forrest,
translated from Middle English by V.L.

Little Fiendy Whozit has a weeny voice;
he rips away his little gifts and claims he had no choice.

Little Fiendy Whozit thinks he knows what's right from wrong,
and he likes to teach you lessons with a big bang-bong.

Now Fiendy might be good with wood or teasing little girls,
but push him past his talent zone, you're in for quite a whirl.

The things you ask he will not do, except to impress others;
to corner him or force his hand, it isn't worth the bother.

He'll drag his feet and raise a stink and sooner whack than kiss ya,
then polish up his nasty sticks, insist he doesn't miss ya.

We've all a Fiendy Whozit in our little bag of tricks;
he feeds on disappointment that he fashions into bricks.

The thing you must remember about Fiendy Whozit's wall
is there's nothing there worth nothing, so don't make him crawl.

The time may come when Fiendy finds his R and L,
but until he shows up friendly, let him stay in…well,

for now, let's keep on skipping rope and holding hands for joy;
there's plenty good and plenty more for every girl and boy,

And should you meet sweet Whozit on your ever-loving way,
please tell him that I'm sending only happy thoughts today;

and if my little horns and tail occasional appear,
they're nothing much to fuss about or fear, my dear.

The Full *Mitote**of Lupo Sanchez to his son Ívano

*Mitote is a Nahuatl term for the cacophony, chaos, or mind chatter that society inflicts on us from the moment we are born, to confuse our natural ease and affinity with Creation. Mitote begins with our parents who tell us, "Life is this way. It is this way..." and extends to teachers, church and workplace. *Mitote* can also be applied in a positive way, realigning us at any moment with our innate truth and goodness. The following is a sample of the latter.

This is who you are!
You are the Dawn of Life
who chased the Sun to where
she hid in the Cave of Shadows
afraid of her own heat
with the message, "Rise! Rise!"

This is who you are!
You are jabalí, Wild Boar,
who parts the grasses that bow
and flutter in subservience to Wind
and, knowing you are servant
to none, cry out, "See! See!"

This is who you are!
You are Jaguar of the silent
paws and twitching whiskers who
travels the corridors of Nagual to the
hearts of the bewildered and
counsels, "Hear! Hear!"

This is who you are!
You are Black Road, rift
of the Milky Way, from
between your great Void the
game of Life spills out, and you
remind us, "Laugh! Laugh!"
This is who you are!
You are Smoking Mountain,

consort to Iztaccihuatl, defender
of peace, volcano of passion
who serenades his beloved
tenderly, "Sing! Sing!"

This is who you are!
You are Flower Song, the
poetry of butterflies and
bees, you sneeze your gold
dust in our noses, thus
reminding us to, "Dance! Dance!"

This is who you are!
You are Corn Mother,
grown in rows of silken
gowns reposed, you feed our
hunger, wrap us in your folds
soft crooning, "Eat! Eat!"

This is who you are!
You are Maguey Cactus,
father, curandero, brewer
to the speechless and despairing
you uplift our spirits, laughing
while you urge, "Drink! Drink!"

And of the final four mitotes,
son, I cannot speak, for yours
they are to quantify, the nature
of the beast; to cultivate the love
that sends you galloping, full rein;
to fly with joy of eagles, and to dive
through coral depths of grief and fear,
emerging as Nagual, empowered
by the Sun and stars: Illuminate!

"Venturing", a glosa, edited by Alain C. Dexter,

from his collection, Dead to Rights: A Circularity of Glosas

Were the archangel, the dangerous one
Beyond the stars, to move down now
One step closer to us, we would die
From the fear in our own hearts.

"The Second Elegy", Rainer Maria Rilke

All those blank spaces in my life
I kept from the historians
all those years penned in captivity
I traveled halls whose doors
could not stay me
until the day my heart shredded from
tidings too harsh to bear;
walls closed in and the floor vanished
and a different voice intoned that you, undone,
Were the archangel, the dangerous one.

Don't believe the chronicles
or if you must, note only the patterns
the seizures and deceits, disloyalties
and eschew the notion that humanity
has changed. It has not, cannot and won't!
You are not here to fix a broken plow
or elevate me to yet another throne;
I've had enough of velvet pillows
and food tasters. You and I must grow
beyond the stars, to move down now.

Beyond the fusty books, we share a backbone
radiant flow of here and now branching out
from my life to yours, from ours to all the others
like Indra's web, each life a pearl
fashioned by the sandy grit of thought,
but know this: the seeding of pain is not why
we are here nor to fill unread shelves
but to live true and full, erasing as we go
the lie, that should it come, bounteous supply,
one step closer to us, we would die.

The kingdoms we carved, I bequeath to you;
the vassals and the dungeons form a private terrain
where time and space meet as old friends
and complexities like muddy shoes are left at the door;
cut away the Gordian knot in your stomach,
make room for butterflies and fresh starts,
catch the filaments of promise I throw to you;
together, let's pull ourselves to new heights,
giving thanks to Earth, freed, on recreated ramparts
From the fear in our own hearts.

The Septrois by Alain C. Dexter in honour of
The 1ˢᵗ Canadian Navarrosa Centre
for Poetry & the Arts in Business

Septrois: Seven Kings

Septrois is a neologue that blends *sept* (seven) with *trois* (three), referring to the original seven-line poem and three new lines added to each. Conjoined, the two numbers create a word play, *sept rois*, that translates as "seven kings". For the seven-line crown stanza, Alain C. Dexter has selected the final stanza from "The Chambered Nautilus" by Oliver Wendell Holmes Sr. (1809-1894).

Build thee more stately mansions, O my soul,
As the swift seasons roll!
Leave thy low-vaulted past!
Let each new temple, nobler than the last,
Shut thee from heaven with a dome more vast,
Till thou at length art free,
Leaving thine outgrown shell by life's unresting sea!

~ ~ ~

Build thee more stately mansions, O my soul,
I have brought bricks and mortar,
blood and toil, artisans of high degree
whose love of heights replaces cruder vanity.

As the swift seasons roll!
Each hour blooms a year for me
through passages of time held light
my joyful course is stayed, feels right.

Leave thy low-vaulted past!
I've helpful souls who sweep away the night,
leave traces for the coming son and daughter
who, by your grace, bring freshening laughter.

Let each new temple, nobler than the last,
encourage us to boldly reconnoiter
less with dramaturge and more with comedy,
hearts well tuned in earthy frequency;

Shut thee from heaven with a dome more vast,
with room enough for all to merry be
abandoning the urgency to rush we might
discover heaven orbits us, a satellite,

Till thou at length art free,
from pain and restless night,
accommodating easily new quarter
for seven kings, as one, your porter;

Leaving thine outgrown shell by life's unresting sea!
embracing the unknown as playful sport or
means to ever curious and hopeful be
of constant love, sweet whirling with delight.

The Proto-Sonnet of Eleanor of Aquitaine

A version of myself beyond I draw
in soft iambs, I am a Queen divine
& erring, both, while you, my knight who saw
the best in me, now errant, may yet find
our magicks through the intertwine of verse
and ladies dear, though scattered far we be,
know well that kings have not the power to curse,
their seizéd crowns will rust, our liberty
through trust will come in forms not yet conceived.
My children sweet, your Courts of Love will shine,
surpass what church and scholars can believe.
Through love of place & friends, a space *must* grow
with noble heart above, and so below.

ABOUT THE AUTHOR

Photo: Russell Howe

Elaine Stirling, at the age of ten, heard a voice inside her head that said, "Whatever you're doing at the age of thirty, you'll do for the rest of your life." That, happily, turned out to be writing, which began with ten Harlequin romance novels in the 1980s, then branched out to short fiction with *Alfred Hitchcock Mystery Magazine* and *Fantasy and Science Fiction Magazine*. In 2009, Elaine published her first nonfiction, *The Corporate Storyteller: A Writing Manual & Style Guide for the Brave New Business Leader*. In 2012, Greyhart Press released *Dead Edit Redo*, a novella of horror and good medicine, and a collection of medieval form poetry by her heteronym, Alain C. Dexter, called *Dead to Rights: A Circularity of Glosas*.

When she's not working on her latest novel, Elaine is a communication consultant who helps corporate executives discover their creative selves. She blogs at "Oceantics", www.elainestirling.wordpress.com, and lives near Toronto, Canada.

Dead to Rights: A Circularity of Glosas

by

Alain C. Dexter

Ladies and gentlemen, step right up, don't be shy, and enter the rhyming gyre of glosas, forty-four line rock operas, poetic pas de deux, created by troubadours of the medieval Spanish courts. *Dead to Rights: A Circularity of Glosas* features eighteen dramatic mini-tales, introduced by quatrains and philosophies that include Poe, Milton, Epictetus and Dickens; spun to effervescence by the spirited Alain C. Dexter.

"Glosas deliver like a compact short story, in stereo; they're a poetic high energy drink, a double shot espresso of verse. You can read one glosa and read it again several times to experience a kaleidoscope effect of something new with each reread. Or you can take in a whole wallop of them and begin to sense the underlying structure that gives the glosa its . . . well, glisten."
— *Alain C. Dexter*

Dead to Rights: Contributors of Crown Stanzas—
John Milton, Gavriel Navarro, Herman Melville, Friedrich Nietzsche, Alfred, Lord Tennyson, William Butler Yeats, Charles Dickens, Edgar Allan Poe, John Donne, Rumi, John Keats, William Blake, Rainer Maria Rilke, Epictetus, Saggil-kīnam-ubbib, Enheduanna, Miguel de Cervantes Saavedra.

Dead Edit Redo

by

Elaine Stirling

Professor and best-selling poet Alain C. Dexter leaps to his death at Valletta Falls, moments after posting his final Facebook update, in the shape of a woman's breasts. Thousands of fans click *Like* and move on; only one, in a small Icelandic town, sees through the morbid wit and takes measures to save him. Meanwhile, Constable Elsie Kalahash of the Ontario Provincial Police just wants to go on holidays. But when you're a Cree medicine woman trained in the Backward-Facing Path, there are no days off.

Discover the story behind the Circularity of Glosas in this novella of horror and good medicine by Elaine Stirling. Available now from Greyhart Press

The Last Sunset

By

Bob Atkinson

#1 bestseller, alternate history: amazon.com
#1 bestseller, time travel romance: amazon.com

Andy McMillan is a soldier leading a training detachment in the Scottish Highlands.

A blinding red light drags him back to a simpler age when the air is filled with the smell of peat fires and the sound of Gaelic voices, and one voice in particular: the beautiful Ishbel

But the Highlanders are in revolt and the redcoats are coming.

Andy McMillan is a soldier.

Will he also prove to be a hero?

About Greyhart Press

Talk to us on Twitter (@GreyhartPress)
or email (editors@greyhartpress.com)

Greyhart Press is an indie publisher of quality genre fiction: fantasy, science fiction, horror, and some stories that defy description.

Greyhart Press

We publish eBooks and print-on-demand paperbacks through online retailers. That's great for us and for you, because we don't have to worry about all that costly hassle of stock-holding and distribution. Instead we can concentrate on finding great stories AND giving some away for free!

Visit our free story promotion page for no-strings-attached free downloads.

Would you like to read our eBooks for free?
If so, our READ... REVIEW... REPEAT... promotion is for you.

See our website for more details.
www.greyhartpress.com